“We’re not here to hurt you,” Bowers was saying, “we’re here to deliver food.”

“You are not welcome here,” said a harsh voice.

Looking over Bowers’s head, Sonek saw that a couple of centurions were pointing disruptors at them. Neither Bowers nor Kedair had taken out their weapons, which was probably wise. This was a situation that required fewer trigger fingers, not more.

Bowers had his hands up in what he probably hoped was a placating gesture. “Our arrival was scheduled. This was arranged with your government.”

“The arrangement has ceased. We no longer require the services of the Federation.”

The centurion and Bowers stared at each other for several seconds.

Sonek finally broke the impasse. “Excuse me, Centurion, but when we flew on down here, I saw a lot of people who looked like they hadn’t had a good meal in a very long time.”

The centurion bellowed, “That is not your concern, human.”

“Well, I’m not human—entirely. But that isn’t really my point—my point is, you all don’t strike me as people who are really in much of a position to be turning down free food. There are children out there who don’t look like they ever had a good meal in their lives. They *could* have one—half a dozen, even—if you take this food. Look, it’s been earmarked for the people on this world. It’s already yours, we’re just delivering it. We *want* you to have it. If you all want to break off the aid agreement between our two nations, then fine, go ahead and do that, but this fo[…] people th[…]

[…]wisting. So[…]se to do wh[…]and not, say, […]

STAR TREK®
DESTINY

A SINGULAR DESTINY

KEITH R.A. DECANDIDO

Based upon

Star Trek and *Star Trek: The Next Generation®*
created by Gene Roddenberry

Star Trek: Deep Space Nine®
created by Rick Berman & Michael Piller

Star Trek: Voyager®
created by Rick Berman & Michael Piller & Jeri Taylor

Star Trek: Enterprise®
created by Rick Berman & Brannon Braga

POCKET BOOKS
New York London Toronto Sydney Thalezra

Pocket Books
A Division of Simon & Schuster, Inc.
1230 Avenue of the Americas
New York, NY 10020

First Pocket Books paperback edition February 2009

Cover art and design by Alan Dingman

Manufactured in the United States of America

10 9 8 7 6 5 4 3

ISBN-13: 978-1-4165-9495-6
ISBN-10: 1-4165-9495-7

Dedicated to the memories of Joseph Pevney,
Alexander Courage, and Robert H. Justman,
who all contributed so much to Star Trek,
and Joan Winston and Robbie Greenberger,
the finest of fans.

All of you are deeply missed.

HISTORIAN'S NOTE

This novel commences in late April 2381, about two months after the conclusion of the *Star Trek: Destiny* trilogy, and a year and a half after the feature film *Star Trek Nemesis.*

Diplomats lie with a heavy sense of destiny.

—Mason Cooley

Blessed are the people whose leaders can look destiny in the eye without flinching but also without attempting to play God.

—Henry Kissinger

A SINGULAR DESTINY

Excerpt from an article by Jack Elliott in the *Times*

The *Zirkiv* only looks like a three-hundred-and-fifty-year-old Earth Cargo Service vessel. The ship's owner, Stammartie Holl, has spent years gathering up the pieces of the hulls of various old ECS ships and putting them on a ship she and her two children built from scratch. Sometimes she hires the ship out for tourists, but mostly she runs cargo with the *Zirkiv.*

It's been in orbit of Cor Caroli IX for a month now, packed to bursting with refugees from T'Khut.

In December of last year, the *Zirkiv* had a contract to bring various goods from Trill to Vulcan. By the time the new year rolled around, they had to make their deliveries with an armed escort for fear of Borg attack.

They had just made their delivery when the word came that a fleet of Borg ships was invading Federation space, including one that was heading straight for Vulcan. While most ships were transporting people away from the main world, there were also more than five hundred people in a habitat on Vulcan's airless sister planet T'Khut. While some were uninterested in abandoning their homes, there were plenty who thought it would be good to be elsewhere if the Borg were coming.

Captain Holl offered them the empty space in her cargo bay. Two hundred and twenty-two Vulcans and forty-seven members of other species took her up on it. Two months later, they're still there.

Starfleet was able to permanently end the Borg threat with the help of a species called the Caeliar, but the damage the Borg did before that was incalculable. T'Khut was one of hundreds of planets devastated, and the people Captain Holl had taken in had no home to go to. Vulcan itself was also attacked by the Borg, with many of its cities vaporized, and it designated the colony at Cor Caroli IX for the overflow of evacuees.

But there was a snag: the Federation finds itself with a significant shortage of topaline, which can't be replicated and is essential for the construction of atmospheric domes.

A new treaty has been signed with Capella IV to mine more topaline, but it's a slow process. And meanwhile, two hundred and sixty-nine citizens of T'Khut must live in the cargo hold of a restored ECS vessel. Oh, they can take trips down to the existing settlement on Cor Caroli IX, but it has limited facilities.

I talked with one of the refugees, and he had this to say. . . .

1

CAPELLA IV

Rebecca Greenblatt hated the fact that the Capellans were so much *taller* than she was.

Not that she minded being short in general. She'd gotten used to it. Although she was born on Benecia, Rebecca had spent most of her childhood on Pangea, a high-gravity world. Living there stunted her growth, so she topped out at a meter and a half. When dealing with most other humanoids, this wasn't too much of an issue, but on Capella the *shortest* native cleared two meters.

She'd spent most of her time on Capella staring up nostrils.

This was not how she had hoped her first job as a supervisor would go.

Not that she was complaining. Hell, right now, she was just thrilled to be alive. Like everyone else, she saw the images on the Federation News Service of thousands of Borg cubes swarming into the Federation—this only seven months after a giant cube entered Earth's solar system, consumed one of its planetoids, and almost destroyed Earth. All things considered, it was good to be alive.

But it was better to be alive and to have finally made supervisor.

She had started working for Janus Mining as an intern while studying structural engineering at Imprek University on Tellar. A tectonic shift under one of Tellar's oceans had led to a discovery of uridium, and Janus had gotten the contract to mine the ore for the Federation. They were eager for staff and so they trolled the universities. Mostly they hired Tellarites, but Imprek had a twenty percent population of non-Tellarites, including Rebecca, who found that her talent and background in structural engineering fit nicely with mining work.

Of course, she didn't do any actual structural engineering on Tellar. Janus mostly wanted people to fetch and carry and run errands, but she did well enough that she was offered a job upon graduation.

That was ten years ago. Last month, she was called into the office of her boss, Torvis-Urzon, at Janus's headquarters on Bre'el IV. The building was small and functional, as was her boss's office, a cramped space with no windows and a desk behind which the Grazerite barely fit.

"Do you recall that promotion we'd discussed?" Torvis-Urzon had asked without preamble as she entered.

Rebecca hadn't been surprised by this. Torvis-Urzon had always viewed politeness as something other people did. "Yes. And I also recall that everything was on hold."

"That was due to our belief that we'd be assimilated. That is hardly a concern now. And in fact, the Borg invasion directly relates to your new job as supervisor."

Her heart racing, Rebecca had said, "What new job?"

"We suddenly find ourselves with a topaline shortage. So you'll be in charge of getting some."

That had made sense to Rebecca. In the wake of the Borg, the need for atmospheric domes had increased a thousandfold, and if you wanted them to *work,* you needed topaline. "Where?"

"Capella IV."

Her heart had slowed considerably. "Capella IV already has a mining operation. In fact, they've had it for more than a century."

"And in all that time, they have yet to perform an upgrade. Capella's topaline production is about a tenth of what it would be with modern facilities."

Rebecca had grinned, then. She'd known nothing about Capella beyond that it was a trading partner with the Federation for topaline, but that was enough. She started scratching her chin. There used to be a mole there, which she'd had removed, but it continued to itch for no good reason long after the mole that caused it had been vaporized. "And the Federation wants us to do it?"

"In fact, the Federation wanted the S.C.E. to do it."

"You're kidding," Rebecca had said with disgust. She hated those Starfleet glory hogs.

"Yes, but the Capellan government refused. Something about an exiled king of theirs or something."

"Exiled king?"

Torvis-Urzon made a noise like a plasma leak, which was how Grazerites shrugged—or, at least, how this one did. "I know nothing of Capellan politics—that is simply what I was told."

"Fine, then. When do I start?"

He dug around the dozens of padds on his desk before finding the right one and handing it to her. "Two days. This has all the information you will require, as well as who is available for you to take."

Now her heart raced again. "I can take who I want?"

"Within reason," Torvis-Urzon said.

Rebecca called up the list in question on the padd's bright display. She immediately noticed that there was no list of options for the post of primary computer technician.

Scowling, she stared at her boss. "You're making me take T'Lis."

"She's the only technician available who has the experience you need."

Waving the padd back and forth as if she wanted to slap Torvis-Urzon with it—which didn't seem like all that bad an idea, then or now—she said, "She creeps me out."

"The translator must have malfunctioned. What did you say?"

Rebecca knew damn well that the universal translator could handle that particular bit of slang, but she also knew that Torvis-Urzon hated people who conversed in slang in any language. "She makes me uncomfortable. She always stares at me like I'm a lab experiment that's gone horribly wrong."

"Perhaps you are." Torvis-Urzon had almost smiled at that one.

With a heavier sigh than the situation really warranted, Rebecca had clutched the padd and left the office, taking it to one of the hotel rooms Janus had reserved for nonlocal staff when they were on-planet.

Within a day, she'd picked her team and contacted most of them. She didn't actually contact T'Lis, figuring that Torvis-Urzon already had—and if he hadn't, maybe she wouldn't come, and Rebecca would be able to get someone else.

But T'Lis did show up, along with the other one hundred and seventy-six people whose job it would be to upgrade the Capellan mining system. They went from Bre'el to Capella in one of Janus's massive carriers, the *Hecate*.

Then she arrived at the capital of Capella and found herself looking up the nostrils of the teer.

In all the material on Capella she'd read over the previous week, none of it mentioned how *tall* they were.

They were also honest to a fault. Their ritual greeting involved open hearts and open hands, and they valued the truth. The teer had said to her on arrival—after the greeting was complete, which put him one up on Torvis-Urzon—"You are welcome on Capella for as long as it takes to restore our ability to trade you for our rocks. You will be welcome for no longer than that."

Realizing that coexisting with the locals wasn't going to be a priority, she threw herself into the task of upgrading Capella's mining operations.

Or, as it turned out, overhauling and/or replacing them. She got a lecture from T'Lis on the subject. "These mines," T'Lis explained, "were built in 2267, at the height of the duotronic age. While these computers were of the best possible quality in 2267, they are woefully antiquated by 2381 standards, as even you might imagine."

Gritting her teeth at the insult but refusing to respond to it, Rebecca instead asked, "Why haven't they upgraded?"

She regretted the question instantly, as the Vulcan woman gave her that damned look. "Since reading the history of Capella that came with our materials is obviously beyond your capabilities, I will tell you. While Capella did agree to a treaty with the Federation in the previous century, relations soured when a group known as the *toora Maab* succeeded in overthrowing the teer, a young man named Leonard Akaar."

Rebecca started scratching her chin. "There's a Capellan named Leonard?" You saw that kind of name mixing in the Federation, of course, but she wouldn't have expected it from snotty isolationists like the Capellans.

"Apparently, he was delivered by a human of that name. In any case, he and his mother were exiled and declared dead. Akaar's tomb is in the capital city."

"City. Right." On Pangea, cities sprawled over thousands of kilometers. On Benecia, cities were built into the mountains. On Capella, what they called a "city" was a few small, poorly constructed buildings that happened to be near each other.

T'Lis went on. "After Akaar's ouster, the Capellans were willing to trade with the Federation but were not willing to allow Federation technicians to perform necessary upgrades."

"So as time went on, the equipment got less efficient, and trade declined."

"Leading to an eventual near-collapse of the Capellan economy," T'Lis said. "It has taken this long only because the mining equipment Starfleet installed a century ago was quite durable. Still, the Borg attack was fortuitous for the Capellans. Without the increase in topaline exports brought about by our presence here, most economists estimated the collapse of the Capellan socioeconomic infrastructure within the decade."

Rebecca excused herself, wishing she had a computer technician who could have simply answered her question by saying that the stuff was old and the Capellans didn't like us enough to let us fix it.

The next day, Rebecca was going over some reports, and called in her assistant, a Zakdorn named Jir Roplik, who had the dual advantages of being incredibly smart and efficient and being one of the few people here who was shorter than her.

"Why is T'Lis taking the computer core offline *again*?"

"Because the diagnostic program works better if she takes it offline."

Scratching her chin, Rebecca said, "Jir, I've worked with computers all my life. In my experience, diagnostics are usually more, ah, *robust* than that."

"T'Lis has been experiencing problems in the changeover to isolinear systems. She says this might be the last time she has to take the core offline for this reason."

" 'Might'? What's the circumstance under which that'll happen?"

"The diagnostic actually *functions*."

"You know, I was only willing to put up with her because she's supposed to be *good* at this," Rebecca said.

Jir blew out a breath, puffing out the folds of his cheeks. "I'm just passing on what she said."

Rebecca looked to the ceiling in supplication, but all it offered was corrugated metal. The living quarters for her people weren't complete yet. Rebecca hadn't requested them to be part of the original manifest because normally on such jobs, you could stay in local housing and not have to waste time building temporary housing, which was usually dreadful in any case.

But living and working in this slapped-together piece of cheap metal needed to improve a whole lot before it got as good as *dreadful,* and Rebecca had requested temporary housing shelters as part of the first resupply shipment from Janus.

Which reminded her . . . "That Ferengi trader yesterday. It was a different ship from the one the first couple of weeks."

"I noticed that, and asked one of the teer's people. Apparently, that's not unusual. The 'big-eared bringers,' as they call them here, change ships all the time. It's rarely the same ship more than three weeks in a row as it is."

"Fine. Also, is Firee still going to be able to meet with me, or is he still pumping out the water?"

"Still pumping out the water. He says they'll be at it until midafternoon."

Rebecca sighed. It had rained the previous night, and although the Capellans built their structures to withstand the elements, they hadn't done the same for the mineshafts that they'd dug since kicking the Federation out. Ironically, the meeting this morning was supposed to be about testing the drainage of the mine in case it rained. Rebecca hadn't expected a practical test to be provided by nature the previous night.

"Greetings!"

Rebecca jumped at the loud voice and turned to the entrance to her office, which was now entirely taken up by a Capellan male. He wore a blue shirt and pants with a dull yellow sash covering his waist and right shoulder, a headdress to match the shirt and pants, black boots, and a weapons belt. His hair was tied in a topknot, which stuck out through the top of the headdress.

Looking up his nostrils, Rebecca asked, "Can I help you?"

"I was sent by the teer. I am Kuun. You are to teach me how to run your new machines."

Scratching her chin almost hard enough to draw blood, Rebecca said, "I'm sorry, Kuun, but we're nowhere near that point yet. Trust me, training you on the mine operation is on our agenda, but it's not finished yet."

"The teer sent me now. You will teach me now."

Was it Rebecca's imagination, or was Kuun growing larger as he spoke? Shaking the notion off, she said, "There's nothing *to* teach. Right now we've got large machines that don't do anything and computers that don't work properly."

"Actually," Jir said, "the refinery is scheduled to be completed today."

Rebecca glowered at her assistant, hoping that her look conveyed her thought: *I wish you hadn't said that.* "Yes, but there's nothing to actually *refine* yet."

Kuun folded a pair of arms that could've been used as support struts for a Pangean building over his huge chest. "You will show me the refinery."

"Tell you what. I'm not free until after lunch, but—"

Jir said, "No, you're free now. I told you, Firee—"

"Cancelled the meeting, right." Rebecca had actually forgotten that. "Fine." She rose from her desk—she had intended to keep it neater than Torvis-Urzon's, at which she had failed rather spectacularly—and approached Kuun. "If you'll come with me. Jir, get in touch with Yinnik and tell him to meet us at the refinery."

"Of course," Jir said with a nod. He went back to his desk—which was pristine, the bastard—while Rebecca led Kuun outside.

For a brief moment, she paused at the threshold and took in the view.

While the people were pains in the ass, and the project was hitting more snags than she was entirely comfortable with, Rebecca had to admit that this was a beautiful planet. The sun shone brightly through a sky that was crystal clear—no doubt due in part to the rainstorm that had passed through. Rain on Pangea had always been a messy affair, as the rain came down at a greater acceleration, and was therefore stinging and uncomfortable. It wasn't until Rebecca moved to Tellar for her university studies that she realized that rain could be beautiful—though after a while, the sodden mess that was Tellarite weather grew wearing.

Here, though, the humidity had washed away, leaving a crisp, clear day. The sun shone, the trees bowed elegantly in the breeze, the distant rocks of the hills to the east glinted in the sunlight, and to the west lay the mine that her people were turning into a state-of-the-art facility that would leave that twenty-third-century anachronism that they had rotting there in the dust.

That was when the refinery blew up.

The force of the explosion pushed against Rebecca, but she did not fall. Her bones and muscles had long since grown accustomed to the pull of Pangea's gravity, and the distant force of an explosion was not enough to uproot her.

The same could not be said for her Capellan companion, who fell backward and on his rear end.

Knowing that Kuun wouldn't accept a hand up, Rebecca instead turned her attention to the refinery. Grabbing the comlink out of her pocket, she said, "Yinnik! What happened? You there?"

"Rebecca, it's Firee. What just happened?"

She started running toward the refinery, her heavy tread making deep impressions in the Capellan dirt. "The refinery just blew up! Emergency Procedure Four, everyone, now!"

Janus Mining had procedures for almost every possible emergency, and when a new one came up, they created a new procedure for the next time. This one, though, had happened plenty of times before, though refineries usually only exploded when refining volatile materials. The problem here was that topaline wasn't volatile, and even if it were, this refinery wasn't active yet.

So what the hell happened?

She put that question aside as she pulled a padd out of her pocket and tied it to the comlink. The first part of every emergency procedure was for everyone who was able to check in to do so.

Of the one hundred and seventy-seven people under Rebecca's supervision, one hundred and sixty-nine checked in. Of the remaining eight, six were Yinnik and five of his staff, who were assigned to the refinery. One was T'Lis. *What was she doing in the refinery?*

The other was the head of security, a native Pangean named Yevgeny Ubekov, with whom Rebecca had gone to school. In fact, she was the one who got him the job with Janus. *And he's the one who's supposed to investigate this. Dammit.*

By the time Rebecca arrived at the refinery, the automatic fire-suppression systems had dealt with the resultant conflagration—which barely had a chance to conflagrate.

The different section chiefs started reporting in that their sections were okay, with the obvious exception of Yinnik regarding the refinery. One of T'Lis's assistants said the computer core was fine. "And," she added, "she was in the refinery because Yinnik said the control consoles weren't working right."

That explains that, at least, Rebecca thought as she noted the fifteen people whose job it was under EP4 to go through the rubble and search for survivors were doing so—aided by Kuun, who was heaving aside rubble and debris without needing to be asked, which Rebecca appreciated.

Also present, but hanging back, was the doctor, a reclusive Bolian named Hruok whom Rebecca had chosen because, of all Janus's medicos, he was the only one who'd worked on a nonindustrial planet.

Hruok was holding a medical tricorder up. "I'm not reading any life signs that aren't the rescue party here." He looked down at Rebecca with sad eyes. "I'm afraid this is recovery, not rescue."

"Then I'll need autopsies," Rebecca said, trying to remember the security procedures. *This is what I had Yevgeny for.* "And we'll scan for explosives."

The doctor stared down at her in confusion. "Explosives?"

"The refinery wasn't operating yet, Doctor. And we're on a planet full of people with a history of disdain for the Federation. If Yevgeny was here, that'd be the first thing he'd check." *I hope.*

Then she got on the comlink. "Jir, contact Torvis-Urzon on the emergency hyperlink and fill him in."

"Of course."

Hruok was back to staring at his tricorder. "I'm picking up Vulcan DNA traces right under where that big person is."

Kuun started digging more thoroughly, yanking out a very large piece of twisted metal that was stained green.

Under it was T'Lis's body. *The last thing I thought about her was unkind.* Rebecca felt awful about that, more so when she realized that *all* her thoughts about T'Lis had been unkind.

One of the engineers, a human named Hugues Staley, walked up to Rebecca. He was holding a modified Starfleet tricorder from about twenty years ago. Hugues loved to take Starfleet surplus and play with it. "Rebecca, I just ran a scan. There's an element that shouldn't be here—it isn't indigenous to Capella, and it's not in anything we use."

"What is it?"

"Cabrodine."

Hugues was speaking as if that would mean something to Rebecca. "Hugues, my last chemistry class was ten years ago, and I've never been involved with mining cabrodine, which is honestly the only way I learn about elements and minerals."

"Well, cabrodine has a bunch of uses, and it's *possible* that the explosion caused a chemical reaction that created it, but . . ."

When Hugues's pause threatened to go on for five seconds, Rebecca prompted him. "But what?"

"It's also a common ingredient of explosives."

Hruok swallowed. "So we're back to sabotage."

"Maybe." Rebecca hit the comlink and cursed Yevgeny for being in the damn refinery. "Jir, have you gotten through to Torvis-Urzon yet?"

"Shroya's looking for him right now."

Rebecca did some quick calculations in her head, belatedly realizing that it was late in the evening in Bre'el IV's capital city. Torvis-Urzon was notoriously difficult to reach once regular business hours concluded.

"Okay, keep me posted."

Looking down at the remains of the refinery as they dug up two more bodies—including that of Yevgeny—Rebecca thought, *This is not how I had hoped my first job as a supervisor would go.*

A letter to Professor Sonek Pran at McKay University, Endurance, Mars, sent by Chief Rupi Yee on the *U.S.S. Sugihara*

To my darling husband:

First of all, happy birthday! I'm sorry I can't be there to celebrate with you. I suppose we could blame the Borg. I think we've gotten to the point where we blame them for everything. Rainy weather? The Borg. The soup from the replicator is watery? The Borg. Hair not behaving itself? The Borg.

We're entering our third week on Ardana. I actually have time to breathe now that we've finally got the planetary transporter system back up and running. The zenite mines are running again, too, now that we finally dug them all out—but that's been someone else's problem. Me, I've had to supervise the rebuilding of a planet's entire transporter system, which was really hard because Ardana has its own system completely different from the rest of the Federation's, and getting it to talk to ours proved a bit of a challenge, especially since a lot of Ardana's computer records were irreparably damaged in the Borg attack. And before you ask if they kept physical backups—those were all incinerated.

But it could've been worse. They're building a statue down here in the shape of the Romulan ship, the Verithrax, *that blew up the Borg cube—and itself—before it could completely wipe the planet out. There are refugee settlements all over the planet and they're* all *calling themselves "the Verithrax settlement." It's driving poor Captain Demitrijian crazy, since she never knows which one anyone's talking about.*

What's really amazing is the Ardanans. They used to have a city that floated in the clouds. It crashed about four years ago, and it was the focus of a huge mess of civil unrest. We came by here last year to help them deal with some crop failures, and I honestly thought that half the citizenry was going to kill the other half. But now? Everybody loves everyone else—and they all love the Romulans, thanks to the Verithrax. *About twenty percent of the Ardanans are wearing their hair in that silly bowl cut that the Romulan military always uses.*

Anyhow, we should only be here another week before we move on to whatever's next. No one has any idea what that might be, of course, though the rumors are flying at warp ten, like usual. Also like usual, nobody pays attention to the transporter operator, so I hear all sorts of odd things. Jomat thinks we'll be assigned to help the Klingons next, while Commander Matsui is convinced they're going to hold us at Ardana, and Ensign Fiore thinks we're going to patrol the Tholian border. Everyone thinks Fiore's nuts, which is good, because I can't imagine defense against the Tholians is such a big priority. Then again, Fiore was the one who didn't see what the big deal was about the Borg anyhow.

As for me, I'm holding out for a solar assignment, since we haven't seen each other in a thousand years. Failing that, I'm hoping we'll be close enough for real-time. Trust me, as soon as I hear an actual order, as opposed to the crazy rumors, I'll let you know.

I assume you heard about Sara's band joining the tour of the refugee stations. You should know also that Ayib's been assigned to P'Jem, since you'd never find out otherwise. I wish you two would just talk *to each other again. I'm tired of being the middle person between my husband and my son.*

Hope to hear from you soon. I love you! And once again, happy birthday, my darling!

Yours always,

Rupi

2

MARS

"Now the trade disputes between the Andorians and the Tellarites were getting ugly, to the point where war was starting to seem pretty much inevitable. Instead, delegates from both sides got themselves together, and they *talked*. These negotiations were spearheaded by Earth and by Vulcan. Right there, you've got yourself the four founding species of the Federation, and it doesn't happen if they decide to start shooting at each other. It's *cooperation* that brought them together."

Professor Sonek Pran stared at the blank faces of the hundred or so students in the lecture hall. They all had padds, though only some were taking notes. And Sonek was sure that some of them were doodling.

Prophets save me from overview classes.

Sonek had had tenure at McKay University's History Department for twenty years, yet he still had to teach these idiotic overview classes, which were filled with undergraduates who were required to take one history class.

He'd managed to avoid teaching the Federation History Overview the past couple of years, but when Jo'Nol got that fellowship, the department chair—who also happened to be Sonek's own grandfather, Tolik of Vulcan—informed him that he would need to take on his overview class.

It was his last class of the day, which made it that much worse. After spending a day talking with students who actually *cared* about history, it was painful to have to deal with a sea of uncaring faces who probably never knew nor cared that the Andorians, Tellarites, Vulcans, and humans were once separate nations, and certainly weren't interested in how they came together.

One of the students—either a Trill or a Kriosian—raised her hand. Seeing a raised hand in an overview class was like a *sehlat* that could speak: very rare. He looked down at the lectern display, which told him who the student was. "Yes, Marva?"

"Wasn't it the Romulans who brought them together, really? The whole thing happened because the Romulans tried to start a war between Andor and Tellar."

A student in an overview class who not only raises her hand but actually goes and says something smart. That's like a sehlat *that speaks Old High Bajoran: even rarer.* "They moved the process along, but the point is, the Romulans set them up, like you said, to start a war—and they *chose* not to. They *chose* to sit themselves down and talk. They *chose* to cooperate. And *that's* the point. That's what the Federation's all about."

Marva seemed unconvinced. "But the Federation didn't form for another few years after that, right? After the Romulan War?"

"Yes, but if the Andorians and Tellarites start fighting, the Coalition doesn't happen. And if the Coalition doesn't happen, the *Federation* doesn't happen." Sonek stared out at the blank faces, which were getting blanker. "You guys *do* remember the Coalition, right? That was this week's reading." Now several of them shifted in their chairs.

Another student spoke up, a Caitian—M'Zeo, according to Sonek's padd. "I did read it, and I believe that it only occurred *because* of the conflict. Changes will only happen due to disaster or war. Like the Dominion War making us ally with the Romulans or Praxis exploding making us ally with the Klingons. And as Marva said, the Federation didn't come together until after the Romulan War."

Sonek held up a finger. "Now, see, two problems. First, nobody 'made' us ally with the Klingons or with the Romulans. Those were choices *we* made—and *they* made, for that matter. Besides, I'm not talking about change. I'm talking about institutions that have lasted a long time. Never mind the external stuff—I'm talking about *the Federation.* Think about it for a moment. A hundred and fifty civilizations, different species that all evolved on different planets, and they all come together and *work* together. *That's* why it lasts. When there's a problem, we cooperate to solve it. When one world's got a crisis, another one goes and lends a hand." He ran a hand through his long white hair, brushing it past his tapered ear. "For that matter, without that cooperation, I don't exist."

A Rhaandarite boy make a strange noise. "How could you not exist?"

Sonek grinned. "I'm what used to be called a quadroon." Several confused faces. "Not too many people say that now. My four grandparents are from four different species. My paternal grandparents are a human and a Betazoid; my maternal ones are a Vulcan and a Bajoran. Leaving aside the notion that my four grandparents probably wouldn't have even *met* without the Federation, there's also the medical end of things. Doctors from different worlds had to get together just so that people from different species *could* have kids."

He glanced down at the time stamp on the lectern display to see that the class was done. "All right, that's it. Now don't forget, I need to know what your final essay topics are going to be. Five of you haven't gotten around to telling me yet, and if you don't by tomorrow, you get docked on the grade." The students were all getting up from their chairs now and gathering their padds. "Oh," Sonek added, "and nobody else is allowed to do the Khitomer Accords." Several groans came from in front of him at that. "Look, now, fifty of you are doing that, and I want to see some variety. Besides, you pick something nobody else did, your paper's more likely to stand out and result in a grade that stays above what's required to actually *count* this class, know what I'm saying?"

Marva walked straight for Sonek's desk. "I didn't know you were part Betazoid also. I should've realized from the eyes."

Sonek smiled. When his long, curly white hair was pulled back, or he tucked it around his ear, his Vulcan heritage was visible, and the faint ridges on the bridge of his nose indicated that he had Bajoran in him, but while most Betazoids had black eyes, not all black-eyed people were necessarily Betazoid.

"So," Marva asked, "does that mean you're telepathic?"

At that, Sonek laughed heartily. As his grandfather was fond of pointing out, that laugh was what told the universe that he was part human, too. "I'm afraid not, Marva. Seems like the Vulcan and Betazoid genes cancelled each other out on that one."

"Too bad. It'd be easier to teach."

I doubt that, Sonek thought, but aloud only said, "Maybe. Never really thought about it all that much. Hey, listen, good points you made in class today."

"I'm actually doing my final paper on how all the important events in Federation history happened because of conflict or strife—starting with the Romulan War and going all the way through to the Borg invasion."

Sonek blinked. "That, uh—that's pretty ambitious for something that's just supposed to be five thousand words. You might be better off trying to focus it a bit more. Besides, the Borg invasion *just* happened. The thing about history is that you need a bit of distance to study it, to even *start* approaching the realm of what happened and why."

Marva made a "hmph" noise, and said, "We'll see." With that, she turned and left.

Sonek shook his head, placing his own padd in the old shoulder satchel that he'd been using since his days as a graduate student long ago. The satchel was blue with red handles and had a (now rather battered) IDIC symbol on both sides in silver and gold. It had been a birthday present from his parents, and he'd always loved it. After forty-four years (to the day, as it happened), the straps nested comfortably on his left shoulder blade. Several doctors had pointed out that his shoulder bone had a divot in it that might cause problems as he got older, but he'd gotten older, and he hardly ever even *used* his left shoulder for anything except pointing at students and carrying his IDIC satchel.

He walked through the corridors of the university, which was located just outside the city of Endurance. He nodded to the occasional student and faculty member who passed him by, but he didn't even remember who it was he'd just nodded to two seconds after passing them.

I just need this day to be done, he thought with more than a little self-pity. He knew that the self-pity was ludicrous, but that rarely stopped him, especially these last couple of years.

He took the turbolift to the second level, where the History Department offices were. He was just going to check for messages, make sure there wasn't anything outstanding he needed to take care of, say good night to his grandfather, and then catch the rail home to his apartment in Valles Marineris.

When the lift doors opened, he realized that wasn't going to happen.

"Surprise!"

Pretty much the entire History Department—including his grandfather, the last person he'd expect to participate in so illogical a pastime as a surprise party—was present, all shouting at once. A sign that read HAPPY 65TH BIRTHDAY SONEK! hung from the ceiling.

Within several seconds, Sonek was receiving congratulations from everyone, and had a piece of cake shoved in his hand.

Haros glasch Yov, whose specialties were pre-Federation Tellarite history and driving his students absolutely crazy, clapped him on the back and said, "Well done, my friend. I honestly did not think you would live to see fifty years, much less sixty-five!"

"Don't be absurd," said Ming Ku, whose History of the Delta Quadrant class had been getting huge class sizes, despite the fact that her syllabus came from the logs of one Starfleet ship that was stuck there for seven years. "Everyone loves Sonek."

"I can tell," Sonek said with as sincere a smile as he could manage.

The party went on for a bit, and he accepted everyone's congratulations and well wishes, and he did his best to accept them graciously.

There was no alcohol, to his regret, but that had been standard for any History Department social function since his grandfather had taken over the chair.

I could murder a bottle of Saurian brandy right about now. Instead he was stuck with *allira* punch, which he certainly enjoyed, but it didn't have quite the kick he was hoping for.

At one point, unable to stand pretending to be cheery any longer, he excused himself to go to his office.

As soon as he entered, the computer intoned, *"You have received four messages."*

"Senders?" he asked as he fell more than sat in the large, flared leather chair and set his punch glass down on his desk.

"Ferin na Yoth, Helena Birgisdottir, Chief Rupi Yee, and Helthari ch'Vress."

The first, second, and fourth were students, and therefore easily put off, especially since the third was from his wife. "Call up message from Chief Yee," he said as he turned the screen so it would face him.

She, of course, started by wishing him a happy birthday, and that just made it worse.

"How fares my granddaughter-in-law?" came a deep voice from the doorway.

Sonek paused the playback of Rupi's letter to look at the voice, which belonged to his grandfather and boss, Tolik.

"She fares just fine, thanks. They're still on Ardana, but it looks like the end's in sight."

"Excellent. Now then—how fares my grandson?"

He affixed the same smile he'd been using at the party. "I'm faring just fine, Gramps. No worries here."

"For someone with as much experience in politics as yourself, Sonek, you are remarkably poor at lying. Your emotional state is obviously in flux, and it is not because you are unable to share this birthday with Rupi."

Sonek shot Tolik a glance. "Of course that's what it is." However, even as he spoke the words, he realized that Tolik was correct. True, he wasn't *happy* that Rupi was off on Ardana, but Captain Demitrijian had cancelled all leaves two months ago out of necessity. The *Sugihara* had taken casualties, after all, and replacements were hard to come by right now.

Tolik said, "You have spent many birthdays without Rupi since her enlistment in Starfleet. Besides which, while the malaise you are in at present is more intense, said malaise has been the norm for several weeks now."

Sonek let out a long breath. "I guess, I—" He took a sip of his punch to cover the gathering of his thoughts. Finally, he said, "I guess I'm just feeling my age."

"I find that statement to be extremely questionable. You are, after all, a hundred years younger than I, and—"

"It's not that I'm feeling *old,* I just feel like—I guess,

I feel like I should've gotten along much further than I have by now. I mean, I've sat in the Palais de la Concorde with councillors and presidents. Governments used to call for me all the time. But now . . ."

"Now the galaxy is in turmoil and you find yourself still here on Mars."

"Yes!" Sonek said almost breathlessly. Now that Tolik had said it out loud, it all made sense to him, the vague unease he'd been feeling since the Borg invasion. "Rupi's out there helping put Ardana back together again. Ayib's probably doing some kind of doctor thing, and Sara's band's playing for the refugees. What the heck am *I* doing?"

"You do not find teaching the youth of the Federation to be a worthwhile cause?"

Sonek shook his head. "I don't know. I'm teaching the same classes I was teaching twenty years ago, giving that same damn lecture about cooperation that I gave when I first got tenure, and—" He shook his head. "I used to be a policy adviser. I used to have all kinds of influence. It wasn't much, really, but it felt like I was an important person. Now, I just feel like a small cog in a tiny wheel nobody cares about outside Endurance."

"There is nothing stopping you from beginning again. President Zife has been out of office for eighteen months."

Sonek twitched just at the mention of the Bolian ex-president. Once the Dominion War commenced, Zife's Zakdorn chief of staff, Koll Azernal, had dismissed Sonek. "You have tremendous skills as a peacemaker," Azernal had said, "but we're now in a state of war. You'll be of more service to the Federation back at the university."

This came after the Zife administration had spent three years ignoring him. For three decades, he'd been an adviser to the Federation government. Presidents T'Pragh, Amitra, and Jaresh-Inyo had all considered his advice and oratory to be invaluable.

But President Zife did not share that opinion, and Sonek had predicted his dismissal by Azernal six months before it happened. He'd stayed on Earth as long as he did only because he desperately wanted to avoid a war with the Dominion. Once that war started, he knew that it was a lost cause.

But Zife had resigned suddenly, and his successor, President Nan Bacco, had served brilliantly, particularly during the Borg mess.

"I suppose I could contact the Palais."

"You could, yes. The question remains," Tolik said, folding his arms over his chest, "why you haven't done so at any point during the past eighteen months—including the fourteen times we have had a variation on this conversation during that time period."

Sonek looked down at the floor, abashed. "Has it really been fourteen times?"

"Fifteen as of now."

"Yeah." Sonek shook his head. "I figured if they wanted me, they'd go ahead and ask. But they *haven't* gone ahead and asked. And I didn't want to seem desperate."

"I do not understand why you do not wish to seem that which you so obviously are."

At that, a laugh exploded from Sonek's lips. "Maybe. I guess I just—"

"Incoming transmission for Professor Pran."

Sonek blinked as he picked up his punch glass. "Who from?"

"From the Palais de la Concorde."

He sputtered, *allira* punch spilling on his desk and getting into his white mustache. "Repeat that?"

"From the Palais de la Concorde."

"You're kidding."

"Message is from the Palais de la Concorde."

"Which office?"

"The office of the chief of staff."

Drawing his sleeve across his mouth to get rid of the last of the punch from his mustache, he looked up at Tolik. "You know anything about this?"

"Negative. It is a most fascinating coincidence, however."

"Yeah."

Tolik started to turn around. "I shall leave you to—"

"No!" Sonek held up a hand. "I'd rather you were standing right there, Gramps. I think I'm gonna be needing some moral support."

"As you wish." Tolik resumed his position in his threshold, arms again folded over his chest.

"Computer, put through the call."

The viewer, which had the frozen image of Sonek's lovely wife, changed to that of the presidential seal, then to that of an olive-skinned man with curly blond hair and a red goatee. *"Professor Pran?"*

"Speaking."

"My name is Zachary Manzanillo. I'm the assistant to Esperanza Piñiero."

Sonek ran his fingers over his mustache. *They weren't kidding about the office of the chief of staff.* "Pleased to make your acquaintance, Mr. Manzanillo. Now, what's this about, exactly?"

"Your presence has been requested at the Palais,

Professor. You're scheduled to meet with Ms. Piñiero at three o'clock local time tomorrow. A shuttle is already en route to Mars, and it will be ready to take you to Earth first thing in the morning."

Sonek shot his grandfather a look. "You *sure* you don't know anything about this, Gramps?"

"Is someone else there?" Manzanillo's tone got rather frosty all of a sudden.

"Dr. Tolik of Vulcan—he's the chair of my department, and also my grandfather. He was here when you called, and there was no reason to believe the call was classified."

"I'm not allowed to make classified calls, Professor Pran. I was merely surprised."

"If you don't mind my asking, Mr. Manzanillo—what, exactly, does the chief of staff want to chat with me about?"

"The president needs your help, Professor. We understand that when presidents have asked you for help in the past, you've provided it. President Bacco wishes you to do likewise for her."

Suddenly, Sonek found that his throat was dry. He took a long sip of *allira* punch and then finally said, "Okay. I guess I'll be seeing you tomorrow afternoon, then."

"I look forward to it, Professor. Your reputation precedes you."

"Now if that were true, Mr. Manzanillo, I doubt you'd want me to come tomorrow," he said with a smile. "Take care, sir."

"Good-bye, Professor."

With that, he signed off.

"Okay, that was just *weird*. We're talking about me getting in touch with the Palais—"

"And they contact you. It would, perhaps, be less weird, as you say, if we had not had this conversation on fourteen occasions during which the Palais did *not* call."

"Yeah." Sonek leaned back in his chair and grabbed the punch, dry-sipping the glass before he realized it was empty. Setting it back down, he said, "Looks like you're gonna have to find someone who can take—"

"I will, of course, distribute your classes among the rest of the department. Your students will be in safe hands."

"Do me a favor, give the overview class to Haros."

One of Tolik's eyebrows shot up. "Did you not characterize Professor Yov once as being 'dumber than a box of stembolts'?"

"Exactly. Just what those kids in the overview class deserve." He got up from his chair, the leather creaking with the release of his weight. "I guess I should go home and start packing."

"Indeed."

Sonek moved past his grandfather to leave his office. As he did so, Tolik put a hand on his grandson's shoulder. "Sonek."

"Yeah, Gramps?" Sonek said, looking right in Tolik's gray eyes.

"Peace and long life."

Sonek broke into a big grin. "Live long and prosper, Gramps. I'll be in touch after I hit Paris."

Excerpt from a Federation News Service report by Emtho Shrik from Gault

Once upon a time, the planet Gault was a pleasant little agricultural world. The settlement was part of the huge Earth colonial boom following the achievement of warp drive and first contact with the Vulcans. The people who settled here were mostly from a group that called themselves the Siberian Collective. They wished to return to an agrarian style of living in the wake of great technology—ironically, the very technology that they wanted to get away from was what allowed them to do so.

Before long, Gault became a thriving world, one of the breadbaskets of the United Earth. With so much farmland lost to overuse, to overpopulation, and to the devastation of Earth's third world war, Gault, and planets like it, became a necessity—first to Earth and then to the Federation.

With the passing of centuries, farming changed. Technology improved, the agrarian back-to-nature colonists grew old, and their children, who had become citizens of the Federation, were more than happy to use the best that technology could offer. Gault became the cream of the crop, as it were.

But then came the replicator age, and Federation citizens could simply ask for a Sackmanov apple instead of having to import one from Gault. However, other nations had less widespread use of replicators, and so trade continued. The Yridians, the Gorn, the Lissepians, the Klingons—they all wanted what Gault produced.

Now, though, Gault has come full circle. This year's harvest is going to be feeding the Federation—specifically, those worlds devastated by the Borg. Replicators have suddenly become hard to come by amid the remains of the pulverized cities of Andor and Coridan and Deneva and Sherman's Planet. Stores that were being saved for fallow years are being taken out of stasis and being sent to refugee camps on worlds that simply cannot handle the sudden need to feed so many so quickly.

Throughout this, Gault is still fulfilling its obligations to the Federation's trading partners. The Yridians are still getting their Horst pears, the Lissepians are still getting their Ulanov spices, and the Klingons are still getting their wheat—apparently Gault wheat is considered by Klingon chefs to be the best base to make *jInjoq* bread. Gault has been providing food for three centuries, and its farmers aren't going to stop now.

3

CESTUS III

"I liked it better when I was lieutenant governor."

"Yes, ma'am."

Governor Yrolla Gari of Cestus III stared up at her assistant, a raven-haired young woman named Therese. Or maybe it was Alda. Gari couldn't remember her name, what with everything else being thrown at her. Her old assistant had quit and moved back to Luna following the Borg invasion, having decided to be closer to her family.

In any case, Therese or Alda or Yvonne or whatever her name was was waiting for her to initial some paperwork. So she did, all the while muttering. "It was so wonderful. Plenty of power, almost no responsibility. The perfect job. Governor Bacco handled the press, handled the district reps, handled everything. She could convince the Gorn to wear sweaters, I swear."

"The Gorn don't wear sweaters?"

Gari looked up at Yvonne or Rita or whomever. "The Gorn don't get cold."

"What if they're on an ice planet?"

"How many more of these do I have to initial?"

The assistant riffled through the padds in her hand. "Fourteen."

"Wonderful." She ran a hand through what was left of her mostly-gray-now hair. "I used to have great hair."

"Your hair's lovely, ma'am."

"It used to be red. Now it's gray. You know whose fault that is?"

"Your parents?"

Gari initialed some more padds. "No, Esperanza bloody Piñiero. She had to come and tell the governor what a *great* idea it would be to run for president. Ten years, she'd been governor. We had this planet running smoother than a starship, the two of us. And Esperanza had to come and mess it all up."

"Don't you think President Bacco is a good president, ma'am?"

"Of *course* she's a good president! Any idiot can see that! That's not the *point!* The point is, she was an even better governor, and that was mainly because I was such a good lieutenant governor. Now look at me. My hair is gray." She sighed, taking some more padds from the assistant. "I'm a behind-the-scenes person, Rita."

"My name's Lucy, ma'am."

Gari blinked. "Really?"

"Yes, ma'am."

"Oh. Well, Lucy, I'm a behind-the-scenes person. I work in the background, make sure things get done. I don't like talking to people."

"I hadn't noticed, ma'am."

A buzzing noise came from the other side of the door.

Lucy went to the door, which slid open to reveal Lin Song, the planetary transportation minister. Normally Lin's job was to make sure the aircars didn't crash into each other and that the transporters all functioned, but recently his job had gotten considerably more complicated. Cestus III was, miraculously, never hit by the Borg. It had become a designated refugee center, partly due to its not being in the line of fire, partly due to having refugee procedures already in place. In fact, Gari had written most of those procedures as lieutenant governor when Cestus III had taken in several thousand refugees from the former Federation colonies near the Cardassian border that had been ceded to the Cardassian Union twelve years earlier.

"I need to see the governor."

Gari put her head in her hands. Lin had taken to his new responsibilities—well, about as well as Gari herself had. If there was even the slightest alteration to what was planned, Lin went to see Gari about it. Since there were about a billion alterations to every plan, this meant Lin had spent more time in Gari's office than he had in his own.

"What is it *this* time, Lin?" Gari asked.

"We've got a refugee ship," he said, barreling past poor Lucy and standing in front of Gari's desk. His black hair was flying off in all directions, and his shirt was untucked, which was a shame, in a way, since Lin had once been very proud of his perfect grooming.

Speaking in slow tones that one would use with a child, Gari said, "Lin, we're a designated refugee planet. We're *supposed* to have refugee ships."

"Yes, but this one isn't on the list."

"What do you mean?"

He held up a padd. "I mean, I'm holding the list right here, and this ship isn't on it."

"What's the ship?"

"It's an Andorian ship, the *Kovlessa*. The captain's name is zh'Ranthi, and she says that she was supposed to go to Zalda, but they were refused."

"So they came *here*? Why?"

Lucy said, "For that matter, why didn't they just stay on Andor?"

Lin shook his head and ran his hand through his hair, making it stick up even more. "They're not *from* Andor, they're from Alrond—it's an Andorian colony in the same star system. The Borg wiped it out on their way to Andor. The planet's now molten slag, and Andor has its hands full with people who actually lived *on* Andor, and the Zaldans out-and-out refused them. And the reason I know all this is I just got an earful from Captain zh'Ranthi on that very subject. I told her we don't have anywhere to put her and the people on her ship, and she insisted I talk to you."

Somehow Gari doubted the latter was true, but believed rather that Lin was trying to pass the buck. On the other hand, if this Andorian was being stubborn, Lin might not have had a choice. *And why the hell did Zalda send them away? Anyone in the sector Andor's in would automatically go to Zalda.*

She looked up at her assistant. "Lucy, put a call through to this ship—"

"The *Kovlessa*," Lin added.

"And tell Captain Zerelli—"

"That's zh'Ranthi."

"Right, her—that Governor Gari wishes to speak

to her. And after that, put a call through to the Palais. We're stretched to the limit here, and I want to know why the *hell* Zalda isn't doing their part."

"Of course," Lucy said with a nod, and went out to her desk.

"Thank you, Governor." Lin turned to leave.

"Where do you think you're going?"

Lin stopped and turned around. "Uhm, well, I have work to do, and—"

"You're the transportation minister, you're standing next to me and helping me figure out where to put these people."

Lin's eyes, amazingly, got wider, which Gari would not have believed possible. "Governor, there's nowhere *to* put them!"

"You're shouting, Lin."

Getting his volume under control, Lin repeated, "Governor, there's nowhere to put them."

"I heard you the first time. In fact, they probably heard you in Johnson City. And it doesn't matter. These people have been flying around in space for weeks now, *and* they were snubbed by Zaldans. We're taking them in."

From her desk, Lucy called out, "I have Captain zh'Ranthi, ma'am!"

Nodding, Gari touched a control on her desk, and the screen on the far wall lit up with the white hair and delicate blue features of an Andorian *zhen*. She wore what appeared to be an old Imperial Guard uniform, stripped of its insignia. Her eyes were bloodshot and her hair askew. Her antennae were pointed straight upward, almost rigid. "Captain, I'm Governor Gari of Cestus III. How can I help you?"

"Governor, I apologize for the imposition, but I have

a ship full of homeless colonists. We came from the Andorian colony of Alrond, and the Borg—"

Gari held up a hand. "I've been told your story, Captain. Why didn't you go to Zalda?"

"We did!" She pounded on her chair arm for emphasis. *"We were told in no uncertain terms that Zalda was refusing any refugees."*

"Did they give a reason?" Lin asked.

Now zh'Ranthi stared angrily with her bloodshot eyes at Lin. *"You again. I told you I didn't wish to speak to you again."*

Before Lin could say something stupid, Gari said, "Captain, Minister Lin is here at my request. He is in charge of placing refugees."

"He informed me that we would not be able to be placed."

"You might not. I'm sorry, Captain, but we're at capacity right now. We will try to do whatever we can to accommodate your people, but it will be difficult."

"Governor, we do not need much. We simply need a shelter and open air. Most of us are Andorians, and we can survive the cold. If you send us to one of your polar regions—"

"I'm afraid our polar regions are uninhabitable, Captain, and incredibly dangerous." Then something occurred to her. "Hold on—Lin, what about the stadiums?"

Lin looked confused. "What?"

"What is a stadium?"

Gari started calling up information on her computer as she spoke. "There's a sport that's rather popular on this world, Captain, called baseball. The game is played in a stadium."

"We've been using Ruth Field as a supplemental hospital," Lin said, "and both New Wrigley and Paige Fields are being used as processing centers."

"That still leaves seven of them. Pick one that will suit Captain zh'Ranthi's needs." Looking at the screen, Gari added, "These are outdoor areas, Captain, but enclosed."

"Arenas?"

"Of a kind, yes. The sport's season was supposed to start earlier this month, but we postponed because of the crisis. I can't promise it'll be all that comfortable, but—"

"Governor, after all these weeks on the Kovlessa, *it will be a relief. This vessel is designed for a crew of fifty, and there are four hundred and twenty-two of us. Open air is precisely what we need."*

"Good. Minister Lin will take care of the details."

Lin's face fell and zh'Ranthi scowled. *"Very well."*

She signed off. Lin looked like he was going to explode. Before he could, Gari said, "We're not turning them away, Lin. Period. Now get to work."

He opened his mouth, closed it, opened it again, then finally said, "Yes, ma'am. Thank you."

After he left, Gari yelled for Lucy. "I need you to put a call through to the Palais."

"I already have," she said, poking her head in.

That surprised Gari. "You did?"

"You told me to after I put you through to the *Kovlessa.*"

Gari put her head in her hands. "God, I did tell you to. I'm losing it."

"Then this probably isn't the best time to remind you about the press conference you have in fifteen minutes."

Her head still in her hands, she said, "Any way I can delegate that to someone else?"

"No, ma'am. It's about the new vehicle restrictions. The people need to hear that from you. The alternative is—"

"Lin, and we don't want that." She sighed. "All right, fine. If the Palais doesn't respond by the time I do the conference, find out what the *hell's* going on on Zalda."

"Yes, ma'am."

A letter to Professor Sonek Pran, sent by Sara Pran Yee on Troyius

Dear Dad:

Happy birthday! Feels like we only celebrated your sixtieth last week, but here it is, your sixty-fifth. You'll be hitting a hundred before you know it.

We made it to Troyius just fine. The Borg apparently left the planet alone because a Starfleet ship made the planet disappear temporarily. I've asked about a dozen people how they did that, and nobody's been able to give me a straight answer. But they're talking about building a statue to the captain of that ship—her name's Sonya Gomez. Didn't we used to know someone named Sonya Gomez? The name's really familiar, but I can't place it.

Anyhow, we got here just fine, like I said. We figured there'd be a lot of people crowded into big spaces, so we just brought along the acoustic instruments. For one thing, they're more portable—we can move from group to group and just play.

The only real problem is that it's midsummer here, and the humidity means I have to keep the autotuner on all *the time, which just drives me* nuts. *Jimmi's* ka'athyra *of course is always in tune, which I just don't understand, since* ka'athyras *are from a desert planet where there's very little humidity, so they couldn't have been built to deal with it very well. I guess Vulcans really are all as smart as G'ampa Tolik. How's he doing, anyhow?*

Where was I? Oh, yeah, the instruments. Fred decided to just bring the bongos, so he can wander with us more easily, A'l'e'r'w'w'o'k is leaving the Elisiar on the ship, but may take it out if we do something more stationary; he's using the rollout for now. Grandpa's on the jirvik, *of course, and Grandma's making sure everything sounds okay, like usual, even though we're staying acoustic for the time being. If nothing else, she'll make sure Fred doesn't hit the bongos too hard.*

We've been doing lots of folk numbers, mostly— things we figure people can sing along to. A lot of the refugees here are from Elas, and A'l'e'r'w'w'o'k knows a lot of Elasian dola *tunes, so he's been taking the lead on those. We've been mixing it in with some Earth sing-alongs and Bajoran spirituals. One guy yesterday requested a Klingon opera— Jimmi was all for it, but the rest of us overruled him. Maybe if we perform with the Elisiar . . .*

Anyhow, it's going very well. These people are scared and miserable, and we're doing what we can to cheer them. A lot of them don't know each other—they're from cities all over Elas, and some are from other worlds, and they don't have much in common, but we're bringing them together by singing. It's really been great.

Gotta go, Dad. For some reason Jimmi wants to practice. Obviously, he never took to heart what G'ampa Byero always said: the last thing you want to do is over-rehearse. The spontaneity is a lot of what's making this fun—except when A'l'e'r'w'w'o'k forgets what key we're in, anyhow. He nearly busted a tentacle when I told him that "Selvarao Maktu" *is in A, not D.*

Anyhow, I'll write soon. Oh, and Ayib is at P'Jem. You should really get in touch with him.

Happy birthday again!

Your loving daughter,

Sara

4

EARTH

Though he traced a quarter of his heritage to the capital of the Federation, Sonek Pran had no great attachment to Earth. However, he did love the view of the Paris skyline as the government shuttle flew through the clouds and headed for the roof of the Palais de la Concorde.

"Palais control," said the pilot, a genial young Benzite woman named Mardral, "this is Shuttle Nine on approach."

"Shuttle Nine, this is Palais control, you are clear to land on the roof. Welcome back. I'll let Zachary know his package is here."

"I'm a 'package,' huh?" Sonek said with a grin.

"Something like that, sir, yes."

"You don't have to call me 'sir,' Mardral, I'm just a college professor on a field trip." He stared at the Benzite woman, who had a breathing unit attached to her chest. " 'Shuttle Nine'? Is that really the best that you people could come up with to name this thing?"

"We leave the fancy names to Starfleet, Professor."

"Fair enough." He stared out the shuttle's portal at the beautiful combination of old and new buildings. There was the Bâtiment Vingt-Troisième Siècle, constructed at the turn of the century eighty-one years ago, the Tour Eiffel, constructed five hundred years earlier, Notre Dame Cathedral, which dated back twelve centuries, and the Palais de la Concorde, which wasn't as old as the Tour Eiffel or Notre Dame, but not as new as the BVTS. Straddling the Champs Élysées, the cylindrical fifteen-story building was the heart of the Federation government.

Sonek had been born in space. His father, Kojo Pran, and maternal grandparents were all part of a travelling troupe of musicians called the A.C. Walden Medicine Show, and his mother, T'Nallis, was the show's sound engineer. They were on a transport taking them to a gig on Betazed—the homeworld of one of those grandparents—but it had suffered some kind of engine problem, and it was stuck at warp one. That meant the four-day trip took a month, and instead of giving birth in a nice hospital in Medara on Betazed, T'Nallis gave birth to Sonek in interstellar space.

That set the tone for the rest of his life. Growing up in a family of musicians, travel was a constant. Once Sonek was old enough to study at a university, he did so, getting his undergraduate degree at YloTrap on Betazed, his master's at Fordham University on Earth, and his doctorate at the V'Shull Institute on Vulcan.

There were times when he missed being with the Medicine Show. Sonek was a decent banjo player, and also could play the harmonica, the *zorvat,* and the *ka'athyra.* But he didn't have the same passion for music that his father and grandparents had—and that his daughter Sara had apparently inherited from them—so he followed his grandfather into academia, even as Sara joined the Medicine Show when she was old enough.

The political element came about somewhat by accident.

Mardral smoothly landed the prosaically named Shuttle Nine onto the circular roof of the Palais. As the door levered open, several people who were obviously crew of some kind went to take care of the shuttle.

Turning to the pilot, Sonek said, "Look, Mardral, I know you don't know me, but I really think you'd be better off if you just gave her an answer."

The Benzite stared at him. "How did you know?"

He pointed at her rebreather. "You've got half a pledge stone on that thing there, and it's the half that says you've been approached. The half that says you've said yes is empty, and you've been fingering it and looking at it this whole trip."

"I just don't know if I'm ready."

Sonek shrugged. "You put the stone on in the first place. Seems to me you think it's worth a shot. Besides, it's not like you're pledged for life."

"True." She smiled. "Thanks, Professor."

"No problem," he said with a smile. Benzite biology was complicated, and had nothing to do with personal relationships and family. The people you reproduced with weren't the same as the people you spent your life with. Sonek had always found it a somewhat liberating system—particularly given his current lack of a relationship with his son.

Putting those unpleasant thoughts aside, he exited the shuttle onto the roof. He was wearing a purple shirt and leather vest, and as he stepped out into the cool spring air, he wished he'd worn something warmer.

The same face Sonek had seen on his desk screen yesterday was attached to the person standing near the roof entrance. Sonek sauntered over toward him, the wind catching his long white hair and blowing it into his face. Brushing it away from his eyes with one hand, he held out the other. "Mr. Manzanillo, it's truly a pleasure to be back in this building."

"How long has it been?" Zachary asked, returning the handshake.

"About eight years now. A couple days after the Dominion took Deep Space 9, President Zife decided that my counsel wasn't needed, seeing as how he wasn't actually listening to any of it anyway."

The pair of them walked to the entrance, which slid aside at their approach to reveal a turbolift. Sonek knew from his many visits here in the past that, as the turbolift took them down into the building, he and Zachary were both being thoroughly scanned.

After going down only two floors, the lift stopped and opened to the usual chaos of the Palais. *No, actually, this is more chaos than usual.* Sonek had last been here during the ramp-up to the Dominion War, and the ambient noise then was about half what it was now. People from dozens of different species were dashing through the halls, walking in and out of offices, reading over padds while walking, shouting at each other, shouting into comscreens, and so on.

Sonek had expected hustle and bustle, but this was the Palais in full crisis mode, and it hit him like a slap on the face. He had to remind himself how easy he'd had it the last couple of months, teaching at a university on a planet that hadn't been hit by the Borg. Mars and Earth had come close—in fact, Sonek, along with Tolik and dozens of other faculty and students from McKay, had joined the thousands at the candlelight vigil at the Settler's Monument in Cydonia when the Borg were on approach, before they surprisingly turned around and headed back to the Azure Nebula.

But life on Mars got fairly normal after that. It was easy, from the hallowed halls of academe, to forget how much carnage there had been—and how much work it would be to fix it.

It was, however, impossible to do so while standing on the fourteenth floor of the Palais.

"So Ms. Piñiero's down here on fourteen, is she?"

"Uh, yes," Zachary said. "That's the traditional spot for the COS."

"Mr. Azernal kept his office up on fifteen alongside the president's."

" 'Traditional' isn't the first word that comes to mind when describing Mr. Azernal," Zachary said with a small smile.

"That's for damn sure."

They arrived at a desk cluttered with padds and a computer station, which was blinking. Touching a control, Zachary said, "Esperanza, he's here."

"Give me a minute, Zachary." The chief of staff sounded haggard.

Indicating the guest chair adjacent to his desk, Zachary said, "Have a seat."

Sonek sat while Zachary started scrolling through

messages on his terminal. Then he snarled and set up a comm line. A Bolian face appeared on the screen. "Jai, what the hell?"

"What the hell, what?"

"I told you that Esperanza can't see your boss until tomorrow. You may find this hard to believe, but upgrading the transporter network on Bolarus isn't her highest priority right now."

"And there's no reason why it should be, but it should be at some *level of priority. Right now our skies are being choked with shuttle traffic. We're doing our part, unlike some planets I could name."*

"They're talking about Zalda downstairs right now."

"Fine, but if we had the transporter upgrades we were supposed to have six months ago, we'd be able to handle the refugees much more easily."

"I know, I know, but we've had bigger problems. Look, if you want to talk to Ashanté Phiri or Myk Bunkrep—"

"The councillor doesn't appreciate being fobbed off on flunkies."

"They're not 'flunkies,' Jai, they're deputy chiefs of staff, and odds are good Esperanza would kick it over to them, anyhow."

"I'll ask the councillor when the session's over."

"And no more threats to pull out of the Federation, please?"

"No promises." With that, the screen went blank.

"You should've called his bluff," Sonek said.

Zachary started, as if he'd forgetten that Sonek was there. "What?"

"It's not like the Bolians are actually going to go ahead and pull out of the Federation. Councillor Nea doesn't really have that kind of authority, and I'm guessing that the Quorum of Bole isn't entirely with her on that, especially if we're just talking about fixing transporters."

"What are you saying?"

"If she's gonna claim to set phasers on kill, make her pull the trigger. Then when she does admit that the thing was on stun all along, she won't be able to make that threat so easily in the future."

The door slid open to reveal the round visage of Esperanza Piñiero. The last time Sonek had seen the woman's face was a few months ago, when she appeared on *Illuminating the City of Light,* a Federation News Service discussion program. In that time, the number of lines on her face and gray hairs had increased. Her brown eyes were bloodshot, and Sonek was half expecting her to collapse in front of him.

"Professor Pran?"

Rising to his feet, Sonek said, "Yes, ma'am."

Holding out her hand, Esperanza said, "It's an honor to meet you, Professor. Your reputation precedes you."

"I doubt that," Sonek said, returning the handshake, "or you'd know that meeting me isn't all that much of an honor at all, Ms. Piñiero."

"Don't sell yourself short, Professor. And it's Esperanza, please."

"Sonek."

Breaking off the handshake—Sonek noted that her grip was firm despite her obvious fatigue—she stepped back from the doorway. "Come in, please."

Zachary said, "Thanks for the advice, Professor."

With a nod, Sonek said, "You're welcome," and entered Esperanza's office.

Sonek gazed around the room. Most of one wall was taken up by a picture window that provided a smaller version of the view from the president's office, which was right above this one. Another wall had a couch with a chair perpendicular to it, a table between them, and a painting of the skyline of Johnson City on Cestus III at sunset over the couch.

The third wall had the door and a closet and a replicator. Esperanza's desk chair was against the fourth wall, giving her a look at both the painting over the couch in front of her and the view of Paris to the right. Two wooden guest chairs sat on the other side of the big metal desk.

Esperanza walked to the replicator first. "Something to drink?"

"*Allira* punch would be wonderful, if you don't mind."

"Not at all." She put her hand on the control. "One *allira* punch, and one Jack Daniel's, neat."

Sonek frowned. "I thought Palais replicators couldn't dispense alcohol during business hours."

The two drinks materialized with a soft hum. Esperanza grabbed them both. "We disabled that feature when the Borg destroyed Deneva. We never got around to restoring it."

"Can't imagine why," Sonek said dryly as he took the tall frosted glass from the chief of staff.

Taking her square, thick-bottomed glass with its amber liquid to the chair perpendicular to the couch, Esperanza said, "Have a seat, Sonek. What was Zachary thanking you for?"

Sonek sat down on the couch, which was incredibly

comfortable. This, he felt, bode well for the meeting. If she wanted him to be comfortable, then it was going to be a pleasant conversation. He knew that the chief of staff had plenty of unpleasant conversations in this room, and he suspected that those took place across the desk.

In answer to her query, Sonek said, "I gave him a bit of advice on dealing with the councillor from Bolarus."

Esperanza winced. "The transporter thing?"

Sonek nodded.

She started to say something, then waved it off. "I can't think about that right now."

"I gotta tell you, Esperanza, I was surprised to hear from the Palais. President Zife and me, well—we didn't exactly see eye to eye, which is why I've been on Mars all this time, but—"

"Your name did actually come up a few times, Sonek, but we weren't sure you'd say yes, given the way things ended with President Zife."

"Esperanza, some thirty-odd years ago or so, President T'Pragh read a monograph I wrote about the Cardassians and called me into this building to talk to me about it. She asked me to serve then, and I've never turned down the call to do so since."

Esperanza smiled, and Sonek had the feeling that it was her first smile of the day. "I'm very glad to hear that, Sonek, because that's exactly what President Bacco is asking you to do now."

Sonek let out a long breath, and his shoulders felt as if two-ton weights had suddenly been removed from them. He actually sank further into the couch, which he wouldn't have believed possible.

Until this moment, he hadn't truly believed that he was going to be asked.

"What can I do for the Federation, Esperanza?"

Setting down her drink on the table, she asked, "How much do you know about the current state of the Romulans?"

"About a year and a half ago—right around the time that President Bacco took office—Praetor Hiren and most of the Senate were killed and usurped by a Reman named Shinzon. Shinzon got himself killed while trying to invade the Federation. One of the surviving senators, Tal'Aura, took over as praetor, but she was the one who wiped out the Senate on Shinzon's behalf, so she wasn't exactly overwhelmed with support. Late last year, a military commander named Donatra set herself up as empress of the Imperial Romulan State, with about half the military and all of the Romulan breadbasket in her pocket. The Federation and the Klingons both went ahead and recognized Donatra's government, and her ships were a big help against the Borg. In fact, one of her ships sacrificed itself to save Ardana. Right now, half the population on Ardana's wearing Romulan military haircuts."

Esperanza's eyes went wide. "Seriously?"

Sonek nodded while sipping his punch. After swallowing, he said, "My wife's the transporter chief on the *Sugihara,* and they're in charge of Ardana's reconstruction efforts."

"Ah." She leaned back in her chair. "Here's the thing: While we do recognize Donatra's government, we're also still providing aid to Romulus, just like we have since Shinzon's coup. Now, though—"

"Now we're stretched kind of thin."

"Yes, and there's a rather obvious trading partner right next door."

"Donatra won't trade with the Star Empire?"

Esperanza shook her head. "Our ambassadors have asked her, Starfleet's asked her, but she's standing firm. And we're the ones who owe *her* a favor after Ardana, which makes it hard to ask for another one with any authority. That's where you come in. I told you your reputation preceded you, and while it may have been your monograph that got you into President T'Pragh's office, it was your ability to convince her that you were right about the Cardassians that kept you there, and made her and three other presidents keep you around, at least for a while. You talked the Brikar into reopening their orbit, you talked the Caitians into staying in the Federation when they were set to leave—again—and you talked the Sulamid energy minister into complying with the Edosian Accords."

"And yet, I can't convince my students to take on sensible essay topics," Sonek said with a smile.

"There's a Starfleet ship, the *Aventine,* that's taking relief supplies to Artaleirh, which is one of Tal'Aura's worlds. After that, they'll take you to Achernar Prime, where you can work your magic on Donatra."

"Now, Esperanza," Sonek started, suddenly nervous, "I can't do magic. I'm no telepath, and I'm no diplomat. I'm just a person who likes to talk to people."

"You're more than that, Sonek, and you know it. And don't worry, we know there's a good chance that you'll fail. Donatra's been pretty ruthless in catering to her own self-interest. Keeping Tal'Aura down is a big part of that, and it's going to be hard to convince her otherwise. The finest minds in the Diplomatic Corps and in Starfleet have already tried. But we've got nothing to lose by trying again with you."

Sonek finished off his punch. The fact was, he was looking forward to the opportunity, but he also didn't want anyone to have unrealistic expectations. From the sounds of it, nobody did, so he was probably safe.

"The *Aventine*'s one of the new *Vestas*, right? Has the slipstream drive?"

Esperanza's mouth hung open for a second. "Uhm—yes. How'd you know that?"

He smiled. "I've still got level-twenty clearance, Esperanza, Don't *use* it much, but it does help me to keep up with things."

"How did you wind up with that high a clearance?" Esperanza asked incredulously.

Sonek shrugged. "I needed it for what President T'Pragh had me do during the Cardassian War, and nobody ever rescinded it."

"Hm." Esperanza grabbed her drink and finished it off. "Well, keep that to yourself. That's the kind of thing that'll probably annoy the other people on the *Aventine*. Anyhow, yes, it does have slipstream, and even without that, it's one of our fastest ships, which is why they're doing relief work right now. You should report to Captain Dax first thing in the morning. You have somewhere to stay tonight?"

"Yeah, I have a standing reservation at the Lutetia. Haven't needed it for eight years, but it's still there."

"Good." Esperanza rose, and Sonek did likewise. "The *Aventine*'s due in late tonight, then they'll be loading up the supplies, then heading out at 0600."

Sonek winced. "Now, just for the record? Starfleet's notions of 'first thing in the morning' are entirely different from *my* notions of 'first thing in the morning.' I'd better head over to the hotel and start catching up on my sleep right now." He held out his hand. "It's an honor to be serving again, Esperanza. Thank you."

"The honor's ours, Sonek, and thank *you*. If you have anything to report or any questions, don't hesitate to contact Zachary. He'll find me. Use code nine eight seven alpha blue six, and you'll be put through straight to him."

"Thanks."

Sonek exited the office, with Esperanza right behind him. Zachary said, "I've got Secretary Offenhouse. He says he has bad news about the Iotians."

"Of *course* he has bad news." Esperanza rolled her eyes. "Does anybody have any other kind?"

"I'll do my best to give you good news, Esperanza."

She smiled again. "Appreciate it, Sonek, truly." To Zachary: "Put Offenhouse through and then escort Professor Pran to the transporter. He's headed to the Lutetia."

Zachary nodded.

Sonek was still smiling, though. He hadn't realized how happy this would make him. *Of course, you should have—you had the stupid conversation with Gramps fifteen times for a reason, after all.* In fact, the voice in his head sounded a lot like Tolik.

Well, you're doing it. You're back in the Palais and you're on your way to Achernar Prime to talk to an empress. This is more like it.

—

President Nanietta Bacco pinched the bridge of her nose as she entered the Federation Council Chambers from her private entrance behind the podium, staving off the current headache. The door slid aside at the approach of two members of her security detail, Agents Wexler and Kistler, and she followed them into the large room on the first floor of the Palais.

Since taking office, Nan Bacco had started to categorize her headaches. Headaches three, six, and seven all were Borg related, and she'd had at least one of them at any given time more or less nonstop since last June. She had been stuck on *Paris One,* the presidential interstellar transport, which had been hit by an unexpected level-ten ion storm en route from Kazar to Earth. Communications, navigation, and warp drive were all down for the count, and Nan was completely out of touch and unable to move for three days while they waited out the storm. During that time, a massive Borg cube invaded the solar system, eliminated Pluto, and almost destroyed Earth, until Captain Picard and the *Enterprise* pulled the latest in a series of rabbits out of their hat to save them all. By the time they cleared the storm and learned what had happened, it was all over. Nan had been less than thrilled with how the Council had handled things in her absence, having apparently sent a diplomatic team to try to negotiate with the Borg, which was about as effective as it would have been had Nan sent such a team to talk to the ion storm.

Today, though, was headache two, which she only got when something happened on Cestus III, and she found herself longing to be governor of the planet again, so she could just deal with it herself, instead of having to listen to her former lieutenant governor talk about it.

The latest harangue from Governor Gari was the cause of this emergency Council session. As she entered, she scanned the galleries on either side of the speaker's floor at the chamber's center, and only about two dozen of the councillors were present. However, the only two who absolutely needed to be here were right in their respective seats: Councillor Molmaan of Zalda and Councillor Djinian of Cestus III. All things being equal, Nan would have raised the issue herself, but it was more appropriate coming from Djinian.

Everyone stood up at Nan's entrance, including the councillors, and several reporters in the gallery. In fact, the reporters outnumbered the councillors, because the majority of the Council members needed to be on or near their homeworlds right now.

With a twinge in her chest, her eyes fell on the seat that belonged to Nerramibus of Alonis. He had been on his way home, with seven members of his staff as well as a pilot and copilot for his personal transport, when he ran into a Borg cube. Alonis had yet to name his successor, nor would they until the mourning period ended.

"Take your seats," Nan said as she stood at the podium. "Council is now in session." The computer then took roll call for the record.

Once that was done, Djinian activated the light in front of her seat, as planned.

"The podium recognizes the councillor from Cestus III."

Djinian was dressed only in a drab gray jumpsuit that looked awful against her dark skin. Usually, she had dressed up for Council sessions, but such things had been much more lax of late.

During full sessions of the Federation Council, the only people who could speak for the record were the person at the podium and anyone on the speaker's floor, who had to be recognized by the podium. There was no limit to the number of people who could be on the floor, though it rarely went above three.

"With the podium's permission," Djinian said, "I would like to play the recording submitted. It's an exchange between Zaldan Orbital Command and the Andorian vessel *Kovlessa* three weeks ago."

"Podium grants permission," Nan said.

Djinian nodded to the clerk, who activated a control. Sound came over the speakers, filling the room.

"Zaldan Orbital Control, this is the Kovlessa. *We have refugees from Alrond, requesting permission to enter orbit and begin transporting."*

"Permission denied, Kovlessa."

"Zalda, your world is the designated planet for refugees in this sector."

"Permission denied. Go elsewhere. Zaldan Orbital Control out."

"Computer," Djinian said to the chamber's interface, "please examine the transponder signals in the just-played communication. What do they correspond to?"

While the computer answered, Molmaan's light predictably went on. *"To the civilian transport vessel* Kovlessa *and to the Orbital Control satellite of planet Zalda."*

"The podium recognizes the councillor from Zalda," Nan said, thinking, *This oughtta be good.*

Molmaan practically stomped down to the floor. Nan imagined smoke coming out of his ears, and his eyes were smoldering. The second his foot touched the floor, he bellowed, "Zalda will *not* allow such lies to be told! I am outraged that such falsehoods are being broadcast in *open council!* Such an insult *cannot* be tolerated!"

Throwing up his webbed hands, he then left the floor—and the chamber.

Nan wasn't expecting that. "Councillor! Please come back so we can—"

"Zalda will not be part of a Federation of liars!" Molmaan cried over his shoulder, and departed.

Nan stared after the door for several seconds. Kistler walked up to her and whispered, "Should someone go after him, Madam President?"

Staring at her bodyguard, Nan deactivated her podium pickup so she'd be off the record and whispered back, "And do what? He's a Federation councillor, not a fugitive. He's welcome to come and go as he pleases, and I'm not about to start holding councillors prisoner in here. Hell, most of the time, I'm happy to be rid of them."

Reactivating the pickup, Nan said, "The councillor from Zalda has yielded the floor, and has presented no explanation."

Djinian said, "In light of this, Madam President, I would like to move that Zalda be stricken from the refugee list until such time as the reasons for refusing the *Kovlessa* can be determined."

Nan asked for a seconding of the motion, which was provided by Councillor Nea of Bolarus. All the remaining councillors present then agreed to the motion, a gesture of unanimity that either bespoke the gravity of the situation or the fact that there was such a small number of councillors present.

Either way, Nan thought, *this doesn't exactly make*

anybody's life easier. The one thing she had been hoping for was that the Council would remain united in this time of crisis. Until now, they had.

The part Nan was least looking forward to was the conversation with Governor Gari. *Headache two is in for the long haul.*

A memo from Federation Transportation Secretary Iliop to President Nan Bacco and Chief of Staff Esperanza Piñiero

As per our discussion earlier today, our latest reports from the Klingon High Council are that they do not require our aid with refugees. While some may, of course, cross the border and ask for assistance, officially, all Klingon nationals are to travel to designated refugee planets. As a matter of fact, the plan the High Council has instituted is remarkably similar to our own. It was apparently suggested by Commander Worf three years ago, during his tenure as Federation Ambassador to the Empire. Designated refugee worlds include Ty'Gokor, Pheben III, Ikalia, and Krios.

Ty'Gokor is specifically for surviving members of the High Council and generals in the Defense Force—as well as the surviving members of their families—whose homes have been lost. That world is serving as the temporary capital of the Empire until the First City is rebuilt—if it can be. Martok is apparently considering making the move to Ty'Gokor permanent.

Pheben III is a farming world, and while farm production has become critical, there are also many wide-open spaces that can be used. In addition, refugees to that planet are being pressed into labor to help with the harvesting of crops, particularly on the northern continent, where it is currently harvest season for *hurkik*, *gonklik*, and *Sovat*.

Ikalia was the site of a battle with the Romulans during which several Starfleet officers were kidnapped twelve years ago. When the Klingons reentered the Khitomer Accords eight years ago, one of the concessions the Federation granted to the Empire was to give them Ikalia. It's been the site of an underfunded research station and little else, so there's plenty of room for refugees, though very little by way of resources. It's the only one of the four that doesn't have some existing structure by which the refugees could possibly survive, and it's likely that lower-class citizens are being diverted there.

Finally, Krios is the refugee world closest to the Federation border. That planet has a massive hunting preserve that is owned by the House of G'mtor. However, G'mtor was killed in action on the *Sword of Kahless* against the Borg, and the Borg wiped out the House G'mtor estates on Qu'Vat during their run through the Empire. Since no one of that House remains alive, the High Council has declared their lands property of the government, and the preserve—which is literally thousands of square kilometers of mostly flat grassland—to be a refugee center, and refugees can apparently hunt their own food.

Should those worlds prove unable to handle the refugee load, we will need to address that issue, though with Zalda apparently no longer accepting refugees, it will be very difficult, since that's the designated world closest to the Klingon border.

5

KRIOS

Captain Drex, son of Martok, could feel the eyes of his first officer boring into the back of his neck.

"Report, Commander," he said.

"We are entering standard orbit of Krios. Convoy settling into orbital pathways as well."

Drex could see that on the forward viewscreen of the *I.K.S. Rovlaq*. While it was standard procedure for the first officer to inform the captain of this, it was hardly necessary. So he turned to face Commander Nidd. "Speak, Commander. What is on your mind?"

Nidd hesitated. Normally, a warrior who hesitated on the bridge of a *Vor'cha*-class battle cruiser would be dead eight seconds later, but Nidd's hesitation was born of confusion. Klingon captains, as a rule, did not ask their subordinates to speak their minds.

But times have changed, Drex thought, *and the old ways may not be best.*

Had the Drex of five years ago heard his present-day self speak those words, he would have been appalled—

and likely homicidal. But as he grew older—and eventually received his own command—he realized that a truly wise warrior knew when to ask questions. While a captain's orders should be obeyed, sometimes a captain's subordinates should be listened to. Every once in a while, wisdom issued forth.

Not that such was likely from Nidd. He was first officer by virtue of the other candidates for the job being dead at the hands of the Borg. The *Rovlaq* was one of only two ships that survived the Borg assault on the Mempa system. Drex's best warriors—and several of his poorer ones—died in the battle. Replacements were few, so the ship was short-handed. For example, though he'd been elevated to first officer—which Drex had done because, well, *somebody* needed to fill the position, and Nidd was the seniormost officer besides Drex on board—the commander was at the ops position behind the captain's chair, as only two warriors on board were capable of operating that particular console with any skill.

Finally, Nidd spoke. "Our current mission is not very glorious, sir. We were among the survivors of Mempa! We destroyed one of the *khest'n* cubes!"

Drex let out a snarl. Yes, technically, the *Rovlaq* fired a torpedo that took out one Borg cube out of the two dozen that ravaged the Mempa system, but it was a minor victory in a massacre.

Nidd went on. "We should not be playing *ghojmoq* to mere civilians!"

Drex turned to the screen again, watching as dozens of small ships of varying designs took on orbital paths proximate to the *Rovlaq*. "What would you have them do, Commander? Fend for themselves? Many of them have paltry weapons and little shielding. Shall we leave subjects of the Empire to die? They have already lost their homes to an honorless foe. Would you abandon them to depredators and pirates?"

"I would have them fight for themselves."

Drex wondered if Nidd had paid attention to a single word he'd said. "We are the Klingon Defense Force, Nidd. Our purpose—our duty—is to safeguard the lives of Klingon nationals throughout the Empire. If we do not do that, then what is our worth, truly?"

Nidd said nothing—which was fine, as the question was rhetorical. Under other circumstances, Drex might have considered killing Nidd for his stupidity and incompetence, but there was literally no one else on board he trusted to stand for the crew.

He had been given this assignment by his father—the first time father and son had had a moment to even speak to each other in months. In fact, it was the first time since Drex had taken command of the *Rovlaq* a year earlier.

This time Drex and Martok had shared a meal on Ty'Gokor. "Your request for crew replacements has been denied, my son," the chancellor had said while chewing his *klongat* leg.

"I understand, Father."

"Still, yours is a *Vor'cha*—it will be sufficient to defend those bound for Krios."

"Of course." Drex had been picking at his *bok-rat* liver.

"You do not like the food, my son?"

Drex smiled. "It is not very well prepared."

"True." Martok rumbled a sigh. "My personal chef perished on Qo'noS, and good replacements are even harder to find in the kitchen than they are in the Defense Force. Still, you will make do with what you have—as we make do now. You will be escorting a convoy of ships from Mempa to Krios. They are relocating there temporarily."

Drex nodded. "There are suvivors from Mempa?"

Smiling wryly, Martok asked, "Did you think your ship to be the only one? No, some were able to escape before the Borg devastated the system. The House of G'mtor's hunting preserve will be their new home for now. Your mission, my son, is to protect them from whoever might crawl out from under a rock."

"The Kinshaya?" Drex guessed the answer, but Martok's quick nod confirmed it.

"They have been quiet since their defeat," the chancellor said, "but that will not last, especially with the Empire weakened."

The Kinshaya were a small nation that had been at war with the Klingon Empire for centuries. Too tenacious to be conquered, too weak to ever achieve victory, the result was a state of constant battle.

However, recently, the Kinshaya had expanded. Another species that had been harassing the Klingons for centuries were the Kreel—though they were more akin to a *kretlach* that picked at Klingon conquests. A year ago, the Kinshaya conquered the Kreel and added their fleet of ships to their own military.

The defeat Martok mentioned had been at the hands of the *I.K.S Gorkon* many months ago, an engagement that left the Kinshaya without a habitable homeworld and earned Klag, son of M'Raq, a promotion to general and command of the Fifth Fleet. But it was only a matter of time before they were done licking their wounds from that defeat and bared their teeth again. Drex had served briefly under Captain Klag, and knew that the son of M'Raq had earned his promotion.

"Father," Drex had asked, "are you well?"

Martok's good eye had widened in shock, and Drex had been perversely pleased to actually surprise his father. "My leg has healed. The rest is politics," he had said with a dismissive wave of his hand. "I have borne politics for five turns now—which frankly is four and a half turns longer than I expected to *remain* as chancellor. I survived the Dominion, I survived Morjod, I survived the Elabrej and the Kinshaya, I survived Tezwa, and I survived the Borg. I shall survive this as well."

Drex spoke with confidence. "You will do more than that, Father—you will thrive."

"You express sentiment like a human, my son."

"Do I? So be it. You are my father, and you are my chancellor. Both of us were almost lost to the most honorless of foes. The Empire has been weakened. If that prompts sentiment, then that is what it does."

Martok had chuckled, moving to bite his *klongat*, then setting it aside. "Weakened we may be—but not diminished. We face difficult times, my son. I have not always been sure that you would be at my side in the dark days ahead." He smiled. "It is good to know that you shall be."

"Always, Father."

"Qapla', Captain Drex—my strong son!"

"Qapla', Father!"

Drex's reverie was interrupted by Nidd. "We are being contacted by the head of the convoy."

"On-screen." Drex faced the viewer and tried not to think about how difficult it would be to stand by his father with Nidd speaking for his crew.

Contempt dripping from his voice, Nidd said, "They do not have visual capability."

"On audio, then."

"Captain Drex, this is Gotlak, son of Gotlak."

Several officers burst out with laughter at that. Most of the convoy were from the rural parts of Mempa VIII, and there was an old tradition among the country dwellers of that world that the first-born son was named for the father, by way of preserving the family name. Drex considered pointing this out to his bridge crew, and that all high-born Klingons used to do that, before the tradition changed and Houses simply changed their name to reflect the House head rather than force the first-born son to keep the same name as his father.

But Drex decided that educating this crew wasn't worth the effort.

Gotlak continued. *"You honor us with your escort, son of Martok, and we thank you for protecting us on our journey to our new home."*

Drex winced. "This is not your new home, Gotlak—it is simply where you and your people are being housed while the High Council determines where to settle you permanently. You will be transported to a hunting preserve until that determination is made."

"Of course, Captain. You have our gratitude. Gotlak out."

Rising to his feet, Drex thought, *But not your comprehension*. Drex had explained the reality of the situation to Gotlak in person when they had met up with the convoy on the outskirts of what was left of the Mempa system. Gotlak's people had been living on their ships for months now.

"Contact Governor Doq and tell him—"

"Sir, multiple ships coming out of warp!"

Drex's complaint about Nidd's interruption died on his lips. "Battle alert! Identify vessels!"

Nidd let out a snarl. "Kinshaya. There are twelve ships approaching on multiple attack vectors."

Drex sat back down in his chair. *It seems Father's concerns were correct.* Nidd had put the ships on the viewer, and Drex saw twelve of the black globe-shaped ships that the Kinshaya favored, each marked with a different design that denoted something about its captain. Drex neither knew nor cared about the specifics—Kinshaya were there to be defeated, nothing more.

"Set course 182 mark 4, full impulse. Train all weapons on multiple targets and fire!"

The course was not ideal—it put them between the Kinshaya and the convoy and limited the *Rovlaq*'s maneuverability—but the convoy needed to be protected at all costs.

"Kinshaya firing." Nidd then looked up suddenly. "Captain, scans show they have Breen disruptors!"

No wonder we haven't heard from them since the Borg attack—they've been refitting their ships. It had been a source of annoyance to Drex that the Empire didn't see fit to conquer the Breen after the Dominion War, and now it was a source of something worse.

"Three enemy vessels destroyed," Nidd said, "and four convoy vessels also destroyed." Disruptor fire impacted with the *Rovlaq*. "Shields at thirty percent!"

"Continuous fire, all weapons! Nidd, send an alert to Command, inform them of this invasion!"

"Captain," said Nidd, "one of the Kinshaya vessels is on course for Governor Doq's satellite!"

Klingon governors often kept their seat of power in orbit. "Pilot, change course to defend the satellite!"

The pilot said, "There are four enemy vessels between us and the satellite, sir."

"Gunner, get them out of our way."

The gunner—an eager young ensign whose name Drex could never remember—said, "It will be a pleasure, Captain."

As expected, the Kinshaya ships closed the gap between them and the *Rovlaq,* even as the latter moved toward them. The Kinshaya ships were small, and a standard battle tactic would be to fly in close to the hull, reducing the effectiveness of the ship's disruptor cannons.

Of course, that was why Defense Force engineers gave the disruptor cannons the ability to rotate, something the Kinshaya either forgot or didn't know about or didn't care about.

However, the Kinshaya had also increased their shielding capabilities. The disruptor fire did not destroy them, and two of the ships crashed into the *Rovlaq*'s port wing, pulverizing the wing's cannon.

"Scans indicate the shields are Romulan," Nidd said.

"I do not care," Drex said. "Target the ship that is after the satellite!"

"Ten seconds to firing range," the pilot said, even as Nidd said, "Kinshaya firing on satellite. Satellite returning fire."

Ten agonizing seconds later, Governor Doq's satellite was destroyed, though not before wiping out its attacker's shields, leaving them vulnerable to a single shot from the *Rovlaq.*

"Three more convoy ships destroyed," Nidd said.

Drex snarled a curse. *We were charged with* protecting *them!*

The gunner said, "Shields down to ten percent!"

"Divert all shield power to the port wing," Drex said. *If we can hold them off long enough to destroy the rest of them, we might survive. Once the shields are down, our damaged wing will leave us vulnerable.*

The remaining six Kinshaya ships all converged on the *Rovlaq,* recognizing that, with the governor's satellite destroyed, the only true threat was Drex's ship.

Naturally, the Kinshaya focused their weapons to port, since those gunports and cannons were gone.

Drex made a decision. "Arm all torpedoes, and target the remaining ships. If it is a good day to die, then it is a good day for *all* of us!"

The gunner did not hesitate. "Yes, sir!"

Perhaps she does not realize that, this close, the torpedoes' detonation will take down what's left of our shields. It was a gamble—that they would destroy all six before their shields went down.

Clenching his fist, Drex said, "Fire!"

The torpedoes spat out of their cannons toward the enemy vessels.

Four of them were consumed by fire. The other two remained intact thanks to their Romulan shields and fired their Breen disruptors on the hole where the *Rovlaq*'s port wing cannon used to be.

Drex turned to look at Nidd. Nidd simply nodded back. "It has been an honor, Captain," he said quietly.

Though he could not bring himself to say likewise, Drex said, "We will meet again in *Sto-Vo-Kor.*"

Consoles began exploding around Drex, and a crack formed in the outer hull. Explosive decompression sent him careening toward it. Just before his head collided with the collapsing hull, Drex thought, *It seems I won't be standing by your side, Father.*

A suicide note left by Augustus Betances

I was pissed about the curtains.

It was the latest in a series of stupid arguments, the kind that couples have all the time, but ultimately, the curtains were the pin that broke the zipthar*'s wing. I could handle her insistence that we send Penelope to the school in Tellerton, even though the school three blocks away was just fine. I could handle her redecorating our bedroom without asking me. I could even handle her sudden conversion to vegetarianism after she did that project with the team of Vulcans.*

But after I specifically said how much I hated the red curtains, she went ahead and got them and put them up in the living room, and went on about how much our friends all liked them.

That was it. I couldn't take it anymore. I took a month's leave from the office, and I told her I was going to Wrigley's Pleasure Planet for a month to calm down.

How stupid is that? To go away from my wife and daughter for a month over curtains*?*

I knew the Borg were starting to attack the Federation, but I managed to get a seat on a transport. They hadn't attacked anywhere near Deneva or *Wrigley's. Everything should've been fine.*

I stood there in the lobby of the hotel, along with everyone else, watching FNS, hearing about the destruction.

I saw the feed from Deneva.

I tried to get home. It took months, and all I found was a pile of ash where our home—where the city we lived in—used to be. All our other friends, what little family either of us had left—all dead.

I checked myself into a hospital on P'Jem, but it hasn't done me any good. I should've been with them. Or maybe they *should have left and* I *should have died. Either way, though, I can't live with the guilt. I can't live with the sheer* stupidity *of it all.*

Elia and Penelope didn't deserve to die. I do. So I'm ending it all. I don't have anyone left anyhow, so what's the point?

Good-bye.

Augustus Betances, former citizen of Deneva

6

U.S.S. AVENTINE

"We're ferrying a *history professor* through Romulan space? Since when are we a tourist liner?"

Captain Ezri Dax sighed at the outburst from her first officer, Commander Sam Bowers, who sat facing her in her ready room off the bridge of the *Aventine*. "He's not just a history professor, Sam, that's just what he does when he's not serving as a government adviser. He's supposed to take a meeting with Donatra."

"Is that going to be before or after we bring food to Artaleirh?"

"After."

Bowers rubbed his temples with his thumbs. "Okay. I'm sorry, I just feel like we're being wasted."

Dax shot her first officer a look.

" 'Wasted' may be too strong a word. . . ."

"Sam, we're taking food to hungry people."

"And I agree that Starfleet should be providing relief to people in the Romulan Star Empire. I just don't see why it has to be us. We're a multimission explorer, not a ferry."

"We're also one of the fastest ships in the fleet. Speed's kind of important when you're on a relief mission, don't you think?"

Bowers shrugged. "Point taken."

Dax finally got to the real reason why she'd summoned her XO. "How soon before we're fully loaded?"

"Half an hour."

Her eyes widening, Dax said, "Really? I got the impression from Lessard that it wouldn't be until 0630."

"Leishman and Helkara had a talk with him."

"Good." When Dax had first signed on to the *Aventine* as second officer, she had had to repeatedly deal with complaints from Cargomaster Alphonse Lessard, who treated the *Aventine*'s cargo bays as if they were a quarter of their actual size.

Several months ago, the captain, first officer, and many others were killed in action against the Borg, with Dax getting a field promotion—and eventual full promotion—to captain. Among other things, that meant her new second officer, a Zakdorn named Gruhn Helkara, had the joyous task of forcing Lessard to actually do his job.

"All right. According to the Palais, Professor Pran—"

"The *Palais*?" Bowers sat up straighter in the guest chair. "This came straight from there?"

Nodding, Dax said, "From the chief of staff herself, though Admiral Akaar was in the room with her when she told me."

"Okay, this *is* serious, if they're hopscotching over the chain of command."

"Nice mixed metaphor." Dax's grin then fell. "Basically, he needs to convince Donatra to open up trade with Tal'Aura, so we don't have to keep doing missions like this."

Sounding dubious, Bowers asked, "And the Palais thinks this notion is realistic?"

"That's what I asked, too, but Ms. Piñiero said that if it was realistic, we wouldn't need Professor Pran."

"Who *is* this guy?"

"Bridge to Captain Dax."

At the interruption from her security chief and tactical officer, Lieutenant Lonnoc Kedair, Dax looked up to the ceiling and said, "Go ahead."

"Transporter room reporting a passenger asking for permission to come aboard. He's beaming up from Paris."

Looking at Bowers, Dax said, "You're about to get the answer to your question." Rising to her feet, she said, "Commander Bowers and I will be right down, Lieutenant."

"Acknowledged."

A short turbolift ride later, and captain and first officer arrived at the transporter room. Chief Spon stood behind the console, manipulating controls with all three arms.

To the Triexian, Dax said, "Energize, Chief."

Nodding her elongated head, Spon activated the transporter.

Seconds later, a sparkle of lights coalesced into a humanoid form. A large canvas bag was slung over his left shoulder. He had a drooping white mustache, and long white hair framing a round, pleasant face. He wore simple civilian clothing: a purple shirt, black vest, black pants, brown boots. The rather unruly head of hair was yoked back into a ponytail, revealing tapered ears that suggested Vulcanoid ancestry. He also had the rhinal ridges of a Bajoran, albeit fainter than usual, and the black eyes of a Betazoid. *That's gotta be an entertaining family tree,* Dax thought as she stepped forward.

"Professor Pran, I presume?"

The grin he let loose was completely human. In all three hundred and sixty-three years of life in nine hosts, the Dax symbiont had never encountered a species that grinned quite the way humans did. "Your presumption is quite correct, Captain Dax. Good to see you again."

She frowned as she shook his hand. "We've met before?"

"Sort of. I spoke with Curzon Dax about thirty, maybe thirty-five years ago at the Altair Conference."

"I'm sorry," Dax said, "I don't remember—but Curzon met a *lot* of people at that conference, and if I remember correctly, he was focused on the negotiations with the Klaestrons."

"Quite all right, Captain. There were a hefty number of people attending that conference, and I think you—or rather, Curzon—met just about everybody. Wouldn't expect you to remember all of them, or even any of them, especially since most of them were even more boring than me."

Indicating Bowers, she said, "This is my first officer, Commander Sam Bowers. He'll be escorting you to your quarters. We should be departing within half an hour."

"Sounds wonderful. I'll do my right damndest to stay completely out of your way, Captain. I just need my stuff to be beamed to my quarters, and I'll try to stay quiet till we reach Artaleirh."

"Chief Spon will take care of that." Dax nodded to the Triexian, who nodded back and started manipulating the controls again.

"Great."

Bowers frowned. "How did you know we were going to Artaleirh first?"

Pran shrugged. "Chief of staff told me. Why, is it supposed to be a secret?"

"It's not something that should be advertised."

"Commander, I was given this information while sitting in the most secure building in the Federation. I'm fairly certain that doesn't entirely fit the definition of 'advertised.'" He clapped his hands. "Anyhow, I think it's best if I get on over to my quarters. You all have work to do, and I'd rather you did that instead of worrying about me."

Pointing to the door, Bowers said, "If you could just wait outside for a second, Professor, I'd like to consult with my captain on ship's business."

"Not at all, Commander. I'll be right out there."

Pran stepped through the door, and as soon as it closed, Bowers turned on his captain. "How, exactly, does Curzon *not* remember *him*?"

"The conference he was referring to had an open bar, and one of the other diplomats present was Kor."

"So?"

Dax smiled, remembering that Bowers didn't report to Deep Space 9 until after Kor's death, and so missed the old *Dahar* master's trips to the station. "No open bar was safe from Kor for very long, and no old friend of Kor's was safe being within a meter of him under those circumstances." She shuddered from the memory.

"I don't remember that night, or meeting Professor Pran, but I'm sure I'll remember that hangover until the day my last host dies."

Bowers chuckled. "All right, but I still don't see how *he's* going to talk Donatra into anything."

"This comes straight from the top, Commander," Dax said firmly, mindful of the transporter chief's presence. "Now, if you please, escort him to his quarters."

"Yes, ma'am." Bowers sighed again. "Ours is not to reason why, right?"

"Something like that."

Bowers stepped out.

As the doors closed, Spon said, "The professor's personal items have been beamed to his quarters."

"What are the items?"

Spon looked down at her display. "Two pieces of luggage containing clothing and toiletries and a banjo."

Dax blinked. "A what?"

"I'm not sure." Spon checked on the computer. "Ah—it's a musical instrument from Earth. I wonder what type of music he plays."

"You're a musician, Chief?"

"Yes, ma'am," Spon said proudly. "I sometimes play the *lood dir,* but I prefer the Elisiar."

Dax recalled Joran attending a concert where an Elisiar was played, and remembered that the music was haunting but effective. "You should play on the ship some time."

Spon hesitated. "Er, I do, Captain—Lieutenant Kandel and I perform regular concerts in the recreation hall, me on the Elisiar, her on a Saar string."

"Oh," Dax said lamely. *Great, I've got concerts on my ship and I don't even know it. Hell, I didn't even know that my transporter chief and beta-shift tactical officer have any musical skills.*

She tried to reassure herself that it was a crew of seven hundred and fifty, and they'd been a bit preoccupied since she signed on, but that was, she felt, a feeble excuse.

Heading toward the door, she said over her shoulder, "Next time you guys play, let me know, all right, Chief?"

"Yes, ma'am."

I wonder what else I don't know about my crew, Dax thought dolefully.

"I'm guessing that the 'ship's business' you wanted to discuss with Captain Dax was asking her what kind of lunatic you were bringing to Romulan space."

Sonek could tell instantly that he was right by the sour expression on Commander Bowers's face in response to his statement.

"It was just ship's business," he said tightly. They entered a turbolift and Bowers said, "Deck five."

As the turbolift moved, Sonek tried to sound reassuring. "This isn't the first starship I've been a passenger on, Commander Bowers. I've been on plenty, and pretty much every single one of the first officers on those ships wanted me *off* the ship as soon as I stepped onto it. I'm fairly well used to it by now, believe me."

Bowers said nothing until they arrived at deck five. "If you need anything, contact the security office. They'll take care of you."

Not "contact me," Sonek noted with amusement. "Any place you can recommend to eat on board?"

At that, Bowers visibly shuddered. "The replicator in your quarters works just fine, Professor."

Sonek took the hint—Bowers didn't want him anywhere near the crew. He was unlikely to put that hint to proper use, but no sense getting the commander up in arms about it just yet. "Yup. Every single one of the first officers. Thank you, Commander. You go on ahead and get back to your actual duties. And don't worry about me."

"Believe me, Professor, I wasn't worried."

The doors parted and Sonek went in, noticing that his luggage and his banjo were both present. "Great! My stuff!"

Bowers peeked inside. "Is that—is that a *banjo*?"

"Yes, sir, it is." Sonek picked it up and started tuning it. The strings made an almost nasal twang that sounded all wrong. "Every single time the thing goes through a transporter, the tuning goes *completely* out of whack. I don't go anywhere without it. Well, all right, that's not entirely true, there are some places where it isn't practical to bring a musical instrument, but I figured it'll take a little while to work our way to Artaleirh and Achernar and back, and the banjo helps me think, on those rare occasions when I find myself with the need to do so."

"Well, have fun." Bowers hesitated, seemed to be warring with himself, and then finally spoke again. "Don't you have an autotuner?"

"Not for this." Sonek shook his head as he continued to manually tune the banjo. "This piece is at least two hundred and fifty years old, and it was handcrafted. I'd have to break it open to put an autotuner in, and I'm just not willing to do that."

"Fine. Enjoy your stay on the *Aventine*." With that insincerity out of the way, Bowers turned and left as fast as he could.

Sonek chuckled and finished tuning the banjo. Once it was in tune, he set it aside. He had a great deal of work to do.

First he walked to the replicator and ordered an *allira* punch. Then he sat down at the desk in the quarters. As was typical for Starfleet, the chairs were not uncomfortable, but nowhere near as nice as the chair in his office on Mars—or, for that matter, the chief of staff's couch.

Still, he had a lot of reading to do. He'd spent all of last night answering correspondence, talking with Tolik over subspace, and sending letters back to Sara and Rupi about what he was doing—at least, the parts he could share.

Now that I'm here, though, it's time for business.

The first thing he did was call up all of the public records regarding the Imperial Romulan State. Following Shinzon's coup, the Romulan Star Empire had been in disarray, and while about half the military was loyal to Tal'Aura, the other half were apparently siding with a commander named Donatra. At the end of last year, Donatra declared herself empress of the Imperial Romulan State, a nation whose purview included Achernar Prime as capital and the worlds of Xanitla, Ralatak, and Virinat—the Romulans' primary agricultural worlds.

The State had appointed an ambassador to the Federation—a former warbird commander named Jovis—and the Federation had likewise sent an ambassador of its own, T'Garas of Vulcan. Sonek had met T'Garas once, and found her to be one of the keener political minds he'd ever met. She'd begun her career as an aide to Councillor T'Latrek, who had represented Vulcan in the Federation Council for decades. *That's as good a pedigree as you can find.*

It also signalled that the Bacco Administration was taking the State seriously as an independent nation, even as it stepped up relief efforts to the Romulan Star Empire. Those efforts had been ongoing since Shinzon's death, and were increased with an emphasis on food after the loss of the Romulans' "breadbasket," which was why a top starship was being sent instead of a freighter—a symbol to Tal'Aura that the Federation took its commitments to *her* seriously as well.

So who is this woman, anyhow? The public information out of the way, Sonek got up, asked the replicator for a bowl of *plomeek* soup, and then called up Starfleet Intelligence's file on Donatra.

"Those files are classified."

Sonek shook his head. "Right. Computer, access code Pran alpha five nine four two green."

"Voiceprint and code verified."

A picture of a very attractive—and surprisingly young looking—Romulan woman appeared on the screen on his desk. Checking her date of birth, he saw that she was only fifty-four years old, which was a mere youth by Romulan standards. *Being a commander at that age is no mean feat—much less an empress.*

Then he read on, including reports filed by deep-cover agents in Romulan territory. Of particular note was her apparent affair with Admiral Braeg and her alliances with both Senator Tal'Aura and Commander Suran, supporting Shinzon's coup. Donatra, however, turned against her conspirators and aided the *U.S.S. Enterprise* against Shinzon. Later, she assisted the *U.S.S. Titan* on their mission to Romulus, and both her ship, the *Valdore,* and *Titan* were trapped in the Small Magellanic Cloud for a time.

Of those four who conspired with Shinzon, only Donatra and Tal'Aura were still alive.

Donatra spent the next ten months building support in the military, even as Tal'Aura consolidated her power elsewhere. She was able to use her influence to reassign patrols so that only ships loyal to her would be in the vicinity of Achernar when she made her move.

The thing that Sonek found interesting was that the Federation and the Klingon Empire were made aware of Donatra's intention to secede a good three weeks before it happened—by Tal'Aura herself, who informed President Bacco and Chancellor Martok at the summit they held on Grisella this past December. This meant that Donatra hadn't been as secret as she'd intended—or she knew Tal'Aura would be impotent to stop her.

Every step of the way, from her aid to the *Enterprise* to her trip to the SMC with *Titan* to her consolidation of power, was geared toward the same goal: weakening Tal'Aura. Perhaps she originally intended to take over as praetor, engaging in a coup of her own, but decided secession was the better choice. Her ambassador to the Federation, Jovis, had long been a critic of the Senate, of both Praetor Hiren and his predecessor Neral, and of the entire government. He always followed orders and came from a particularly rich family, and his complaints never developed into actions. The Tal Shiar apparently had a huge file on him, but never acted on it.

Another member of Donatra's inner circle was a woman named Toreth, whom she had appointed the head of the State military. The former commander of the *Khazara*, Toreth had long been an opponent of the Tal Shiar, and was also the victim of a deception on the part of the Vulcan underground led by Ambassador Spock, one that allowed several Romulan defectors to escape to the Federation. Toreth had been censured for her role in that, ameliorated by her assassination of N'Vek, the traitor on her ship.

Toreth did not rise to prominence again until the Dominion War, where she was single-handedly responsible for several victories for the allies. There was also no record of any kind of dissent following the *Khazara* incident—until she allied with Donatra.

Perhaps the most telling piece of information Sonek saw in the file was a report filed by the handler for one of the deep-cover agents. "Commander Donatra's support is widely known to include a few dozen ships, though that support has appeared to be more of a lack of support for Tal'Aura. That her support is truly this widespread has apparently caught everyone by surprise—except for the empress herself."

That told Sonek a very important piece of information: This was not a woman who'd be easy to convince of much of anything.

Several nights later, on her way to her cabin for some sleep, Dax was walking past the rec hall when she heard music.

Her first thought was, *Spon's doing a concert and didn't tell me.* Then she realized that there was much more than an Elisiar and a Saar string. She could pick out several other instruments.

Standing on her toes, Dax peered into the glass circle in the door, which was etched with the Starfleet delta. It didn't appear to be a formal concert, since there were several musicians seated on stools or on the floor. All of them, though, were centered around a giant triple-keyboarded instrument that had a Möbius strip of keys at the feet. Spon was sitting at it, playing away, and there were people with instruments all around her: Kandel with her Saar string, which rested on the lap and had ten strings that were plucked with fingers; Lieutenant Tovak, also from beta shift, on a *ka'athyra,* a traditional Vulcan lyre; Ensign Erin Constantino, rounding out the beta-shift bridge crew, on an acoustic guitar; someone from either engineering or security whom Dax didn't recognize on a roll-out keyboard that was in front of him on the floor; and Sonek Pran on what Dax assumed to be his banjo.

Resting back on her heels, Dax contemplated whether or not to go in. It looked like everyone was having a good time. Tomorrow at approximately 1100, they would be crossing into Romulan space, and they were going to be on yellow alert from then until they left Romulan space a week (or more, depending on how things went) later. As a former counselor, Dax understood the importance of blowing off steam before an anticipated tense time.

Will everyone tighten up as soon as I walk in? Will I ruin the party? Jadzia and Curzon would tell her she was being insane, and of *course* she should go to the party, as would Emony. Tobin would avoid the party like the plague, and Lela would think it inappropriate. Joran would go in just to upstage the other musicians. As for Torias and Audrid—

Enough. You're Ezri Dax, you're captain of the Aventine, *and it's your damn ship. Go in, already.* She walked toward the doors with a determined look screwed to her face.

As they slid open, she heard a cacophony of sound that was mostly coherent. Kandel and Spon were singing something in what Dax was fairly certain was Deltan.

The song ended moments later, and everyone—save for Professor Pran—got to their feet. Kedair bellowed out, "Captain on deck!"

Dax sighed and reminded herself to have a talk with Bowers. While she understood and appreciated his desire for more formality on duty, there was no reason for it to apply to the rec hall at midnight. "Oh for pity's sake, at ease, everyone. I was just coming in to see what all the fuss was about."

Pran said, "Just having ourselves a little jam session."

"Well, don't stop on my account."

Dax went over to sit next to Kedair. The Takaran woman was wearing civilian clothes—which made her leaping to attention moments ago even sillier, to Dax's mind—which for her consisted of a red and blue one-piece outfit that looked remarkably like a sarong and went from her armpits to her knees. The colors brought out the teal in her skin. Next to her was Susan Hyatt, the ship's counselor, who was wearing a big blue sweater and black leggings.

Pran asked, "Anybody know 'Crossroad Blues'? It's in A."

"I do," Constantino said.

"We can fake it," Spon added.

The professor started plucking a blues rhythm on his banjo, and the others followed along. "This is an old blues song from Earth—it was playing the night that my wife and I had our first kiss."

Dax leaned across her security chief to say to Hyatt, "It's good to see Ensign Constantino doing well."

Hyatt shook her head. "She isn't. She's been acting as if nothing is wrong."

Frowning, Dax looked down at Constantino, sitting on the floor with her guitar. The ensign was from Deneva, and that planet's population had been practically wiped out by the Borg. Her family was gone, including her parents, grandparents, husband, and daughter. Dax had been willing to give her leave time, but she had insisted on going back to work—with Dax's proviso that she see Counselor Hyatt. It apparently wasn't doing as much good as she'd hoped.

They went through a few more songs, only one of which Dax recognized—it was an old Vulcan desert chant that Audrid had learned once—and then Pran said, "I've got one I'd like to try if it's all right with you guys. The words are in Spanish—it was written by a human by the name of Victor Jara back on Earth before it was united. He was a singer and a poet and he lived under a military dictatorship and was imprisoned for being too radical. They put him in a soccer stadium called *Estadio Chile,* and later on they renamed the place *Estadio Victor Jara* after him. Place is still standing, actually—I saw a game there about twenty years ago or so. Anyhow, Victor Jara, when he was imprisoned there, he sang to keep the other prisoners' spirits up, and when the guards told him to stop, he wouldn't. They went ahead and shot him the next morning. This was the last song he wrote. It's not what you'd call a happy song, but it's one that's been on my mind the last couple of months."

Pran started plucking on the banjo. Prior to this, he'd been picking lightly, the instrument's tone airy and bright, and sticking with high notes on the bottom strings. Now, though, the notes were longer and lower and sadder. The song was slow and deliberate, like a dirge.

He sang in Spanish; Dax's combadge translated it for her:

We are five thouand, in this small part of the city.
We are five thousand. I wonder how many we are
in all.
In the cities, in the country, here alone,
Ten thousand hands that plant seeds and make
the factories run.
How much humanity exposed to hunger, cold,
panic, pain, and terror?

Dax looked over at Constantino and saw tears welling in her eyes. Looking around, the captain saw that the words were having a similar, if less extreme, impact on the rest of the audience. Spon started a low humming background noise on the Elisiar that sounded like the wail of a dying bird.

Six of us were lost as if into starry space.
One dead, one beaten as I never knew a human
being could be beaten.
The other four wanted to end their terror,
One jumping into nothingness,
Another beating his head against a wall,
But all with the fixed stare of death.

Dax thought about the pulverized surface of Deneva, the ravaged cities on Pandril, the boiling deserts of

Vulcan, the graveyard of ships in the Azure Nebula. *So many dead . . .*

How hard it is to sing when I must sing of horror.
Horror which I am living, horror which I am
dying.
To see myself among so much and so many
moments of infinity
In which silence and screams are the end of my
song.

Throughout the other songs, there had been a pretty high level of ambient noise, as people continued to talk under the music. Also throughout the other songs, all the musicians were participating, creating a unique blend of sounds.

This time, though, it was just Sonek Pran and his banjo, and Spon and the Elisiar. The room was silent beyond that.

What I see, I have never seen,
What I have felt and what I feel
Will give birth to the moment.

After he sang the last line, the room was utterly quiet.

Hyatt broke it with applause, which broke the dam, as the whole room was cheering after that.

Constantino climbed to her feet and, with the neck of the guitar gripped tightly in her left hand, walked over to Hyatt. "Counselor, you have a minute?" Her cheeks, Dax noticed, were streaked with tears.

Hyatt put a hand on her shoulder, got up from her stool, and said, "Of course, Erin. Let's go."

Spon lightened the mood by performing a Triexian patter song. The engineer/security guard/whoever followed with a silly folk song that was actually Betazoid in origin, and Kandel did a lovely rendition of "Beyond Antares."

After that, things broke up. Kedair looked at Dax. "Good of you to join us, Captain."

"I'm glad I did."

"Hey, Captain—who *is* that guy, anyhow? I thought we were taking on a diplomat of some kind."

"He is." Dax hopped off the stool and walked over to Pran, who was setting his banjo down and getting an *allira* punch from the replicator. "Nicely done, Professor."

"Thank you very kindly, Captain. It wasn't much, but after everything this ship's been through, I figured a little catharsis couldn't really hurt all that much. I grew up with music, you see, and that was always how we went and solved our problems."

"Singing?"

Pran nodded and sipped his punch. "It's always worked fine for me."

Kedair had walked up behind Dax. "How do you know what this ship's been through?"

"Uh," Dax quickly said, "Professor Sonek Pran, this is my chief of security, Lieutenant Lonnoc Kedair."

"Pleasure, Lieutenant." Pran offered his hand, which Kedair shook. "To answer your question, I've been on this ship for three days. Hard not to know what's been happening after that much time. Besides, it's what everybody's going through. The specifics don't matter so much as the fact that it's a shared trauma, to some extent. Some people's losses have been a whole lot worse than others. I was lucky, I didn't lose too many people. Ensign Constantino wasn't so lucky."

"You know about her?" Dax asked.

"I know she's from Deneva. That's enough, really." Pran gulped down the rest of his punch and then set the glass down on one of the tables. "Well, if we're getting into Romulan territory tomorrow, I'd best get some sleep. Captain, if it's all right with you, I'd like to observe the delivery of the food supplies to Artaleirh. It'll help me when I'm talking to Donatra to have some real-world context, not just a bunch of secondhand reports."

Dax looked at Kedair. "Assuming my chief of security doesn't have an objection?"

"No objection, but you're going to have a guard assigned to you pretty much from the moment we enter Romulan space."

Grinning, Pran asked, "Don't trust me, Lieutenant?"

"Don't trust the Romulans. They don't like having to take charity and they don't like Federation politicians very much."

"Well, neither do I, so we'll have that in common, at least. Good night, both of you."

Pran turned and left, saying good-bye to virtually the entire room.

This is going to be an interesting mission, Dax thought. "I'm off to bed as well."

"Good night, Captain," Kedair said. "I'm gonna stay up a bit and make sure everyone stumbles back to their cabin okay."

Nodding, Dax left the rec hall.

Federation News Service report by Yrik Ulfthar

Riots have broken out in New Samarkand, the capital city of Alpha Centauri. The riots' origins appear to have been in Our Lady of Significant Mercy Hospital, where people started fighting over medication—although tensions all over the planet in general and in New Samarkand in particular have been escalating since the Borg invasion. It is unknown who the participants in the fight at the hospital were, but the violence spread remarkably quickly, with hundreds of citizens looting, destroying property, and shouting epithets against recent arrivals on Alpha Centauri, against Starfleet, and against the Borg.

Alpha Centauri Police are attempting to get the situation under control, and we're receiving reports that Starfleet has been called in to aid ACP forces. There has been no comment as yet from Governor Barrile's office.

Thus far, no fatalities have been reported. Mercy Hospital has closed to trauma, and victims are being sent to the Archer University Hospital.

More on this story as it develops.

7

U.S.S. MUSGRAVE

Fabian Stevens stared at the beautiful porcelain features of his wife on the viewscreen, blond hair severely tied back, framing her ice-blue eyes. "So how you liking the red collar?"

Commander Domenica Corsi rolled those ice-blue eyes. *"Are you gonna ask that* every *time we talk?"*

"No, just when you're in uniform," Stevens said with a cheeky grin. "Consider it an incentive to contact me in a slinky negligee or something."

"I don't have a slinky negligee."

The grin widened. "Consider it an incentive to get one."

"Very funny. How are things over there?"

"They're *still* trying to get me to tell them how you guys made Troyius disappear."

Corsi smiled. *"Did you tell them?"*

"Hell, no. First of all, I don't know how you did it, though I have a few guesses. Secondly, even if I did know, I wouldn't tell *these* garbanzos. I'm loyal to my wife and my ship."

"Fabe, the Musgrave *is your ship."*

"That's just a technicality because I lost the damn coin toss," Stevens muttered.

Stevens had served as a tactical systems specialist on the Starfleet Corps of Engineers ship *U.S.S. da Vinci* since the Dominion War, during much of which he'd been in a relationship with Corsi, at the time the ship's chief of security. However, Corsi grew increasingly uncomfortable with the possibility that her feelings for Stevens would interfere with her ability to properly protect the *da Vinci* and its crew. They agreed that one of them would have to transfer off—they also agreed to marry, to solidify their commitment to each other even as they were separating physically.

In the interests of fairness, and because both were important parts of the *da Vinci* team, they flipped a latinum strip to see who would be the one to transfer off after the wedding. Stevens lost, so he went to the *Musgrave,* which was another *Sabre*-class ship assigned to the S.C.E.

Changing the subject, Stevens asked, "Did they let you guys paw over the *Columbia*?"

Corsi snorted. *"They practically had to pry it out of Gomez's hands. But everyone had a grand old time crawling around it while we towed it back from the Gamma Quadrant. And, of course, we had to stay at warp three to keep the tractor, so it took a while. Tev tried to insist that we could go warp four, but that defeated the whole point of taking longer to play with it."*

Stevens shook his head. Five years on the *da Vinci,* and Tev still was missing half a dozen clues.

"Oh, and we saw the captain."

At that, Stevens smiled. Sonya Gomez was now the

commanding officer of the *da Vinci,* and also in charge of its S.C.E. team—she was the only ship captain in Starfleet with a gold collar—with Corsi as her first officer and also the person in charge of day-to-day operations of the vessel, but despite having retired last June, her predecessor as CO, David Gold, would always be "the captain." He was the one who performed their wedding, in fact, in the *da Vinci* shuttlebay.

"A bunch of us had dinner at the house while we were on Earth. Retirement suits him. Suits Rachel, too."

"I can imagine," Stevens said, his stomach grumbling at the thought of the missed feast. Rabbi Rachel Gilman was one of the finest chefs in the universe, and occasionally getting to eat her cooking was one of the best fringe benefits of serving on the *da Vinci.*

"He's been consulting on Earth's defense—fitting, since that was why he retired."

Stevens nodded. After a massive Borg cube nearly destroyed Earth—and would have killed Rachel had it been successful—Gold chose to retire so that they could be together in case something like that happened again. And then something like that almost did a couple of months ago.

"Conlon was at the house, too. She's taking over Voyager*'s engine room. In fact, she went straight to Utopia Planitia after dinner."*

"Good for her! *Voyager*'s lucky to have her."

"And we're unlucky not to anymore. I may need to kill Bennett. I don't suppose we could poach your Belandrid."

"Don't even think about it—Lolo's my favorite person on this ship."

"S.C.E. team, report to observation, please."

Looking up at the voice of Lieutenant Commander Bojan Hadžić, Stevens sighed and said, "Looks like I gotta go. Give my best to everyone. And tell Hawk to keep you guys safe."

"Will do."

"I love you."

"I love you, too."

Corsi's face faded from the viewer. Stevens tapped his combadge and said, "On my way, Bojan."

One way in which the *Musgrave* was like the *da Vinci* was that relations were casual. In fact, they were more so: Stevens would never refer to the first officer by anything other than "Commander" or "sir" on any other ship—but Bojan Hadžić preferred to be called by his first name, mostly because he was incredibly uncomfortable with the rank.

Stevens arrived at the observation lounge to find that most of the team was there. As on the *da Vinci,* the S.C.E. team was led by two officers, with five enlisted specialists. All of them were present and most were seated.

Sitting with their backs to the viewport—which showed that the *Musgrave* was moving at high warp—were the placid Lieutenant T'Eama, a Vulcan woman who served as second officer and second-in-command of the S.C.E. contingent, and the excitable Trill woman Jira Trin, their computer and cryptography specialist. Stevens took his seat next to Trin and hoped she wouldn't bounce too much.

Facing Stevens were their anthropologist, Dr. Mrodile, a Bolian with a tendency to rub his ridge; structural systems specialist Ysalda, an amphibious Aquan woman whose skin was the same color as her gold collar, which came right up to the gills on her elongated neck; and their newest arrival, warp specialist Grazna, a Denobulan woman with long brown hair. Grazna replaced Thrantira zh'Zulis, an Andorian warp specialist whose enlistment had ended and who would only reenlist if she was assigned to the reconstruction on Andor. Stevens was impressed that they even got a replacement, but apparently Grazna had served with Captain Dayrit on the *Discovery*.

Standing at the head of the table next to the viewer was the only human besides Stevens on the team: Hadžić, his unruly mop of brown hair flopping into his face and brushing his bulbous nose. The image on the viewer was of a star system, labelled MAXIA ZETA.

The doors parted to allow the last attendee of the meeting to arrive: the ship's diminutive chief engineer and recent target of Corsi's desire for a new chief engineer, Lieutenant Commander Lolo. A Belandrid, the blue-skinned engineer only came up to the average human's waist, and appeared far too fragile to survive in Starfleet. However, over the past year, Stevens had learned to trust the Belandrid to be able to take care of himself.

"Good, good," Hadžić said as Lolo took his seat at the foot of the table between Stevens and Grazna, "everyone is here." The lieutenant commander spoke with a slight Croatian accent.

Stevens managed to refrain from pointing out that Captain Dayrit wasn't here, nor was the security chief, the chief medical officer, or any of the other thirty-odd people assigned to the ship, but it was a close call.

"How many of you are familiar with Maxia Zeta IV?"

This time, Stevens couldn't hold back. "Well, it's the fourth planet in the Maxia Zeta system."

Hadžić glowered at Stevens. "Yes, thank you, Fabian," he said dryly.

"Isn't there a dilithium mine there?" Grazna asked.

"Yes, there is—at least in theory." Hadžić touched a control, and the image zoomed in to the fourth planet. "They opened up a new dig site after the Borg invasion, since there are a lot of new ships being built, and they uncovered a farantine deposit."

At that, Stevens winced. "Oy."

Mrodile scratched his ridge. "I'm not familiar with that substance."

T'Eama looked at the Bolian as if he were diseased—a look T'Eama used fairly often, if it came to that—and said, "Farantine creates a duonetic field."

"Which," Stevens said quickly before Mrodile asked another dumb question, "basically stops anything electronic from working."

"Okay. That's bad, I take it."

"Very much so, yes," Hadžić said, brushing his hair off his face. "We only know about it because there's a station on one of the planet's moons, and it's unaffected. They were the ones who sent the call for help."

Waving her arms back and forth, Trin asked, "How could there be farantine on that planet and they don't know it?"

Stevens said, "It doesn't always show up on a scan. We had to deal with farantine contamination when I was on the *da Vinci.*"

"That," T'Eama said, "was when you dealt with the Androssi on Maeglin?"

Of course she can quote the mission. "Yup. And we had no idea the Androssi machines would create a chemical reaction that resulted in farantine until they were activated, and we scanned those suckers down to the last subatomic particle."

"Obviously, you did not," T'Eama said.

"In any case," Hadžić said before Stevens had the chance to try to defend himself and his former shipmates, "our job is to remove the farantine contamination from the atmosphere without the use of any technology whatsoever."

Silence spread across the table. Stevens tried very hard not to be the first one to laugh.

Ysalda saved him from that, with a full-throated guffaw. She followed it with, "Are we to use shovels, perhaps?"

Lolo looked at Stevens and spoke with his circular mouth in a voice that sounded like it was coming through a water cooler. "Hhhhhhow did you fffix on Mmmmaeglin?"

I was really hoping nobody would ask that. "We didn't. We cleared enough of the farantine to allow equipment to work *sometimes,* but it wasn't a perfect solution." Then he recalled something. "Our chief engineer came up with a paint that was resistant. It should be on file."

"Pppppaint?" Lolo asked.

Grazna said, "You suggest painting our equipment?"

"Yes." Stevens held up a hand. "And before you ask what to do with things like tricorders and padds that have displays, you don't paint them, but you do paint a force field generator. You keep the tricorder and padd inside the force field, and everything's ducky."

"That's *really* complicated," Trin said.

"So is what we need to accomplish," Hadžić said. "Fabian, if you would be so kind as to re-create your *da Vinci* paint."

Again, Stevens showed restraint by not making a Mona Lisa joke.

Looking around the table, Hadžić added, "The rest of you have one day to come up with other options."

Trin asked, "Is throwing up our hands and saying we should get our dilithium elsewhere an option?"

"No," Hadžić said. "We need all the sources of dilithium we can get, and there's the matter of this being an order."

Grazna gave a distressingly wide smile. "Details, details."

Hadžić made a "shoo" gesture with his hands. "Go. Do this. We'll meet tomorrow at 0900 to see what we have come up with."

Stevens got up from his chair and nearly crashed into Trin. "Sorry!" she cried even as she barreled past him toward the door.

"No, no," Stevens said to the door as it closed on her, "I'm fine, really."

Hadžić had left the room even faster than Trin had, with most of the others all leaving behind him. After a moment, only Grazna, Ysalda, and Stevens were left.

"Okay, I'm new to the S.C.E.," the Denobulan woman said. "Is this normal?"

"Is what normal?" Stevens asked.

"Being asked to do something completely impossible."

"Nope." Stevens smiled. "On a normal day, we'd have to do three or four things that are impossible."

Grazna shook her head. "I walked right into that, didn't I?"

Stevens nodded. "With both feet, your eyes wide open, and a bull's eye painted on your face. That's something else you'll have to get used to."

"What?"

"Be prepared for the consequences if you leave straight lines lying around."

"Also," Ysalda added, "be prepared for your suggestions to be ignored. Bojan usually comes up with something on his own and then we wind up implementing his plan, regardless of whether or not it's the best plan."

"Really?" Grazna asked.

Feeling the need to defend his CO, Stevens said, "It should be pointed out that his plan is almost always the best one."

"That's one opinion," Ysalda said, and then left before Stevens could respond.

After the door closed on her, Stevens said, "And another opinion is that you're a twit."

Chuckling, Grazna said, "Okay. I'm gonna go read the telemetry from that moon base, see if I can come up with something better than paint."

"Hey, don't knock the paint until you see it in action."

They both left the meeting room, and Stevens turned his mind to the problem at hand. The fact was, the paint in question hadn't been completely effective even in the reduced farantine concentration that was left on Maeglin. If this was worse—and it seemed to be; he too would need to look at the telemetry to be sure—then he'd need a different miracle.

But hey, that's what we do. . . .

CASUALTY REPORT 92792382 BAKER

Addendum to list of confirmed dead reported to Starfleet Command in Sector 22093 since Stardate 58222.9

(For previous reported casualties in this sector, refer to Casualty Report 92792382 Alpha.)

1100110
1100111
Alroniaks of Alonis
Daniela Bruner
Michael Burns
B'w'e'd'l'e'r
Cartominkwano of Alonis
Hessretheress ch'Lan
Themnorsith ch'Lessa
Tharantana ch'Nora
Elefthor ch'Rin
Shritharia ch'Vrun
Lieutenant Commander Thomas Alan Chafin
Benjamin Cruz Jr.

Benjamin Cruz Sr.
Ryon Daley
Alto Dex
Garo Dex
Okin Dex
Major Efrimtiran of Alonis
Frak
Elizabeth Fredericksen
Matt Gagnon
Rey Garcia
Michael Gitlin
Lieutenant Dorian Giughan
Emrik glasch Gral
Ensign Griztrakar
Ensign Christina Grosso
H'a'e'd't'd'o'i'r
Cordelia Hawkins
Cornelia Hawkins
Lisa-Karen Hawkins
Orenthal V. Hawkins
Vernetha Hawkins
Wallie Hawkins
Wanjuri Hawkins
Zik Heltrigum
Christine Hendler
Claiborne Henry
Tor glasch Hok
Lionel Iturralde
Jorialotnik of Alonis
Kan
Karak of Vulcan
Brian Keane
Charles Keane

Tracey Keane
Elizabeth Kearney
Kelav
Elizabeth A. King
Ensign Liza Lagdanen
Monique Lang
Leslie Lannon
Liezakranor of Alonis
Lieutenant Commander Shira Lipkin
Mak Brin
Mak Sefrin
Mak Torin
Mak Yarin
Jorge Martinez
Allyn McWhirter
Henry McWhirter
Thomas McWhirter
Una McWhirter
Christopher Metzen
Kenneth Minaya
Miraboria of Alonis
Margaret Mitchell
Amanda Molina
Luis Molina
Gram glasch Mort
Zik chim Mort
Evin Nadaner
Masusaka Nakadai
Asano Nakamura
Mariko Nakamura
Yukio Nakamura
Lieutenant Alberto Natale
Michael Neilson

Councillor Nerramibus of Alonis
Jack Ousmanova
Nicole Ousmanova
Olga Ousmanova
Roy Ousmanova
Lieutenant Mika Oyama
Sem glasch Pak
Miral Paris
Maria Patterson
Ensign Phira
Pott
Lieutenant (j.g.) E. Richard Price
Q'o'l'r't'r'e'z'a'k
Quirimirkis of Alonis
Rolik of Vulcan
Lieutenant Commander Yukio Sakai
Captain George Sanders
Dayana Sandoval
Rachelle Sandoval
Sanek of Vulcan
Semtek of Vulcan
Sentir of Vulcan
Kiramassala sh'Lan
Thriazhrovarasa sh'Meth
Shivas of Vulcan
Sik
Ensign Stephen Soohoo
Sorlak of Vulcan
Sossamirak of Alonis
Sprinc of Vulcan
T'Brals of Vulcan
T'Darin of Vulcan
T'Latt of Vulcan

T'Lor of Vulcan
T'Maro of Vulcan
Temnik 42
Thantarishran th'Lan
Commander Katherine Toomajian
B'Elanna Torres
Turak of Vulcan
Lieutenant Colonel Urikmilagro of Alonis
Brian Victor
Thrintarno zh'Lan
Sellessi zh'Lessa
Ziralor 26

8

U.S.S. AVENTINE

Sonek slugged down the last of his morning tea—the *Aventine* replicator made a decent Irish breakfast tea—and slung his IDIC canvas bag over his shoulder.

The door to his guest quarters slid aside at his approach to reveal a tall Efrosian woman, her hair tied in an elaborate bun atop her head, the same color as her copper skin.

"Let me guess," Sonek said with a smile, "you're my security guard?"

"Yes, sir," the woman said. "I'm Ensign Altoss."

Chuckling as he walked out into the corridor, Altoss falling into step behind him and to the right, Sonek said, "You really don't have to call me 'sir,' Ensign. Sonek is fine, and if you absolutely *have* to be formal, then you can call me 'Professor,' or even 'Doctor,' since I have one of those too."

"Whatever you say, Professor."

"Any ground rules I should know about?"

"Do whatever I tell you to do."

"Simple enough."

"Also do whatever Commander Bowers tells you to do."

"Okay."

"For that matter—"

They arrived at the turbolift, and Sonek held up a hand while they waited for a car. "I know, I know—do whatever anyone on the away team tells me to do, and don't do anything without checking with you or one of them first, up to and including using the commode."

"Exactly. And I will be with you at all times." Altoss cracked a small smile. "Including in the commode."

The lift door slid open. "I have been duly warned."

"Shuttlebay one," Altoss said.

Sonek frowned. "We're not beaming down?"

Altoss shook her head. "The food supplies are being delivered to a secure warehouse that's transporter-proof as a security measure."

"Makes sense," Sonek said with a nod. "Hungry people have a tendency to get just a little bit desperate. Of course, that causes other problems, especially if people think that the government's hiding food from them, or keeping it locked up or something. Then you have to protect it even more, and people start to get cranky. Vicious little circle, isn't it?"

Altoss stared straight ahead. "I suppose, Professor."

Looking sheepish, Sonek said, "Sorry. I'm an academic first and foremost, which means I have a tendency to run on at the mouth. Feel free to have one of those things you tell me to do be to shut the hell up, all right?"

"Not at all, sir. I'm led to understand that your mission is to talk to Empress Donatra?"

"That's the notion, yeah."

"Then you should absolutely talk all you wish." The door parted, and Altoss stared at Sonek. "My job is to make sure you live long enough to keep talking."

She moved past him to the corridor. Chuckling as he followed, Sonek said, "Well, good."

Sonek knew that the *Aventine* had a decent-sized fleet of runabouts and shuttlecraft. One of the shuttles had a large cargo module attached to it.

He also knew that the shuttle they'd be using seated only four, which meant that only two other people were heading down: Bowers, who was leading the team, and Kedair. When the large shuttlebay doors parted, Sonek saw that they were both present, along with Dax, while the ship's chief engineer, Mikaela Leishman, and second officer, Gruhn Helkara, were checking over the cargo module and the containers therein.

"Good morning, Professor," Dax said. "You'll be launching in five minutes."

"Great." He looked at the shuttle, which had the name KOR stencilled on the hull. Gazing at two other craft parked nearby, he saw they were named *Kang* and *Koloth*. "You don't normally see Starfleet shuttles named after Klingon heroes."

Dax looked down in mild embarrassment. "Captain's privilege. Kor, Kang, and Koloth were three of my dearest friends—Kang and Koloth through two hosts and Kor through three."

Leishman walked over to the group, brushing a lock of brown hair out of her face with one hand and popping something into her mouth with the other. "We're good to go," she said while chewing.

Dax gave the chief engineer a lopsided smile. "I assume that's from your stash and not the Romulan food supply?"

"Aye, Captain." Leishman swallowed her treat, and then said, "Romulan candy is *nasty* tasting stuff."

"That's just the stuff they export," Sonek said. "What you gotta do is go to Romii and have one of the tree candies. Best confection I've ever had, and I've been eating sweets all my life."

Leishman raised an eyebrow at him. "Well, next time I'm on Romii, I'll be sure to check it out."

"I've actually got a source for the stuff I might be able to call on while we're in the neighborhood. I'll keep you posted."

Bowers walked up to Sonek. "Professor? I just want you to know that I objected to your accompanying us on this away team."

"I would've been stunned if you hadn't, Commander. I'm a civilian and I'm a security risk, plus honestly, I can be a bit of a pain in the ass when I become focused on something. I wouldn't be at all surprised if Ensign Altoss here needs to put me in irons at some point or other."

"We don't put people in irons," Bowers said.

Kedair smiled, exposing white teeth that contrasted sharply with her teal skin. "We just shoot them."

Altoss asked, "Doesn't that mean I'll have to carry him?"

"Part of life in security," Kedair said with mock gravity.

Dax smiled. "Have a safe trip."

"Thank you, Captain," Bowers said. "Let's go."

The cargo module door levered shut even as the *Kor*'s side door rose to allow the away team ingress.

Well, the away team and the civilian observer. Sonek knew he wasn't part of the team, and that Altoss's primary job would probably be just to keep Sonek out of the way.

As she settled into the copilot's seat and started running through the preflight checklist, Kedair said, "I checked with air control on Artaleirh, and they approved us for the landing coordinates—but they didn't sound too pleased about it."

"That's not all that surprising," Sonek said. "Romulans are particularly lousy at taking charity. They come by that trait honestly, what with spending decades flying around in a bunch of badly maintained ships until they found Romulus and Remus. Self-sufficiency is a seriously important quality, and to not have it is to lose your honor and I'm babbling again," he finished quickly and with a sheepish grin. "Sorry."

"It wasn't just that," Kedair said. "The air controller seemed to think we weren't needed. I insisted that we had scheduled this delivery, and she said we could land, but—honestly, I don't think they want us here."

"Well, they're stuck with us," Bowers said.

What the *Aventine* first officer lacked in pleasantness—though Sonek had no doubt that he was a decent sort of person off duty—he made up for in piloting skills. Even with the added burden of the cargo module, the *Kor* flew smoothly out of the shuttlebay and headed to the atmosphere.

The inertial dampers did their job, as the turbulence of entering the upper atmosphere and the cloud layer was not transferred to the passengers. Sonek was seated next to a window, and so was able to see the clouds and sky and pollutants. Artaleirh had been one of the primary ship-building worlds of the Romulan Star Empire, though many of their facilities were collecting mothballs. The Empire's economy was in the proverbial waste extractor. A lesson Sonek had tried very hard to beat into his students—and he was only partially successful, since people who grew up with replicators in the Federation's moneyless economy tended to miss the nuances of such things—was that if nothing grows in the ground, you don't have an economy. Right now, all the places that grew things in the ground were under Donatra's aegis.

As if to accentuate the point, the *Kor* broke through the cloud cover and flew over the city of Trilakas. It was centrally located on this continent, which made it an ideal distribution point for the food.

Trilakas was composed primarily of round, one-story homes that seemed to be made out of some kind of clay. Sonek wasn't sure what the weather was like, but he knew mountainous regions tended toward wind, and he wondered how much proof against the wind those homes were.

As they descended, Sonek was able to make out people, and he winced as he saw how emaciated many of them were. He'd lived all his life in the Federation, and the notion of somebody going hungry was foreign to his personal experience; the notion of being well-fed was obviously equally foreign to the personal experiences of anyone in Trilakas right now. That fact probably extended to the rest of Artaleirh.

Some of the homes had small attempts at gardens—or pots with plants in them. None of them looked particularly healthy or flourishing. A few animals roamed about—he recognized *travit,* which was served as a delicacy on Romulus, but which also provided milk. Sonek suspected the latter was of more use right now than the former, since that was a more continuous supply. There weren't a lot of *travit*—doubtful that there were enough of them to even provide milk for most of these people.

Good thing we're bringing food, he thought as the shuttle came in for a very smooth landing on a large paved circle in front of a massive warehouse.

Kedair looked up from her display at Bowers. "That thing's sensor-proof, just like they said. I don't know what's in there."

"Not our problem, Lieutenant—we're just here to add to it. Let's go."

The door rose open. Kedair stepped out first, followed by Bowers, then Altoss, then finally Sonek. For some reason, they all stopped short after stepping down out of the shuttle, and it took Sonek a moment to figure out why.

"We're not here to hurt you," Bowers was saying, "we're here to deliver food."

"You are not welcome here," said a harsh voice.

Looking over Bowers's head, Sonek saw that a couple of centurions were pointing disruptors at them. Altoss had moved to stand between the centurions and Sonek, her hand on her phaser, but at a head shake from Kedair, she did not unholster it. Neither Bowers nor Kedair had taken out their weapons, which was probably wise. This was a situation that required fewer trigger fingers, not more.

Bowers had his hands up in what he probably hoped was a placating gesture. "Our arrival was scheduled. This was arranged with your government."

Not sounding in the least bit placated, the centurion

said, "The arrangement has ceased. We no longer require the services of the Federation."

The centurion and Bowers stared at each other for several seconds.

Sonek finally broke the impasse, stepping out from behind Altoss. "Excuse me, Centurion, but when we flew on down here, I saw a whole lot of people who looked like they hadn't had a good meal in a very long time."

Altoss moved again to stand between the disruptors and Sonek, and she added an annoyed glare at him.

The centurion bellowed, "That is not your concern, human."

Staying behind Altoss, Sonek said, "Well, I'm not human—entirely. But that isn't really my point—my point is, you all don't strike me as people who are really in much of a position to be turning down free food. There are children out there who don't look like they ever had a good meal in their lives. They *could* have one—half a dozen, even—if you take this food. Look, it's been earmarked for the people on this world. It's already yours, we're just delivering it. We *want* you to have it. If you want to break off the aid agreement between our two nations, then fine, go ahead and do that, but this food's *here*. Why take it out of the mouths of the people that you're supposed to be protecting?"

The centurion glowered at Sonek, his mouth twisting. Sonek had the feeling that this was a decision that was usually made very far over his head. He was obviously going over it in his mind. Sonek hoped that he was trying to find an excuse to do what was right within the confines of his orders—and not, say, trying to find an excuse to shoot all four of them.

Finally, the centurion said, "The Romulan people no longer need the charity of the Federation—but we will accept this one final gift."

"Thank you," Bowers said. He turned to Kedair. "Let's get this cargo unloaded."

Sonek lent a hand with bringing the containers of food into the warehouse—which had a bunch of other containers inside as well, all with the Empire's symbol emblazoned on them. The unloading was done in silence, something that always made Sonek nervous, so he tried to speak to one of the centurions. "Excuse me, but—"

"You've said enough, human."

This time, Sonek brushed his hair away from his ear to, as it were, make a point.

The Romulan's face compressed into a scowl. "You are Vulcan?"

"As much as I am human. I'm a quarter Vulcan, quarter human, quarter Betazoid, quarter Bajoran."

The scowl deepened. "And that is why your Federation is weak—you interbreed like *hnoiyiku* rutting in the dirt."

With that, he stomped off. Only when he was seemingly out of earshot did Bowers say, "If we're weak, why are *we* bringing *them* food?"

"Because of a *human!*" the centurion replied, pointing an accusatory finger and apparently *not* out of earshot. "Shinzon was one of your mongrel species."

So much for that idea, Sonek thought. However, he was more interested in the hand that was pointing at him.

"Maybe Shinzon was genetically human," Bowers said, "but he was exactly what you all made him."

The centurion made a disparaging noise and walked off.

Kedair approached another centurion. "When you're ready to distribute—"

"We are familiar with the workings of your stasis containers, Lieutenant. We are not invalids who need the Federation to walk us to our beds."

Putting her hands on her hips, Kedair said, "Well, I don't know what that means, exactly, but I was just trying to help."

"Yes, that is all you humans do is help."

"Actually, I'm not human, either. I would've thought the green skin would give it away."

"It does not matter. You are all *lloann'mhrahel,* and you must leave—now."

The away team boarded the *Kor* in silence. Nobody said anything until they were in the upper atmosphere, which was when Bowers said, "Thanks, Professor. I think you cut through their pride a little."

He shook his head. "That wasn't pride, Commander."

"Of course it was," Kedair said. "Typical Romulan bluster, if you ask me. Hey, what was that he called us, anyhow? My translator didn't catch it."

"What, *lloann'mhrahel*?" Sonek asked. "It's what they usually call the Federation, but the literal translation's 'them, from there.' Kinda like the original meaning of 'barbarian' was 'people who aren't Greek.' "

"And you don't think it's pride?" Bowers asked, shaking his head.

"I'm not saying they don't have a ton of pride, Commander—what I *am* saying is that they weren't trying to kick us out because of pride. It isn't like they didn't need the food. Pride's usually the first thing to go right out the airlock when your belly's grumbling."

"Those centurions looked well fed to me," Bowers said.

"No, honestly, Commander, they weren't. Those padded uniforms they wear make it look like they're bulked up, but that's just clever tailoring. Their hands, though, were gaunt and bony and arthritic. That only happens to Romulans that young when they aren't getting enough protein." He stared out the window but saw only clouds, which blocked the surface. "There's more going on here than them being tired of charity, I can guarantee that."

When they arrived at the shuttlebay, Bowers and Kedair went off to report to Dax, while Altoss escorted Sonek back to his quarters. "I should be more or less okay until we get to Achernar Prime," he told her. "Unless you want to come in and have yourself a drink."

"I'm on duty," Altoss said, "and I'm not really interested in—in fraternizing."

"I'm happily married, thanks. I was just making a friendly gesture—no fraternizing intended."

"Sorry." She smiled. "Instinctive reaction."

Sonek smiled. "Not a problem. I'm thinking you get hit on quite a bit?"

"More than I'm comfortable with. People assume that because Efrosians aren't monogamous that they're automatically promiscuous. It gets tiresome. In any event, I need to report to the security office." She nodded and added, "It was a pleasure protecting you."

"It was a pleasure being protected. I'm allergic to disruptor fire."

Altoss went off, and Sonek ordered an *allira* punch from the replicator.

Why would they turn down aid? This is aid they've been getting for a year and a half, and more so since December, and from the looks of things, they need more, not less. What's changed?

Realizing he needed more information, he sat down at his desk. "Computer, most recent stories from FNS."

The computer obligingly provided him with abstracts from the twenty latest stories filed with the Federation News Service.

He wasn't looking for anything in particular, but one item caught his eye: MINE EXPLOSION ON CAPELLA IV.

Calling up the story, he read the report, saw the images taken from the wreckage, saw the list of casualties.

Then there was the verbal report from the reporter on the scene, a Coridanite named Thorik. *"An isolationist faction known as the* toora Maab *has claimed responsibility for the explosion, which has set back topaline mining by at least three months—though the supervisor for Janus Mining, Rebecca Greenblatt, said that she will endeavor to reduce that delay by at least a month. Still, experts do not believe that the damage can be repaired and the mine brought to full operating efficiency in any less time than that. When told this, Greenblatt said that the experts, and I quote, don't know their asses from their elbows."*

Sonek ended the report and closed the images off the screen—he really didn't need to look at more wrecked buildings and dead bodies.

Two thoughts entered his head. The first was that he would like to meet this Rebecca Greenblatt.

The other was more troubling. *The* toora Maab *hasn't*

been active for a hundred years. They haven't needed to be, because they won. *They deposed the teer and his mother, exiled them, and severed all alliances with the Federation* and *the Klingon Empire. Now their economy's tanking and they're getting a lifeline with free upgrades to the mine. Why would they sabotage that? And why dig up a hundred-year-old movement?*

Sonek didn't have any answers, and he really hated that.

The door chime rang. "Come on in," he said, and the door slid open to reveal Captain Dax.

"I'm told I owe you thanks."

Shrugging, Sonek said, "Not really. I don't think that centurion entirely *wanted* to turn down the food, but he was under orders. I just gave him a good excuse to go where he wanted."

"My first officer disagrees with you. He thinks the Romulans are just being stubborn and that you're showing off."

"Well, he could be right."

"You think so?"

"Honestly? No, I don't. But I don't know *what's* going on, just that *something* is."

"Is it going to affect your talk with Donatra?"

Sonek shrugged again. "Inform it, maybe, but that's about it. I'm sorry, my manners just fly out the airlock when I start chewing on a problem. Can I get you something to drink?"

Holding up her hands, Dax said, "No, that's not necessary. We're breaking orbit and heading to Achernar now."

Whirling around, Sonek saw the warp effect outside his window. "Now, how about that? Usually I notice when the ship I'm standing in goes to warp." He grinned. "Means one of two things. Either I'm getting old, or I'm really tied up in trying to figure these problems out."

" 'These'?"

Sonek filled Dax in on the news report about Capella.

Dax nodded. "I remember the *toora Maab.* Probably somebody on Capella just wanted to use a familiar name. I'm sure there are plenty of people who aren't happy about the Federation being back on the planet."

"Maybe. But the pattern doesn't fit."

"Events don't always fit into a pattern, Professor."

He smiled. "Maybe not. Anyhow, I'd better do a once-over of what I've got on Donatra. When'll we be getting there?"

"Our ETA is 1930 tomorrow."

"Great."

Dax excused herself and left. Sonek sat back at his desk. He dry-sipped his glass before he realized that he'd finished his punch, but he didn't bother getting up to get a new one. If he was going to talk Donatra into helping her greatest enemy, he'd need serious ammunition.

The first thing Sonek noticed about Donatra's chambers on Achernar Prime was that they looked absolutely nothing like the Senate floor on Romulus. Where the latter was circular, with high ceilings and light from Eisn, Romulus's sun, streaming in to illuminate both the Senate and the central floor, Donatra had chosen a long, low-ceilinged room deep within a massive edifice built into a cliff face on the edge of Achernar Prime's western continent. Donatra sat in a huge, high-backed chair that was two steps up from the floor and situated against the north wall. According to the map provided by the *Aventine*'s sensors, the other side of the south wall was a sheer drop of a hundred kilometers to the ocean. The very long east and west walls were decorated with ancient (or at least ancient-looking) swords and shields of both Romulan and Vulcan design.

Sonek beamed down accompanied only by Altoss. That had been the subject of a protracted discussion in the *Aventine* observation lounge as they were on approach to Achernar.

"We can't just turn over two people to the Romulans like that," Bowers had said.

"First of all," Sonek had said, " 'the Romulans' isn't quite what we're talking about anymore. We've got two separate political entities, and the one we're in right now is the one that's been allied with us. The woman into whose chamber I'm beaming down put her life on the line to help out *Enterprise* and *Titan* both, and her military sacrificed itself to save Ardana. Also, we're the ones asking *her* for a favor. Under those circumstances, I really don't think beaming down a security squad is going to do much for our chances of getting that favor, or of keeping the alliance."

"There isn't an alliance," Dax had pointed out before Bowers could object, "but your point's well taken. Ensign Altoss will beam down with you—I assume even Donatra will understand your having a bodyguard?"

"That's fine, but it shouldn't be any more than that." Sonek had noticed Bowers almost squirming in his chair. "Look, Commander, I get what you're saying, believe me. If I was the one sitting where you're sitting, I'd be saying the same thing. But we can't make it look like we're asking for this favor at the point of a phaser. We've got a heavily armed ship in orbit—that ought to be more than enough to let Donatra know that we're serious about this."

"All right," Bowers had said, "it's your funeral."

Sonek had laughed at that. "I sure hope it isn't, Commander."

If it was to be Sonek's funeral, it was likely to be initiated by one of the two guards standing on either side of Donatra's throne, disruptors drawn and pointed forward. *No,* he realized, *one of them's pointed at me, the other one at Altoss.*

The most recent image of Donatra on file was from *Titan*'s communication logs over a year ago. She had let her hair grow out, and Sonek noted that neither of her two guards had the bowl-cut that had been favored by the Romulan military in recent times. If Donatra had relaxed that rule, it made the new fashions on Ardana more ironic. Sonek made a mental note to mention that in his next letter to Rupi.

The guards' uniforms were also different from the gray padded outfits that the centurions on Artaleirh wore. Donatra had gone back to an older style, dotted gray jumpsuits and black boots, but without the colored sash over the right shoulder indicating rank. Instead, rank was denoted by a pin on the chest.

The empress herself wore a black cloak that looked more Vulcan than Romulan, with a red stole draped over her shoulders and down her front. Sonek's written Romulan was a little rusty, but he was pretty sure the characters stitched in green on the stole spelled out the phrase "Imperial Romulan State."

Sonek approached the throne, head lowered. "Empress Donatra. Thank you for agreeing to see me. I am Professor Sonek Pran."

"You are the emissary from the Federation?"

Sonek considered. "I guess that's one way of putting it. President Bacco asked me to come and chat with you about some things."

"Has she? Interesting." Donatra rose to her feet. "I assume the topic of this—this chat—to be the same as that which I discussed with Starfleet captains and Federation diplomats over the past two months?"

"I believe so, yes, ma'am. Er—" He hesitated. "How do I address you? 'Empress'? 'Highness'? 'Your worship'?"

Donatra smiled. " 'Empress' is sufficient. Tell me, Professor Sonek Pran of the Federation—how are you to convince me where others have not?"

"Well, I honestly don't know that, Empress. I'm a student of history, and I'm hoping that maybe we can talk a little bit *about* history and about the future and about what our places in it will be."

"A student of history, you say?"

"And a teacher of it, yes."

"And a student of Romulans, I understand."

Sonek frowned. "Ma'am?"

Donatra stepped down from her throne and approached Sonek. She was, Sonek noticed, quite lovely, far more so in person than her images indicated. Her eyes seemed to bore right through you, and yet you could lose yourself in them if you weren't careful.

Then again, you don't get to shatter a millennia-old empire if you don't have yourself a goodly amount of charisma.

Donatra continued. "Your name was familiar to me when Ambassador T'Garas informed me that you wanted to meet with me. You were the one who wrote the monograph on Admiral Jarok."

That caught Sonek off guard. He had written that monograph at the request of the Federation Council when the Romulans had ended their self-imposed removal from galactic affairs at the end of 2364. Alidar Jarok was a Romulan admiral of many years' standing. Sonek had done the best he could with the information available, both from intelligence reports and a smuggled-out copy of Jarok's official biography—the latter of which was significantly exaggerated, of course, but reading between the lines was always one of Sonek's gifts.

"Yes, I did write that."

"It was bilious tripe. You completely misunderstood Jarok's entire life."

"There are some folks in Starfleet Command who'd agree with you. When Jarok tried to defect fifteen years ago, a big reason why Starfleet didn't trust him was because of what I wrote in my monograph, since one of my conclusions was that he was a patriot of the highest order, and would never betray the Romulan Empire for any reason whatsoever."

"And he didn't. Jarok did what he did to *preserve* the Empire. In a sense, so did I." She gestured for Sonek to follow her as she moved toward a door on the east wall. "Come. We shall share fire and water and we will speak of history and the future."

Altoss moved in step behind Sonek, which prompted Donatra to stop moving and the two guards to step forward.

"Your bodyguard will remain here. As will my sentries. You are a guest, here under diplomatic privilege. You will not be harmed."

Sonek turned to Altoss. "I'll be fine, Ensign."

"Professor, I'm under orders to stay by your side at all times."

"I'm under diplomatic privilege. If any harm comes to me, Donatra's honor bound to commit suicide."

"That won't be much comfort to *you,* though."

Sonek grinned. "Probably not, but it'll be fine. Really."

"Under protest, Professor," the Efrosian woman said angrily.

Donatra led Sonek into a small room where two servants stood. He noticed also that there was a brazier in the center of the room with a low fire burning. Against one wall was a small table with two chairs. As she moved toward it, Donatra asked, "Would you like a drink?"

"Whatever you're having, Empress," Sonek said with a small bow.

To one servant, she said, "A flagon of ale and two glasses."

I was afraid of that, Sonek thought. The last time he'd had Romulan ale was at a diplomatic function on Pacifica. He couldn't see for two days. *Still, when in Rome . . .*

"I noticed," he said, waiting for Donatra to sit down before taking the seat opposite her, "that you offered me fire and water, which is a traditional Vulcan manner of offering hospitality. The robe you're wearing is very much like that of a high Vulcan official. Half the weapons on the wall out there are Vulcan." He smiled across the table at her. "Going back to your roots?"

"In a manner of speaking. I do not agree with your Ambassador Spock that our people should be reunited.

But too much of early Romulan history was given over to an effort to *not* be Vulcan. When the coronet of Karatek was uncovered five years ago, it revealed much about our common history with our sundered cousins, and I believe we should embrace that aspect of our heritage. Vulcan is a part of us, whether we admit it or not."

Sonek nodded. "Makes sense. Logic probably dictated what you did late last year."

Donatra raised an eyebrow. "Interesting that you say that, since one of Tal'Aura's many arguments against me is that I split off from Romulus in a petulant display of emotion."

"Tal'Aura's trying to hold what's left of the Star Empire together. Of course she's going to say that. But I'm sure she knows better. You could've tried to do what Shinzon did—made a power grab of your own, overthrown Tal'Aura, and replaced her with your own leadership. But if you did that, you'd pit yourself against a sitting praetor, and that didn't work so well against Hiren. So instead, you went ahead and built a coalition of support for seceding. Now it's not you against Tal'Aura in a one-on-one fight, it's the two of you in separate corners and saying to the people, 'Pick one of us.' "

The servant came back with the ale, pouring some into each of the glasses. Sonek tried not to notice the sparks that seemed to shoot up from the blue liquid.

Donatra raised her glass. "To the future."

Sonek did likewise. "To history, which used to be the future."

At that, Donatra laughed. It was a pleasant laugh, and that actually made Sonek a little nervous. Then again, if she was relaxed enough to laugh, it meant that she might be taking him seriously. Or it might have meant that she was just humoring him.

He sipped the ale and tried not to let it show on his face that he felt like a phaser had overloaded in the base of his neck.

Setting her glass down with an authoritative thunk, Donatra said, "It is true that Tal'Aura and I are not at war, but we *are* enemies. That is why I will not help her."

"Respectfully, Empress, that's where I think your logic is falling down on the job. You don't want to help Tal'Aura because you'd rather hurt her. That's pretty much what it all boils down to, doesn't it?"

Now Donatra was scowling. "If one wishes to be crude about it."

"My apologies for being crude, but my point is simply that you think there's still a battle between you and Tal'Aura, and there really isn't—because, Empress, *you've already won.*"

"Have I?" The laugh came back, but it was harsh and bitter this time. "Shall I recount to you all the assassination attempts that have been made at me since the formation of the Imperial Romulan State?"

"I don't mean to make light of this, but that's pretty much the norm for a monarch. Besides, those probably weren't Tal'Aura's agents trying to kill you, they were likely just your garden-variety crazy people and folks inside the State who want your throne for themselves. That's, to coin a phrase, the cost of doing business. But what I'm talking about is the fact that Tal'Aura knew what you were going to do before you did it."

Donatra frowned. "I beg your pardon?"

Sonek leaned forward in his chair. "Tal'Aura told President Bacco and Chancellor Martok about your plans to form the Imperial Romulan State at the summit they had on Grisella. That was a couple of weeks or so before you announced it. Tal'Aura knew about it—and didn't do anything about it because she *couldn't.* She didn't have the forces, and she knew it. Plus, you've already got the support of your people."

"You seem very sure of that for someone who has spent the last several years at a university on Mars." At Sonek's lack of reaction to this, Donatra added, "You do not seem surprised."

"I would've been a lot more surprised if you *didn't* do a full background check on me. And the reason I know you have the people's support is that, just as Tal'Aura doesn't have enough of the military on her side to go to war against you, *you* don't have enough military to put occupying forces on all the planets you've seized—which means the people on those planets are going along with being citizens of a new nation. Now, the way I see it, you figure that Tal'Aura will slowly lose her power, and more planets will go over to your side, and you'll all be one big happy Romulan family again, right?"

Donatra said nothing.

"Fine, don't confirm it, but it's kind of obvious that that's in the back of your mind—or the front of it. The best part is, you get to accomplish your long-term goal without having to lift a single finger. In fact, that plan works best with a lack of action on your part—just stand by and watch Tal'Aura's regime fall apart."

Sonek cleared his throat and wished he'd asked for something nonalcoholic before he went on. "But the problem with that plan is that the people who suffer the most *aren't* the people you want to hurt. Tal'Aura and the Senate are going to keep their bellies full no matter what. I just came from Artaleirh. The people there aren't getting their food from Virinat like they used to because Virinat's loyal to you, not them." Sonek took a breath. "Empress, if you offer to trade with Tal'Aura now, the people of the Romulan Empire will know who it was who fed them. And they'll know that it wasn't Tal'Aura."

"And when Tal'Aura claims that this food is her right?"

Sonek shrugged. "She can claim it all she wants. What matters is, her people will get fed." Throwing caution to the wind and figuring that some liquid was better than none, he took another sip of ale, then waited for his neck to finish disintegrating. "Not only that, but the Federation will know who alleviated our burden. We don't forget our friends, you know."

"Yes, we've all seen that with the way you've treated the Klingon Empire—despite how appallingly they have often treated you."

"We don't hold grudges. We prefer to look to the future. Oh, and something else—Xanitla, Ralatak, and Virinat used to produce enough food to feed everybody in the empire, plus whoever you might've been exporting to. That first number has been cut in half—which leads me to think that there's gonna be a bit of a surplus anyhow. Seems to me you'd want to make use of that to trade for some of the things you *do* need." Sonek blinked a few times, trying to keep his head clear. The ale was getting to him, but he didn't dare show it.

Donatra then laughed again. "You hide the ale's effect on you poorly."

"Sorry—just trying to keep whatever's left of my dignity intact."

"Your dignity lies in your words, Professor Sonek Pran." Donatra got to her feet. "Very well. I will consider your proposal. How long will the *Aventine* remain in orbit?"

Sonek also rose. "That depends—how long do you need to consider my proposal?"

"I will contact you at first light."

With a bow, Sonek said, "Thank you, Empress."

"There is a third possibility that you have not mentioned."

Cutting off his bow halfway back up, Sonek frowned. "I'm sorry?"

"Either I will go along with your plan and begin trade with Tal'Aura, or I will reject your plan and continue as before."

Sonek nodded. "The third possibility is that you go ahead and offer this agreement to Tal'Aura and she says no."

"In which case, I will look a fool."

"Not really. Tal'Aura will look a fool for taking food out of the mouths of her own people, and her popularity will plummet even further." Sonek thought it best not to mention that Tal'Aura was apparently casting off the Federation's aid already. That still bothered him.

"Await a summons from me in the morning, Professor Sonek Pran of the Federation."

"I'll count the minutes, Empress." With another bow, Sonek left the room, wondering if Donatra would continue to call him by his full name and title and nation of origin tomorrow.

Altoss was waiting only semi-patiently. Sonek didn't

need any particular skills in reading body language to see that the Efrosian ensign was ready to jump out of her skin. Her hand was hovering near her phaser, and Sonek guessed that it was taking a Herculean effort for her not to draw it—an effort not aided by the two soldiers, who still stood on either side of Donatra's throne and who had their sidearms pointed right at her.

"Ready to go home?" Sonek asked brightly.

Scowling, Altoss said, "Gladly."

Smiling at the two guards, Sonek said, "Thanks for keeping an eye on my friend here. Take care!"

As they walked toward the back of the room to the lift that would take them to the surface, Altoss whispered, "Why do you feel the need to talk to them?"

"I like talking to people."

"I've noticed. It's probably going to get you killed."

"Yeah, but it's what I do for a living. You worry too much."

They entered the lift, which started moving up as soon as they both entered it—the lift only went in two directions: up to the surface and down to Donatra's chambers. As it ascended, Altoss said, "Worrying too much is what *I* do for a living."

"And it's likely to get *you* killed." Sonek grinned. "No wonder we get along."

"Speak for yourself, Professor," Altoss said as the door opened onto the reception area on the surface. She tapped her combadge. "Altoss to *Aventine*. Two to beam up."

The next morning, Sonek once again sat in the observation lounge of the *Aventine* with Dax and Bowers. They were all waiting for Donatra to get in touch.

"Do you think she'll go for it?" Dax asked.

"I have to say that I really don't have the foggiest idea."

Bowers rolled his eyes. "That's encouraging."

Sonek smirked. "You'd rather I lied, Commander?"

"I'd rather you did what you were supposed to do."

Throwing up his hands, Sonek said, "I did, Commander. The Palais sent me here to talk to Donatra, and yesterday I beamed on down and I talked to Donatra. I'm none too clear on what more you want from me."

Bowers blew out a breath. "What I want, Professor, is for this mission to be over, so we can move on to something *important*."

Sonek could see from the look on Bowers's face that he regretted the words as soon as he said them, but that didn't stop Dax from saying, "That's enough, Commander!"

Wincing, Bowers said, "I'm sorry, Captain."

Dax was a small, unintimidating woman, for the most part, so the iron in her voice as she spoke to her first officer caught Sonek off guard. "You should be. You were the one who wrote in your report about the starving children on Artaleirh. We're trying to come up with a way to feed them, and I'm *very* curious as to how that qualifies as unimportant."

Bowers got to his feet and stood at attention. "It doesn't, Captain. I'm just—"

The iron now gone, Dax said, "Frustrated?"

Sonek said, "He was probably going to say 'tired.' I can see it in all of you, to be honest: you're exhausted. You've been working without a real break for months." Smiling at Bowers, he added, "That's why I haven't taken any of the potshots you've been lobbing at me the past few days personally. That's also why I had that jam session the other night. You gotta blow off steam every once in a while. The commander here's been blowing it at me, and that's fine. I'm not gonna be on this ship too long, so I'm an easy target, someone Commander Bowers doesn't have to work with every day."

Dax smirked. "I thought you were a history professor, not a counselor."

"I'm not, I'm just nosy."

"Bridge to Captain Dax."

Looking up at Kedair's voice, Dax said, "Go ahead, Lieutenant."

"Incoming message from the surface, Captain. It's Empress Donatra."

"This ought to be good. Send it in here, Lieutenant."

Sonek turned to face the viewer, and Donatra's face appeared.

"Empress, I'm Captain Ezri Dax of the Starship *Aventine*. How may I help you?"

Donatra inclined her head. *"Captain. I was wondering if I might ask your indulgence for a tour of your ship. I understand it is a new class of vessel."*

"Yes, it is."

"Excellent. Then I would like to beam aboard—and perhaps Professor Pran and I might continue our discussion of yesterday."

Dax glanced at Sonek, then said, "We'd be honored, Empress. Can you come aboard in two hours?"

"Three would be preferable, as I have several matters of state to attend to this morning before my advisers will let me go off-planet even for a short time."

Dax nodded. "I understand. Please signal us when you're ready to come up, Empress."

After Donatra signed off, Bowers looked at Sonek. "I guess she's still thinking about it."

"Looks like it, yeah."

Dax tapped her combadge. "Dax to Kedair. Empress Donatra is going to be coming on board at 1100 hours. Prepare an honor guard for that time in transporter room one. Also, any sensitive areas of the ship are to be made completely off limits to any non-Starfleet personnel."

"Aye, Captain."

Bowers looked at Sonek. "Professor, I—I'm sorry."

Getting to his feet, Sonek said, "What for? You were just doing your job, Commander. I think we're all better off if you keep on doing that."

"Glad we got that straight," Dax said dryly. "Commander, you'll have the bridge while the professor and I give the empress her tour."

Bowers nodded.

Dax added, "Let's hope, Professor, that your powers of persuasion are all they're cracked up to be."

"I understand that your vessel has been equipped with an experimental new faster-than-light drive," Donatra said as Dax led her down a corridor.

Donatra had beamed aboard fifteen minutes late, which bothered neither Dax nor Pran even a little bit. Dax knew from her time as Curzon that heads of state were, at best, on time for their first appointment of the day only. Pran had joked in the transporter room while they waited that a mere fifteen minutes constituted early by most standards.

She had come aboard with one bodyguard only—the same as Pran had beamed down with, a consideration Dax appreciated—and Dax matched that by having Kedair send her deputy security chief, Lieutenant Naomi Darrow. The five of them proceeded to the parts of the ship Dax was willing to show off, including the hydroponics bay, the various science labs, the arboretum, and the holodeck. They were on their way now to the rec hall.

Dax, of course, could not answer the empress's question in the affirmative, even though they both knew it was true. "I'm afraid I don't know what you're talking about, Empress. The *Aventine* is outfitted with a standard warp drive."

Donatra smiled. "Of course it is. I understand, Captain, that you are not allowed to speak with me of classified things. I mention it merely to point out that secrets are difficult to keep in the best of times—and these are far from the best of times. Nations that are trying to relocate and reconstruct such a large percentage of their population and planetary resources tend to leak intelligence like a punctured boat."

I was already aware of that, thanks. "Nonetheless, Empress, I still have no idea what you're talking about."

"As you say." Donatra then looked down directly at Dax. "My ability to measure Trill aging patterns is not what it might be, but you do appear to be rather young to be a starship captain. Were you promoted due to the shortage of captains following the Borg invasion? Oh, no," Donatra said suddenly, before Dax could answer. "You were at the forefront of the final defeat of the Borg, alongside my good friends Captains Picard and Riker. I take it Starfleet thinks very highly of your abilities."

"Yes, they do." Dax smiled. "And I'm a lot older than I look."

Donatra blinked. "You're joined? I wasn't aware that

there were any such left after the . . . unpleasantness some years ago."

Dax had no interest in discussing the intricacies of Trill politics, or the rather unpleasant revelations four years ago that resulted in a moratorium on joinings. Even if she were, she was spared having to do so by their arrival at the rec hall.

"This," the captain said as the doors parted, "is our recreation hall."

Spon's Elisiar, Dax noted, was still in the center of the room. The large instrument wasn't very portable, and Dax figured that Chief Spon wanted to keep it handy for as long as Pran was on board.

"Is that an Elisiar?"

For the first time since they left the transporter room, Pran spoke up. Only then did Dax realize that that was the longest he'd been quiet in her presence. "You know about Elisiars?"

"Yes. During the Dominion War, as part of the treaty between Romulus and the Federation, a musical group that called itself the A.C. Walden Medicine Show played on Romii."

"You were at that show? So was I." Pran smiled. "Family privilege. I'm related to half the people in that group." Looking at Dax, he added, "That's where I first had tree candy, actually."

"You should be proud of your family, Professor," Donatra said. "They performed quite well. I was particularly impressed with their interpretation of *'Tr'owiluhfe Mnei'sahe.'* It was not a melody I would have imagined being played on an Elisiar. Traditionally, it is only played on the *ka'athyra*."

"That's part of what the group likes to do—take songs

that everyone knows and put a completely different spin on them. It's a good way to really *listen* to the song. A lot of times, taking a new look at an old thing is the best way to appreciate it, and get something new out of it you weren't expecting."

Not exactly subtle, Dax thought. But Donatra did lead him right to it.

The empress then turned to Dax. "Captain, I would ask a favor of you. I wish to open a dialogue with Praetor Tal'Aura to discuss the opening of trade relations between our two nations. I believe that a direct communication from me would not be answered."

Dax nodded. "But one from a Federation starship that just provided aid to her people would be?"

"Yes."

"Empress, I would be honored. If you wish, we can go to the bridge right now."

"Excellent. And I thank you for the tour." She turned to Pran. "And thank you, Professor, for allowing me to see my relationship with the praetor in a new light."

Pran bowed his head. "Happy to be of service, Empress."

The quintet made their way to the bridge, Pran and Donatra talking about some musical trivia or other.

When the turbolift arrived, Bowers got to his feet. "Captain on deck!" He turned toward the lift.

"Empress Donatra," Dax said, "this my first officer, Commander Sam Bowers."

Inclining his head, Bowers said, "Welcome aboard the *Aventine,* Empress."

"Thank you, Commander."

Dax led Donatra to the tactical station toward the bridge's aft section. Both Darrow and Donatra's guard took up position on either side of the turbolift doors. Pran lingered behind Dax and Donatra.

To the security chief, Dax said, "Lieutenant Kedair, please open a channel to the Hall of State on Romulus. Tell them that Captain Dax of the *Aventine* is at Achernar Prime and requests an audience with the praetor."

"Aye, Captain."

Turning to Donatra, she said, "Empress, this will take a few minutes. Let me show you around the bridge."

By the time Dax finished showing Donatra all the consoles and explaining their functions, Kedair had navigated through several different intermediaries before finally getting Praetor Tal'Aura on the screen.

"Madam Praetor, I'm Captain Ezri Dax of the *Aventine.*"

"So I was told. I was also told that you were at the planet where the traitor has based her illegal empire. Ah, and I see she is standing with you. May I assume that you are about to set course to Romulus and deliver the traitor to the Senate, where she may stand trial for her numerous crimes?"

Dax swallowed a sigh. *This wasn't how I wanted this to go.* "Madam Praetor, Empress Donatra wishes to discuss the opening of trade relations with—"

Holding up a hand, Tal'Aura said, *"Stop right there, Captain. I am afraid that any talk of trade relations would be pointless. The Romulan Star Empire has no need for trade relations—not with your Federation, and* certainly *not with that* veruul *on your bridge."*

Stepping forward, Donatra said, "Your people are starving, Tal'Aura. I can feed them."

"You will address me properly!"

Donatra smiled. "You first. I see no reason to provide a respectful title for one who calls a fellow head of state a *veruul*."

"This is pointless. Captain Dax, I thank you for the goods your ship delivered to Artaleirh. Our ambassador will be informing your president of this formally, but all aid agreements between your government and mine are now officially terminated. Your ship may travel safely through our space to return home. Romulus out."

The bridge was silent for several seconds.

Finally, Dax said, "That didn't go very well, did it?"

Donatra turned to Dax. "It went exactly as I expected it would. Tal'Aura is a stubborn fool."

Bowers looked at Pran. "I'm surprised you didn't jump in to try to talk her out of it."

Pran shook his head. "There wasn't really much of a point to talking. It just would've made that whole conversation go on longer, and get the exact same result. I don't have magic powers, Commander. If I'm capable of convincing people of something, it's because either they don't have all the information, or because they believe it to some extent already. Or both." Glancing over at Donatra, he said, "With respect, Empress, you don't want to see Romulans starving, even if they're not your subjects. That helped make my argument for me." Then he pointed at the screen, which now showed Achernar Prime below their orbital path. "But Tal'Aura had already made her decision, and nothing I said, the captain said, the empress said, or the Elements Themselves might've said would have made a helluva lot of difference. And that's because *she* knows something we don't. I, for one, would like to know what it is."

"Whereas I," Donatra said, moving toward the turbolift, "could not possibly care less. I have done what I can. If Tal'Aura is too stubborn to accept my offer, then she will eventually pay the price."

"Maybe," Pran said. "And maybe she already has."

Dax didn't like the sound of that at all.

Final log entry by Captain George Sanders, commanding officer, *U.S.S. Malinche,* Stardate 58199.3

The *Malinche* is en route to the Andorian system, but our long-range sensors have detected half a dozen Borg cubes between us and Andor. The plan was to join the fleet being led by the *Venture,* but we'll actually reach the Borg *before* they arrive at Andor.

I've decided to engage the enemy in interstellar space. One *Excelsior*-class ship isn't going to make a whole lot of difference in a fleet of two dozen. But if we can sneak in behind the Borg, we *might*—and I freely admit, it's a big *might*—soften them up for the fleet.

It's a long shot, but those are the only kind of shots we've really got left. This day's been coming for sixteen years, and the only thing we can do, cliché though it may be, is to go down fighting.

The crew is aware of the fact that we are very unlikely to survive this mission. They are all performing their duties brilliantly. I would like to recommend that they all, from my first officer Commander Toomajian on down, receive posthumous commendations for bravery—assuming there's still a Federation after all this is done.

Who knows? Maybe we'll even survive.

Since this is likely my final log entry, I would like to indulge myself and add a personal message to my family. I love you all.

End log entry.

9

H'ATORIA

Archbishop Retej, leader of the Seventh Holy Kinshaya Attack Fleet, entered the circular flight deck of his flagship. His first mate, Bishop Ador, stood at attention and spread his wings. They were decent-sized wings, tattooed with the blue-and-white crest of his order, and he spread them to gain the attention of the rest of the bridge crew. The Devout had evolved beyond the need to use the wings for flight, and now they were used solely to denote one's station.

" *'Aya!* Make respect!" Ador bellowed.

Keeping his own wings furled, Retej said, "Be as you were." Despite this admonition, most of the bridge crew still lowered their stances, bending all four knees out of respect for their commander.

The flight deck was in a circle, that purest of shapes, just as the ship and all its important rooms were. Consoles lined the walls, with either loyal servants of the Devout or Kreel slaves standing at each of them, facing the center, which was both a holographic projector and a transporter.

Retej strode to the console that faced the entryway to the flight deck, where his first mate was stationed. "What is our status, Bishop?"

Ador's wings folded back down. " *'Aya.* We have reduced to sublight speeds and we shall achieve orbit of H'atoria in seven units, my Lord."

"Excellent. What do scans say of the planet? How many of the demons' ships defend that world?"

For a moment, Ador hesitated, and his ears flattened. " *'Aya*, my Lord—none."

Retej's wings flared, showing the red-and-black crest of his own order. "None?"

" *'Aya*, my Lord. We have used the scanner that can penetrate their cloaks. There is *nothing.*"

This disturbed Retej. H'atoria was a world on the border between the Klingon Empire—the realm of the demons—and the Federation. Retej knew little of the Federation, as they shared no border with the Kinshaya, not even now that they had conquered the heretic Kreel, but he did know that this world was an important trading post between the two nations.

Of course, that was before the Borg.

"Place tactical analysis on the viewer," Retej said, folding his wings back down.

Turning to the weapons master, Ador said, "Deacon Adasop, obey the archbishop's direction."

" *'Aya,* Bishop, it will be done." Adasop, who had the plain wings of the lower classes, manipulated the controls with his forelegs. Moments later, a holographic image appeared in the center of the flight deck, showing the world of H'atoria and its two tiny moons.

And nothing else. No ships, no artificial satellites, nothing.

However, the space surrounding the planet was of less interest to Retej than what the scans were showing of the planet itself. Life-form readings were given in red, and there were precious few of them—most in the northern polar region. Bodies of water were indicated in white, and there was only one such, in that same region.

Retej's ears flattened. " *'Aya.* We were not told that this was among the worlds devastated by the Borg. It would seem that that intelligence was faulty."

"We were also told," Ador added, "that this planet was primarily covered in oceans."

Adasop said, " *'Aya,* Bishop, I have a report."

Ador looked at Retej, who raised his ears, indicating that he should proceed.

"Provide your report, Deacon."

" *'Aya.* Scans show the same traces of weapons fire as on other worlds destroyed by the Borg. There are no constructions, no electromagnetic emissions, no indications of an industrialized society."

Retej stared at the hologram. "What species are the life-form readings from?"

Ador said, " *'Aya,* my Lord, they match the readings of the Selsseress, the species native to the planet."

"Tell me about them, Bishop."

Turning to the chief scientist, Ador said, "Vicar Noca, report to the archbishop."

From the science station, Noca stood on all fours and spread his wings, which were wider even than Retej's. The vicar's tiresome insistence on showing them off grew wearisome, as did his refusal to say " *'Aya*" to

Retej out of respect, as was his due as archbishop, but Noca's crèche was one of the noblest of all Kinshaya, as indicated by the three-colored crest on his wings, in black and purple and green. And he had a brilliant scientific mind. Retej knew he was a valuable asset, which meant he had to put up with his arrogance.

"The Selsseress are an amphibious people who can thrive only in high humidity, preferably near water. According to the planetary survey we were provided with, they lived all over the world, both on the few landmasses and swimming in the oceans. They are also barely sentient, providing a workforce that is capable only of the most menial of labors. Several of the demons' wealthier citizens have holdings on this world, but Deacon Adasop's scans would seem to indicate that they are no more."

This caused Ador's ears to flatten further. " *'Aya.* We have been sent to conquer a worthless planet."

"Not quite, Bishop," Retej said, spreading his wings wide. "The value of this planet was never in its inhabitants or its resources, but in its location. And given how many of our fellow Devout were killed in the taking of Krios, I am just as happy to find this planet ripe for the taking. Enter orbit, have the fleet take up conquest positions. We will claim this world for the Holy Order of the Kinshaya."

Despite his bravado, he felt some disappointment. While it was never a good day for the Devout to die, he had been looking forward to removing more demons from the universe of life and sending them to the purgatory they so richly deserved. In particular, he was hoping that the *kro-vak,* the destroyer of worlds, the demon known as Klag, would be present to defend H'atoria so

Retej would have the pleasure of killing that particular demon himself.

On the other hand, it seemed as if the Borg had done plenty for them in that regard with the Klingons of this world.

Retej had always been fascinated by the concept of the Borg. Creatures who were subsumed to one purpose only. He had always imagined that, if they could capture one, they could figure out how to engineer their cybernetics and their drive and use it for their own purposes, to further the glory of the Devout.

Now, though, it was too late. From all reports—which were generally reliable—the Borg were no more.

Ador's voice drew him from his thoughts. "We have achieved orbit, my Lord."

"Good. Have survey teams transport to the surface and report on the status of the world. In particular, I wish to know more about the remaining Selsseress. And be sure that each team has an armed escort—the demons may yet have tricks to play on us."

" *'Aya,* my Lord, it will be done."

Personal log of Counselor Brian Ellis, Starbase 22, Stardate 58322.2

I've been working nonstop for seven weeks now. No breaks, no leave, nothing. The joys of being a counselor specializing in post-traumatic stress after the Borg have killed sixty billion people—at least—are such that my guest chair is occupied pretty regularly.

I had a patient today who completely stunned and horrified me. Hard to believe, really, as I honestly thought I'd heard it all at this point: Crewperson Alhan Jago, an engineer from the *Lexington,* who's suffering from survivor's guilt because the rest of the engineering staff was killed, but he survived because he was in sickbay being treated for what he kept insisting was a minor wound (the *Lexington* CMO's report is that his leg was broken); Chief Thaddeus Samson, the cargomaster of the *Venture,* whose entire family lived on Deneva; Ensigns Seareg and Yoralig, two science officers from the *Phoenix,* who were the only survivors of that ship's failed defense of Coridan, having been the only ones to be able to make use of escape pods—and who are both

Coridanites; medical officers from the *Lexington,* the *Atlas,* the *Prometheus,* the *Khwarizimi,* the *Monarch,* and the *Thantasaras,* who have all been overwhelmed with casualties and are having trouble dealing with it; Lieutenant Commander Byron Fantomos, the recreation officer of the *Sovereign,* who simply *cannot* get his mind around the death count; Lieutenant (j.g.) Valak, an operations officer on the *Monarch,* who was in the midst of *Pon farr,* and whose wife, Lieutenant (j.g.) T'Mura, was killed during the *Monarch*'s engagement of the Borg at Lorillia, and whose emotional control is in complete tatters; Lieutenant Commander Kara na Miin, the second officer of the *Kearsarge,* who had to take command when the captain had a nervous breakdown and the first officer was killed during the defense of Vulcan; and Captain Tando of the *Kearsarge,* with whom I've had ten sessions, during which he has yet to say a single word—or, indeed, do much of anything beyond stare straight ahead, his mouth hanging open.

With all that, I still managed to be caught off guard today. My appointments have been pretty heavy, as this has been a popular repair station, plus it's been designated as a transfer point, so we get a lot of people on their way to new assignments. Still, I haven't had a lot of space for new people, and often have to send new patients to one of the other counselors on the starbase or on one of the ships in dock. But I had a postponement—Chief Samson had to deal with a crisis on the *Venture*—so I talked to Ensign Dmitri Nakahara, the deputy security chief on the *Hood.*

The *Hood* was responding to a distress signal a couple of weeks ago. It turned out to be the remains of a Borg scout sphere that had crashed on a planetoid. There were seven drones in that sphere—except, of course, thanks to the Caeliar, they were all restored to themselves again. The *Hood*'s short-handed, with the security chief also acting as first officer, so Nakahara was assigned to lead the away team that had to secure the site.

I just sat there and listened to Nakahara talk calmly and coolly about this away mission he led, and then he got to the part where he fired his phaser at each of the seven ex-drones, killing them. I was horrified, not because of what he did—okay, yes, in part because of what he did—but because he was utterly unrepentant about it. Well, no, he was unrepentant about the action. What he felt bad about was lying to his superiors. He ordered the enlisted security guards who went down with him to stick to his story, which was that there were no survivors and that the distress signal was automated.

But that wasn't the worst part.

The ex-drones *asked them for help.* They talked about how they were themselves again, and one of them even identified himself as Starfleet security, a man named Soon-Tek Han, who was assigned to the *Enterprise*-D sixteen years ago when they first encountered the Borg.

And Nakahara shot them.

His reasoning was that the Borg committed despicable acts of atrocity, and they needed to pay for that. Never mind that they were under the control of their Queen and that they were no more individually responsible for their actions than—well, than Nakahara's trigger finger alone was responsible for killing Han and the rest of those former drones.

What stunned me, and what scares me, is that Nakahara is convinced of the rightness of his actions. His only concern is that he doesn't think that Captain DeSoto will understand his actions, so he lied in his official report.

I should, of course, report him. Confidentiality does not extend to such heinous crimes. Nakahara's a murderer, and his subordinates are accessories.

And yet, is he? There are over *sixty billion people* who are dead now. Thousands of ships, both Starfleet and not, were destroyed. Vulcan and Andor are both badly scarred, Sherman's Planet and Rhaandarel were wiped out. . . . Commander Fantomos isn't the only one who finds the numbers simply mind-boggling.

It's the greatest tragedy in the history of the galaxy. How can we judge someone like Nakahara, whose job is to protect us from threats like the Borg? How can we judge any of us?

And how bad is it that a very big part of me is defending the actions of a man who murdered seven people in cold blood?

I have to report it to Captain DeSoto and Admiral T'r'w'o'l'h'o'r, of course. But merely the fact that I've considered not doing so is an indication of just how bad things are right now.

10

EARTH

The assorted councillors and cabinet members and staffers all rose to their feet as the meeting *finally* came to an end. President Nan Bacco tried to keep her poker face, but it was hard these days, especially given that she hadn't had a good night's sleep since the Borg attacked Barolia.

Secretary Iliop—the secretary of transportation, who'd been obscenely busy these past months—muttered to Toshiro Czierniewski, the assistant technology secretary, as he walked toward the door, "If we could only put more slipstream drives in."

Toshiro looked at Iliop and said, "It's still not a hundred percent, Ili. And most civilian ships aren't anywhere near as adaptable to the new components as Starfleet, and some of the Starfleet ships are having problems."

"Yes, but . . ."

The two Cabinet members' conversation became lost as they exited the president's office. Which was fine with Nan, as the Berellian had been on this kick for the past month, arguing it with Toshiro, Toshiro's boss, Fleet Admiral Akaar, and anybody else in range, and Nan was bored with it after the *first* dozen times.

The only person who didn't leave was her chief of staff. Esperanza Piñiero waited until the door slid shut behind the last Cabinet member, and then said, "We've got some news on Capella. Akaar, C29, and Forzrat are working downstairs in the Vanderbilt Room. I'd like Sivak to bring them up."

"I assume it's bad news?"

"Not entirely."

Rubbing her temples in the hopes of staving off headache five, Nan said, "Don't play games with me, Esperanza, is it good news or bad news?"

"It carries the potential for good news."

"Be still, my beating heart." She reached down to her desk and touched the intercom. "Sivak, what's next?"

Her assistant's deep voice sounded over the speaker. *"You are scheduled to meet with Ambassador K'mtok in five minutes—however, his shuttle was delayed, and he will not arrive for another twenty minutes."*

"Dandy," Nan muttered. She was not looking forward to her conversation with the Klingon ambassador to the Federation.

"What're you meeting with K'mtok about?" Esperanza asked.

"He's probably gonna express his displeasure about the number of Starfleet ships we're sending to help the Defense Force retake H'atoria and Krios from the Kinshaya—especially since that number is zero."

"Better you than me, ma'am."

"I get that a lot."

Nan was about to tell Sivak to send Akaar and the other two up, but the Vulcan didn't give her a chance. *"Ma'am, Ambassador Kalavak arrived while your meeting was ongoing. I informed him that you were busy, but he said it was urgent that you two speak."*

Nan stared at Esperanza. Kalavak was the Romulan Star Empire's ambassador to the Federation, and her last conversation with him was even less pleasant than the forthcoming one with K'mtok was likely to be. Nan had all but bullied the Empire (as well as the Cardassian Union and the Gorn Hegemony) to join the Federation, Klingon, Talarian, Ferengi, and Imperial Romulan State forces at the Azure Nebula. (She had tried and failed to do likewise with the Tholian Assembly, whose ambassador had left the Palais in what could generously be called a huff.) That armada was wiped out by the seven thousand Borg cubes that invaded the Alpha Quadrant, and the one time she'd met with Kalavak since the massacre, the ambassador told the president that she was personally responsible for the murder of thousands of loyal Romulan soldiers.

Looking at Esperanza, Nan said, "Five'll get you ten he wants to yell at me again."

"Maybe. But given what we've got Professor Pran doing, I think he might have something worthwhile to say."

"First time for everything. Sivak, send him in. And have Admiral Akaar, Secretary Forzrat, and Councillor C29 Green come up here. They should all be together in the Vanderbilt Room. I'll talk to them when I'm done with the ambassador."

"Very well."

A moment later, the door opened to reveal the hard

face and tall form of Ambassador Kalavak. "Good afternoon, Madam President."

Already he's more polite than last time, Nan thought as she walked around the desk. "Mr. Ambassador—what can I do for you?"

"I convey a message from the Romulan Senate. While we appreciate the aid that the Federation has provided to the Empire since the fall of Shinzon, that aid will no longer be required. Furthermore, while any Federation ships within Romulan space may travel freely until they finish their particular journeys, from this point forward no Federation ships will be allowed to enter Romulan space without permission."

Esperanza blinked. "You're closing your borders?"

"No," Kalavak said, "simply monitoring them."

Nan rubbed her hands together. Headache one was coming on, which was the one reserved for diplomats who came into her office and made her life miserable. "Mr. Ambassador, I find this very distressing. The reports from the ships that have provided aid have painted a very unpleasant picture."

"With respect, Madam President, that is no longer your concern." He smiled. "I would think you would be relieved—we are lifting what must be a terrible burden for you in this time of crisis."

"We're not in the habit of abandoning people we're trying to help—the burden to us notwithstanding."

"Unless they ask you to abandon them, which is what we are doing."

Nan let out a long breath. "Mr. Ambassador, if that is your wish, we will, of course, honor it, but I beg you to reconsider."

For the first time since he was assigned to this post

last year, Kalavak's mask of imperiousness fell, and he spoke in an almost-conspiratorial tone. "Were the decision mine, I would surely do so. But I merely convey the wishes of the praetor and the Senate." Then the mask came back on, and he bowed. "Thank you, Madam President."

With that, he turned and left.

Nan looked at Esperanza. "Well, isn't that a kick in the teeth?"

"Ma'am, Kalavak was right, this is a *huge* relief. The ships we've been sending to Romulus can be diverted to internal issues. Hell, we sent Pran to Donatra so we could get this very result."

"And what if Pran can't talk Donatra into it?"

"To be honest, ma'am, that's their problem. We can't force them to accept our help."

"Maybe, but I sure as hell don't like it. And having to accept things I don't like has become *way* too common lately." She sighed again, something else that had become too common, then hit the intercom. "Sivak, are Akaar and the others up here yet?"

"They are awaiting your pleasure, Madam President."

Running a wrinkled hand through her bone-white hair, Nan muttered, "My pleasure hasn't been an issue since I was sworn in."

"Excuse me, ma'am? I'm afraid you're mumbling again. There are Vulcan rhetorical techniques that I would be happy to—"

"Just send them in," Nan snapped. Putting up with Sivak used to be worth it because he was so good at his job, but lately, her patience had been wearing thin with him. *Hell, and everything else . . .*

When the doors parted and the trio entered, Nan had to suppress a giggle. *Which is more proof that I need more sleep,* she thought ruefully, but all she could think as they came in was, *Small, medium, and large.*

Small was C29 Green, the councillor from Nasat, who was on the technology council. Like all Nasats, C29 looked like a big pillbug, with eight legs, a round face with a protuberance where his nose would be, and a large carapace. Though enormous by bug standards, he only came up to Nan's chest when walking upright on his back legs. Nasats, Nan knew, could also skitter on all eights, and compress themselves into their carapace and roll—though she couldn't imagine the staid C29 doing that.

Medium was the short Androsian woman, Forzrat, the secretary of technology, whose work on this was why she had sent her assistant to the previous meeting. While humanoid, Androsians were cyclopean, with a giant eye in the center of their foreheads, nostril slits with no nose, and ear canals with no ears. Her long hair was colored bright green, which was what signified her office, as Androsians used hair color rather than insignia on clothing. Though she was shorter than Nan, she still towered over the Nasat councillor.

And the third person towered over everybody. Fleet Admiral Leonard Akaar, who had been the Starfleet liaison to the president since Admiral Ross's retirement last year, was from Capella IV, where they bred them big. The admiral—who had passed his centennial birthday—was two and a half meters tall, with long white hair and the face of a man who had pretty much seen everything.

Today he looked even more hangdog than usual,

which didn't surprise Nan, since this was about the homeworld that he'd been exiled from as a youth. Born to the teer of the Ten Tribes, Akaar and his mother Eleen were cast out before he came of age and could take on the mantle of teer himself. He was delivered by (and named for) a Starfleet doctor, so he joined Starfleet in his exile, eventually rising to the captaincy of the *Wyoming* before ascending to the admiralty.

"Talk to me," Nan said as they all sat down. Akaar and Esperanza took one of the two parallel couches, with Forzrat facing them on the other couch and C29 on the special chair that was used for Nasats, of whom there were several working in the Palais. Nan herself took the comfortable chair situated perpendicular to both sofas.

"The situation on Capella is dire," Akaar said. "Apparently the terrorists who were responsible for my mother's and my exile have re-formed and are targeting the mine." The admiral's blasé tone belied the pain that Nan knew he must be feeling. That tone became somewhat more angry when he added, "And the Capellans still refuse to allow Starfleet to aid them because of me."

Nan smirked. "I don't suppose we could tell them you've resigned."

"It would not matter, or I *would* have resigned, Madam President. But Starfleet's acceptance of me into their ranks has forever poisoned the organization in the minds of my people. Even were I to undergo the *w'lash'nogot,* it would probably not matter."

Pointing a finger at him, Nan said, "Let's not find out, all right, Leonard? You are *not* committing suicide. I've gone to too many funerals this year, thanks."

"I have no intention of doing so, ma'am."

"Good." Nan knew of the Capellan suicide ritual from Akaar's file, as he had attempted to kill himself in such a ritual when he was captain of the *Wyoming* and was stranded on a planetoid with another crew member, who wound up saving Akaar's life.

"However," Forzrat said, "we have some good news. Starfleet, Janus Mining, and a few other mining companies have donated equipment, and the S.C.E. has fabricated some more. It's all at Starbase 10, and we simply need a ship to transport it to the Capella system."

C29 said, "I've spoken with Rebecca Greenblatt—she's the person in charge for Janus on the planet. She's convinced the teer to let a Starfleet ship in-system to deliver the material, as long as no Starfleet officers set foot on their world."

"That must have taken some doing," Esperanza said.

Making a clicking noise, C29 said, "Ms. Greenblatt can be very persuasive—and stubborn. Besides, this is her first time as a supervisor, and she doesn't want it to be a failure."

"Well, it's my first time as president," Nan said, "and I get where she's coming from, believe me."

Esperanza asked, "Do we have a ship at the starbase?"

"Not at present," Akaar said. "And there are no ships, Starfleet or civilian, in the vicinity that can carry the load, but many of our ships are not where they are scheduled to be."

Angrily, Nan asked, "Why the hell not?"

"Missions are taking longer than expected—or less time, in some cases—and keeping track of timetables is difficult. Also, many of our vessels are shorthanded, and replacements are—"

Nan cut him off, feeling like an idiot for getting angry. "Right, of course. Sorry."

"Excuse me, Madam President?" That was Sivak.

Getting up and walking to her desk, Nan activated the intercom. Sivak wouldn't interrupt without good reason. "What is it?"

"Mr. Manzanillo has a message for Ms. Piñiero. He says that the Aventine *is calling."*

Before Nan could yell at Esperanza for her dumb-ass assistant's inability to take a message, her chief of staff said, "I told Zachary to find me whenever we heard from them, ma'am. That's the ship that's carrying Professor Pran."

"Are they still in Romulan space?" Akaar asked.

"Presumably," Esperanza said.

"Starbase 10 is proximate to the Romulan border, and the *Aventine* is one of our fastest ships. It would be the perfect vessel to bring the equipment to Capella."

"Let's hope the professor has good news, then," Nan said. "Sivak, tell Zachary to put the *Aventine* through to my office."

"Very well."

Moments later, the viewscreen on the west wall lit up with the Federation emblem, then showed a humanoid with long white hair, and a Trill Starfleet officer whom Nan recognized instantly as Captain Ezri Dax of the *Aventine*—one of the three (or four, really) starship captains who pretty much saved all their asses from the Borg.

The latter's eyes went wide. *"Madam President! I'm sorry, we didn't mean to interrupt—"*

"It's okay, Captain Dax," Nan said, holding up a hand. "We meant for you to interrupt. I'm here with Esperanza

Piñiero, Fleet Admiral Akaar, Councillor C29 Green, and Secretary Forzrat."

"This is Professor Sonek Pran."

Pran smiled. *"A pleasure, Madam President. And if it's all right, I'd like to personally thank you for giving me this opportunity."* The smile fell. *"I wish I could report more success."*

"Give it to me, Professor—hearing bad news has become my best skill these last few months."

"Donatra was more than willing to open up trade talks with Tal'Aura, but Tal'Aura wasn't interested. Her people practically had to be put in a headlock before they'd take the food we brought to Artaleirh."

Nan exchanged a glance with Esperanza, then looked back at the screen. "We just had a conversation with the Romulan ambassador—they're cutting off all aid from us."

"Dammit," Esperanza muttered. "I'm sorry, ma'am."

Confused, Nan asked, "For what?"

"It was my idea to try to get Donatra to do this, and after going to all the trouble of sending the professor out there and strong-arming her into it, it winds up being for nothing. This has probably given our credibility with Donatra a huge hit."

"I wouldn't worry about that too terribly much, Ms. Piñiero," Pran said. *"The Federation's far too valuable an ally for her to simply abandon. The only person who's lost credibility with her is Tal'Aura, and she wasn't overburdened with much of that anyway."*

Dax said, *"Madam President, I'm more concerned about the Romulans themselves. We saw hundreds of starving people just in one region of Artaleirh, and I can't imagine it's any better elsewhere."*

"Not a helluva lot we can do, unfortunately," Nan said. "We can't force people to accept help, and frankly, we've got our own problems right now."

Akaar said, "Perhaps they are receiving aid from elsewhere."

"Yeah," Pran said, *"but from who? The only nation that wasn't clobbered by the Borg is the Tholians, and I don't entirely see them as the types to provide food to Romulans, do you, Admiral?"*

"No," Akaar said. "But I do not believe that Praetor Tal'Aura would simply allow her empire to fall into ruin."

"I don't know," C29 said, "she's been doing a fine job of it so far."

Akaar turned to Nan. "Ma'am, with respect—"

"Right," Nan said. "Captain, you're still in Romulan space?"

"Yes, ma'am," Dax said.

"I'm afraid we need to ask you to take a little detour. Admiral?"

Rising to his feet, Akaar said, "Captain Dax, I need you to go to Starbase 10 and take on some mining equipment that needs to be delivered immediately to Capella. And time is of the essence—you are authorized to use the slipstream drive once you've departed the starbase. You will rendezvous with a Janus Mining vessel called the *Hecate* at Capella. Under no circumstances are any of your personnel to set foot on Capella IV, Captain, is that understood?"

Dax's eyes widened in surprise—so, Nan noticed, did Pran's. The captain said, *"Of course, Admiral. Excuse me a moment."*

She stepped away from the viewer, presumably to order her ship's pilot to change course.

Pran then spoke. *"I'm sorry, Admiral, Madam President, but I'd like to know, if you don't mind: is this related to the mine explosion?"*

"Yes," Akaar said. "The equipment the *Aventine* will be delivering will be replacement parts for those that were destroyed in the hopes of getting the topaline mining back on schedule."

"That strikes me as kind of optimistic, based on the reports I've been reading."

"Maybe," Forzrat said, "but it's necessary. We have millions of refugees that need somewhere to go both here and in Klingon space."

"And it's worse now," Esperanza said, "since the Klingons lost H'atoria and Krios and we lost Zalda."

"Uhm—I'm sorry, but what? What happened to those planets?"

Nan answered the question. "The Kinshaya moved in on H'atoria and Krios, and the Defense Force has been stretched too thin to do anything about that. In fact, when I'm done with you people, I expect Ambassador K'mtok's going to be scolding me on the subject."

"And Zalda?"

Quickly, Nan filled the professor in on Zalda's apparent withdrawal from the Federation.

"None of this makes anything like sense."

"You're only just figuring that out now?" Nan asked wryly.

Pran smiled. *"Oh, I'm very much aware of what kind of sense of the absurd the universe has, Madam President. But Zalda refusing refugees? That just doesn't track. And I get why the Kinshaya would want Krios, but H'atoria was hit by the Borg and has no real value. And it's nowhere* near *the Kinshaya's sphere of influence. What would they want with it?"*

Esperanza quickly said, "Those are all good questions, Professor, but we have bigger fish to fry. I'm sorry you'll have to delay your trip home, but you can probably grab a shuttle to Mars from Starbase 10."

"That's all right, Ms. Piñiero. If Captain Dax doesn't mind, I'd like to stick around. If nothing else, I've never actually been to Capella."

Dax came back into view. *"We're en route to Starbase 10 at maximum warp. We'll be there in twenty hours."* She turned to Pran. *"And you're welcome to stay as long as you like, Professor."*

"Thank you both," Nan said. "And godspeed."

Both captain and professor said, *"Thank you, Madam President."* Then the screen reverted to the Federation emblem, and went dark.

C29 and Forzrat both rose from the couch. The Nasat councillor was actually "standing" on all eights. "If you'll excuse me, ma'am, I'd like to contact Ms. Greenblatt on Capella and let her know that help is on the way."

"And," the Androsian said, "I will contact Admiral Hao and alert him to the *Aventine*'s arrival."

Nan nodded. "Of course."

"Thank you, Madam President," they both said before departing.

Akaar was still standing and said, "I should depart as well."

"Stay just a minute, would you, Leonard?" Nan said. "I have a meeting with K'mtok, and I think it'll go better if I have a Starfleet officer from a warrior culture around."

"Ma'am, K'mtok respects you," Esperanza said. "I don't think you need the admiral to be your bodyguard."

"No," Akaar said, "but Klingon warriors also respect the military, and I can provide more specific reasons why Starfleet cannot aid the Defense Force."

"Which is why I asked him to stay in the first place. I do actually think about these things, you know," Nan said grouchily.

"So you keep insisting, ma'am," Esperanza said with a small smile. "I need to go meet with the Deltan delegation."

"Fine, go. I'll see you at the Cabinet meeting tonight."

"Thank you, Madam President."

As Esperanza departed, Nan went to the intercom. "Sivak, has Ambassador K'mtok arrived yet?"

"No, ma'am, as I would have informed you if he had."

I swear, I will kill him. "Any word on when—?"

"His shuttle is on final approach to the roof. Agent Kistler is awaiting his arrival, and will escort him to this floor."

"Thank you. Send him right in as soon as he gets here."

"Very well."

Nan went to sit at her desk, and turned the chair so she could see the view of Paris.

Behind her, Akaar said, "The view is impressive, Madam President, yet it always makes me sad."

That piqued her curiosity, though she did not turn from staring at the skyline. "Why is that?"

"My people live in what you would consider shacks. They fight with *kligats,* they dress in clothing that they sew themselves, they plant and hunt and gather their own food. Contact with the Federation should have been the dawning of a new age for the Ten Tribes, but instead my people are still ruled by superstition and foolishness, and have made appallingly little progress in the past century. We should have been able to create a city like this."

Now she did turn to look at him, and for the first time in their acquaintance, Nan saw sadness in the admiral's eyes. "You really miss it, don't you?" she asked quietly.

"With my very soul. I have not set foot on my homeworld in a hundred years, yet a day does not pass when I do not think of it."

Nan tried to imagine what it would be like if she could never set foot on Cestus III, and found she couldn't. Nor could she imagine what it was like for all the refugees from Pandril, Coridan, Deneva, and all the other worlds that had been devastated.

But Akaar could. She wondered if that knowledge helped him in coordinating the endless relief efforts in the wake of the Borg invasion. She wondered if having such an experience would help her.

And then she looked into Akaar's eyes, and decided that she was just as happy never to find out.

The doors parted, and K'mtok came storming in, Kistler trailing behind him. The latter was part of Nan's security detail, and he would remain in the room for as long as K'mtok was there.

The ambassador himself was a broad-shouldered, gray-bearded Klingon with unusually sharp incisors even for a species that sharpened its teeth. He also had a metaphorical cloud over his head. Nan had been on the receiving end of K'mtok's wrath on more than one occasion, starting with the time he stormed into her office and tried to order her to deny aid to Reman refugees heading to Outpost 22. She slapped him down in fairly short order, and over the course of the next few months, she gained his respect, to the point that he did not hesitate to support her when she assembled an armada to fight the Borg at the Azure Nebula.

Now, though, he was back to the fire and brimstone she'd gotten at their first meeting.

"Why has the delivery of topaline been delayed?"

That brought Nan up short. She had been expecting a different harangue. "Mr. Ambassador, the topaline mine on Capella was bombed, and—"

"I am aware of that!"

In a calm voice, Nan said, "Please let me finish, Mr. Ambassador, or I will have Agent Kistler restrain you."

K'mtok's jaw twisted. "Madam President, our need for topaline is great. The treaty between our two nations—"

"I'm aware of the terms of the Khitomer Accords, Mr. Ambassador, and right now the *Aventine* is on its way to Capella to deliver material to allow Janus Mining to reconstruct the topaline mine."

At the mention of the ship, K'mtok's entire demeanor changed. "The *Aventine*? Excellent! I assume that Captain Dax is still in command of that vessel?"

Not sure why it mattered, Nan said, "Uhm, yes, she is."

Akaar said, "One of the previous hosts of the Dax symbiont was a Federation diplomat."

"The Great Curzon," K'mtok said, almost reverently.

"And the host previous to Ezri was married to a member of the House of Martok," Akaar continued. "Ezri is still considered part of the chancellor's House."

"I have confidence," K'mtok said, "that Captain Dax will do all that she can."

The thing I love about this job, Nan thought wryly, *is that you find yourself dodging phaser beams you didn't even know were being fired.* She had no idea that Captain Dax had this kind of pedigree, but she was suddenly very grateful that she was the one they were sending to Capella. "Glad to be of service, Mr. Ambassador. If that's all there is . . ."

"No, it is not. May I sit?"

"Of course." Nan indicated the couch. K'mtok sat, with Akaar taking the seat opposite him and Nan returning to the chair.

"Chancellor Martok and the High Council respectfully request that you reconsider your decision not to send Starfleet ships to aid in our battle against the Kinshaya."

So much for dodging all the phaser beams. "I'm sorry, Mr. Ambassador, but it wasn't a question of 'deciding' not to send ships. The fact of the matter is, we don't have any to spare."

Akaar added, "We might be able to send a half-dozen ships in approximately two weeks—and I must emphasize the word *might*."

A growl started to rumble in K'mtok's throat. "When you requested the Defense Force be added to your fleet in the Azure Nebula, Madam President, we did not hesitate to do so!"

"Yes," Nan said, "and in that battle, we lost a huge number of ships—and we lost more after that, as did you. We're both stretched to the limit." She leaned forward. "K'mtok, I'm sorry, truly. If there was *any* way to send ships to help you, I'd send them, but we're running the ships we *do* have ragged. In two weeks' time, if you haven't succeeded in retaking H'atoria and Krios yourselves—"

"H'atoria is of no consequence," K'mtok said dismissively. "Its presence on the border with your Federation is the only reason for its existence. But the planet no longer has a use to us. Krios, however, is a different matter. The warrior who died defending that world was Martok's only son."

Nan winced. The report she'd been given hadn't been specific about who was in charge of Klingon forces at Krios, only that they were routed and destroyed.

She turned to Akaar. "Leonard, is there anything we can spare?"

The Capellan shook his head. "Nothing that is close enough to Klingon space to be of immediate use."

K'mtok got to his feet. "I will convey your . . . your regrets to the High Council. And we will remember this day."

With that, the ambassador left, Kistler trailing behind once again.

Nan leaned back and looked to the ceiling in supplication. "Well, that went really lousy."

"Klingons do not ask for help easily," Akaar said. "To have refused it—"

"Believe me, Leonard, the last year and a half have given me quite the crash course in the nuances of how Klingons act. But I didn't have a choice. You said it yourself, we can't spare anyone. I can't let the Federation fall apart while we help the Klingons fight their battles." She looked at him. "Who can we send in two weeks?"

"Assuming their current missions finish in a timely manner, the *Kearsarge,* the *Sugihara,* the *Intrepid,* and the *Hood.*"

"That's four—you told K'mtok a half dozen."

Akaar actually smiled. "I lied."

"To the face of a Klingon warrior? That takes *kajunpakt.*"

Nodding in recognition of the Klingon word for effrontery, Akaar said, "One does not become a Starfleet admiral without a certain amount of *kajunpakt,* Madam President."

"Yeah, it's a prerequisite of this job, too." She got up and went to her desk. "Thanks for sharing the view, Leonard."

The admiral put his right hand to his chest and then extended his arm, his hand open—a standard Capellan salute. "Thank you, Madam President."

As Akaar departed, Nan touched the intercom. "What's next?"

A letter to Chief Rupi Yee on the *U.S.S. Sugihara*, sent by Dr. Ayib Yee Pran on P'Jem

Dear Mom:

This is the first break I've had since I got here, so I thought I'd fill you in.

We were brought over here on a hospital ship, the S.S. Shostakovich, *which was named after the guy who discovered the cure for cancer back in the twenty-first century—that's your useless fact for the day. It was about a third civilian doctors from Vulcan or its colonies, about a third Starfleet doctors, and about a third of us folks from* Médecins Sans Frontières. *I got to share my cabin with a cranky Gallamite surgeon who spent most of the trip asleep, for which I was very grateful. He's also* MSF, *but we hadn't met prior to this.*

Unfortunately, I got some bad news. I asked Yvrig before we left if she'd heard from Sortek yet, and she told me that they just confirmed that he was definitely in ShiKahr when the Borg bombarded Vulcan. There'll never be any way to confirm it, which I hate, but it's the only—you'll pardon the expression—logical explanation of why we haven't heard from him for three months. Honestly, we all figured that was what happened, but they only just were able to track down a communication he made from ShiKahr to Cor Caroli about two hours before the Borg hit. He had family on Cor Caroli, so that makes sense, but it's been a mess over there.

In any case, I know you liked Sortek, and I wanted you to know. I'm really sorry—he was a great doctor and a good friend.

Anyhow, we got to P'Jem, and one of the Starfleet doctors was this wizened old human admiral, who immediately took charge of everything. I got a little peevish when he did that—this wasn't a Starfleet operation, they were just helping out—but I didn't say anything, since his plan actually made perfect sense. My Gallamite roomie said that the old man was more than a hundred and fifty years old. I laughed and said he was still younger than my great-grandfather, and the Gallamite just stared at me with those eyes and that see-through head.

Never did get his name. Or the admiral's for that matter. I think someone called him Leonard, but I'm not sure.

Anyhow, the vast majority of my patients were Vulcanoid, since they're prevalent in that region: lots of Vulcans, a dozen Rigellians, half a dozen Romulans, and a group of Watraii pilgrims. I told the admiral that I'd been to the Watraii homeworld, back when that plague hit them two years ago, so I could take care of them, and he made a grumbling noise that I interpreted as a yes.

The Watraii I'm treating were actually visiting Vulcan when the Borg attacked. Later on, they told me that a bunch of the people who were on Vulcan but survived were evac'd here, because half of Vulcan's hospitals are piles of radioactive ash, and the other half are full to bursting. Most of the complaints were radiation sickness—fallout from the Borg attack—but then I discovered that they were all suffering from a virus that most Vulcans were immune to: shevrak, *it's called. The first human delegation to Vulcan, way back when, all got it, and now these Watraii have it. The doctors on P'Jem had missed it, and were confused as to why the hyronalin treatments weren't working.* Shevrak *feeds on hyronalin, so it not only wasn't curing the radiation poisoning, it was making the virus worse. Unfortunately, the alternative is arithrazine, and they didn't have any, and the replicators were down.*

So I got to do something I haven't done since that lovely trip to Kefor VI in medical school: sit in a lab and synthesize a cure, in this case, arithrazine. The admiral even poked his head in at one point, said, "How about that? Real medicine," and walked out.

Anyhow, the Watraii are resting comfortably, everyone else is more or less stable, and we're not getting a fresh batch of refugees until tomorrow—these are people whose ship was a clapped-out old Horizon-*class monstrosity with an engine that could only go warp three for nine hours at a pop.*

Took them three months just to get to this system, and they're suffering from malnutrition and other fun things, so we'll be busy when they get here.

I hope they let you leave Ardana eventually. And despite what you might think, I really do hope you are able to get back home and see Dad.

Love you, Mom.

Ayib

11

MAXIA ZETA IV

Every morning when Bojan Hadžić got out of bed, it took him a moment to remember where he was. He kept hoping that he'd be back home in Novalja, in his house on the beach, his German shepherd Radek lying on his feet.

But he wasn't home. He was in his cabin on the *U.S.S. Musgrave,* just as he had been most every morning since the Dominion War.

As he climbed out of bed he did the next thing he did every morning: cursed Benjamin Sisko.

Bojan had never met Sisko. While not a violent man, Bojan would gladly punch the man in the nose if ever he did meet him. Sisko was the one who discovered the Bajoran wormhole, a passageway to the Gamma Quadrant, and that started a chain of events that led to the war with the Dominion, a superpower in that quadrant.

A few months after the Dominion took the Bajoran system, signalling the beginning of the conflict, Bojan—who had been quite content being a leading civilian scientist with specialties in astrophysics and engineering, doing work for the United Earth government and teaching at al-Rashid University in Siena—decided to enlist in Starfleet as an engineer. He knew that Starfleet needed people, and he knew the Dominion was a threat. He'd been living on Earth when a rogue Starfleet admiral convinced President Jaresh-Inyo to declare martial law, and he'd also had a friend at the Antwerp Conference when the Dominion bombed it.

His enlistment was for five years. True, the war would likely be over by then, one way or the other, but that was the standard enlistment at the time, and Bojan was willing.

At first, he was assigned to Starbase 375, but that only lasted a few weeks until the *U.S.S. Tecumseh* limped into the starbase with half its crew killed in action. The ship was repaired and restaffed, with Bojan as one of the engineers, serving under a pompous ass of a Bolian named Gorvrat.

When the *Tecumseh* went back into action, they ran into a Jem'Hadar patrol in Cardassian space. Bojan was assigned to the bridge engineering station, while all three shifts of engineering were in the engine room, trying to keep the ship in one piece as the Jem'Hadar cut them to pieces.

He still remembered that day with perfect clarity. Even in the chaos the bridge had become, he distinctly heard the tactical officer, a Vulcan woman named Larak, say, "Shields down—Jem'Hadar firing on engineering."

The first officer was also a Vulcan, and he ordered evasive maneuvers, but it was too late.

Bojan looked away from the main viewer, but the sensor schematic on his console told him what happened:

the Jem'Hadar's phased polaron beam sliced open the hull right outside engineering. All of decks twenty-nine, thirty, and thirty-one had been exposed to the vacuum of space.

Quickly, Bojan checked the structural integrity field, reconstituting it so that it would keep the ship intact with this new hole in its secondary hull. Bulkheads dropped to protect the rest of the ship.

The entire engineering staff, from that jackass Gorvrat on down, was killed, with six exceptions: two people in sickbay, three more in various Jefferies tubes, and Bojan.

Captain Flannagan wasted no time in giving Bojan a battlefield commission to lieutenant, junior grade, and putting him in charge of engineering. Bojan had argued strenuously against this notion, but the only surviving officer was an ensign two weeks out of the Academy on his first assignment. The others were also enlisted, and none of them had anything like Bojan's experience. Regulations also stated that a chief engineer on an *Excelsior*-class ship had to be a lieutenant, junior grade, or higher. Finally, Bojan accepted it as a temporary assignment until they got back to Federation space, something to make the paperwork all nice and tidy—he was an academic; he understood the need for tidy paperwork.

They had gotten away from the Jem'Hadar, but they were still behind enemy lines and had to maintain radio silence to avoid detection, which meant they were on their own to get home. Bojan and his five-person staff managed to repair the warp drive enough to achieve warp one-point-two, but it took a month at that speed to return to Starbase 375. Four interminable weeks during which Bojan rarely slept and kept sane only through thoughts of some day returning to his beach house.

Instead he received a commendation for his work in getting the *Tecumseh* back to Federation space, and not only did Admiral Ross make his commission permanent, he promoted him to full lieutenant.

Stuck with being an officer, Bojan remained on the *Tecumseh,* now with a full staff. His original plan was to serve the five years he'd enlisted for and then resign. After the war, he transferred to the *Musgrave,* initially as second officer, then first officer, having been promoted to lieutenant commander despite having spent no time at the Academy and insisting that he wasn't an officer, not really.

He actually *liked* the work the S.C.E. did, and decided to stay on board a bit past his five years. Just long enough to finish the various projects he had going on aboard the *Musgrave.*

Then, seven months after his five years had ended, when Bojan was thinking it was time to resign and let T'Eama take over the S.C.E. team, the Borg came back. It was the Dominion all over again. Bojan couldn't leave now. He was needed on the *Musgrave.* Too many people were dead. Too many of them were friends and colleagues, from his predecessor as *Musgrave* first officer, who was on Starbase 234 when it was destroyed, to one of his former colleagues at al-Rashid, who was on Vulcan for a lecture tour, to his sister Marija, who was vacationing on Risa.

The work the S.C.E. was doing was important. Bojan knew that, and so he stayed.

But every morning, for just a few moments, he

thought about home and wished he was back there.

Once that was out of the way, and he'd finished with his morning ablutions and his cursing of Benjamin Sisko, he put on his uniform, sighing heavily at the two solid pips and one hollow pip on his collar, which he still didn't think he'd done anything to earn. He just happened to be on bridge duty. Everything else, he would've done in any case.

He exited his small cabin. One of the perks of being first officer on a *Sabre*-class ship: he was one of three people who got single quarters, the other two being Captain Dayrit and Lieutenant T'Eama. The other thirty-eight members of the *Musgrave*'s complement had to double up. Making a beeline for the turbolift, he nodded absently to a crewperson who said hello to him, without remembering who it was two seconds later.

"Bridge," he muttered as he entered the lift, prompting the computer to ask him to repeat his request. "Bridge!" he yelled this time, then muttered in Croatian about the need to make the vocal pickups more sensitive on the turbolifts.

Upon arrival, he went straight to the aft science station. A voice said, "Good morning, Bojan," and he muttered a reply.

Belatedly realizing that it was the captain who said that, Bojan turned to the center seat and said, "Good morning, Captain Dayrit."

The dark-haired, broad-shouldered Filipino smiled. "How're we doing on the farantine problem?"

"I had a planetary scan of Maxia Zeta III and two simulations running overnight, which might help. The others are doing whatever they are doing, and we will be meeting at 0930 to discuss options."

"Good." Dayrit turned to look at his first officer. "Why a scan of Maxia Zeta III?"

"Geologically speaking, the third and fourth planets in this system are identical. And the last mineral survey was done when the dilithium mine was constructed on the fourth planet twenty years ago."

"Hold on, if the two planets are identical, why can't we mine dilithium on the third planet?"

"The mineral compositions of both planets are the same, but the third planet is more tectonically unstable. A dilithium mine would just make that worse—the place would be uninhabitable within days of the mine becoming operational."

"And that would be bad." Dayrit nodded. "In any case, we've got a ship coming by to bring some food and other supplies. They've got emergency rations down there, but they're running out pretty quick."

Bojan didn't have anything in particular to say in response to that—that was someone else's problem—and he sat at the console and called up the results of the analysis of Maxia Zeta III and of his simulation.

The latter, to his disappointment but not to his surprise, had also failed—just as the other four he'd run yesterday did. No matter how he changed the parameters, he could not get a shuttlecraft to land safely on Maxia Zeta IV.

He turned to the other report and quickly noticed something—or, more accurately, didn't notice something.

"Computer," he said, "verify that this analysis of Maxia Zeta is complete."

"Verified."

"Oh, dear. Oh, dear dear dear."

"What is it, Bojan?" Dayrit asked.

"Captain, there may be more to this than we thought."

Half an hour later, Bojan was once again standing in the observation lounge with the rest of the team. He never thought of them as "his" team, even though Dayrit often referred to the S.C.E. contingent on the *Musgrave* as "your guys" to Bojan. But generally, he was happy to delegate most of the leadership tasks to T'Eama.

The only difference between this meeting and yesterday's was the added presence of the ship's security chief, Lieutenant Brian Cormack.

"We have two problems," Bojan said without preamble, once everyone had taken their seats. "I've completed a full scan of the Maxia Zeta star—and farantine is nowhere to be found."

"So what?" Ysalda asked. "Just because an element isn't in a star doesn't mean it can't be on a planet."

"Yes, but I was concerned when I learned that, so I scanned Maxia Zeta III."

Ysalda was still questioning him. "What for?"

T'Eama raised an eyebrow and answered before Bojan could. "Current theory holds that the third and fourth planets in this system were once one world, but suffered a cataclysm that split them in two."

"And before you ask," Bojan said quickly, "we can't construct a mine on the third planet as it's too unstable. The place is riddled with earthquakes and the like." Waving his hand back and forth, he went on. "In any case, that does not matter so much as what the scan turned up: no farantine on the third planet."

"And again," Ysalda said, "I ask, so what? We didn't find the farantine on the fourth planet, either."

"That is not quite the case. The last mineralogical survey was done twenty years ago."

Fabian nodded. "Sensors are a lot better now—especially on an S.C.E. ship."

"Exactly," Bojan said. "When we did our standard planetary scan upon entering orbit, we not only found the farantine that the mine uncovered, but a goodly portion that was still buried besides."

"I'm sorry," Mrodile said, rubbing his ridge, "I don't understand what—"

"If there's no farantine on the third planet," Fabian said, "it means that the farantine on the fourth planet isn't natural—it was put there on purpose."

The anthropologist's blue face became slightly pale. "Oh."

Bojan blew out a breath. " 'Oh' is right. This has gone from a terrible accident to an act of sabotage."

"That changes everything, doesn't it?" Brian said. "I'm assuming that's why the captain put us on yellow alert?" The security chief's Liverpool accent got thicker, as it often did when things got interesting.

"Actually," T'Eama said, "it changes very little. Our mission remains the same regardless of the source of the farantine, to wit, we must get rid of it."

Fabian said, "Yeah, but what if whoever put it there is still around? They might get a little peevish when we take their sabotage away."

"Assuming we even *can,*" Jira said in her usual harried tone. "Nothing we've tried is working."

"Don't be so sure," Fabian said with a smile.

Ysalda stared at him. "You're not still on that paint notion, are you?"

"It worked in the lab—which is more than I can say

for any of your bright ideas." Fabian turned to Bojan. "The next step is to go down and collect some farantine."

"And *that* is where things are different, yeah?" Cormack said. "Because if this *is* a case of sabotage, it's a right nasty one—goin' after a prime source of dilithium right when we need to rebuild an entire fleet? Any away teams that go down to Maxia Zeta, I'd like one security guard per, plus one supervisor, either myself or Ensign Rivera."

Bojan nodded. "That's probably a good idea, yes."

"Which brings us to the next problem," Ysalda said. "We've done tests in the hololab, but farantine is notoriously unstable. We need to test the actual farantine—*especially* if it's artificial. It might have properties we aren't expecting."

Mrodile rubbed his ridge again. "So we bring some up, right?"

"How?" Ysalda asked. "As soon as we beam it aboard, the ship stops working."

"And once again," Fabian said, "we come to the paint. We go down, collect some in a sample case that I've covered with the Magical Paint of Doom, and bring it back. As long as it's in the sample case, it won't affect the ship."

"You're assuming the paint will work," T'Eama said.

Fabian shrugged. "Like I said, it worked in the hololab."

"Which is more than the rest of us can say," Jira said. "We tried force fields, we tried astatine particles, we tried weaponry."

Bojan frowned. "Weaponry did not work?"

"After a fashion," T'Eama said. "It would be effective

in destroying the farantine—and equally effective in destroying much of Maxia Zeta IV, including the dilithium mine itself, which would need to be rebuilt."

"I also tried something we built on Argo a few years back," Ysalda said, "a special structural integrity field that would lessen the pressures of the deep sea, but we can't shield it against the farantine."

T'Eama stared at Bojan with that penetrating stare of hers. At first, Bojan had thought that T'Eama didn't respect him, but he soon realized that she didn't really respect anyone, and so he stopped taking it personally. "You mentioned, Commander, that there were two problems."

The Vulcan woman was also the only person on board who insisted on addressing him by his hated rank, but that was because she was a stickler for protocol.

She also had a good memory, as Bojan himself had forgotten about the other problem. "Thank you, T'Eama. The second problem, which I was wrestling with during the night, is this: We cannot beam down to the surface—or rather, we can, but we cannot beam back."

Jira bounced in her chair. "So? We take a shuttle—no, wait, once it's in the atmosphere, it can't take off again."

"Exactly. I have attempted several modifications to the shuttle, and also to the transporter, but the former has resulted in the shuttle crashing, and the latter has resulted in the away team either being trapped on the planet or dissolved into atoms."

"That would suck," Fabian said.

"Nnnnnnnnno problem," Lolo said from the other end of the table. "Eeeeeeeasy fix."

Bojan blinked. "I'm sorry?"

"Uuuuuuuse thrusters." Lolo picked up a padd and started typing furiously with his seven webbed fingers.

Frowning, Bojan said, "Thrusters will not work, either, Lolo, they—"

"Nnnnnnnot standard tttttthrusters. Cccccccchemical." Lolo then put something on the main viewer in the lounge.

Bojan turned to see a schematic of the *Erickson,* one of the *Musgrave*'s two shuttlecraft, with large devices that looked like exhaust ports placed on the four corners of the craft.

Fabian grinned. "You wanna stick a rocket on the *Erickson*?"

"Ffffffffour rockets," Lolo said.

Bojan nodded. "When the duonetic field renders the shuttle inoperable, the rockets take over."

T'Eama asked, "How will the rockets be controlled? Standard panels will not function."

"Nnnnnnnonstandard panel," Lolo said, and he called up another image onto the viewer: a large box covered in switches and levers.

Shaking his head, Bojan thought of the old rockets that were used to fly into space before Zefram Cochrane invented warp drive—and even afterward, since rockets were still used to achieve escape velocity for at least a few years after that.

Raising his hand, Brian said, "I'd like to make a request, all right?"

"Yes?" Bojan asked.

"I think all the testing you lot do should be done on the *Erickson.* The farantine is too risky to work with on the *Musgrave,* and the danger's much less if it's on a shuttle."

Waving her hands back and forth, Jira said, "Hang on, this is getting ridiculous. Rockets? Panels with levers and switches? Risking a dead shuttle crashing into Maxia Zeta?"

"The shuttle won't crash," Ysalda said. "It'll be near enough to the *Musgrave* that it can be towed with a tractor. And if the farantine does interfere, we can always jettison it."

"Even so, though, this is a *huge* risk just to get a test sample. Is this really worth it?"

Bojan set his jaw. "Jira, there are dozens of ships being built at Utopia Planitia right now. They need dilithium to channel the matter/antimatter reaction that allows their warp drives to work, and the reason *why* they need them is so they can travel fast enough to send relief to the *hundreds* of planets that require assistance. There are people *starving* all over the Federation and beyond right now, and living in deplorable conditions, and the only way that will change is if we replenish the ships we lost to the Borg!"

Everyone stared at Bojan incredulously (except for T'Eama), which was when he realized that he was shouting. To the best of his knowledge, he'd never shouted in front of his shipmates before. In fact, the last time he could remember yelling at anyone was on the *Tecumseh,* but that was after they'd been limping along for two weeks behind enemy lines, and tensions were *incredibly* high.

Looking down and brushing his hair out of his face, he said in a quiet voice, "I'm sorry. But this planet is of critical import right now, and we *must* get those mines up and running. Make the modifications to the *Erickson*."

With that, Bojan turned and left observation. He found himself with the need for a cup of chamomile tea—his stomach was tied up in knots.

I truly miss my beach house right now. . . .

A classified report from Lieutenant Commander Kareem Mussad, Starfleet Corps of Engineers, Station Deep Space 3, to Captain Montgomery Scott, S.C.E. Headquarters, Tucker Memorial Building, San Francisco, Earth

As of this writing, we have recovered remains of Borg vessels and other Borg technology from seventy-three different sites, and I was just informed that the *U.S.S. Khwarizimi* is delivering material from a seventy-fourth. With the obvious exception of Commander Gong, all personnel on DS3 who are not under my direct command are not aware of what we are studying here, and many of the ships that have brought Borg material here were also kept unaware, as per the directive from Starfleet Security.

I understand your objections to those security measures, Captain, but I feel it is necessary. Feelings about the Borg are running *extremely* high right now. The entire quadrant has been living in active fear of the Borg for a year now, and they caused a huge amount of destruction when they finally invaded in force. People are—justifiably, in my opinion—scared of the Borg and angry at the Borg, and a lot of those people would be even more upset if they found out we were doing research into Borg technology to try to—you'll pardon the expression—assimilate it into our own. In fact, several members of my team have expressed those very reservations.

On top of that, there is significant doubt in many circles—again, including some members of my own team—that the Borg threat is truly finished, and a worry that examining their technology in depth will lead somehow to the Borg being revived. One of my people, Ensign Xi, has a recurring nightmare that she will be attacked by nanoprobes while working on Borg tech, be assimilated, and become a new Borg Queen. Yes, all the evidence suggests strongly that that won't happen, but evidence has a bad track record against fear, in my experience.

All of this is by way of saying that Starfleet Security is, in my opinion, right to keep Project Reassimilation classified. The public outcry would be huge, and would get in the way of actually accomplishing any work.

As for the results of that work—well, that's a bigger problem. The only Borg technology that was still intact after the Caeliar did whatever it was they did was the material that's *completely* inert and powerless. The first time we tried to power up something, it immediately disintegrated into ash. We've been examining this new collection of Borg tech for months now, but it's not adding anything to our base of knowledge. Because the Borg integrated *everything,* it means there are no qualitative differences among (to give four random examples) the material salvaged in orbit of Earth fifteen years ago after the *Enterprise* blew up a cube, the wreckage found by the *Defiant* in the Gamma Quadrant five years ago, the technology acquired by *Voyager* during its seven years in the Delta Quadrant, and the remains of the ship destroyed by *Excalibur* at Starbase 343.

Lieutenant Baldvinsson is in charge of the team that is attempting to reverse-engineer the Borg's self-repair technology. Her full report is appended, but the upshot is that it will take years to even begin to figure it all out without the ability to power the components. Determining how to separate the self-repair from the direct access that made the Borg subservient to the tyrant consciousness of the Caeliar will take considerable doing. The lieutenant says that ten years would be a conservative estimate.

This is a very long-winded way of reporting that I have nothing to report—yet. We're only just starting to understand how this all works, and it will take a lot of very smart people a very long time to comprehend it. But I have faith that we will figure it all out eventually.

12

U.S.S. AVENTINE

Sam Bowers stood in a *makuso* pose—heels together, feet at forty-five degree angles relative to his torso; hands in front of him, his right hand inside his left, with his left thumb tucked under his right palm; eyes closed—and tried to empty his mind.

At that, he was not remotely successful.

Still, he opened his eyes and got into a ready position, hands now at his sides, feet separated. Then he began the form.

He was doing *Tsuki No Kata,* which some translated as "punching form," others as "fortune and luck form." It was developed by Mas Oyama of the *Kyokushin* discipline of karate three hundred years earlier.

Bowers had first studied the martial arts as a teenager on Mantilles. He'd been having anger issues, and the school counselor recommended the martial arts to help keep his temper under control. It turned out to be a good fit, and Bowers was able to use the discipline of karate to help keep his temper reined in.

He kept up with it until he left home to attend Starfleet Academy, having gotten as far as brown belt, one step shy of a black belt. His studies didn't really give him much time to continue, although he did put his training to good use during self-defense classes at the Academy.

When he served on the *Budapest,* the deputy chief of security, who was a fifth-degree black belt, started a regular class on the ship, which Bowers attended, working his way back up from beginner (white belt) status, but once again falling short of a black belt when he was transferred.

Since coming to the *Aventine,* he'd noticed that he was starting to have issues with his temper again. By the time he was a cadet, Bowers had achieved a certain equanimity, so to find himself reverting to adolescent form now was disconcerting to say the least.

Then again, since coming to the *Aventine,* he'd been hip-deep in Borg.

So he started up his karate training again. No one on the *Aventine* was offering any classes in karate—the deputy security chief, Naomi Darrow, ran an *aikido* class, but that was it, really—so he did the training on his own.

However, as he moved through the *kata,* he realized that *Tsuki No* was the wrong one to be doing in his current state of mind. Most of the moves in the *kata* were hard and fast, and Bowers found himself rushing through them, making them sloppy and unfocused. When he got to the eighth move of the twenty-move program, he slowed down, as was expected, changing his stance and then slowly doing a forearm block.

Then he started to step forward, remembered that he'd skipped a move, stopped, stepped back, and then let out a curse that would've gotten him reprimanded by *Shihan* Williams back on Mantilles.

"I don't know, Commander. Looked like you were doing all right from here."

Whirling around, Bowers saw Sonek Pran standing off to the side of the *Aventine* gym, observing. The professor had his long white hair tied back in a ponytail, exposing his tapered ears, and was wearing loose-fitting workout clothes. He and Bowers were among the few in the gym at this early hour. Some people were scattered about here and there, but they had all given the first officer a wide berth.

It figures that Pran doesn't give me the same consideration. As soon as he had the thought, Bowers dismissed it as unfair. In fact, his knee-jerk negative reaction to Pran was one of the indications that he was out of sorts.

"You've obviously never studied the martial arts," Bowers said with a smile, "or you'd know I was very far from all right."

"You've got me there. I never went much for the martial arts, really. Had a problem with the whole concept."

Bowers walked over to the wall, where he'd kept a towel, and daubed his forehead. "What do you mean?"

"Well, not the *whole* concept, exactly—just the first word."

"Martial?"

Pran nodded. "The thing that makes sentient life different from all the other kinds of life that are out there is that violence isn't actually necessary to solve our problems. We can *talk* about them. Or we can agree to disagree. Or we can compromise. There's no problem anywhere that can't be solved by two or more rational people sitting down and talking, and it means people get to live longer. There's an old human saying: 'I don't want to achieve immortality through my work, I want to achieve immortality through not dying.' Nonviolence is a good way to accomplish that, seems to me."

Bowers shrugged, setting the towel back down. "No offense, Professor, but that strikes me as more than a little naïve."

Pran raised an eyebrow. That gesture, along with the fact that his ears were more visible than normal, made him look Vulcan for the first time since he'd beamed aboard. "You think so, Commander? I don't know. Look at where we live. The current crisis notwithstanding, the Federation is a nation of no poverty, no want, no hunger. I mean, yeah, there's a lot of that right now, and probably will be for a good while, but for the last couple centuries, this Federation has managed to live a nearly ideal life. Yes, we've fought wars, but only as a last resort, and never because we started them."

Shaking his head, Bowers said, "So that's how you justify the Federation's wars? 'They started it.' That's a little kid's defense."

"I'm not justifying a single thing, Commander. I'm just explaining *why* we do what we do. My point is, that's not what I'm shooting for. I've spent my entire life trying to prove what I just told you. I've never held a weapon, I've never raised my arms in violence—I've always talked my way out of everything."

Thinking back to Artaleirh, Bowers said, "Even when centurions are pointing disruptors at you?"

"Especially then." Pran started doing some stretches.

Bowers watched him for a second, then realized he'd never done any proper warming up. *Something else that* Shihan *Williams wouldn't have liked.* "Mind if I join you, Professor?"

"Not at all, Commander."

As they both started their stretches of legs, arms, and torso, Pran said, "How soon before we head to Capella?"

"Depends."

Frowning, Pran asked, "On what?"

Bowers smiled tightly. "On how well Helkara can force Lessard to do his job."

"Okay." Pran obviously had no idea what Bowers was talking about, but he didn't pursue it. The *Aventine* had arrived at Starbase 10 late last night, and Bowers had instructed Gruhn Helkara to get the cargo bays loaded as fast as possible. Unfortunately, half of the equipment had to be loaded manually, as it was either too large even for a cargo transporter or made of material that couldn't safely be transported.

"By the way, even if you wanted to leave, looks like you couldn't have," Bowers said as he bent over to touch his toes. "We're the only Starfleet ship here, and none of the civilian transports are headed anywhere near Mars."

"That's fine." Pran also bent over; Bowers took some small amusement in the fact that he couldn't reach his toes without bending his knees. "I'd actually like to take a good look at what's happening on Capella anyway." He stood upright. "I'd also like to know what's happening on Romulus."

"Isn't it obvious?" Bowers also rolled his torso upward. "They're trading with someone else."

"Yeah, but who? Everybody was hit hard by the Borg, and the ones who weren't aren't in any kind of shape to provide Tal'Aura with the same level of support the Federation was providing—or that Donatra could've provided. Who does that leave? The Klingons wouldn't help Tal'Aura if you put a disruptor to Martok's head. The Tholians are even less likely than the Klingons. The Gorn, Cardassians, and Breen don't have the resources, and Tal'Aura can't afford the Ferengi."

Unable to help being impressed, Bowers said, "You've given this some thought."

"And done some research. Honestly, it's the only thing I *have* been thinking about since we left Achernar. And then there's all the other weird stuff, like the Kinshaya taking H'atoria and Krios. I can understand Krios, but H'atoria? It's a pile of sand right now."

"It's also the primary shipping lane between us and the Empire." Bowers was surprised that Pran didn't know that.

"I know that," Pran said, and Bowers couldn't help but bark a short laugh that he covered with a cough. Pran continued: "But the Kinshaya have never given much of a damn about the Federation. There've been *maybe* two contacts between the Kinshaya and Starfleet in the last two hundred years, and the Kinshaya ambassador hasn't set foot in the embassy on Earth in a decade. So why are they all of a sudden horning in on our trade routes? For that matter, how do they expect to hold the planet? It's nowhere near their usual sphere of influence, and it'd take a Defense Force fleet all of five minutes to take it back."

"Assuming they bother," Bowers said as he leaned against the wall and pulled his right knee up to his right shoulder. "The world's been practically wiped clean, and the Empire's a lot more likely to just give up on it."

Pran shook his head. "H'atoria was never all that valuable in the first place. The Empire conquered it only because it was close to the Federation, and they wanted to use it as a staging area for a war against us. After the Organian Peace Treaty was signed, they mostly abandoned it, and then after the Khitomer Accords, it became a major trading post. It's smack in the middle of the fastest, most efficient trade route between our two borders, and right now it's in enemy hands. There's gotta be a reason for that."

Bowers felt like he had been left out of the conversation—either that, or Pran was acting as if he was teaching one of his history classes. "Disrupting trade, presumably."

Pran looked at him. "Yeah, but for how long? Like I said, H'atoria's way out of Kinshaya territory, and the only way they have enough military force to hold the planet for any length of time is if they leave their own territory undefended, and I can't see the Klingons passing up *that* chance."

"Maybe the Kinshaya are overconfident. They *did* just conquer the Kreel last year."

"True, and the Klingons bloodied their nose right after." Pran let out a long sigh, then started doing neck rolls. "They could just be pissed off about the whole thing."

"Besides, there are other trade routes," Bowers said. "Through— Oh, hell."

Pran grinned as he rolled his head counterclockwise. "Right, through Zalda—which just left the Federation in a snit."

"House of cards." Bowers spoke the cliché without even realizing why.

"What do you mean?"

Bowers thought a moment. "If you picture the Alpha Quadrant as a house of cards, the Borg knocked a bunch of them out—so the rest of it's collapsing."

"Yeah, but . . ." Pran tugged on his mustache. "Problem is, that doesn't really work. With a house of cards, you take out one card and everything collapses. But this is only certain cards collapsing."

"It happens," Bowers said. "Things go wrong in circumstances like this. There doesn't need to be a pattern."

"Maybe not." Pran didn't sound like he believed it.

But Bowers was sure he was imagining things.

I'm probably just imagining things, Sonek thought as he emerged from the shower in his cabin. The workout had been excellent, and he'd enjoyed talking to Bowers a lot more when the commander was treating him like a person instead of an annoyance.

And he was probably right—this was probably just the chaos one would expect after events that wreaked so much devastation. But Sonek couldn't help but wonder why these things in particular were happening.

After throwing a comfortable jumpsuit on, he sat at the desk. "Computer, show all Starfleet dispatches for the past week in reverse order, access code Pran alpha five nine four two green."

"Voiceprint and code verified."

The screen lit up with an abstract of the most recent dispatch, which was a routine report from the *U.S.S. Io*'s survey of an asteroid field.

He continued to scroll through them. The *U.S.S. Cheiron* was being sent to Cestus III to aid in their difficulties dealing with refugees, since they were getting a great deal of overflow from Zalda. The *U.S.S. Titan* was continuing to map the Kavrot Sector, reporting that they would be reaching uncharted territory within the week. Admiral Leonard McCoy, who was in charge of the delegation of Starfleet and civilian doctors on P'Jem, reported that the *shevrak* outbreak was under control. (Dimly, Sonek recalled Rupi saying something about P'Jem in her last letter—or was it Sara?—and he made a mental note to check back later.) Utopia Planitia was reporting that the *U.S.S. Galen*, the *U.S.S. Esquiline,* and the *U.S.S. Achilles* all had their slipstream drives installed, with the other six ships in that particular fleet still in the process of having it done. Deep Space 4 reported an unusually high volume of warp activity in and out of the Typhon Expanse. The *S.S. Esperanto* was being recalled from Tezwa and reassigned to Andor, as relief efforts on Tezwa were being scaled back. Starbase 375 reported that the assimilation of the Argaya, Lyshan, and Solarion systems into the Cardassian Union—as promised to the Cardassian government in exchange for their ships joining the fleet at the Azure Nebula—was behind schedule. Starbase 24 had several reports from Klingon space, in particular on the attempts to terraform the planets in the Mempa system so it would be habitable again, and on the defeat at Krios, in which the Kinshaya ships were using Breen disruptors. The *U.S.S. Musgrave* was reporting that the farantine on Maxia Zeta

IV was *not* natural, but had been placed there, probably to sabotage the dilithium mine.

Those last two got Sonek's attention. He called up both reports. The first had been made by the base commandant, Commander Peter Abraham, and gave detailed scan reports provided by the Klingon Defense Force, which had been transmitted from the Krios governor's satellite and the *I.K.S. Rovlaq* before they were destroyed. *Since when do the Breen trade with the Kinshaya? Since when do the Kinshaya have anything the Breen want? Since when do the Kinshaya even acknowledge the existence of the Breen?*

Setting that particular confusion aside for the time being, he went on to the S.C.E. report, made by a Lieutenant Commander Bojan Hadžić, which stated that someone had, in essence, injected artificial farantine into one of the dilithium mines on Maxia Zeta IV. The upshot of this was a halt in dilithium mining, which would have a cascade effect on the efforts at the Utopia Planitia shipyards to replenish the fleet.

Or rather, *fleets,* as about half of Maxia Zeta's yield of dilithium was earmarked for the Klingon Empire, just as half of Capella's topaline was also bound for the Empire.

Sonek got to his feet and started pacing around his cabin. *We've got the two best shipping lanes between the Federation and the Empire closed off, which will slow up trade, since the supply ships will have to take more roundabout routes.* A third route, through the Azure Nebula, had been effectively cut off by the Borg invasion, since there were hundreds of ship hulks and radiation making it an even worse navigation hazard than usual. Salvaging those ships hadn't been a priority for any save the Ferengi.

He walked past his banjo and decided to pick it up. Tuning it, he went over what he'd just read. Most of it was about what you'd expect in the wake of the Borg invasion. But Zalda pulling out of the Federation and going quiet, H'atoria being taken for no obvious reason, Kinshaya using Breen weapons, and deliberate sabotage of both the Federation's and the Klingons' attempts to build atmospheric domes and new ships. None of it would be fatal, but it would slow things down at a time when both nations needed to rebuild as fast as possible.

After tuning the banjo up, he started playing an old human folk song called "Golden Vanity."

Is there a connection here? Or is Bowers right and I'm looking for patterns that aren't there?

Shaking his head, he started singing the lyrics.

Then he swum back to his ship, he beat upon the side,
Cried, "Captain, pick me up, for I'm wearied with the tide,
"And I'm sinking in the low and lonesome low,
"I am sinking in the lonesome sea."

"No, I will not pick you up," the Captain then replied.
"I'll shoot you, I'll drown you, I'll sink you in the tide.
"I will sink you in the low and lonesome low,
"I will sink you in the lonesome sea."

And then, for no good reason that he could articulate, he said, "Computer, call up all police records from Federation worlds from the last two years and search for references to farantine."

"Working."

Knowing the search would take a while, Sonek went back to the song, then moved to a Bajoran spiritual that was in the same key. He was about to start playing a song his father wrote when the computer said, *"Search complete."*

Setting the banjo gently down, Sonek walked over to the desk again and called up the search results. There were four, but he quickly realized that the mention of farantine in three of them was incidental.

The fourth, though, was of interest. A Ferengi woman named Sekki was arrested for fraud for trying to pass off artificial farantine as real. She sold it, along with a special containment unit, to a group of scientists from an independent group called the Matter of Everything. They had set up shop on Alpha Proxima II, a Federation world, so local authorities were called in. However, since the farantine worked exactly the same way real farantine did, the MOE researchers asked that the charges be dropped.

"Computer, call up all information in all databases about a Ferengi named Sekki."

"Working."

Sonek walked over to the replicator and got himself an *allira* punch. He seriously doubted that there wasn't a connection between a Ferengi who had created artificial farantine and a sudden influx of artificial farantine on Maxia Zeta IV.

"Search complete."

Gulping down some punch, Sonek sat down and read over what there was to know about Sekki.

Then he read it again.

After the second reading, he walked over to a com-panel. "Computer, put a call through to Captain Dax, please."

An interminable amount of time later, the captain's voice finally sounded over the speaker. *"Dax here."*

"Captain, it's Sonek. We need to talk—right now."

Personal log of Counselor Kaimi Pumehana of the *U.S.S. Massachusetts,* Stardate 58321.0

The myth is that Vulcans don't have emotions.

It's a common enough mistake. They spend so much time mastering their emotions and disdaining emotionalism—but the reason why isn't because they don't feel them, it's because they *suppress* them. And Vulcan emotions are far far far more turbulent than anyone's this sidc of the Klingons. And honestly, if I was given a choice between confronting a pissed-off Vulcan or a pissed-off Klingon, I'd take the Klingon without hesitation.

As a case in point, one of the reasons why I've been asked to help out with some of the civilians on Vulcan since the *Massachusetts* arrived here is because one of the civilian counselors at the hospital in Vulcana Regar was killed by one of her patients. The other counselors all had full workloads, and so I took on hers (with the exception of the one who killed his counselor, who is being held in custody and is a problem for the Vulcan authorities). I've had them beamed up here at Captain Long's insistence—she doesn't trust the security on Vulcan right now, and feels I'll be safer from any more potential murderers on the ship instead of in a chaos-ridden hospital. I can't really say I blame her.

There was one patient who baffled me for the first forty minutes of our one-hour session. He seemed fine, showed no obvious—or even not-so-obvious—signs of mental distress. I've counseled literally dozens of Vulcans over the years, including the six currently serving on the *Massachusetts,* so I know what to look for.

And then, suddenly, it came out: Frustration. Anger. Resentment. Toward the Borg, as it turned out, but not for the reasons you might think. He said he'd always admired the Borg, because they were the ultimate triumph of logic. They had achieved what hundreds of Vulcans have tried to achieve through *Kolinahr,* to a degree that no Vulcan ever had: the perfect mastery of logic over emotion.

His resentment wasn't at himself for thinking so highly of an enemy of the Federation, though—rather it was at the Borg themselves, for violating what he saw as their logical mandate by attacking the Federation the way they did. "Revenge," he said, "is not logical."

I have to admit, I was *very* glad that he was my last appointment for the day. He's an ordinary person, a civil servant, a hard worker, single, one hundred seventy-five years old, no anomalies in his record. And yet, he's a borderline sociopath. He believes that the loss of life to the Borg was deserved—at least prior to their recent attacks on the Federation—because those people all got in the way of the Borg's logic.

He was the most extreme case, but there are a lot of Vulcans who are struggling with their emotional control. One therapy that I suggested—and which only some of the counselors in Vulcana Regar are following through with—is to have the patients act out for a brief period—let their emotions run free for, say, ten minutes while alone in a room. Drop the barriers and let it all out. Dr. T'Haro pointed out the risk that they might not be able to erect the barriers again, but I insisted that the alternative would be for the barriers to fall unexpectedly. If it's done under controlled conditions, there's less risk.

Vulcan hasn't suffered a catastrophe along these lines since Surak's time, and hasn't even had such a full-scale invasion of their space since the Federation formed. There is not a single living Vulcan who has had to deal with a trauma on this scale before, and the emotional control that they use for everyday life is no longer sufficient.

I will keep trying to help them. I just hope it's enough.

13

TY'GOKOR

Martok's leg hurt.

The limb had been fully healed from being broken during the Borg invasion when Chancellor Martok's flagship, the *Sword of Kahless,* engaged the Borg and lost rather handily. Only a small fraction of the ship's crew of three thousand survived, including Martok.

Eventually, the leg was fully repaired, by a KMA-licensed doctor working in the Hall of Warriors on Ty'Gokor—which had become the temporary seat of the Empire's government. Martok himself had incorporated the Klingon Medical Authority some four-and-a-half turns ago after determining that the previous medical association, the Klingon Physicians Enclave, was little more than an excuse for doctors to get together and drink a great deal.

For several years, Martok was stationed on a Federation-run starbase in the Bajoran sector, and he soon grew to appreciate the benefits of returning whole warriors to the field of battle. Ever so slowly during the years of his reign, he had been striving to improve the state of Klingon medicine.

Which made him wonder why in the name of Kahless's hand his leg *hurt* so damned much.

He was about to summon his aide—a young warrior whose name Martok had yet to remember—to call for the doctor when she came in herself. "General Klag has arrived, sir."

"Send him in," Martok said, putting the pain in his leg aside.

The son of M'Raq strode confidently into the chancellor's makeshift office. Martok was still in the process of putting together a new High Council, and still was not sure whether to keep the Empire's capital on Ty'Gokor or to rebuild the Great Hall on Qo'noS yet *again*. It had already been destroyed once before since he took office, and it was quite possible that the Empire could not afford to rebuild Qo'noS to its former glory.

As a result, the chancellor's space was a room with a desk, and nothing more beyond the workstation on that desk.

Klag stood at attention before Martok. He wore the cassock of his office well; it was decorated with numerous medals earned as a commander during the Dominion War—when he slew half a dozen Jem'Hadar single-handedly on Marcan V—as a captain, and most recently as a general. Martok noted that the medal that had the most prominent spot was his medallion symbolizing his membership in the Order of the *Bat'leth*, which Klag had earned five turns earlier.

"What do you want?" Martok asked by way of greeting.

"The *Gorkon* is ready to lead the Fifth Fleet once

again. Praxis Station has released the ship, and all my fleet captains are standing by for your orders, Chancellor."

The ache started in Martok's leg again, and only then did he realize that the pain had nothing to do with his injury, but was rather his body's way of expressing its displeasure with his current situation. "You will have to split your fleet, General. The *Gorkon* and no more than four other vessels will go to Krios to reclaim that world from the Kinshaya. The remainder of your fleet must be committed to protecting the convoy headed for the Mempa system."

Klag stiffened. "Protection duty? Surely that is a duty of less import than—"

Martok slammed a hand on his desk. "Nothing is more important than the Klingon *people,* General! Mempa was our most populous system, and your assignment is to make sure that the people and materials to rebuild it arrive safely. Or do you not believe you can destroy the Kinshaya with only five ships?"

Slowly, Klag said, "Sir, I was going to say of less import than avenging the death of your son."

Martok let out a long breath through his jagged teeth. "Do not try my patience, General. My blood cries out for vengeance against the filthy *petaQpu'* who have taken my son from me. If I could, I would lead the battle myself in the *Sword of Kahless.*" He rose to his feet, ignoring the pain that shot through his leg. "But I am leader of the Klingon people, and I will not shirk my responsibility for them, not even for our most sacred right."

Klag nodded. "Of course, Chancellor. We will depart immediately."

"Good."

"Will we receive any additional assistance from Starfleet?"

"No," Martok said in a low rumble. "Ambassador K'mtok informs me that Starfleet can spare no vessels for another two weeks, and we *cannot* allow Kinshaya to occupy Krios for that long."

"Indeed."

"And, General? The Fifth Fleet only needs to escort the convoy *to* Mempa. Once the convoy arrives, the forces already present can protect it. If the Fleet ships are still required to assist you in retaking Krios, they will be available then."

"Very well," Klag said with a nod.

Martok waved his hand, indicating that Klag could depart.

The general turned and moved to the exit, then stopped. "Chancellor? Your son died well."

"Thank you, my friend," Martok said quietly. "I know you and he were not the staunchest of comrades."

Klag grinned at that. When Klag was first assigned to the *I.K.S. Gorkon* as captain, Drex was his first officer, but Klag had him transferred off after their first mission, as he had not been comfortable with the chancellor's son being so close. "Quite the opposite. But then, that was true of you and me, as well, Chancellor. In the end, though, my former first officer comported himself as a warrior of honor. I am sure he sails in the Black Fleet with distinction."

"Alongside his mother, no doubt." Martok thought fondly of his mate, Sirella, who died five turns ago during the attempted coup against Martok by the usurper Morjod. "So many dead at the hands of those cyborgs, yet the two I think of the most died in unrelated conflicts. A Klingon is his work, not his family."

"Perhaps," Klag said. "But family remains with us always."

Martok looked at the general, who had stood by while Martok condemned both Klag's brother and his mother after they conspired to have Klag killed. The chancellor could not read the general's face, and Martok wondered if the general was thinking of that, or of his mate and two-year-old son.

"Qapla', son of M'Raq. Bring Krios back to us."

"It will be done, Chancellor." And with that, Klag departed.

As soon as Klag left the confines of the chancellor's office, he headed into the hallway of the Hall of Warriors. Leader Morr, who had been his bodyguard since he was first assigned to the *Gorkon,* followed silently behind. With unabashed pride, Klag looked upon the statue of himself, which had been commissioned after the *Gorkon* devastated the Kinshaya homeworld. The sculptor J'lang had received the commission, and Klag had yet to grow tired of looking at his likeness rendered in stone, standing with one arm raised, holding the *mek'leth* that he had used to slay the dishonorable General Talak on San-Tarah.

Enough self-indulgence, Klag thought. He had survived and thrived, and his enemies had died—but a Klingon warrior's work was not done until he drew his last breath in battle. Activating his wrist communicator, he contacted the ship that he insisted be his flagship when he was given the Fifth Fleet. "Klag to *Gorkon.*"

His first officer answered promptly. *"Laneth."*

"I am ready to beam aboard. Have all ship commanders meet me in the wardroom immediately."

"Yes, General."

Moments later, Klag felt the pull of the transporter beam, which took him and Morr away from the statues of the Empire's heroes and into the transporter room of the *Gorkon.*

As much pride as he took in being enshrined alongside such great warriors as Martok, Kor, Gorkon, Kerla, Koloth, Jurva, Azetbur, Kravokh, Koord, and Kang, Klag took even more in the *I.K.S. Gorkon.* It was rare that a Klingon warrior was able to keep a vessel intact for so long, even rarer for one with a record of battle as lengthy as Klag's.

As he made his way to the wardroom, he said to Morr, "Have the quartermaster send a barrel of bloodwine from my personal stock to the wardroom."

Morr nodded and spoke quietly into his communicator as they strode.

The Fifth Fleet had been devastated by the Borg, but Klag had spent the last several months reconstructing it according to his own standards. Previously composed of fifteen vessels, it now contained seventeen. Besides the Chancellor-class *Gorkon,* the fleet included two *Vor'cha*-class attack cruisers (the *Roval* and the *Hopliq*), two *K'Vort*-class battleships (the *Kreltek* and the *Kolvad*), three *Karas*-class strike ships (the *Gowchok,* the *Chi'dor,* and the *Haproq*), and nine birds-of-prey, which travelled in three groups of three, each group under one commander.

Seven of the eight commanders, as well as Commander Laneth of the *Gorkon,* had all served under Klag on the bridge of this vessel in some capacity or other. The exception was Captain Huss, a fellow member of the Order of the *Bat'leth,* who had fought at Klag's side at San-Tarah against the traitor Talak. All nine were loyal to Klag, and he knew he could trust them all to fight at his side and under his command.

They filed into the wardroom one by one, greeting each other with cheers and laughs and head-butts. Captains Leskit and Toq of the *Hopliq* and *Kreltek,* respectively, head-butted most enthusiastically as the elderly Leskit and the young Toq had formed the strongest of bonds in their time together as pilot and second officer of the *Gorkon,* and both had served as first officer under Klag before gaining their own commands.

Eventually, Klag called the meeting to order, holding up his flagon of bloodwine. "A toast!" he bellowed, and the others either held up their flagons or refilled them and then held them up. "To the Fifth Fleet! To victory! To honor!"

All the assembled captains and commanders cried, "To the Fifth Fleet!"

They all drank heartily, then tossed aside their flagons.

Leskit fell more than sat in a seat and drawled, "So is our esteemed chancellor sending us to avenge his son's untimely demise at Krios?"

"After a fashion," Klag said. "I will take the *Gorkon,* along with the *Kolvad* and Captain Huss's strike ships, to Krios and engage the Kinshaya. Captain K'Nir, you will lead the remainder of the fleet to the Oort cloud of this system and meet with a convoy that is travelling to Mempa."

Strictly speaking, Leskit was the senior of the three

remaining captains—the birds-of-prey were all led by warriors of commander rank—and Toq was the one who had achieved a captaincy first, but despite having matured considerably since his days as Klag's second officer, Toq was still young and impulsive, and Leskit was a captain only under extreme protest. K'Nir was best suited to lead the fleet in Klag's absence. What's more, every warrior in the room knew she was, and so there was no questioning of Klag's orders, no complaints, no posturing on the part of either Leskit or Toq.

As it should be, Klag thought with satisfaction.

"As soon as the convoy is safely in the Mempa system, set course immediately for Krios."

K'Nir nodded. "Understood, General."

Huss spoke up. "General, why are a dozen vessels needed to escort a mere convoy?"

"Because there is nothing 'mere' about the convoy," Klag said. "It is two score ships carrying personnel and material that will be used to rebuild the Mempa system. The equipment is quite valuable and an easy target for pirates. We will *not* allow it to be looted."

"It won't," K'Nir said with confidence.

"Besides," Commander Koxx, who lead the birds-of-prey *Jor, Nukmay,* and *Khich,* said, "the general will have defeated the *khest'n* Kinshaya long before we get there."

Toq went to the floor and picked up his flagon. "To victory!"

Everyone shouted back: "To victory!"

After Toq had slugged down his drink, Klag said, "Return to your ships. We depart in twenty minutes."

The commanders all filed out, only Leskit lingering behind. The old razorbeast was fondling the Cardassian neckbones that he still—more than five turns after the end of the Dominion War—wore on a chain around his neck. "Ironic, really."

"What is?"

"Every first officer you ever had who's still drawing breath is serving in this fleet—except Drex, your first one. You kicked him off the *Gorkon,* and now we go to avenge his death."

Klag smirked. "The irony is not lost on me, old friend." He clasped Leskit's shoulder. "Go to the *Hopliq*. Keep our people safe. I will retake Krios."

Leskit rose and made an exaggerated bow. "As the general commands."

As the old captain moved to the door, Klag called out, "And make sure Toq doesn't do anything foolish!"

"Don't I always?" Leskit said with a chuckle that made his neckbones rattle.

After the door rumbled shut behind Leskit, Klag sat for a moment in the wardroom alone. Ideally, two fleets would handle this, but shipbuilding had been slowed by a dilithium shortage, exacerbated by delays in imported dilithium from the Federation, and the topaline shortage meant that many ships were being used as refugee ferries until atmospheric domes could be completed.

But there were thousands of Klingon nationals on Krios who were living under the thumb of the Kinshaya fanatics, and that, Klag could not tolerate. The Kinshaya referred to the Klingons as demons, and Klag knew that, after what happened last year, he was the most demonic of all to them. Rumor had it that the Kinshaya called him *kro-vak,* which translated from their gutter tongue as "destroyer of worlds."

No worlds will be destroyed, Klag thought, *but many more Kinshaya will ride the Barge of the Dead to* Gre'thor *when I'm through with them.*

Excerpt from the first contact report made by Commander Samir al-Halak, first officer, *U.S.S. Enterprise*-C, Stardate 16883.1

The Zaldans are a humanoid people, following the same bipedal, bilateral symmetry that we have seen throughout the galaxy. The only external physical difference between them and humans is the fact that their hands—and, we later learned, their feet—are webbed. Dr. Stern reports that their internal organs are composed differently, but not to any greater or lesser degree than many other humanoid species.

Their culture, though, is a different matter. The Zaldans despise falsehood to a degree that I've never seen before. Dr. Stern—who's never had any problems being truthful and blunt—wound up taking the lead in the away party's discussions with the Zaldan government.

Lieutenant Commander Bat-Levi joked that the Tellarites would be best for making contact with them, but I quickly realized that that wasn't the case. Tellarites are aggressive and like to argue, and it's easy to mistake the Zaldans for having similar tendencies, but Tellarites are still quite capable of falsehood, as are most other species. Legend has it that

Vulcans never lie, though it's more a goal than a reality. For Zaldans, though, the very *idea* of falsehood is repugnant.

They've already had several encounters with both the Klingons and the Romulans—the latter were a surprise, since they're supposed to have closed their borders, but the Zaldan Leader (that's how the translator rendered his title, "leader") said that it was a civilian trading ship—and despite the fact that the Federation is, in their words, "full of those who speak falsehood," they are interested in pursuing membership. Their previous encounters with alien life-forms have convinced them that they are the only sane people in the galaxy, and everyone else is a collection of liars. Apparently, their attitude is that the only way to change the universe is to become part of it.

On the one hand, the prohibition against lying really plays merry hell with conversation. Polite compliments are just as taboo as outright lies. On the other hand, Zalda has almost no crime, either.

I think they are a very interesting people, and I think we can benefit from further contact with them, and possibly consider them for membership.

14

U.S.S. AVENTINE

Dax peered across the desk of her ready room at Sonek. "So let me get this straight," she said very slowly. "You want me to divert to Zalda because you think there's a Ferengi conspiracy to drive a wedge between the Klingons and the Federation?"

Sonek nodded. "And to destabilize the Federation, yes. But I don't need the *Aventine* to divert—just give me a runabout."

"Can you *fly* a runabout?"

"Okay, just give me a runabout and a pilot."

With a frown, Dax looked over at Bowers, sitting in the other guest chair in the ready room. The first officer just shrugged, and Dax turned her gaze back on Sonek. "Do you have *any* evidence to support this claim?"

"Not in the least." Sonek said those words—the last ones Dax was expecting him to say—with a bright smile on his face. "But the pattern looks pretty obvious, once you know where to look."

Dax leaned back in her chair and stared up at the

bat'leth that hung on the far wall. The Klingon weapon had belonged to Jadzia, the previous host of the Dax symbiont, a gift from her husband. It was perfectly balanced and weighted for her. As Ezri was twenty centimeters shorter than her previous host, she was having a much harder time mastering it. However, she felt confident enough in wielding it that she could easily use it to decapitate Sonek if what he was about to say annoyed her as much as she suspected it would.

Not that she *would,* of course, but she felt a certain satisfaction in thinking about it.

She stared hard at him and said, "Fine. Convince me. Who's the Ferengi?"

Shifting in his seat as if to get more comfortable, Sonek started gesturing with his hands. Dax recognized it as a standard rhetorical gesture, often used by college professors when they were lecturing. "Remember when President Bacco assembled the fleet that got sent to the Azure Nebula?"

"We were part of that fleet."

"Right, of course. Well, the Ferengi ambassador, Derro, he went right along with the notion, but the Breen didn't. So the president went and convinced Derro to hire the Breen as mercenaries. This had what you'd call a double benefit—killing two birds with just the one stone. See, the Tholians were likely to hire the Breen for their own defense, and this was the president's way of punishing the Tholians for refusing to go along. Pissed off the Tholian ambassador something fierce, too."

Waving his hands in front of his chest, Bowers said, "Hold on. How do you know all this? This is all back-room Palais stuff."

Sonek shrugged. "I've got level-twenty clearance."

"*You* have level-twenty clearance?" Bowers was shaking his head, and Dax couldn't help but smile. She already knew that Sonek had enough clout to interrupt a meeting in the president's office, so the fact that he had such a high clearance wasn't much of a surprise.

Sonek said, "President T'Pragh gave me that clearance. I needed it during the Cardassian War, and it was never rescinded."

Bowers was rolling his eyes now. "Go on please, Professor."

"All right. Derro was planning to sell torpedoes and disruptors to the Breen mercenaries also. There's just one little problem with that, and that's that he was outbid by a woman named Sekki."

"So Ambassador Derro isn't our Ferengi?" Dax asked.

Sonek shook his head. "No, it's Sekki. I checked, and she sold them quantum torpedoes—Derro was only offering photon—and she also had type-9 disruptors."

Bowers pursed his lips. "The Breen use type-8, I thought."

"Not these Breen. Mind you, the difference isn't all that much, and it's not like it mattered against the Borg—but the interesting part is that not only did the mercenaries in the Azure Nebula use those, but so did the Kinshaya who took Krios—and probably H'atoria, too."

"We don't know for sure about H'atoria?"

"There isn't any sensor data to look at. We're lucky there was any from Krios, honestly. Luckily, the captain of the *Rovlaq* and someone on the governor's satellite had the presence of mind to send a databurst back to Defense Force Command."

"I still don't see—" Dax started.

But Sonek held up a hand. "I'm getting to it, honest, just bear with me, please. Now this Sekki woman also has a criminal record."

Bowers snorted. "For a Ferengi businessperson, that's a badge of honor."

"Yeah." Sonek chuckled. "But it's what the record's for that's interesting: she was arrested for fraud for trying to pass off artificial farantine as real. Now, before you ask, they just uncovered some artificial farantine on Maxia Zeta IV—it's gone and crippled the dilithium mining. That's *two* of the weird things going on that can be tied to Sekki. Not only that, but the refinery explosion on Capella IV was attributed to a terrorist group that hasn't even existed for a hundred years—which is the sort of thing that might be there to cover up the truth. I think this whole thing is a real complicated campaign, engineered by Sekki, to destabilize relations between the Federation and the Klingons, to cripple our rebuilding efforts."

Dax asked what she thought was the obvious question: "And why would a Ferengi want to do this? There's not much profit in it. Sure, both nations are delayed in rebuilding, but it's not like either is going to turn to a Ferengi to buy dilithium or topaline. So what's the angle?"

"I don't know yet, but I think that Zalda's the key."

That got Dax to blink in confusion. "Excuse me? What does Zalda have to do with this? They're just having their usual snit."

"Yeah, but it fits the pattern."

"What pattern?"

It was, to Dax's surprise, Bowers who answered. "The disruption of the Federation and the Klingons.

H'atoria and Zalda are the two main trade routes. We've got plenty of others, but they'll take longer in terms of transit time."

Sonek shot Bowers a grateful look, then said to Dax, "Just one more thing to make our lives more complicated. And look at what happened with Zalda. Them refusing refugees makes no sense on the face of it. But everyone's willing to believe it because the Zaldans, to be pretty blunt about it, are really annoying."

Dax barked an involuntary laugh at that. Curzon had been present for the signing ceremony when Zalda entered the Federation. Many described the Zaldans as "refreshing," but Dax recalled that Curzon's description was much closer to Sonek's.

"The thing is, the main reason *why* Molmaan would storm out of the Council chambers in a snit is if he thought he was being lied to."

"Why didn't President Bacco or the Council think of this?"

"Because the planet being hit with the overflow of refugees is Cestus III."

Nodding, Dax said, "The president's home."

"That would make her own attitude toward the Zaldans more aggressive, and leave her less likely to examine motives—especially since she's got eighteen or nineteen other things on her mind right present. Besides, nobody really *likes* the Zaldans all that much. I mean, sure, they're members—have been for decades. But that's as much due to their proximity to the two empires as anything. It's real easy to put them in one of their snits, and I think that's what happened here."

Stealing a quick longing look at the *bat'leth* again, Dax asked, "Okay, let's say for a second I buy all this—

and right now I can't say that I do—what do you need the runabout for?"

"To go to Zalda. You need to get yourselves to Capella as soon as the stuff's loaded, and there aren't any other ships that could take me hereabouts, so I need to borrow one of yours. But I'll bring it back, honest, and I think I can talk Molmaan into reopening talks with the Council."

"I've never met Molmaan," Dax said, "but why do you think that?"

"We go back a ways."

"You're friends?"

"Not exactly—more like former colleagues. He was on the Security Council during the Cardassian War, and we worked together a few times. He once told me he respected me, and that's not something he would say unless he meant it, being Zaldan and all."

Dax nodded. "You think you can play on that."

"It's worth a shot. Both for refugees and trade with the Empire, we need Zalda back."

Dax folded her hands on her desk. When Mikaela Leishman first reported on board, her first task was to create a new desk for Dax, as Captain Dexar was two meters tall, with short legs for his height, so he liked a nice high desk. The first time Dax sat at it, she felt like a child, and quickly ordered the desk replaced.

"I'll be honest with you, Sonek. I don't buy your conspiracy theory. After what just happened, chaos is the order of the day, and everything that's gone on since is within the realm of possibility of just happening. Having said that, it's precisely *because* of that chaos that you could be right, as someone could be using the chaos to mask their plan." Unfolding her hands, she placed them flat on the desk. "But the one thing you did convince me of is that you might be able to talk the Zaldans into coming back, which would be immensely useful for the reasons you gave. For that reason, and that reason only, I'm going to let you have the *Seine,* as well as a pilot and the security guard who's been assigned to you."

Sonek let loose with a particularly wide grin. "Thank you, Captain."

"You're to proceed to Zalda immediately, then rendezvous with us at Capella."

"Will do." Sonek got to his feet. "I need to pack a few things. Thanks very much, Captain, I appreciate it."

With that, he left. Dax stared with annoyance at the door. "Dismissed," she said dryly.

"He's not Starfleet," Bowers said, "what do you expect?"

Nodding to concede the point, Dax gave her XO an inquisitive look. "What do you think?"

"I think he's a crazy academic spouting conspiracy theories. But I know that I didn't think Donatra would agree to trade with Tal'Aura in a million years, and I also know that on Artaleirh he talked two centurions who were pointing disruptors at him to go against their orders." Bowers leaned back and threw up his hands. "I guess what I think is that you were right to give him the runabout."

Dax chuckled. "Well, thanks for that. And I agree with everything else you said—especially the first part. I used to *be* the crazy academic spouting conspiracy theories, after all, so I know the type."

"Tobin?"

Nodding, Dax said, "And Sonek reminds me a little too much of that particular host." She considered. "Of course, he also reminds me of Curzon, and Curzon's crazy theories were usually right." Also throwing up her hands, she got to her feet. "Either way, give him whichever shuttle pilot's up on the duty roster and whichever guard Kedair gave him at Artaleirh, and send him on his way. How soon until we can get under way to Capella?"

Also rising, Bowers said, "I checked with Helkara before I came in here, and he said half an hour."

"And he isn't taking any crap from Lessard?"

"Oh no," Bowers said emphatically. "In fact, the last time I saw Lessard, he was sweating like a pig and muttering invocations to God, Jesus Christ, the Virgin Mary, and the Great Bird of the Galaxy."

"Oh, I wish I could've seen that. What a pity."

Frowning, Bowers asked, "Why a pity?"

"Well, I'm the captain. I have to maintain a certain dignity, so publicly I can't really take joy in the suffering of my crew."

"Yeah, but it's just you and me in private."

Grinning, Dax said, "Exactly." Then she dropped the grin and got back to business. "Tell Mikaela to warm up the slipstream drive."

Bowers smiled. "She's been wanting to road-test the upgraded drive since they put it in. And Tharp's been eager to use it, too."

While she understood her chief engineer's eagerness to use the new, improved slipstream drive that replaced the one that burned out after an assault on the Borg, Dax was more confused about the mention of Lieutenant Tharp. "Why him?"

"Navigation is completely different with slipstream—the variables are different, the routes change, the subspace variances are off-kilter, and plotting a course is a hundred and eighty degrees from what it is in warp, so to speak. Captain Hernandez made it look easy, but it's not. In fact, Tharp, Constantino, and Mavroidis have been running about a thousand different simulations each."

Bowers had just named the conn officers for alpha, beta, and gamma shifts, respectively. Another of her previous hosts, Torias, was a pilot, and she vividly recalled the pilot's tendency toward "new-toy-itis" (a phrase Torias had first heard from a human colleague). Slipstream was the next new thing to fly, and it only made sense that her three top pilots were eager to get their hands on it—especially since the replacement drive had incorporated some upgrades suggested by the Caeliar-enhanced Captain Erika Hernandez while she was on board.

"Well," she said, "best speed to Capella as soon as Helkara reports ready, Sam. Dismissed."

Nodding, Bowers took his leave.

Dax started pacing her ready room, stealing glances at the *bat'leth* as she did so.

It's a stupid theory. Hell, it's not even a theory, it's a hypothesis, and not a very good one. The Capellans have always been well stocked with fanatics. We're just there to drop off some equipment.

Even as she tried to convince herself of that, she found herself saying, "Computer, call up all information regarding current mining operations on Capella IV."

An article by Ozla Graniv in *Seeker*

Yesterday, the *S.S. Esperanto* was recalled from Tezwa. It is not being replaced.

The *Esperanto,* which has been one of the vessels that has made regular supply runs to Tezwa, is leaving that planet behind, as so many others did—including me. This independent world near the Klingon-Federation border was the victim of a coup d'état, and almost became the flashpoint for renewed hostilities between the Federation and the Klingon Empire. Ex-Prime Minister Kinchawn used illegally obtained experimental weapons to wipe out a Klingon fleet, and the Klingon Defense Force retaliated with extreme prejudice.

Once a vibrant, thriving spacefaring world, Tezwa was quickly reduced by quantum torpedoes and disruptors to preindustrial levels, dependent on Federation relief teams and cleanup efforts in order to survive.

Which was all well and good until the Borg came.

Aid suddenly was cut back. Ships were recalled from Tezwa

in order to bolster the Federation's defenses against the Borg invasion.

And then seven thousand cubes poured out of the Azure Nebula, devastating so many worlds. The survivors of Deneva—those few who were lucky enough to be off-world when the Borg ravaged the planet—wish they had it as good as the people of Tezwa.

These sentiments are understandable, but dangerous—because they assume that Tezwa has it at all "good." The people responsible for this nightmare existence on Tezwa are no longer in the picture, but their legacy lives on in the pain and suffering of the survivors.

Now it's just going to get worse because the Federation is more concerned with internal matters, and not without reason. But it's hard to look at the people who were counting on the aqueduct that was left half-finished and now may never be completed. The agricultural consultants here to help make the land arable again have left, leaving the Tezwans to hope that they don't suffer complications come harvest time.

It's easy to forget about Tezwa. I know I did. I spent several months on this world in the wake of Kinchawn's madness, and was saddened by what I saw. I felt for the people of this world, who had had everything taken from them.

But then I left, and I moved on to other things. Now the Federation has been forced to reassess its relief efforts, not just for Tezwa, but for Romulus and for any other planet that isn't actually part of the Federation. Our own house needs to be in order before we can help our neighbors.

We cannot forget the face of this suffering. There are Tezwan children rummaging through rubble looking for food. When a water purifier is damaged during one of the many incidents of violence that have broken out all over the planet, there is no longer anyone qualified to fix it, leaving whole villages to drink dirty water to survive. Hospitals need to ration their supplies, since they no longer know when, or even if, the shelves will be restocked.

The Borg invasion didn't just damage the worlds that the cyborgs fired on.

15

RUNABOUT *SEINE*

Ensign Altoss was dreading no longer having the fore compartment of the *Seine* to herself. Professor Pran she didn't mind, but she was about ready to kill Lieutenant Trabka.

It was a twenty-seven-hour journey from Starbase 10 to Zalda at the runabout's top speed, so everyone got to sleep. Altoss had volunteered to pilot the runabout while the other two slept, which was necessary since she and Trabka were the only ones qualified to do so. Technically, the *Seine* could be put on autopilot, but Altoss felt that it was best for someone to be on duty at all times.

Besides, it meant that sixteen of the twenty-seven hours would be spent with either herself or Trabka asleep, which meant that Altoss would be spared listening to her.

Though Altoss was born on Triex, the daughter of a travel writer, she spent most of her life going from planet to planet. She never even set foot on the Efrosian homeworld until the death-march for her mother, which was after Altoss's enrollment in Starfleet Academy. Her mother had been on Betazed when it was taken by the Dominion, and killed during the initial assault on that world. In fact, it was the death-march for all the Efrosians who died on Betazed—all thirty-nine of them, including her mother.

By the time she graduated, the Dominion War was over. Altoss regretted not having the opportunity to fight to avenge her mother's death, but she was also grateful that the conflict had ended. She was assigned to the *U.S.S. Centaur* for a time before signing on to the *Aventine* for its maiden voyage.

The aft compartment door slid open, and Altoss whirled around, praying that it was Professor Pran. She had been dreading the assignment to protect a civilian, but he had turned out to be quite interesting. It was only in part because of her orders to stay by his side that she had tried to accompany him into the anteroom with Donatra—the chance to see that conversation was too good to pass up.

Unfortunately, it was Stephanie Trabka. *Wonderful.*

Without preamble, the junior-grade lieutenant said, "They're probably at Capella already. I bet that Constantino did the whole shift herself, too."

"Lieutenant—" Altoss started, but Trabka was, of course, on a roll.

"Do you know how long I've waited for something like slipstream drive?"

"Yes," Altoss said, "because you've spoken of nothing else since we came aboard the *Seine*."

That brought Trabka up short. She sat in the copilot's seat next to Altoss. "That's not true."

"Lieutenant, you have spoken on precisely two subjects for the past twenty-six and a half hours: the *Aventine*'s slipstream drive and the fact that you're not on the ship when it's in use."

Trabka shook her head. "It's just not fair. I applied to be transferred to the *Aventine* the minute I heard it was being constructed, but I got wait-listed. I finally get assigned *after* the Borg invasion, and what happens? They make me a *shuttle pilot*. Oh sure, I'm also the relief conn officer for gamma shift, but when does *anything* ever happen on *gamma* shift?"

Altoss tugged on her eyebrows in frustration. "The *Aventine* isn't going anywhere, Lieutenant. I'm sure your chance will come."

The aft door opened again, this time letting Professor Pran in. *At last.* Suffering was always better shared, in Altoss's considered opinion.

"Morning, everybody. How we set for time?"

Trabka sat up straighter as she took over the helm controls. "We'll be dropping out of warp in ten minutes, and then it'll be twenty minutes to the planet."

"Good." Settling into one of the passenger chairs, Pran said, "If it's all right, I'd like to contact Zalda soon as we drop to impulse."

Frowning, Trabka asked, "You don't want to wait until we're in orbit?"

Pran looked at her quizzically. "What for?"

"Er, nothing, I guess."

Altoss rolled her eyes.

Fearing that Trabka would go off on another rant, Altoss turned to Pran. "Professor, what did you and Donatra talk about?"

Grinning, Pran said, "And here I thought you just wanted to come along to keep me from getting shot."

"Well, that, too. But that was history there. I wanted to be part of it."

"We're all part of history, Ensign. Everybody has a part to play."

Trabka muttered, "Some more than others."

Pran looked at Trabka, then turned to Altoss. "She still carrying on about not getting to play with the slip-stream?"

Altoss practically hissed the word, "Yes."

Sighing dramatically, Trabka said, "I'm sorry, but I did my graduating thesis at the Academy on slipstream drive. I've been fascinated by the technology for ages. It's been my life, and then I finally get on the *Aventine,* and what happens?"

"They use it when you're off-ship," Pran said. "I'm sorry, Lieutenant, truly I am. If I had known that—well, I doubt I would've been able to do anything about it, since I suspect that my influence over the duty roster is negligible, but I would've at least complained about it."

For the first time since they left the *Aventine,* Trabka smiled. She had a small, shy smile that, oddly, reminded Altoss of her mother. "Thank you, Professor."

For the change of subject, if for no other reason, Altoss said, "Lieutenant, when you smile, you look a lot like my mother."

"Really?" Trabka seemed understandably confused by that.

"Just the smile—no other way," Altoss said quickly. "Even so, you look more like her than I do."

Trabka looked down at her console. "Coming out of warp. Do you look more like your father?"

"Don't know," Altoss said, doing a standard scan of the system as the *Seine* came out of warp. If nothing else, regulations stated that they had to verify that they were actually in the Zaldan system—which they were.

"You don't know your father?"

"Why would I?"

Pran said, "Efrosians don't really have the same system of parenting as some other folks, Lieutenant. If we were talking in Efrosian right now, the word for 'mother' would more accurately translate to 'parent.' 'Father,' though, that translates to 'seed donor.' Kids are raised by their mothers, and people only know who their father—or, I guess, seed donor—is if they need to for medical reasons."

"Oh. That's too bad," Trabka said. "My father raised me by himself. My mother died in a shuttle accident when I was two months old."

"I'm sorry," Altoss said, meaning it. To lose one's mother was the worst possible thing that could happen to a child.

"It's okay. I just have a hard time imagining life without a father."

Smiling, Altoss said, "I have a similar difficulty conceiving of life without a mother."

"On approach to Zalda," Trabka said.

Altoss opened up a channel. "Zalda Orbital Control, this is the Starfleet runabout *U.S.S. Seine* on a diplomatic mission from the Federation Council. Professor Sonek Pran requests an audience with Councillor Molmaan immediately." Pran had told her to use that precise language the previous day. Altoss pointed out that that was technically a lie—Pran's only assignment from the Palais was to talk to Donatra—but Pran said that what Molmaan didn't know wouldn't hurt him.

Many seconds passed with no response. Altoss put

the message on auto-repeat and turned to Pran. "They may not answer."

"Give it a couple minutes," Pran said.

"It's not true, you know," Trabka said.

"What isn't?" Altoss asked.

Trabka glanced back at Pran. "Not everyone has a part to play. Some people are just there and history goes zooming by them at warp speed."

"Well now, you're certainly entitled to think that way, Lieutenant, but I don't agree with you in the least. Everyone takes part in history, whether they know it or not. Matter of fact, most of them don't know it at all, seeing as how they're too busy living it to pay much attention. When Surak preached logic and mastery of emotion, he wasn't trying to make history, he was trying to save his people from annihilating each other. His only realistic expectation was to get himself killed by the folks on Vulcan who didn't agree with him. Who makes history depends on what history you're trying to find out about."

"Yeah, but Surak was special," Trabka said.

"Maybe, but we only know that now in hindsight. And becoming famous isn't the only way to be part of history. Let me give you an example—there's an old human story they tell on Earth sometimes from millennia ago. Parts of it are based in fact, actually. There were these brothers. One of them was named Joseph, and the other brothers didn't really like him all that much, because he could interpret dreams. And because of that, their parents liked him more than the other brothers—or, at least, that's what the brothers thought. So one day, Joseph went out looking for his brothers, and couldn't find them. He walked down the road, and a man told Joseph, 'They went that way.' And Joseph followed the man's directions, and found his brothers. Now his brothers decided they'd had enough of him and sold him off into slavery. He became a slave in another country, and wound up in jail, and while he was there, he interpreted the dreams of his cellmates and one of the prison guards. Now the leader of that other country started having bad dreams, and he didn't know what they meant. One of the prison guards got himself promoted, and he was working at the palace now, and he told the leader that he knew this man in jail who could tell him what the dreams meant.

"Eventually, our boy Joseph was freed and made an adviser to the leader. He predicted a famine that would come, so the leader was able to stockpile food against it. Back home, though, his brothers weren't so lucky, and they were starving—until Joseph invited them to where he was.

"Joseph and his brothers had a really big family, and their descendants eventually made up an entire race of people on Earth. Two of the biggest religions humans ever had had the story of Joseph as part of their mythology. And *none* of that would've happened, except for this one guy who said, 'They went that way.' " Pran grinned. "I always tell my students that story when they doubt the idea that one person can make a big difference in the universe."

Altoss was about to comment on the story when her console beeped. "Zalda's replying."

"Runabout Seine, *you are not welcome in Zaldan space. Leave now."*

The transmission ceased.

Shaking his head, Pran got up from his seat. "I am *not* giving up that easy. Open the channel back up."

Altoss did so. "Go ahead."

"This is Sonek Pran. I'm here on official business from the Palais de la Concorde on Earth, and I'm here to see Councillor Molmaan. This is a formal diplomatic visit, and if you refuse it, then I'll have to report to President Bacco that Zalda has declared itself an enemy of the Federation. Which, by the way, will also make you an enemy of the Klingon Empire, and I hear they're looking for new worlds."

There was no response.

"We're approaching the planet," Trabka said. "Should I enter orbit?"

"We can't," Altoss said before Pran could say anything. "We don't have permission and, more to the point, we haven't been given an orbital path. We could completely disrupt their orbit traffic—or crash."

"Well," Pran said, "the first part doesn't bother me all that much, but I get what you mean about the second part. I think—"

"Pran, what are you doing here?"

That got Pran to grin. "Good to hear your voice, Councillor."

"Do you bear an apology from the president?"

"I bear about a hundred questions from the president before an apology gets to the table."

"Then let me ask a question. Are you insulting me once again by lying, or are you truly so stupid as to believe that the Federation will declare Zalda an enemy when we have so many refugees on our world?"

Altoss shot Pran a look. "They have refugees?"

"Who is that?"

"Ensign Altoss," Pran said. "She's from the *Aventine*'s security detail. I've also got a pilot here, Lieutenant Stephanie Trabka."

Molmaan didn't bother with pleasantries. *"Of course we have refugees. What possible reason would we have for refusing them?"*

"I don't know, but the Council got itself some very compelling evidence."

"Lies!"

"Were they? You didn't exactly go out of your way to refute them."

"Lies are lies—they are not to be tolerated!"

"Oh, cut that out, Molmaan. You've been looking for an excuse to back out of the Federation for years."

"I do not deny that I have advocated secession, as I find the tiresome prevarication of other species to be a tremendous irritation. But I do not believe now is the proper time, after such a major crisis—and I do not believe that anyone would think that of us."

"Like I said, Councillor, they had evidence. Maybe it was faked, but if it was, it was a damn good fake. Now, if you ask me, the best bet is for you to go back to Earth and *talk* to President Bacco and the Council. Straighten this mess out, before it gets worse."

There was a long pause before Molmaan spoke again. *"What assurances do I have that I will not be lied to again?"*

"None whatsoever."

Altoss shot Pran another look at that—then remembered who he was talking to. Blunt honesty was the way to go here.

Pran went on. "What I *can* assure you is that you'll be *listened* to—but you have to actually be willing to *talk* first."

Another long pause. *"Why were we not believed in the first place?"*

"Because the evidence was compelling, and because that evidence pointed to Cestus III being the planet to bear the brunt of your apparent refusal to take refugees. You know President Bacco a lot better than I do, and *I* know how important her homeworld is to her. Whoever set this up did it on purpose, and knew both how the president would respond with Cestus III involved and how you'd respond to something you knew was a lie."

Yet another long pause. Altoss saw Trabka readjust their course again, since they still didn't have an orbital path to take.

"I will return to Earth," Molmaan finally said. *"I will speak to the rest of the Council and to the president. I do not promise that we will forgive this insult, but I do promise that I will consider it."*

"That's all we're asking, Councillor. Thank you."

"The president was wise to send you, Pran. I know you are a creature of truth, unlike so many other outsiders. If you believe this to be a ruse, then I believe that it might well be so."

"I appreciate the vote of confidence, Molmaan. One more thing?"

"What?" Molmaan sounded even more peevish now.

"The refugees. We've been diverting them, but—"

"They may come here. We will not turn away people in need. We only refused your runabout because you are not in that manner of need."

"Fair enough. Thanks again, Councillor. Have a safe trip back to Earth."

Molmaan didn't bother with a signoff, but just ended communications.

Altoss looked up at Pran, who was still standing between her and Trabka. "That went better than expected."

"Hope so. Do me a favor, Ensign, and call the Palais for me. I need to let the chief of staff and the president know what's happening."

Her nose flaring with surprise, Altoss said, "Excuse me? The Palais?"

Pran grinned. "The one and only. Hurry, will you, I want the refugee ships to be able to move sooner rather than later."

"Okay." Altoss started going through the various security protocols necessary to contact so secure a location as the Palais de la Concorde.

After about a minute of that, and of Pran giving a code, a human face appeared on the screen. "Zachary, it's Sonek. Is Esperanza around?"

"Absolutely. Hang on a second."

The human's face went away, and minutes later, Altoss found herself looking at the president's office on the top floor of the Palais. She had, of course, seen images of the room many times, and even went on a tour of the Palais that included the office when she was a cadet. All those times, it felt like a museum exhibit. Now, though, they were seeing it *as an office,* and Altoss found herself more than a little intimidated.

More so when she saw who was on the screen: President Bacco herself, along with an olive-skinned woman that she assumed to be Esperanza Piñiero, the chief of staff, Fleet Admiral Leonard Akaar, whom she'd met briefly at her Academy graduation, and a tall, thin Bajoran man whom she recognized as the Palais press liaison, Kant Jorel.

The president was not a young woman, but she looked much older than she seemed on the Federation News Service reports Altoss had seen. Her hair—as white as an Efrosian man's—was thinner, and she had a lot more lines on her face.

"Professor," President Bacco said, *"I wasn't expecting to hear from you so soon."*

"I actually have some good news for you, Madam President."

"Don't keep me in suspense, dammit. I've had maybe four pieces of good news since I took office. Tell me!"

"Zalda's open for the refugee business, and turns out they always have been. Molmaan's on his way to Earth to hash out what went on on Cestus."

There was a silence that was as long as Molmaan's pauses.

Finally the chief of staff broke it. *"Say that again, please, Sonek?"*

His grin as wide as she'd ever seen it, Pran said, "Zalda's back in play, Ms. Piñiero. Molmaan and I have a history, and I talked Captain Dax into lending me a runabout to go have a chat with him. They're off on Capella now."

"Well." The president shook her head. *"Professor, I don't know what to say. This definitely falls into the category of above and beyond."*

"Not at all, ma'am. Just doing what I can to help."

Akaar rose to his feet, reminding Altoss just how

tall the admiral was. *"I will see to the refugee situation immediately, with your permission, ma'am."*

Waving her hand in a "shoo" motion, the president said, *"Absolutely with my permission. Go, go!"*

"Thank you, Madam President."

As Akaar left, the Bajoran, Kant, asked, *"Does this mean I can tell the room that the rumors of Zalda's departure were greatly exaggerated?"*

"Uh, I wouldn't," Pran said. "Molmaan did say they won't refuse anyone in need, but if you say anything beyond that, it may get him aggravated all over again."

"And heaven forfend Councillor Molmaan be aggravated," the president said. *"All right, fine, just say that Zalda's taking refugees and leave it at that."*

Kant nodded.

Piñiero looked at the screen. *"Good work, Professor. Thank you."*

"You're very welcome, Ms. Piñiero. And thank you, Madam President."

Altoss closed the connection.

Trabka said, "She looks a lot older in real life."

At that, Altoss laughed, since she had thought the same thing.

"Borg invasions'll do that to you," Pran said. "All right, next stop is Maxia Zeta."

For the third time, Altoss shot Pran a surprised look. The professor seemed to have a knack for it. "Excuse me?"

"Uh, Professor," Trabka said, "our orders were just to take you to Zalda."

"I know that, and I'm sorry, but this is important. Now that we know for sure that the whole thing with Zalda was a setup, that means it's even *more* likely that what happened on Maxia Zeta IV is part of it, too. Look, someone's trying to destabilize the Federation at a time when we're really vulnerable. Captain Dax'll live without the runabout for another couple days—but we *have* to go to Maxia Zeta IV."

Trabka looked helplessly at Altoss, who just shrugged. "You're the ranking officer, Lieutenant. It's your call."

The pilot then looked up at Pran. "You're thinking we might be the people who said 'they went that way'?"

Pran chuckled. "Maybe. Only one way to find out."

"All right—but if Captain Dax or Commander Bowers asks, I'm saying that you made me do it." With that, Trabka set a course for the Maxia Zeta system. "This'd be a lot faster with slipstream," she muttered as she engaged.

Altoss resisted the urge to shoot her.

A homily given by Prylar Hon Avid at a vigil on Berengaria, 28 February 2381

Thank you all for coming today.

A year ago, the Vedek Assembly summoned me and told me that the population of Bajorans living here on Berengaria had grown sufficiently large that a temple was to be constructed, and I was asked to be its caretaker. The congregation is not large, certainly very small compared to those on Bajor and its colonies, but I still usually see a few dozen faces during services.

Today, at this vigil we hold in memory of the billions who died at the hands of the Borg, I see hundreds of faces. Most of you do not believe the Prophets to be divine, do not follow the faith that I espouse, and do not consider this temple to be your chosen place of worship.

But we have come together because of the greatest tragedy the galaxy has ever known. In times like these, it is common to question one's faith, and to contemplate the nature of a universe that has been so cruel, and to take solace in one's beliefs.

My own faith grew out of a time when Bajor was not an equal member of the Federation, but a subject world of the Cardassian Union. I worked in the Voria mines, doing backbreaking labor that led to the deaths of many of my friends and family. Throughout that appalling experience, faith in the Prophets kept me going when it would have been easy to give up. One of our greatest spiritual leaders from many centuries ago, a kai named Dava Nikende, once said, "It is in the time of struggle that we must become as one." Kai Dava was speaking of Bajor, but his words apply equally well to those of us—both in the Federation and out—who were victimized by the Borg invasion.

I see the devastation on Vulcan, on Andor, on Deneva, on Risa, on Sherman's Planet, on Pandril, on Qo'noS, and on so many other worlds, I see the graveyard of starships in the Azure Nebula, and I see that we all are as I was—laboring in the mines, under the thumb of an awful oppressor.

I am not here to tell you that you should believe in the Prophets. I am not here to tell you that you should believe in anything. I *am* here to tell you to embrace your faith, and to embrace each other. It is easy to suddenly believe in the Prophets, in Allah, in Uzaveh, in the Blessed Exchequer, in Kahless, in Shariel when the bad times come, and it is just as easy to renounce them. But as time goes on, as the wounds slowly start to heal—as you come out of the mine and start a new life—do not forget that your faith is what keeps you living, not just in your gods or your beliefs, but in one another.

Thank you, and walk with the Prophets.

16

U.S.S. AVENTINE

Dax looked away from the screen on her desk, blinking several times. She'd been reading the reports on the Capella IV mine explosion for an hour now, and she was starting to get bleary-eyed. She got up and started pacing back and forth across her ready room.

Her eye once again caught the *bat'leth* Worf had given her. Worf had been Jadzia's husband—her *mate* in Klingon terms—and had remained a good friend to Ezri. She had aided him when Morjod tried to overthrow Martok after the Dominion War, and more recently they'd fought side by side against the Borg, she on the *Aventine,* he in his current post of first officer of the *Enterprise.* Worf had spent seven years as a security chief, and another four as a diplomat, and she found herself wondering what he'd think of what she just read.

The door chime rang. "Come," she said, turning away from the weapon on the wall to face her ready-room door, which slid aside to reveal Lieutenant Kedair.

"Captain, we've just heard from the *Hecate.* They're

waiting at Capella's Oort cloud, and are ready for the transfer as soon as we arrive."

"Which will be?"

"Ten minutes at current speed of warp two."

"Good." The *Aventine* had traversed most of the distance between Starbase 10 and Capella via slipstream, but the drive was not quite as precise as one would like. The Caeliar-enhanced Captain Hernandez had been able to navigate with pinpoint accuracy, but the regular humanoids at the conn weren't so fortunate. As a result, the *Aventine* had come out of slipstream a couple of light-years shy of Capella, and they were covering the rest of it by warp drive.

"Commander Bowers, Lieutenant Leishman, Lieutenant Tharp, and Ensign Constantino are going over the telemetry from the slip drive right now."

Dax nodded and moved to sit back at her desk. *I don't have Worf, but I do have a perfectly good security chief.* "Have a seat, Lonnoc."

"Uh, sure." Kedair seemed surprised by the invitation, or perhaps by the informality, and acceded to her request tentatively.

In case it was the informality, Dax said, "I don't bite, Lieutenant. I just need a second opinion on something—specifically, a security chief's opinion."

Now appearing more at ease, Kedair said, "What can I do for you, Captain?"

"Professor Pran thinks that what happened on Capella is part of a larger plan to destabilize both the Federation and the Klingons."

"I thought it was just an explosion in a mine—a hundred-year-old mine at that."

"Me, too." Dax turned her screen so that Kedair could

see it. "But it was the new refinery that exploded, and it did so before it had a chance to refine anything. What's more, the scans found cabrodine."

Kedair nodded. "Okay, so it was an explosive. Doesn't Capella have a history of extremism and terrorism along these lines?"

"A long time ago, sure, but—" Dax shook her head. "It doesn't feel right. This mine is coming at the best possible time for Capella. Their economy is on the verge of collapse. Conversely, the teer is immensely popular."

"That doesn't make any sense. Don't the people blame him?"

"Sadly, it's not that unusual." Dax shook her head, remembering the bizarreness of politics that she'd encountered in all her various lifetimes. "A charismatic enough leader can escape blame even as the cliff's falling out from under everyone's feet."

"Oh, I know that. Trust me, we've had our share of incompetents serving as immensely popular high thanes on Takara. It still doesn't make any sense." Kedair folded her hands on her lap. "So you think this is outside sabotage."

"I think there's enough doubt that we need to investigate more closely—and more objectively than the Janus Mining people would be willing to."

Kedair nodded. "Yeah, their primary concern would be to get the refinery back up and running. And the Capellans presumably don't have the resources to do a proper investigation."

"Neither does Janus, actually—most of their scanning equipment is at least five years behind ours, if not more." Dax shrugged. "To be fair, it doesn't need to be any better than that, generally. This is the sort of thing that would normally be handled by local authorities—but that brings us back to a people who are still mostly preindustrial."

"Uh, Captain?" Kedair looked uncomfortable again.

"Yes?"

"Well—don't we have orders not to set foot on Capella IV?"

Dax nodded. "The Capellans are willing to have Federation civilians on their world, but not Starfleet. It's because of Admiral Akaar, actually. He was supposed to be the teer, but he was exiled. After he joined Starfleet—"

"Oh, you're kidding?" Kedair now looked appalled. "That's even more ridiculous than the current teer being popular."

"Be that as it may, the only way to get a proper investigation of this incident is to do it ourselves. Which means we'll have to violate those orders."

"On the basis of a hunch from a college professor?"

Dax let out a long breath. "Yeah, I know. You think it's a bad idea?"

"Violating orders is never a good idea—but the impression I've gotten from Pran is that he doesn't make judgments without giving some considerable thought to it. And honestly? The notion of eight people being killed without a complete investigation rankles me." Kedair shook her head. "It's your decision, Captain. Whatever you decide, I'm right behind you—and if you ask me to, I'll make sure the truth behind that explosion comes out."

Dax was glad to see that her security chief was so determined. Kedair had been involved in a friendly fire incident on a Borg ship, and Dax had been concerned that she wouldn't recover from it. "Consider yourself asked."

The pair of them exited the ready room to the bridge. Helkara rose from the command chair and said, "Captain on the bridge."

The Zakdorn second officer moved to the operations console, while Kedair took over at tactical. Dax settled into the command chair and said, "Open a channel to the *Hecate.* And bring Commander Bowers up to speed."

From behind her at tactical, Kedair said, "Channel open."

"Hecate, this is Captain Dax of the *Aventine."*

The face of a dark-skinned human appeared on the forward viewer. *"My name is Hugues Staley, Captain. Are you ready to transfer the equipment?"*

"I'm afraid not, Mr. Staley. I regret to inform you that I am not satisfied with the investigation of the explosion."

Staley blinked. *"Excuse me?"*

"Eight Federation citizens are dead, Mr. Staley, and we need to know why before I can release this equipment."

"We know why, Captain, we—"

"No, we know how. That's not good enough. If you'll be so kind as to escort us into orbit of Capella IV, I'll be sending down a security team to fully investigate the explosion."

"That would be a very bad idea, Captain. The teer—"

"The teer needs this mine to be operational. That won't happen until I have been assured by my chief of security that there is no more danger to Federation citizens on the planet."

Staley just stared at Dax for several seconds. Then he said, *"Hold on a moment, please."*

The screen reverted back to the warp-affected starfield.

While Dax waited, Bowers and Tharp entered the bridge from the door that led to the observation lounge. Taking his seat next to Dax's, Bowers said in a low voice that only she could hear, "You're taking a big chance, Captain."

In a like tone, Dax asked, "If you have any objections, Sam, now's the time."

Bowers shook his head. "Honestly, this whole thing has felt hinky to me, too."

"Thanks for the support. And some day, you'll have to give me the etymology of 'hinky.' "

Even as Bowers smiled, the screen changed again, this time to a short, squat woman, whom Dax recognized from the files she'd read as the Janus Mining supervisor on Capella IV, Rebecca Greenblatt. *"Captain Dax, why are you refusing delivery of the equipment we need?"*

"And you are?" Even though she knew the answer, Dax thought a *bit* of decorum was required.

"Extremely pissed off that Starfleet is sticking their nose in my project. I'm Rebecca Greenblatt, I'm running this show for Janus Mining, and I don't appreciate you refusing delivery."

"I'm not refusing delivery, Ms. Greenblatt, I'm simply delaying it until I'm satisfied that conditions on Capella IV are safe."

"There are two-meter tall men walking around with kligats, *Captain. It's not remotely safe. But I have a job to do, and you're impeding my ability to do it."*

"Ms. Greenblatt, I have reason to believe that the *toora Maab* is not responsible for your refinery exploding."

"And that reason would be?"

"Mine. I'm not at liberty to discuss it with you until our investigation is complete—and you won't be getting the equipment until then."

Greenblatt scratched her chin. *"This is insane. Look, you people aren't even* allowed *on the planet. The teer won't permit it."*

"If the teer wants the mine, he'll have to permit it. There's a great deal at stake, Ms. Greenblatt. I only need one of my people to beam down: my security chief, Lieutenant Kedair. No other Starfleet personnel will set foot on Capella, I promise you that."

Rolling her eyes, Greenblatt said, *"Oh, you* promise, *do you? Well, that makes* all *the difference. Hang on a moment."*

Again, the screen reverted to the starfield, which reverted to a normal view. "Coming out of warp," Tharp said, having taken over the conn.

"How'd the slipstream function?" Dax asked her XO.

"Not bad. Mikaela's concerned about some of the phase variances, but nothing untoward. We also can't use it for another couple of days at least. She's writing up a full report now. Oh, and the structural integrity field took a bigger hit than expected—it's down to sixty-three percent. Constantino had some suggestions about the angle of entry that would smooth the transition and ease the strain on the SIF."

Dax winced. When they used the slipstream against the Borg, the SIF suffered only a fifteen percent loss of power, and that was quickly restored. The specs for the drive called for a loss of no more than twenty percent, so one of thirty-seven percent was cause for concern. "I'm looking forward to that report."

The screen changed again, and this time Greenblatt had company: a large man with long black hair and penetrating green eyes. *"You are Earth people?"* the man asked.

"No, actually," Dax said. "I'm from the planet Trill. I'm Captain Dax of the Federation Starship *Aventine.*" She rose to her feet, put her fist to her chest, then opened the fist and extended that arm. "We come with open hearts and open hands."

"I am Keen, the teer of the Ten Tribes. You are not from Earth?"

"No. Neither is my chief of security—she is from a planet that is not part of the Federation, called Takara."

"Very well. Your chief of security may set foot on our world. If any others do so, they will be slain on sight."

"Understood, Teer. Thank you."

"When this task is completed, you will provide this woman with what she requires?"

"Absolutely. You have my word."

"I do not know you, Captain Dax of the Aventine, *and therefore I will trust your word. If you give me reason not to, there will be a grave price to pay."*

With that, the screen went blank.

Kedair let out a grunt from the tactical station. "I guess I'm good to go, Captain?"

Dax nodded. "Go down unarmed. Be sure to greet them the way I did."

"Unarmed?" Kedair sounded as if she was about to object further, but Dax cut her off.

"If you bring down a weapon, they'll confiscate it. Just bring a tricorder."

"Aye, Captain." Kedair did not sound happy.

Dax didn't care. She was going out on a limb as it was. *Sonek, if this turns out not to be what you say it is, I swear I will kill you.*

The first thing Rebecca Greenblatt said to Lonnoc Kedair when she materialized on Capella IV was: "You Starfleet people and your power trips. You just think the entire galaxy rotates around you guys, don't you? Let me tell you, there's nothing you can do that civilians can't do just as well, all right?"

This did very little to endear the Janus Mining supervisor to Kedair. Neither did the next thing she said. "I'm going to be with you every step of the way for this pointless exercise of yours."

"Joy," was all Kedair could muster in reply.

She followed standard procedure for such investigations, which was to examine the site of the explosion—much of which had long since been cleaned up—and to interview the witnesses.

The former confirmed the traces of cabrodine, specifically a ninety-six percent match for cabrodine. While that was within the margin for error, Kedair asked Greenblatt, "When you guys did your scan, what did it turn up for the cabrodine?"

"What do you mean?"

"What percentage match was it?"

"A hundred, why?"

Kedair frowned. The *Vesta*-class ships were fresh off the line with the same top-of-the-line sensors as the

Luna class, and that extended to the tricorders. She tapped her combadge. "Kedair to Helkara."

The Zakdorn second officer replied. *"Helkara here, go ahead."*

"Gruhn, I'm transmitting a scan to you." She matched action to words. "Could you do a detailed breakdown of the scan?"

"Sure, but it'll take an hour."

"That's fine. Thanks. Kedair out."

Greenblatt scratched her chin. "It's cabrodine. What's the big deal?"

"I don't know yet," Kedair said honestly. "If I did, I wouldn't have asked for the scan."

The interviews were more problematic because the employees of Janus Mining constantly looked to Greenblatt for guidance in how to answer and the Capellans didn't have the first notion what was really going on—and didn't particularly care.

Only one fact of potential interest came up, during the interview with the supply person, an elderly Zakdorn, who mentioned that the supply vessel was different from the last few times—but the ship had changed several times, so this wasn't unusual. Kedair might not have even bothered thinking about that, but the supply ship in question was Ferengi.

After the interviews—which told her very little that the reports didn't—Kedair turned to Greenblatt to ask about something the reports didn't mention. "What evidence did you have to implicate the *toora Maab* in the explosion?"

"Two things. One was a message sent to the teer by the *toora Maab* claiming responsibility. The other is the graffiti."

Kedair's translator didn't render that final word. "I'm sorry?"

"We found writing on the walls of the refinery. When we pieced it together, it spelled out *'toora Maab kligaro.'* Whichever member of the *toora Maab* did this probably committed the vandalism while leaving the explosive."

Looking out over the countryside of Capella, unblemished by industry, Kedair asked, "What was used to create the lettering?"

"A red dye from a local plant—they use it to color their clothing."

Entering commands into her tricorder, she asked, "What plant?"

Putting her hands on her hips, Greenblatt asked, "What *difference* does it make? Lieutenant, this is a waste of time. The *jorni* bush is all up and down the river. You can find it *anywhere.*"

Kedair whirled around. "Which is it?"

"Which is what?"

"You said you can find it anywhere, but that it's up and down the river. Which is it?"

Greenblatt closed her eyes and let out an annoyed sigh that made Kedair want to punch her in the throat. "It's only found on riverbanks. But this continent alone is covered in them."

"Good, that gives me search parameters." Kedair entered the molecular structure of the *jorni* bush, which was in the tricorder's database along with all the other information they had about Capella IV in the *Aventine* computer, and then did a search for it in a two-kilometer radius, one that excluded the coastal areas.

"What are you doing?" Greenblatt asked.

"With luck, finding our saboteur."

"How?"

Smiling sweetly, Kedair said, "Gee, Ms. Greenblatt, you said there's nothing we can do that civilians can't do just as well, so why don't you tell me?" Her tricorder beeped. "Ah, here we go. According to this, there's a concentration of *jorni* on a rock face about half a kilometer from here—and nowhere near a river."

Greenblatt moved to stand next to Kedair and held out her hand. "Let me see that."

Rather than hand the tricorder to her, Kedair simply held it up for Greenblatt to see the display.

"That's the *voskiz* rock—there are caves in there, which were formed by rivers," Greenblatt said.

"So?"

"What makes the *jorni* plant unique, and the reason why it only grows by the river is that there's a mineral in the rivers on this continent that alters the plants. That's also why it's such a good dye. There could be trace deposits of that mineral in the cave, and that might lead to *jorni*."

Despite herself, Kedair was impressed. "You may be right—but the only way for me to find out is to go to that rock and look for myself."

"Ourselves, Lieutenant. You're not going anywhere on Capella without me."

"Like hell. Ms. Greenblatt, I appreciate your need to supervise, but I'm about to explore a cave that may contain the saboteur who killed eight of your people. I'm trained in this."

Greenblatt folded her squat arms defiantly over her barrel chest. The supervisor had been raised on Pangea, which made her short, but also broad and tough. Not that Kedair was all that impressed—non-Takarans were appallingly fragile—but she could at least appreciate Greenblatt's determination.

"If you don't take me with you," Greenblatt continued, "I'll tell the teer you haven't cooperated by the terms of the agreement, and you'll be forcibly removed from this planet."

"I'd like to see them try." Kedair sighed and threw up her hands. "Fine, come with, but don't say I didn't warn you."

The hike to the *voskiz* rock took about an hour. The two women walked in not-so-companionable silence.

Just as they were approaching the cave indicated by the tricorder, Greenblatt finally spoke. "I'm surprised you didn't try to use your pheremones on my people."

Kedair stepped up onto an outcropping that was right in front of the mouth of the cave, and then stared down at Greenblatt as she clambered upward to join her. "Excuse me?"

"Your pheremones."

"I have no idea what you're talking about."

"Don't get cute with me, Lieutenant. I know all about Orion women and—"

Unable to help herself, Kedair burst out laughing. "I'm not Orion."

"What?"

"Don't let the skin color fool you, Ms. Greenblatt. I'm Takaran."

"I don't know that species."

"Which is why you shouldn't make assumptions." Kedair peered at her tricorder, which was scanning the cave interior, then closed it and reached for a phaser that wasn't there. *Damn stupid native customs.* "Stay behind me," she told Greenblatt.

"What for?"

Because if you don't, I'll hit you over the head with a rock. Somehow, Kedair managed not to say that out loud. "Just do it. There's someone in there."

Greenblatt didn't say anything in response to that, which came to Kedair as something of a relief. The Takaran woman slowly moved into the cave. She was about to pull out her tricorder and activate its lamp when she noticed flickering inside. *Someone lit a fire.*

Moving farther in, she saw sconces on the cave wall, holding wooden torches. The flames flickered toward the entryway she'd just used, indicating another entrance on the far side.

Turning a corner, she saw dozens of pieces of paper with sloppy writing on it that she assumed to be the Capellan script, a bucket filled with dye, several dried-out branches from a *jorni* bush, and a male figure lying on his side, his back toward Kedair.

Reaching behind her, she made as if to push the air back. She hoped that Greenblatt was bright enough to realize that that meant to stay where she was. She didn't know much about how Capellans slept, but this person was breathing so lightly that he was probably faking sleep.

Sure enough, the person rolled over with amazing speed. Kedair heard a whistling noise as a *kligat*—a three-bladed circular weapon—flew through the air and impaled itself right in her chest.

Her face spreading into a large grin, she said to her would-be assailant, "Thanks! I've been wanting one of these."

Said assailant had sprung to a kneeling position, but now he had a look of pure shock on his face, as Kedair had not done any of the things the Capellan no doubt expected her to do with a *kligat* buried in her thoracic region—which, primarily, was fall down and die.

"How are you not dead?"

"By still being alive." Kedair grabbed the *kligat* by its center and yanked it out. The impact had still hurt, and pulling it out actually hurt even more, but she didn't show that pain on her face. Placing the weapon in her empty phaser holster, she said, "You must be the *toora Maab*."

"Yes! Yes, I am! And I will show everyone that outsiders are not to be trusted! They lie!"

"I'm sure they do. You're coming with me, friend." Kedair reached for the man, who recoiled.

"I will go nowhere with you, alien filth!"

Kedair brandished the *kligat*. "I'll use this if you want. I guarantee that I'll get a better result than you got from throwing it at me."

The young man considered, and then said, "I will come with you. But the teer will see that my actions were correct!"

Not bloody likely, Kedair thought.

Within an hour, the young man—whose name was Tlaar—had been imprisoned, awaiting the teer's judgment.

The entire time back down the rock, Greenblatt kept going on about Kedair's ability to survive a direct hit from a *kligat*. At first, she had thought it was some kind of armor, right until she saw that Kedair's uniform was ripped open, exposing green flesh that was obviously damaged but healing.

"How do you *do* that?"

"One of the many ways in which I'm not an Orion," was all Kedair was willing to say. After the attitude she'd gotten from Greenblatt, she wasn't of a turn of mind to explain the specifics of Takaran biology and how very difficult—by the standards of most other species in the galaxy—they were to kill, or even hurt, thanks to a lack of localization of vital organs and an ability to regenerate.

After they had left Tlaar to the tender mercies of the Ten Tribes, a voice sounded from Kedair's combadge. *"Helkara to Kedair."*

"Go ahead."

"That sample you examined isn't cabrodine."

Greenblatt said, "That's impossible."

"I'm afraid it's not impossible. The sample on the debris has a changeable molecular structure, and it's been altered to look like cabrodine to most standard scans. Honestly, whoever did this has access to state-of-the-art equipment. I'd heard of research being done into this by the Breen, but I didn't think they'd gotten to the point of perfecting it."

The voice of Captain Dax sounded over the comlink. *"Can you tell what the substance was originally?"*

"Not beyond a doubt, but all indications are that it's nitrilin."

"Damn," Kedair said.

"I don't understand," Greenblatt said. "Instead of one explosive, it's another one. What difference does it make?"

"Cabrodine's fairly common," Kedair said. "Even a Capellan lunatic in a cave could probably get his hands on it. But nitrilin? That only originates from the Oorfar system in the Ferengi Alliance, and it's very expensive to obtain. And, Captain? I located our *toora Maab* terrorist."

"Terrorist, singular?" Dax said.

"Yes. It was a young man named Tlaar. He's the lunatic in the cave I just mentioned. There just isn't any way he has the know-how to make nitrilin look like cabrodine. He might have set the explosives, but it's impossible to believe that he obtained them without significant help. Also, the mining operation gets supplies from a Ferengi service, and the person who did the supply run was different than usual."

"Was it a male or a female Ferengi?" Dax asked.

Greenblatt said, "The latest one? A woman. I never got her name. It was the first time we got a woman, actually."

There was a pause before Dax said, *"Good work, Lieutenant. Ms. Greenblatt, we'll be beaming down your equipment shortly."*

"That's it?" Greenblatt sounded confused. "I don't understand. What's changed?"

Kedair looked down at Greenblatt. "Your mine was a target, Ms. Greenblatt, one of many. You might want to tighten security on this place."

"That's already happened, and will continue. We'll have topaline within a couple of weeks."

"Glad to hear it," Dax said. *"Let's leave Ms. Greenblatt to her work, Lieutenant."*

"Aye, Captain." Kedair looked at Greenblatt and tried to sound pleasant. "Thanks for your help."

Holding up a pudgy hand, Greenblatt said, "Hold it, Lieutenant. I still don't get it—why would somebody off Capella target this mine?"

"To keep us from getting topaline with any speed."

Greenblatt shook her head. "So—what? Eight of my people died for some political bullshit?"

"Something like that," Kedair said. "I'm sorry."

"Yeah, me, too." Greenblatt looked away, then right at Kedair. "Thanks, Lieutenant. And do me a favor?"

"Uh, sure."

"Get the bastards, would you? This is my first job as a supervisor, and it *wasn't* supposed to go like this."

Kedair smiled. "I'll do my best." She tapped her combadge. "One to beam up."

The transporter whisked her back to the *Aventine*. Her last view of Capella IV was a very angry-looking Rebecca Greenblatt.

Arrest report filed by Sergeant Hildegard Silverman, Johnson City Police Department, Cestus III

Torethirala zh'Vres, a.k.a. "Captain Altheria zh'Ranthi," has been arrested on charges of fraud and conspiracy, with other charges possibly to be added later. Zh'Vres was arrested at Explorer Field and taken to JCPD Headquarters; she has refused to speak to authorities and has demanded counsel.

Suspicions were raised when the arresting officer perused a casualty list from the Andorian sector that included Captain Altheria zh'Ranthi, the name and rank given by the commander of the *Kovlessa,* a refugee ship that claimed to have come to Cestus III after being refused by Zalda. Shortly thereafter, a routine DNA scan of "zh'Ranthi's" blood (taken while she received medical treatment at Explorer Field) revealed that her DNA profile had been altered with a drug that was put on the market two years ago, and which JCPD computers were programmed to recognize only six months ago. When JCPD scientists removed the drug from the suspect's blood, it was revealed that "zh'Ranthi" was, in fact, Torethirala zh'Vres. She was listed in the database as being wanted by the Ferengi for fraud, though those charges were recently dropped after the Ferengi authorities were bribed. The source of the bribe remains anonymous, though we are continuing to attempt to learn the identity of zh'Vres's benefactor.

The passengers on the *Kovlessa* are being held at Explorer Field, and may be arrested as well, pending the results of the ongoing investigation.

17

RUNABOUT *SEINE*

Sonek sat in the aft compartment of the *Seine,* picking on his banjo.

So what, exactly, are you trying to prove? he asked himself. *The Palais just asked you to talk to Donatra. You talked to Donatra. There is absolutely no reason why you shouldn't have gone home. Okay, so talking to Molmaan probably helped, but why are you dragging this runabout and these two young officers all over half the galaxy?*

He heard his grandfather's voice in his head in response: *You want to prove that you're still useful.*

The problem was, of course, that he already *did* prove that. Not only did he do what was asked, he did a little extra besides. Wasn't that enough?

But then there's another problem: what if I'm right?

It was looking increasingly likely that this Ferengi woman was trying to destabilize, or at least stall, the rebuilding.

Of course, Captain Dax's question is still nagging. Why is she doing this?

He started playing a song called *"Miloraz Silbonni,"* a Talarian song that was written for a *sontra,* a pipe instrument that was played via foot pedals. Sonek had always loved the song, and his daughter Sara had created a banjo arrangement for it as part of a birthday present for him several years back. Sonek still remembered the look on the face of the Talarian ambassador when he'd played it for him at a conference on Pacifica—

Sara.

Suddenly it hit him. Days ago, when he saw the report on the medical problems with the refugees on P'Jem, he knew there was something familiar, and thinking of his daughter finally made it click: his son, Ayib, was part of the *Médecins Sans Frontières* delegation sent to P'Jem.

Setting the banjo down, he said, "Computer, call up all Starfleet reports and news stories regarding P'Jem since the end of the Borg invasion—access code Pran alpha five nine four two green."

He scrolled through the various reports, again finding the one by Admiral McCoy. Sure enough, the doctor who solved the *shevrak* outbreak was Dr. Ayib Yee Pran.

Should've realized he was doing something useful.

The door to the fore compartment slid open, and Altoss came in. "Professor, we're coming out of warp. We'll be at Maxia Zeta IV soon."

"Thanks, Ensign."

"You okay, Professor?"

Sonek looked up at the Efrosian, and realized that he spoke those two words in as subdued a voice as he'd used in all the time since he left Mars. "I'm just sitting here reading up on what my son's been doing." He quickly told her about what he did on P'Jem.

"We're a little far from P'Jem," Altoss said when he was done, "but I think I can punch through a signal if you want to contact him."

"Thanks, Ensign," Sonek said, "that's very kind of you, but—well, I don't think that'd be the greatest idea, really."

"Why not?"

Taking a deep breath, Sonek said, "Because Ayib and I haven't spoken a word to each other in about seven years."

Altoss smiled. "I hate to repeat myself but, why not?"

"There isn't really a good reason. Whole lotta bad ones, but not a single good one. We just—we just don't get along. You put us in a room together, and I swear to you, Ensign, we wouldn't agree that space was black. It's been like this since he was a little kid. I don't know why, but that's just the way it's been. Drives my wife crazy, as you might imagine, and my daughter isn't too thrilled about it, either. But every time the two of us try to reconcile, it lasts for maybe a day or two, and then we start screaming at each other." He shook his head. "Nothing to be done about it."

"Uh, Professor?" Altoss was speaking tentatively. "I—I don't want to overstep, but—"

Sonek grinned. "You're my protector, Ensign. I don't think there's much that qualifies as overstepping as far as you're concerned."

"You're being an idiot."

That brought Sonek up short. "Okay."

"In the past week, you've talked an armed centurion into disobeying his orders, you've talked an empress into offering a deal to a person she despises, and you talked a Zaldan into not being an ass. You're telling me you can't convince your own offspring to get along with you?"

"Apparently not," Sonek said with a sigh. "The technical term for that is irony. We've tried talking to each other. *Believe* me, we've tried. But so far nothing's worked."

A beeping noise was followed by Trabka's voice over the speakers. *"Professor, we're in hailing range of the* Musgrave. *They're in a high orbit."*

"Probably trying to avoid the farantine," Altoss said.

Nodding, Sonek cleared the computer screen. "We'll be right in, Lieutenant."

Sonek and Altoss went into the forward compartment as Trabka said, "Hailing the *Musgrave* now." There was the sound of a channel being opened, followed by Trabka's hail: "This is the Runabout *Seine* with an emissary from Earth, calling the *Musgrave*."

The screen lit up a moment later, showing two humans sitting at a table in what looked like a typical starship observation lounge. One human had short, well-combed dark hair and no obvious neck, with a red collar containing four pips. The other had an unruly mop of brown hair, with two solid pips and one hollow pip on his gold collar.

"This is interesting—we were about to call Earth," the captain said. *"I'm Manolet Dayrit, captain of the* Musgrave. *This is my first officer, Bojan Hadžić."*

"Captain, Commander, my name's Sonek Pran. I'm here on behalf of the Palais de la Concorde, and we're here to let you know that we think we know how and why the farantine was placed on Maxia Zeta IV."

"If you're referring to the Ferengi woman Sekki, we're already on it," Dayrit said with what Sonek thought to be an amused smile. *"That's why we were going to call Earth. We were going to contact S.C.E. headquarters and see if it would be possible to track down this Sekki woman."*

"Oh." Sonek just stared at the screen for a second. Then he admonished himself. *These people are smart. Give them a little credit for figuring out what you figured out.* "Well, Captain, I'm afraid this needs to go a little bit higher up the food chain than the Tucker Building on Earth. This is much bigger than someone trying to sabotage the dilithium mining down there."

Hadžić spoke then. *"That's not enough?"*

Sonek shook his head. "If you don't mind my asking, I'm curious to know how you folks figured it all out."

"It was not that difficult," Hadžić said. *"Jira, our computer expert, did a search, and she found the arrest record in question. That did not guarantee that she was the person responsible, but it seemed likely—and even if she was not, the report mentioned a containment unit, and that would be extremely useful to us just at the moment."*

"I don't think she'd be inclined to give you any help, Commander. I'm fairly certain this is a small part of a much larger plan."

"Uh, Professor?"

Sonek looked down at Trabka, who suddenly looked very nervous. Several bad thoughts went through Sonek's head, not least being a hostile ship in Sekki's employ showing up. "What is it, Ensign?"

"We're being hailed by the *Aventine*."

Now her nerves made sense. "Don't worry, Lieutenant. I'll take the brunt of this one."

"What's going on here, Mr. Pran?" Dayrit asked.

"The *Seine*'s assigned to the *Aventine,* Captain," Sonek said. "Probably just checking in and wondering why we aren't at Zalda."

"And that would be?"

"Well, honestly," Sonek said a little sheepishly, "it was to warn you folks about Sekki."

"Then I suggest you take that call, Mr. Pran," Dayrit said rather sternly.

"Yeah. Put it on through, Lieutenant, and tie the *Musgrave* in. Might as well all talk together."

The screen switched from a single view of the *Musgrave* observation lounge to a split screen, the *Musgrave* on the left, the *Aventine* bridge, centered on Captain Dax, on the right.

To say Dax's aspect was that of a very angry person would be grossly understated. She was generally pleasant, small and unassuming, but she had a fire in her that probably came from three centuries of experience with not suffering fools gladly. *And I'm doing a fine job of being foolish right present.*

"Professor, would you mind explaining to me what you're doing at Maxia Zeta IV instead of Capella?"

Dayrit grinned. *"I thought you were supposed to be at Zalda. I'm Captain Manolet Dayrit of the* Musgrave*—you must be Captain Dax. It's an honor to meet you, ma'am."*

Caught momentarily off guard by this additional participant in the conversation, Dax quickly said, *"Uh, thank you, Captain. And yes, the* Seine *was supposed to be at Zalda—and then rendezvous with the* Aventine *at Capella. So you can imagine how surprised I was to check the* Seine*'s transponder and learn that it was in the Maxia Zeta system."*

"It's entirely on me, Captain. Lieutenant Trabka and Ensign Altoss were—"

"Were derelict in their duty. I'll deal with them later, Professor, but for now, I'm directing most of my ire at you. The conditions under which I allowed you use of the runabout were made quite clear, I thought."

"They were, and I'm truly sorry, Captain, but—"

Holding up a hand, Dax said, *"No, no, there's no 'but' at the end of that. The sentence ends with 'I'm truly sorry.' You're a civilian, Professor, and right now I'm sorely tempted to have Captain Dayrit's security chief put you under arrest for theft of Starfleet property."*

"And I freely admit that you'd be within your rights to do that," Sonek said. "If you do, I'll go to the *Musgrave* brig and subject myself to whatever punishment is appropriate. Really, Captain, I am sorry. It's just—" He hesitated, wondering if he should be this frank on an open channel, then deciding, *what the hell.* "This is my first time in the field in a very long time. I guess I just let myself get a little carried away."

There was a long, very uncomfortable pause before Dax finally spoke. *"We'll revisit arresting you later. And that is* not *me trying to save face, Professor. We* will *be discussing this at length. However, right now I think we're facing something of a crisis. It looks like the explosion at the refinery on Capella wasn't done by anyone on-planet."*

Hadžić said, *"I thought that was the old mine that blew up?"*

"No," Sonek said, "it was the brand-new refinery. Are you saying there's been a new investigation?"

"I had Lieutenant Kedair look into it as a condition of our delivering the new equipment to Janus."

Sonek winced. Dax, he knew, only did that because she was starting to believe Sonek's own hypothesis, so it made his flaunting of her authority even worse. *I owe that woman a lot more than an apology.*

"The best part?" Dax continued. *"They get supplies from a Ferengi cargo carrier, and the most recent carrier captain was a woman—the first woman to bring the delivery. Not only that, but it wasn't cabrodine that caused the explosion; it was nitrilin altered to look like cabrodine in a standard scan."*

"Do you have those, Captain?" Hadžić asked eagerly. *"Right now, we have a team on one of our shuttlecraft studying the artificial farantine, and anything you can give us might be of assistance."*

"Of course," Dax said. She instructed Helkara to send over the data.

"Captain," Sonek said slowly, "I was just saying to Captain Dayrit here that we need to bring this to a higher authority. With your permission, I'd like to get in touch with the Palais, fill them in on all this."

"The Palais?" Dayrit said. *"How big is this, exactly?"*

"That's what we're all trying very hard to figure out," Sonek said.

"So," Dax said sourly, *"now you're asking permission?"*

"Captain—"

Again holding up a hand, Dax said, *"Forget it. I'll put the call through."*

"Use code nine eight seven alpha blue six—that'll put you right on through to the chief of staff's office."

While they waited, Sonek tried very hard to ignore the nasty look that Altoss was giving him. He recalled what Trabka had said, seemingly jokingly, about how she would blame Sonek if Dax or Bowers asked why they diverted, and now it seemed that that wasn't going to be enough. *I owe a bunch of apologies. . . .*

Eventually a third image appeared on the screen, taking up most of the screen, with Dax and the *Aventine,* and Dayrit and Hadžić both inset in the lower right and left corners, respectively. That image was of the chief of staff's office, with Esperanza sitting at her desk and the massive, imposing form of Fleet Admiral Akaar in her guest chair.

Sonek quickly did the introductions. "Esperanza Piñiero, chief of staff, I've got Captain Dayrit and Lieutenant Commander Bojan Hadžić of the *Musgrave* in orbit of Maxia Zeta IV, plus also Captain Dax, who's in orbit of Capella IV."

"I assume you have news," Esperanza said dryly.

Quickly, Dax filled in the chief of staff and the admiral regarding Kedair's investigation, and Hadžić did likewise for what they'd discovered on Maxia Zeta IV. Sonek then asked, "Have you heard from Councillor Molmaan?"

Esperanza nodded. *"He addressed the Council via subspace while en route back to Earth."*

"Good," Sonek said.

"One of these days, you're going to have to tell me how you managed to talk him into it."

In a sweet, deadly voice, Dax said, *"I've found, Ms. Piñiero, that Professor Pran has an uncanny ability to talk people into doing things you wouldn't expect them to."*

Next to him, Trabka sank further into the pilot's chair, and Sonek could feel Altoss's eyes boring into the back of his neck.

"Molmaan was actually as conciliatory as he's likely to be, especially after Councillor Djinian testified before the Council regarding an arrest and investigation going on on Cestus III."

That piqued Sonek's interest. "Oh?"

"The person claiming to be Altheria zh'Ranthi, captain of the Kovlessa, *was, in fact, a known criminal named Torethirala zh'Vres. She had altered her appearance and DNA profile to match that of zh'Ranthi. Among other things, the investigation revealed that the evidence was a forgery, and that the* Kovlessa*'s logs had been tampered with to make it seem like they'd been to Zalda."*

"Another setup," Sonek said. "Did the fake captain actually provide any information?"

Esperanza shook her head. *"She's refused to talk since her arrest. The Johnson City Police are looking into her finances, but they're a little overwhelmed right now."*

"Aren't we all?" Dayrit said.

"If she changed her DNA profile, how'd they find out?" Sonek asked.

"Somebody happened to notice a list of casualties from the Andorian sector that had zh'Ranthi's name on it."

"Yeah, that'll do it." Sonek sighed. "This is starting to come together."

"Maybe," Dax said. *"Right now, it's all circumstantial. And there's still one big question that needs to be answered: why?"*

Dayrit asked, *"Why what, Captain?"*

"Why is this Sekki woman—assuming that she really is the one responsible for the farantine and the explosion and the Breen weapons the Kinshaya are using and for the Kovlessa*—doing all this?"*

"That is an excellent question," Akaar said.

"Seems to me," Sonek said, "that the obvious thing to do next is find this Sekki woman."

"In fact," Dayrit said, *"we were about to attempt that. Even if she isn't responsible, she might be able to help us."*

Sonek shook his head. "Like I said, Captain, that isn't very likely. Captain Dax asked a good question, and I think the obvious answer is that someone hired her to do all this. If that is the case, she's about as likely to tell us who her employer is as a *sehlat* is to speak Old High Bajoran."

"It is also academic," Akaar said, *"if we cannot find her in the first place. It is a very large galaxy, and many people are not where they are supposed to be."*

Suddenly, Dax smiled. *"Sonek, you said that Sekki outbid Ambassador Derro in making the deal with the Breen, right?"*

Heartened by the fact that she was being familiar once more, Sonek said, "Yes, I did."

The smile widened. *"In that case, we should have no trouble finding her. Just ask the person who lost out to her on a lucrative contract."*

Sonek couldn't help but laugh at that. "Now why didn't I think of that?"

"Fine," Esperanza said, *"I'll put you in touch with Ambassador Derro."*

"Thanks very much, Ms. Piñiero."

"Captain Dayrit," Akaar said, *"how fare your attempts to work around the farantine?"*

With a sigh, Dayrit replied, *"Slowly, I'm afraid, Admiral. But I have faith in Commander Hadžić's team. They haven't let me down yet."*

Dax added, *"The Janus people seem to think they'll have the mine up and running in a week's time, Admiral."*

"You sound unconvinced." Akaar's words echoed Sonek's thoughts.

"The impression I got from the supervisor is that she's trying a little too hard—an impression that my security chief agrees with."

"Let's hope you're wrong," Esperanza said. *"That topaline mining needs to start yesterday. I'll have Zachary track down the ambassador and tell you how to reach him. Piñiero out."*

The chief of staff's office disappeared from the screen, returning to the double-image of the *Musgrave* and *Aventine*.

"That was a first for me," Dayrit said.

Hadžić added, *"For me as well."*

Dax shrugged. *"They're just people doing a job like the rest of us."*

Sonek chuckled. *Leave it to the one with the three-hundred-year-old slug in her belly to take the philosophical view.* "Now all we have to do is wait to hear from Zachary."

"We'll leave you to that," Dayrit said. *"We have a mine of our own to save.* Musgrave *out."*

Now the image returned to just Dax. *"I wasn't kidding about revisiting this conversation later, Sonek. Lieutenant Trabka?"*

"Yes, Captain?" Trabka said in a small voice.

"Hold station at Maxia Zeta for now. Until we know where Sekki is, there's not much sense in either of our ships moving. We'll set a course of action once we've tracked her down."

"Aye, Captain."

"Aventine out."

Dax's face disappeared from the screen.

"I'm gonna get transferred off," Trabka said, "and I'll *never* get to fly slipstream. They'll put me on the damn Jovian run after this."

Altoss was still staring angrily at Sonek. "Professor, I deferred to Lieutenant Trabka—which was obviously a mistake." That last was said while transferring her angry stare to the pilot. "I'm sorry I did that. There was *no* reason to come here, and I should have insisted that we go to Capella IV." She shook her head. "When we report back to the *Aventine,* I want off your detail."

"I don't really think that'll be all that much of an issue, Ensign. By the time you're back on the *Aventine,* I'll likely be long gone. I can't imagine Captain Dax is going to want me back on board in any case."

Shaking her head, Altoss said, "I don't blame her. Excuse me." She strode to the aft compartment.

Trabka looked up at Sonek. "She's right, you know. I shouldn't have agreed."

Sonek let out a long breath. "No, you shouldn't have. But I was all hell-bent on figuring this whole thing out, and I knew that you resented being sent on a milk run—I figured I could play on that a little bit and get you to go along with me. I'm sorry about that, Lieutenant, really."

"Ah, it's okay. It was my fault. I'm the ranking officer, like Altoss said, and I should've been more responsible. It's done."

"Yeah." Sonek felt the need to pluck on the banjo, but somehow he didn't think it would be a good idea to go aft and face Altoss again.

So he sat down in one of the passenger seats and started thinking about what he would ask Ambassador Derro. Better that than to think about how he'd screwed up.

Log entry by Captain Janna Demitrijian, commanding officer, *U.S.S. Sugihara*, Stardate 58307.7

It is with a heavy heart that I must report the deaths of four members of my crew. Engineering crewpersons Jomat and Linnea Palmer, Transporter Chief Rupi Yee, and Ensign Letitia Shawan were among the casualties when a building collapsed in the city of Lejico here on Ardana, following an earthquake.

Based on the preliminary reports made by local authorities—and confirmed by my security chief's scans of the area—the Borg attack apparently led to some tectonic instability in the crust under Lejico, as well as its surrounding towns and villages. The continent hasn't suffered earthquakes of any kind in over a thousand years; today's quake reached 9.5 on the Richter scale. The building itself had also been hit during the firefight between the Borg cube and the *Verithrax,* and its foundation was already weakened. It was targeted to be repaired next week.

Ensign Shawan, Chief Yee, Jomat, and Palmer were having lunch across the street from the building when the quake struck. In addition to my four crew members, two hundred and three Ardanans were killed.

All four have done superlative work during this mission to Ardana. Shawan was in charge of several of Commander Barbanti's engineering repair teams, on which both Jomat and Palmer served. As for Chief Yee, she was able to restore Ardana's unique transporter system, which had been destroyed by the Borg. They will receive posthumous commendations, though that will be small comfort to their families—or to me.

It's not enough that we lost so much to the Borg. The casualty lists we've received keep getting longer, not just from bodies that have at last been identified from attack sites, but because the aftermath of this invasion threatens to claim its share of lives as well.

18

KRIOS

"The cloak is working to expected parameters, General."

Those words were music to Klag's ears. Cloaking technology was in a constant state of war with sensors. One side develops a cloak that cannot be detected, so the other side develops sensors that could penetrate it. The most recent victor for the sensor side was the Dominion, who had developed antiproton scans that could detect cloaked ships.

The Science Institute had been working for many turns to try to overcome the antiproton problem, and they finally appeared to have solved the issue shortly before the Borg invasion.

Implementation had to wait, as the institute was located on Mempa V. Everyone had been forced to evacuate, and while they were able to take all their computer files with them, the physical equipment and machinery had to remain behind.

A new institute was quickly set up on Ty'Gokor, the

Empire's temporary capital after the bombardment of Qo'noS, and the staff set to work re-creating that which had been destroyed.

The Fifth Fleet was given the honor of being the first to have the new cloaks installed, a privilege Klag had been able to obtain because the head of the institute was a former member of his crew, Kurak, daughter of Haleka. During her time as an officer in the Defense Force, Kurak had been the *Gorkon*'s chief engineer; after she resigned, the institute snatched her up. Kurak had been the one who designed Chancellor Gowron's flagship, the *Negh'Var,* and she had been the one to develop countermeasures against the Dominion's cloak-defeating scans.

From the operations console behind his chair, Lieutenant B'Olgana continued her report. "We're picking up several Kinshaya ships, all of which are making constant antiproton scans."

Next to Klag, Commander Laneth said, "The Kinshaya have certainly been making friends."

Klag nodded. First Breen weapons and Romulan shields, now antiproton scans. It was possible that the Kinshaya developed the latter on their own, but it wasn't consistent with the way their technology had developed, and the Kinshaya had never been ones to concern themselves with any part of the galaxy beyond their immediate border.

Of course, that was before they conquered the Kreel.

Laneth then turned to look behind her. "Number of enemy vessels, Lieutenant?"

B'Olgana peered at her console. "Six, Commander."

Klag tugged at his beard. "They have reinforced their

position, but still have fewer ships than they used to invade. Any indication that we have been detected?"

"Their search pattern hasn't changed—there's no indication that they've seen us."

"Formation *wej,* Lieutenant," Klag said.

"Transmitting to fleet on secure channel," B'Olgana replied. That formation had the *Gorkon* and the *Kolvad* approaching the planet from opposite directions, with Huss's strike ships remaining in reserve—two hovering over the north pole, one over the south pole, both blind to sensors even while decloaked.

"Captain B'Eruk has received transmission, and is changing course." After a pause, B'Olgana added, "As has Captain Huss."

"Good." Klag had been concerned that Huss would object to a strategy that would delay her entry into battle. But this way the Kinshaya would be overconfident, thinking only two ships were being sent to take back the planet.

Not that five ships is much of an improvement, he thought bitterly.

"Arm all weapons, prepare to decloak and fire as soon as we are in position."

The gunner, *Bekk* Lojar, said, "Arming weapons."

Gripping the arm of his chair, Klag peered at the forward viewscreen, which showed a tactical image displaying the Klingon ships moving as if to the points of a compass. "North" were the *Gowchok* and the *Chi'dor,* heading toward Krios's north pole. "South" was the *Haproq,* the third of Huss's birds-of-prey. The *Kolvad* moved "west," going the long way around Krios, with the *Gorkon* moving directly into orbit "east."

"Reading multiple Kinshaya and Kreel life signs on the surface," B'Olgana said. "It is an occupying force. However, I am also reading isolated pockets of disruptor fire."

"Excellent," Laneth said with a grin. "That means their hold is already weakening. Let us loosen their grip further."

The pilot looked up from his console. "We are in position."

"Wait for it," Klag said, holding up a hand.

Several seconds passed. Klag could feel the tension on the bridge, but he felt quite calm. *Soon we will have another great victory for the Empire to add to our record of battle.* In more than five turns he had led the *Gorkon* to many victories, and he was looking forward to the latest.

Finally, B'Olgana spoke. "*Kolvad* reports they are in position, General."

"Proceed with attack."

The lights on the bridge brightened, indicating that the cloak was dropped. The *Gorkon* had multiple disruptor cannons and quantum torpedo launchers, and they all fired the second the cloak dropped. Lojar had calculated a most efficient firing solution, as three of the six Kinshaya vessels were destroyed almost immediately by the *Gorkon,* with another eliminated by the *Kolvad.*

Victory will soon be ours.

The ears of Bishop Uerba, one of the ship commanders of the Tenth Holy Kinshaya Attack Fleet, flattened in anger as he saw two-thirds of Archbishop Yklem's fleet—including the archbishop's flagship—eliminated by two demon vessels that had not been detected.

His wings flaring, Uerba faced his weapons master,

Deacon Anilom. "Open fire on the demons immediately!"

" *'Aya,* my Lord, it will be done," the deacon said quickly, his plain wings also flaring as his forelegs manipulated the console.

Turning to his first mate, Vicar Seguh, Uerba asked, "What happened? How were the demons not detected?"

" *'Aya,* my Lord, I do not know. We were scanning continuously with the cloaking detection system. We should have seen them coming."

His ears flattening, even as his wings flared further, Uerba said, "Continuous fire!"

Again, Anilom said, " *'Aya,* my Lord, it will be done." After a moment: " *'Aya.* Shields of the smaller demon vessel are reduced considerably."

Seguh approached Uerba and spoke in a soft voice. " *'Aya,* my Lord, we could summon the reinforcements."

Uerba bared his teeth at his first mate, and Seguh backed away. Bending his knees, the vicar quickly said, " *'Aya,* my Lord, truly I meant no disrespect, but the demons have killed many Devout, including the archbishop. They must be avenged."

"And we shall avenge them," Uerba said quietly.

Deacon Rendrag, who had achieved the position of chief scientist despite being of the lower classes, then spoke out of turn. " *'Aya,* my Lord, I have identified the demon ships."

Seguh, no doubt smarting from Uerba's displeasure at his offensive suggestion, bared his teeth at the deacon. "What does it matter? They are demons, and they must be destroyed."

" *'Aya,* Vicar, I am sorry, but it *does* matter. The larger ship—it is the one named *Gorkon.*"

Uerba turned to stare hungrily at the holographic display at the center of the flight deck. "The *kro-vak.* The Devout shall be avenged this day!" Turning to one of the Kreel slaves, he said, "Contact the reinforcements!"

The Kreel knew better than to say anything—Kreel who spoke didn't live very long—but simply carried out the order.

" *'Aya,* my Lord?" Seguh sounded confused.

"I have every faith in the Devout's ability to exact revenge on ordinary demons—but this is the *kro-vak.* We must guarantee his destruction!"

Anilom's ears flattened. " *'Aya,* my Lord, the *kro-vak* continues to resist our weaponry. However, the smaller ship's shields are almost gone."

Having returned to his console, Seguh looked down at it and then reported. " *'Aya,* my Lord, the reinforcements will arrive in three units."

The bishop stared at the display, which showed the smaller ship—Rendrag had apparently identified it, too, as the display labelled it *Kolvad*—with very little of its shielding left. He almost didn't care about that other ship, with the destroyer of worlds right there.

But the *Gorkon* remained all but undamaged, and they were inflicting their own damage on the two remaining vessels of the Devout.

Finally, he looked at Anilom. " *'Aya*. Let the *kro-vak* see his fellow demon destroyed before we eliminate him."

As Uerba watched, weapons fire leapt from his vessel, striking the demon ship and destroying it in blessed fire that was consumed by the vacuum of space. Bishop Uerba had not been part of the original fleet that took Krios from the demons. The two ships that remained of that fleet had landed on the planet, and their Devout and slaves were used as ground troops on the surface. Even now, Archbishop Elyk was pacifying the forces and dealing with the demons' rebellion on Krios.

Archbishop Yklem's fleet had been sent in to take over the orbital domination of Krios, and to defend against the demons' attempts to reclaim the world.

" *'Aya!"* Anilom cried.

But even as the weapons master spoke, Uerba saw what had happened on the display in the center of the flight deck. Three more demon ships had emerged from the polar regions of Krios and were firing.

"How soon until reinforcements arrive?" Seguh asked.

Rendrag's wings sagged. " *'Aya.* One more unit."

" *'Aya.* The *kro-vak* has taken Bishop Rensar's ship in tow," Anilom said.

His wings flaring, Uerba cried, "Destroy the *kro-vak!* Now!"

Seguh bared his teeth in anger. " *'Aya,* my Lord, the three new demon ships are hemming us in."

Muttering a damnation, Uerba then said, "Hold them off until the reinforcements arrive."

" *'Aya,* my Lord, it will be done." Anilom continued to fire his weapons.

Then the six reinforcement vessels decloaked. The wings of all the Devout on the flight deck flared with respect.

At last, Uerba thought, *the homeworld shall be avenged.*

Klag rose to his feet in shock as he saw the six ships decloak in orbit of Krios.

It was not enough that the *khest'n* Kinshaya had destroyed the *Kolvad.* B'Eruk had been one of the finest gunners who ever served under him, and she had commanded the *Kolvad* with honor for months before Klag had brought her into his fleet.

Now half a dozen new ships had entered the fray. But that was not what had shocked him. No, it was the fact that these were not Kinshaya ships.

Two were Breen. Two were Gorn. And two were Tzenkethi. And they decloaked *together*.

B'Olgana angrily said, "Four vessels are targeting their weapons on us, General. The Tzenkethi are targeting Captain Huss's ships."

Turning to Lojar, Laneth said, "Make *sure* that Kinshaya ship is brought aboard. As soon as it's secured, put Commander Lokor in charge of the prisoners."

Klag continued to watch the viewer. The *Gorkon* was now taking fire from several vessels at once. The two Tzenkethi ships were being harried by the *Gowchok, Chi'dor,* and *Haproq.* Obviously the Gorn, Tzenkethi, and Breen were here to aid the Kinshaya in their invasion of the Empire.

The general whirled to face his bridge. "Continuous fire on the Kinshaya with torpedoes. Use cannons on the others. And send a priority message to Ty'Gokor. It seems that many nations have declared war on us."

B'Olgana looked down at her console. "Message away—and the Kinshaya vessel is in the shuttlebay."

Laneth looked at the pilot. "Set course 197 mark 4."

Klag nodded his approval. That would give the *Gorkon* some distance and more maneuvering room. By contrast, he saw that Huss was taking her strike ships deeper into Krios's atmosphere. None of the enemy ships were designed for atmospheric entry.

But then one of the Breen ships fired on the *Gowchok*

and destroyed it. Shrapnel from the explosive sent the *Chi'dor* off course, and it crashed into the *Haproq*. Klag howled in outrage—Huss was one of the finest captains in the Defense Force, and in the space of mere moments, she was gone.

Do well in Sto-Vo-Kor, Klag thought to both Huss and B'Eruk. *It seems I may be joining you shortly.*

"We have destroyed both Gorn ships and one Tzenkethi," Lojar said. "However, shields are down to forty percent! The remaining Kinshaya vessel is depowered."

"They may be depowered, but they are hailing us!" B'Olgana sounded surprised.

"We do not need to hear the words of Kinshaya filth," Laneth said dismissively.

Klag, though, was curious. "On-screen, Lieutenant."

The fur-covered face and tall ears of a Kinshaya was obscured by blood and burns. Klag was especially entertained to see that this particular Kinshaya's wings were damaged. " 'Aya, *demons. I am . . . I am Bishop Uerba. I may die . . . die this day, but . . . but I die knowing we destroyed you,* kro-vak."

"I am still here, Bishop. Which is more than can be said for you. Fire!"

Lojar obeyed Klag's order, and Uerba's face disappeared from the screen a second after he screamed, the flight deck of his spherical vessel disintegrating around him.

Laneth got to her feet and stood next to Klag. "General, our supply of torpedoes is almost depleted. We are still only one ship against three. We may need to retreat, if for no other reason than to make sure that Command learns of this new alliance."

Much as he hated to admit it, Klag knew the commander was right. He could not liberate Krios with only one ship, and not only Command but the High Council needed to know about these vessels that came to the Kinshaya's defense—while cloaked, no less. *"QI'yaH,"* he muttered.

"General!"

Klag turned around to see B'Olgana smiling.

"Three Defense Force vessels decloaking!"

Turning back to the screen, Klag saw three shimmers that coalesced into a trio of battle cruisers—two *Vor'cha* class and one *K'Vort* class.

Throwing his head back and laughing, Klag regretted his cowardice. He should have known that his fleet wouldn't let him down.

"Captain Leskit is hailing us," B'Olgana added.

"You didn't really think we'd let you get massacred, did you, General?"

"Leskit, you old razorbeast—when the High Council condemns you to death for insubordination, I promise to commend you to *Sto-Vo-Kor* myself."

"What more could a warrior possibly ask, General? But no orders were disobeyed . . . entirely."

Toq's voice then sounded over the speaker. *"We will explain after we have sent these invaders to* Gre'thor, *General."*

The *Hopliq,* the *Roval,* and the *Kreltek* all moved into formation alongside the *Gorkon,* their fully charged disruptor cannons and fully loaded torpedo bays emptying out at the three remaining ships. What had looked to be a need for retreat suddenly became a rout. Within minutes, the *Kreltek* had destroyed one of the Breen ships, with the *Hopliq* destroying the other. The *Roval* did considerable damage to the remaining Tzenkethi vessel before they cloaked and warped away.

From the bridge of the *Roval,* Captain K'Nir asked, *"Shall I pursue, General?"*

Klag considered it. "No," he finally said. "Let them report back to their superiors that the Fifth Fleet took Krios back!"

A cheer went up all across the bridge. Laneth started singing: *"Qoy qeylIs puqloD. Qoy puqbe'pu'."*

Lojar and the pilot joined her on the next line: *"yoH-bogh matlhbogh je SuvwI'."*

With the third line, virtually the entire bridge—as well as the bridges of the other three ships—joined in:

nI'be' yInmaj 'ach wovqu'.
batlh maHeghbej 'ej yo' qIjDaq
vavpu'ma' DImuv.

As the singing was going on, Klag walked to B'Olgana's station and spoke under the din to the operations officer. "Have *QaS DevwI'* Wol assemble troops. They will deal with the Kinshaya ground forces."

"Yes, General."

As B'Olgana followed his order, Klag then joined in with the rest of the song.

pa' reH maSuvtaHqu'.
mamevQo'. maSuvtaH. ma'ov.

Even before the last word was sung, the bridge erupted in loud cheers and head-butts all around.

"It is my hope," Klag said as the celebrations died

down, "that the Mempa convoy will not suffer for your absence, Captains."

"They will not," K'Nir said. *"When we arrived at Ty'Gokor's Oort cloud, there were two Defense Force ships in addition to the convoy: the* Ditagh *and the* Sturka. *Captains Vikagh and K'Draq said they would take over the convoy. We left the birds-of-prey to support them, and came to aid you."*

Again, Klag threw his head back and laughed. Like the *Gorkon,* the *Ditagh* and *Sturka* were Chancellor-class vessels, among the finest in the Defense Force. Vikagh and K'Draq were both honorable warriors, and Klag made a mental note to drown them both in bloodwine the next time he saw them.

Laneth said, "General, *QaS DevwI'* Wol is ready to start beaming down troops. With your permission . . ."

Klag nodded, and Laneth departed to see the ground troops off. As the door rumbled shut behind the commander, Klag said, "Lieutenant B'Olgana."

"Sir!"

"Send a message to Ty'Gokor. Inform Chancellor Martok that his son has been avenged!"

"Gladly, sir." B'Olgana was grinning as she obeyed the order.

"If Wol is handling the surface," Leskit said, *"it should be under control within an hour."*

"If that long," Klag said with a smile. "I believe this calls for a celebration, Captains. The wardroom in half an hour—and we will drink to our fallen comrades who have joined the Black Fleet this day!"

Transcript of interrogation by Commander Lokor, head of security, *I.K.S. Gorkon*, of Vicar Errot of the Kinshaya, the 180th day of the Year of Kahless 1007

ERROT: *'Aya,* demon, I will reveal nothing to you.

LOKOR: I've no doubt that you think that, Kinshaya. And in truth there is very little I would need to hear from you, under normal circumstances. Our people have been at war for longer than either of us have been alive.

ERROT: It will always be so, until such time as the demonic infestation is eradicated.

LOKOR: So you insist. And yet, now you have help.

ERROT: We need no help to kill demons, nor to destroy the *kro-vak.*

LOKOR: Ah yes, your nickname for General Klag.

ERROT: General? Typical demon—you reward those who attempt genocide. He will suffer the Torments for what he did to our holy place.

LOKOR: And what torments will you suffer, Vicar?

ERROT: I am of the Devout. I will suffer no Torments, but be rewarded with warmth and joy at the end of my days.

LOKOR: Hardly. Does not your holy writ say that none of the Devout shall sully themselves by associating with heretics?

ERROT: What do you know of our holy writ, demon?

LOKOR: I know that those words I spoke are not what one might call compatible with utilizing Breen disruptors or Romulan shields—not to mention allying yourselves with the Gorn, Tzenkethi, and Breen. Are they not all heretics as well?

ERROT: Of course.

LOKOR: Yet you fight alongside them. You violate your tenets.

ERROT: *'Aya,* demon, you know *nothing.* Like all demons, you twist the holy writ to serve your own purposes, but you reveal your ignorance.

LOKOR: Do I?

ERROT: Holy writ also states that the Devout may forgive the heretics and be at peace with them if it be for the greater good.

LOKOR: Interesting. The text that I've read uses the word *altash.* I was under the impression that that term did not mean "be at peace," but rather "leave alone."

ERROT: You know nothing of the tongue of the Devout, and to hear it from your filthy mouth disgusts me, demon!

LOKOR: I am sure that it does. And I have proven you wrong.

ERROT: What do you mean?

LOKOR: When I came into this room, you said you would reveal nothing. Instead, you have revealed quite a bit. I believe you mentioned a reward at the end of your days?

ERROT: Yes.

LOKOR: It's time you were on your way then. [Sound of disruptor fire.]

19

RUNABOUT *SEINE*

"Well, Professor, you want the good news or the bad news?"

Sonek didn't like the sound of that. He stared up at Lieutenant Trabka, who had just entered the aft compartment, interrupting Sonek picking at his banjo. He wasn't playing any particular song, just sliding around until he found a note he liked.

When confronted with good news/bad news questions like the one Trabka had just asked, Sonek tended to ask for the good news first, since it would then serve to make the bad news seem not so bad. It didn't always work that way, but he figured he'd go for that. "Good news first, I guess."

"We've received a message from Ambassador Derro."

Setting the banjo down, Sonek got to his feet. "Finally." It had been two days since Esperanza said she'd have the Ferengi ambassador get in touch with them.

Before Sonek could move forward to the door, Trabka

winced. "Uh, you didn't need to get up. See, the bad news is the contents of the message."

Letting out a long sigh as he sat back down, Sonek said, "Which were?"

" 'I have nothing to say to the human Pran.' Those were the ambassador's exact words, actually."

"Huh." Sonek hadn't been expecting that. "Guess he didn't see a picture, or he'd know he was only twenty-five percent right. Any chance of me talking to him anyway?"

Trabka shook her head. "It wasn't a live communication, he just sent that message. I don't think he wants to talk to you."

Thinking about Ensign Altoss, who hadn't said a word to him since they signed off with the Palais two days ago, Sonek said, "There's a good deal of that going around, isn't there?" He sighed. "Better get in touch with the *Aventine,* talk to Captain Dax."

Nodding, Trabka moved back to the fore. Altoss passed her in the doorway, muttered something to the lieutenant, then made a beeline for the replicator without even making eye contact with Sonek.

Deciding to throw caution to the winds, he initiated contact. "Still mad at me, aren't you, Ensign?"

Whirling around and pointing an accusatory finger at Sonek, she said, "Don't. Just—just don't."

Now Sonek was confused. "Don't what?"

"Don't try to make this out to be something trivial. That I'm just a little miffed at you right now, but it will pass. This won't." Turning back around, she spoke to the replicator. "*Fozat* juice, iced." After the drink materialized in the replicator tray, Altoss grabbed it and took a sip before looking back at Sonek. "There's a chain of command for a *reason,* Professor. This runabout is one of the *least* capable of all the ships in Starfleet, and *it* could slice one of Maxia Zeta IV's continents in half. We fly around in ships that could destroy entire planets—that's a *huge* amount of power, and it's so incredibly easy to abuse. That's why we *have* to have a chain of command, because we have to have some way to regulate that."

"Ensign, I'm sorry, truly," Sonek said, meaning it. "I guess I just wanted to do what was right, and I got caught up in it."

"Who cares what *you* thought was right?" Altoss was yelling now. "First of all, you're not even *in* Starfleet. And even if you were, what gives you the right to make that decision? Nobody ever disobeyed an order thinking they were in the *wrong.* But if people just do whatever they want, if they disregard their orders, if they ignore the hierarchy and the chain of command, you know what you get? The Borg. And I think we've all gotten a good idea what happens when *they* run amok."

Before Sonek could even consider formulating a response to that, Trabka's voice came over the speaker. *"Professor, I have the* Aventine."

Without a word, they both moved fore—Altoss no doubt because she had said her piece, Sonek because he found he had nothing to say to Altoss beyond the rather obvious "You're right"—and Sonek saw that Captain Dax's face was on the viewer.

She looked unhappy, which Sonek assumed at first to be because of her continued displeasure with Sonek's commandeering the runabout to go to Maxia Zeta. Then he realized that she looked sad, not angry. "Captain, I'm afraid we have some pretty bad news."

"So do I. Sonek, I'm so sorry, but we just got a message—your wife was killed on Ardana."

For several seconds, Sonek didn't say anything. He couldn't make his mouth move. His heart started beating like a trip-hammer, and he felt sweat break out on his forehead.

"What—what happened?" he said in a hoarse whisper, as his throat had suddenly dried up.

"I'm not sure of the specifics, I'm afraid. We got this fourth-hand—they alerted your grandfather on Mars, and he forwarded it to the Palais, who forwarded it to Starfleet Command, who forwarded it to us. The only thing I know for sure is that she was one of four people who died in some kind of accident."

"An accident?" Rupi had always said that there were no accidents, just things that happened because people weren't careful.

Oh, Prophets, how can she be dead?

"I need to talk to my daughter—and my son, I guess, too."

To Trabka, Dax said, *"Put the professor through to whoever he needs to contact, Lieutenant."*

"Aye, Captain."

I just got a letter from her the other day, she can't possibly be dead.

Sonek looked up at the viewer, only then realizing that somewhere along the line he'd sat down. "Thanks for . . . for passing that on, Captain. As for our bad news—"

Dax held up a hand. *"It can wait."*

"No, it can't," Sonek said firmly, even though a voice in his mind was crying out to run aft and curl up into a ball. "I've got a mission to carry out, and Rupi'll be just as dead whether or not I carry it out. Besides, someone just reminded me about the importance of one's duty." He gave Altoss a sidelong glance. "In any case—it looks like Derro isn't all that interested in having a chat with me. He didn't give a reason, he just said no."

"He did, did he?" Now Dax had a rather enigmatic smile on her face. *"Give me an hour."* The smile fell. *"Once again, Sonek, I speak for the entire crew when I say we're sorry for your loss."*

"Thank you, Captain."

"Aventine *out*."

The screen switched back to Maxia Zeta IV.

Altoss put a hand on Sonek's shoulder. He looked up to see a softness he hadn't seen in the security guard since they first met on the *Aventine*. "I feel your loss, Professor."

Sonek put his hand on top of hers. "Thank you, Ensign."

"Who do you need to contact?" Trabka asked.

"Uh, well, I guess Sara. She's on Troyius."

Trabka nodded. "It'll take a few minutes."

Nodding back, Sonek rose unsteadily to his feet. "I'll be in back."

Moving aft, Sonek went straight for the replicator. All four species that made up his background had wildly varying death rituals, from the Bajoran death chant to a Betazoid memory ceremony. But there was one tradition that his grandmother had always insisted on. It was done when each of his great-grandparents died, as well as several aunts, uncles, and cousins—most recently, a great-uncle, Tolik's brother, who died in the Borg attack on Vulcan.

Approaching the replicator, he said, "Computer, Talisker, eighteen years old, alcoholic."

"This unit cannot produce alcoholic drinks."

Sonek sighed, but wasn't surprised. The chief of staff could reprogram her own replicator how she wanted, but Starfleet runabouts weren't as flexible. "Same drink, then, syntheholic."

A flat-bottomed, rectangular glass materialized with an amber liquid in it. Grabbing it, Sonek held it up to the air. "You will be missed, my love."

Then he drank down the Scotch. It tasted wretched—a proper Talisker 18 was a thing of beauty, but this tasted akin to phaser coolant—but he drank it anyhow. Normally, the last two words weren't part of it, but he was willing to make an exception for Rupi. Had there been anyone else present, a Vulcan salutation would have been added: "I grieve with thee."

He thought back to when he first met Rupi, at a bar on Altair VI. She was a civilian transporter technician on vacation with her boyfriend; he was there for the world's most boring academic conference. In fact, the boyfriend, a Trill named Farin Zak, was with her when they met, and the three of them got along very well. Sonek hadn't had any romantic thoughts toward Rupi—at least in part because she and Farin seemed quite a happy couple—but simply considered her a friend.

They'd stayed in touch for about a year. Rupi and Farin broke up during that time, and she dated a few more people. In fact, Sonek introduced her to one of them, a fellow teacher named Matthew Zavitz.

And then, after she and Matt broke up, Sonek took her out to dinner to console her, and they talked all night, until the restaurant kicked them out because they wanted to close. He took her home, she put "Crossroad Blues" on her music system, and they kissed passionately.

They'd been together ever since.

"Professor, I have your daughter."

He gulped down the rest of the drink—it wasn't meant to be gulped, but he felt better after slugging it down—and then said to Trabka, "Thanks, Lieutenant. I'll take it in here."

Altoss had been hoping that the music would soothe her.

She had requested that the computer play a random selection of works by Satlin Ra-Graveness. Trabka hadn't objected—she'd never heard Satlin's work, and was curious—and Altoss had always found that his music helped her relax.

Not today, however.

On the one hand, she grieved for Professor Pran's loss. While Efrosians were not monogamous, she understood the tendency of many other sentients to form permanent bonds with people. She also knew how difficult it would likely be for the professor's two children, to lose their mother like that. She also felt bad for yelling at Pran the way she did.

On the other hand, she wasn't *that* sorry, mostly because she was right. She probably could have phrased it more diplomatically. Pran wasn't a bad person—far from it—but he *had* made a mistake. Also, she actually liked Pran.

On the third hand (which she supposed she had to borrow from Chief Spon), she wasn't supposed to like the protectee. That was the first thing they told you in security training, that if you're performing any kind of bodyguard duty, the absolute worst thing you could do was get close to the person you're protecting.

For a moment, she considered talking with Trabka about it, but Altoss found she was enjoying the respectful silence the lieutenant had engaged in since the news about Pran's wife came in. She was just as happy to keep it going.

She was curious about one thing, however, so she turned to Trabka, who had put several calls through for Pran. "Where else did you put communications through for the professor besides Troyius?"

"Mars and to the *Sugihara.*"

Altoss frowned. "Not P'Jem?"

Trabka shook her head.

The door slid open to let Pran in. Both officers turned and stood. Altoss asked, "Are you all right, Professor?"

"Gonna be a while before I can give a yes to that question, Ensign, but I'm working on it."

"Why didn't you talk to your son?"

Pran raised an eyebrow, a shockingly Vulcan gesture. Altoss tended to forget that particular quarter of the professor's heritage, given how few characteristics of that species he showed, even his pointed ears being covered by his long, white hair.

"Sara's gonna get in touch with him," he said rather lamely.

"You should really be the one to tell him."

Before Pran could reply, the comm system beeped. Trabka sat back down. "It's the Ferengi embassy on Earth."

"The what now?" Pran asked.

Altoss checked the chronometer. "Captain Dax did say to give her an hour, and that was fifty-nine minutes ago."

Pran took a very deep breath through his nose and then exhaled it through his mouth. "All right, then, let's not go keeping the ambassador waiting. I'm sure he's a busy man. Put him on through, Lieutenant."

The view of Maxia Zeta IV, which also now included the *Musgrave* in orbit, switched to that of a big-eared, very pudgy Ferengi. Altoss wasn't entirely surprised to see that a Ferengi diplomat would be someone well-endowed in the lobe department—Ferengi put a lot of stock in such things—but also someone well fed.

"Greetings! Do I have the pleasure of speaking to Professor Sonek Pran?"

The professor stepped forward. "Uh, that'd be me, actually, Your Excellency. It's an honor to meet you."

"I understand that you are trying to seek out a business associate of mine."

Pran tilted his head to the right. "I guess that's one way of looking at it—though from what I've been given to understand, she's more of a competitor."

"Ah," Derro said with a lascivious smile, *"a female."*

Altoss frowned. She would have thought that the captain would have specified who it was that Pran needed to talk to, but apparently not. Then again, that might have been part of how she got Derro to make the call.

"Her name is Sekki," Pran said.

The smile fell into a scowl with remarkable speed. *"What is it you wish to know about that foul creature?"*

"Well, where to find her might be a pretty good start, I think."

And then the scowl turned into a smile again, but this one Altoss recognized as the one they'd been trained at the Academy to look out for. She recalled the exact words of Commander Zbigniew: "If you're in a room with a smiling Ferengi, get out of the room." The commander followed that by quoting from the Ferengi's own Rules of Acquisition, specifically the forty-eighth one: "The bigger the smile, the sharper the knife."

"What possible reason could you have to find that—that female?" That last word was spoken with an impressive amount of derision—so much so that Altoss almost took it personally. Derro continued: *"I'm sure that I can provide whatever service* she *claims to be able to perform, and can do so at a more reasonable price."*

"I'm afraid that we need to talk to her about a very specific business dealing."

Now Derro nodded knowingly. *"Ah, of course. The wench cheated you, didn't she?"* He shook his head. *"You have my sympathies, Professor. The darkest day in Ferengi history was when* females *were permitted to do business. They do not have the lobes for it. Grand Nagus Gint was wise when he wrote the Ninety-fourth Rule of Acquisition."*

" 'Females and finances don't mix,' " Pran said with a nod.

Derro's beady eyes widened a bit. *"You know the Rules?"*

"Oh sure. I've found that they can be quite a good guide to how to live your life."

"It is rare to find a non-Ferengi who appreciates the value of the Rules—especially one who comes from the—" The disgust on Derro's face now made his expression when he used the word "female" look downright joyous. *"—moneyless economy of the Federation."*

"I know what you mean, Your Excellency, believe me. Now, I heard through the grapevine that Sekki outbid you on a contract with the Breen, so I thought you might have a way to get in touch with her."

"As it happens, I do not. However, I might be able to tell you where *she is."*

"I assume, as per the Ninety-Eighth Rule, there's a price for this information?"

Derro chuckled. *"Don't push your luck, Professor. Quoting the Rules just proves you're intelligent, and it's never good to do business with someone more intelligent than you."*

"Which," Pran said with a smile, "is the Two Hundred and First Rule."

Another chuckle. *"In fact, the only price I will extract for this information is simply this: you must tell Captain Dax that the information was of value to you."*

Altoss's first thought was, *That's it?* But Pran showed no surprise, he merely nodded. "I will gladly pay that price, Your Excellency. If you want, we can contact the *Aventine* right now."

"I do want, yes. It's not that I don't trust you, Professor, it's simply that I don't trust anyone."

"That makes you a wise businessman *and* a wise diplomat, Your Excellency."

"Yes, it does."

There was a pause.

Finally, Pran prompted the ambassador. "Well?"

"Well what?"

"Your Excellency, I'm afraid I can't tell Captain Dax that the information's of value when I don't even *have* the information."

Derro sighed. Altoss had the feeling he was hoping Pran wouldn't have noticed that, making her wonder if he had already forgotten the Two Hundred and First Rule that he'd just quoted. *"Very well. The female you seek has recently purchased a mansion on Thalezra."*

Altoss squinted at the screen, recalling a mission from her first assignment aboard the *Aventine* under Captain Dexar. "That's an independent world. They have no treaties with *any* outside government, and they also have an open immigration policy. It's a popular place for people to retire to, and also a popular destination for fugitives. Oh, and they like to build things, so it's probably a very nice mansion."

"Your female is well informed," Derro said dully.

"That's one of the many reasons why we keep her around, Your Excellency," Pran said with a smile before looking down at Trabka. "Lieutenant, if you'd be so kind as to do the honors?"

"Contacting the *Aventine* now."

Shortly, there were two images on the screen: Derro on the left, Dax on the right, the latter in her ready room. *"Hello, Derro."*

"Greetings, Ezri. Professor?"

Pran cleared his throat. "The ambassador wishes me to inform you that his information was useful."

"Good," the captain said with a pleasant smile.

"May I assume now, Ezri, that my debt to you is at last paid in full?"

"You're kidding, right, Derro? You've got a long *way to go before it's paid in* full."

Derro muttered something. *"Very well."* And without another word, his face disappeared, leaving only Dax.

"Debt, huh?"

"The ambassador and I go back a ways."

Grinning, Pran said, "All right, then. Derro's information is that our friend Sekki's on Thalezra."

"Why am I not surprised?" Dax then snapped her fingers. *"Oh, before I forget, you may want to look over the*

latest from the Klingons. They took Krios back, but how they did so was . . . interesting."

Pran raised an eyebrow. "Really?"

"Yes, really. We're setting course for Thalezra, also."

Altoss said, "We'll be able to get there much sooner—ETA is twenty hours."

"Not quite," Dax said with a smile.

Trabka muttered something under her breath, then said, "Slipstream?"

Dax nodded. *"We might even beat you there. Whoever* does *arrive first, check in as soon as you know something."*

"Will do, Captain. Thanks. *Seine* out."

Dax's face was replaced by the planet once again.

Pran then looked at Trabka, who looked like someone had killed her pet. "Lieutenant, set a course for Thalezra, and contact the *Musgrave*." When nothing happened, Pran again was forced to prompt. "Lieutenant?"

"Hm?" Trabka looked up blankly. "Oh, uh, right, of course. Setting course."

Altoss sat in the copilot's chair and glowered at Trabka. "Contacting the *Musgrave*." As she opened the channel, she thought, *Just when I thought she was done complaining, this happens. I really am going to have to kill her.*

Dayrit's face appeared on the screen where Dax and Derro had been.

"Captain," Pran said, "it looks like we'll be heading on out."

"All right, Seine. *Good luck to you. Oh, and the next time you talk to Captain Dax, thank her for me."*

"Uh—be happy to." Pran sounded as confused as Altoss felt. "What for, exactly?"

"The sensor data she sent on Capella IV was a huge help. According to Bojan—er, that's Commander Hadžić—it provided a roadmap to fixing the farantine problem. We should have the dilithium mine back up and running within twenty-four hours—at least, according to Mr. Stevens. We'll see."

"That's excellent news, Captain," Pran said with a grin. "We'll pass it on."

Dayrit nodded. "Musgrave *out.*"

Pran moved toward the rear. "I'm gonna go get myself a nap. Let me know when we reach Thalezra."

Altoss watched him go as Trabka moved the runabout out of orbit. *He puts up a good front, I'll give him that—but he's probably in agony right now.*

With a sigh, she turned back to the copilot's console. *Best to just leave him alone. Let him grieve.*

Trabka shook her head. "I can't believe they're using slipstream *again,* and I'm not there."

And I'm in my own kind of agony up here.

She called up the library computer. If she was going to be stuck up here with Trabka, at least she could do something useful.

Sonek sat staring at the computer screen for more than an hour.

He had napped for about seven hours—which really made it a full night's sleep, rather than a nap—after crying himself to sleep, and spent the entire time dreaming about Rupi.

After he awakened, he read up on the taking back of Krios by the Klingon Defense Force's Fifth Fleet—which was done despite the fact that the Kinshaya were aided by the Breen, the Tzenkethi, and the Gorn.

That finished, he stared at the screen and tried to figure out if he wanted to contact Ayib or not.

Sara had said she would do it, and Sonek had thanked her for it. The A.C. Walden Medicine Show would be prematurely ending their time on Troyius playing for the refugees and would take their transport back to Mars for the funeral. From what Captain Demitrijian had said when Sonek talked to her, there was very little left of Rupi after the building collapse in Lejico—enough to identify her DNA, but not much beyond that—so there was no real time frame for when the services had to take place. Once the entire family was home on Mars, they'd have the service Rupi had specified in her will.

Part of that family was Ayib.

He picked up the banjo and started strumming. But no matter what he tried to play, it didn't sound right. Music had always been his refuge, but he'd never had to respond to anything like this before.

It had been so easy in the *Aventine* rec hall when it was other people's suffering he was trying to alleviate. For all the devastation wreaked by the Borg, very little of it had touched Sonek all that closely. One great-uncle whom he didn't even know all that well, plenty of friends, several of Rupi's shipmates—but nobody *that* close to him.

The plucking of the banjo just sounded like noise.

Finally, he contacted the fore section. "Ensign Altoss, could you do me a favor?"

"That would depend on the favor."

"Smart woman," he said with a grim smile. "A couple days back, you offered to put through a call to P'Jem for me, and I was wondering if that offer still stood."

"Absolutely. I assume the call is for Dr. Ayib Pran?"

"Yeah."

About a minute later, the screen lit up with the face of an elderly human, wearing a turtleneck that was decorated with admiral's bars. *"What do you want?"*

Wondering if the old man knew that he had just given the standard ritual Klingon greeting, Sonek said, "Uh, I'm trying to find Dr. Ayib Pran?"

"Ayib's a little busy right now. Maybe I can help you?"

"I doubt that, Admiral. I'm Ayib's father, and I need to talk to him."

The admiral's face softened. *"Oh. All right, hang on a second."*

He walked away from the screen, eventually replaced by the round face and big blue eyes—that he'd inherited from his mother—of his son. His cheeks were puffed, so he'd obviously been crying.

"Hello, Ayib."

"Dad. I wasn't expecting you. Sara said—"

"I know what Sara said, but that was just me being an idiot—you know, like usual. Your mother's dead, and it's pretty ridiculous that I'd fob off telling you that on Sara. She's got enough grief without me adding to it."

"It's okay, Dad. Look, you don't have to do this. I've got a lot to keep me busy here, and I assume you're busy teaching or whatever."

"Actually, I'm back to working for the Palais. Right now, I'm on a Starfleet runabout heading out of Federation space for some—well, some work."

Ayib frowned. *"I thought you were done with that."*

"More like it was done with me, honestly. But it's not anymore." He hesitated. "Your mother and Sara both told me about what you're doing on P'Jem—and I read the report about the *shevrak* thing. That was some nice work."

Shrugging, Ayib said, *"I was lucky."* He ran a hand across a tearing eye. *"I was telling Mom about it in my last letter to her. I don't even know if she got it or not."*

Sonek stared at the screen. He and Sara had talked for a good twenty minutes, yet here he was less than two minutes into talking with Ayib, and he had nothing left to say. "Look, Ayib—I'll see you on Mars, all right? The Medicine Show's headed back there, and you—"

"I won't be able to leave for a couple of days. Admiral McCoy's fine with letting me go, but not until a replacement shows up. The Sylvania*'s on its way to drop off my replacement, and they'll take me to Mars. Should be here in a couple of days."*

"So you said. I guess I'll see you there, then."

"Dad?"

"Yeah, Ayib?" His son sounded pained.

"You had a Talisker, right?"

That got a smile out of Sonek. "Of course I did."

Ayib nodded. *"Me, too. Had it with Admiral McCoy. In fact, that's when I found out his name—nobody told me, even though he's in charge. It's really been crazy here. He hated the Scotch, and kept trying to get me to make it a mint julep instead. But tradition is tradition, right?"*

"Yeah." Sonek felt a tear run down his right cheek into his mustache. "You take care, okay, Ayib? I'll see you when we're both home."

"Sure, Dad. And thanks for getting in touch, okay?" A tear was running down his cheek as well.

A few minutes later, after the call was ended, Sonek

wiped his eyes dry, set the banjo down on his bunk, and went fore.

"Professor," Altoss said, "I have some good news for you."

"There's a nice change." Sonek was referring as much to the Efrosian woman's tone as her words—this was the most pleasant she'd been since Captain Dax reamed him out over the runabout. Sonek had actually been tempted to point out that the *Musgrave* received the *Aventine*'s sensor data from Capella only because the *Seine* had come to Maxia Zeta, and that was what helped them to apparently solve the farantine problem—but he also knew mentioning that would be pushing his luck, and besides, it wouldn't have altered Altoss's point regarding the chain of command, which was absolutely right.

"The reason I recognized Thalezra is because I've been there. One of the *Aventine*'s earliest missions was to track someone down on Thalezra. Since they don't have any treaties, there's no way to get the local Thal authorities to cooperate with a legal search. So Lieutenant Kedair made a less-than-legal search."

"I knew I liked that young woman for a reason," Sonek said with a smile. "What did she do, exactly?"

"She found a back door into the Thal database. Thing is, it's been a while—I was worried that they may have found it and closed it." Altoss then broke into a smile. "But they didn't. I was able to track down a requisition made by a Ferengi woman named Sekki to have a mansion constructed. There are also some orders for various pieces of furniture and artwork, food replicators, and a search for someone to grow bugs for her."

Trabka made a face. "Bugs?"

"For snacks," Sonek said. "Ferengi like to eat them."

"Okay, I really did not need to know that."

Under her breath, Altoss muttered, "Now you know how we felt."

"What was that, Ensign?" Trabka asked.

"Nothing, Lieutenant," Altoss said quickly. "She also requisitioned a sensor screen. Thing is—I've found all the requests, but I haven't found any invoices or receipts to indicate that the work was completed."

Sonek shrugged. "Only one way to find out, really. How soon till we get there?"

Trabka double-checked her console. "About eleven hours."

"All right. I assume that a Starfleet ship won't be welcome?"

Altoss nodded. "The *Aventine* was challenged the moment we entered the system. However, we can reconfigure the shields so that we'll appear to be a Lissepian planet-hopper."

Frowning, Sonek asked, "Why that, of all things?"

"They're almost the same size as a runabout, so it's an easier sell. As long as we stay far enough from any artificial satellites in orbit that can get a visual fix, we should be fine."

That last part was said with a glance at Trabka, who nodded. "That won't be a problem."

"Great." Sonek clapped his hands once. "Let's hope we can pull this off."

Eleven hours later, they had reached Thalezra. Sonek had spent most of that time wondering how he was going to convince Sekki to talk to him. He doubted he could rely on Captain Dax to pull another rabbit out of her hat, and while Sonek had a well-deserved reputation for talking people into things, he wasn't always terrifically successful with Ferengi, who tended to be rather single-minded: pay them, and they'll talk. Since Sonek didn't have any latinum with him, and no real leverage, he wasn't sure how to go about it.

For her part, Altoss had been working on the shields, and she said as they came out of warp, "We are now officially Lissepian tourists."

Trabka added, "We're in orbit, and there's nothing closer than five hundred kilometers. We should be safe. And we should be in scanning range of where that paperwork you found said the mansion is."

Altoss nodded. "Scanning the surface."

Several seconds passed. Sonek tried not to fidget.

Frowning, Altoss said, "I've got the mansion—I think. I'm picking up a very faint Ferengi life sign."

"Is the sensor screen up?" Trabka asked.

"I don't think so."

With a sigh, Sonek said, "All right, let's beam down."

"Are you sure that's a good idea?" Trabka asked. "I mean, won't the local authorities complain?"

As if on cue, the communications console beeped. Altoss glanced at the readout. "We're being hailed by Thal Orbital Control."

"Figures. Let's see how my Lissepian is. Put them on."

"Lissepian vessel, this is Orbital Control. State your business, please."

In Lissepian—which would be translated by the runabout comm systems, but Sonek wanted them to hear the accent—he said, "Hello to you! I am named Kom Traya, and the vessel I am in is named *Traya Nall.*"

"What is your business, Traya Nall?"

"There is a Ferengi woman who is a friend of Kom Traya. She is named Sekki and I desire to meet with her. Is that agreeable to yourselves, Orbital Control?"

There was a pause, the length of which was making Sonek nervous. However, eventually there was a response. *"We will be monitoring your ship very closely,* Traya Nall. *If you transport to any location other than the mansion belonging to Sekki, you will be fired upon. Is that understood?"*

"If this is what is necessary to visit my good friend named Sekki then that is what I shall do."

"Very well. Orbital Control out."

Trabka let out a very long breath, while Altoss glared at Sonek. "That was a big risk you took."

"Telling the truth would've been a bigger risk. The fact that I'm on a diplomatic mission wouldn't mean a damn thing to them, and if they knew this was a Starfleet ship, they'd be on the defensive and trying to hinder us as much as possible. Now they'll be keeping an eye on us, but they're not really worried. We're not likely to be here all that long, so it probably won't make that much difference, but all things considered, I'd rather the Thals think this is just a Lissepian here to visit a friend."

"I hope you're right." Altoss rose. "Shall we beam down?"

Sonek smiled. "Yes, indeed. Lieutenant, stay in touch, and if you hear anything from our new friends at Orbital Control, you let me know, all right?"

Trabka nodded as Sonek followed Altoss to the small transporter in the rear of the fore compartment.

Seconds later they were in Sekki's mansion. The place was huge, but also empty. It looked as if the structure was finished, but the furnishings hadn't arrived yet. Altoss had beamed them into a hallway near the front door—which was wood gilded with gold-pressed latinum in the images of assorted flowers—and walls made of what looked to Sonek's untrained eye as either *jorvik* from Risa or marble from Earth. If it was the former, it was quite valuable, given that Risa wasn't likely to be exporting much after being devastated by the Borg.

The fact that she can afford jorvik *also means she's been well compensated.* Then again, she was doing good work, from what Sonek could tell.

Altoss had her tricorder out. "I'm not getting the Ferengi life sign anymore. Very few EM emissions, either—this place isn't really habitable yet." Her words echoed hollowly off the blank walls.

They checked the rest of the ground floor, finding a lot of large empty rooms, and one room with a big table and a hole in the wall roughly the size of a standard food replicator.

"Where are the EM emissions coming from, anyhow?" Sonek asked.

Peering at the tricorder, Altoss said, "Upstairs."

The staircase had a latinum banister and the stairs were covered in plush orange carpeting. Altoss went up first, Sonek right behind. The second floor, they soon realized, was in similar shape to the first: almost no furnishings, and a lot of empty rooms. The orange carpet, to Sonek's eyes' regret, continued over the floor of the hallway, and there were a dozen small rooms that were probably intended as bedrooms. At the end of the hall was the largest of them.

"The emissions are coming from in there," Altoss

said, pointing at the large wooden double doors that led to that large room.

"Let's go, then."

Nodding, Altoss slowly opened the door, hand on her phaser. After looking around, she opened the doors all the way and went in. Sonek followed, and saw that this was the only room up here that had anything in it: a huge four-poster bed, a desk, a workstation, a hideous painting depicting what looked like a rainy day on Ferenginar on the wall, and a door to a commode.

Suddenly, Altoss ran to the other side of the bed. She knelt down, looking at something on the floor that Sonek could not see. "Well, now I know why there's no life sign anymore."

Sonek moved to join her at the other side of the bed to see a Ferengi female lying on her back, staring with dead eyes at the ceiling, a multicolored Tholian silk dress marred by the gaping wound in her chest. It looked as if someone had scooped out Sekki's rib cage. *Assuming this is Sekki, anyhow.* He hadn't been able to find a picture of her, but given that she was wearing Tholian silk—which was *not* cheap—he was willing to bet that it was the owner of the house. Besides, who else would be in the master bedroom?

He looked away fairly quickly, as the presence of so much blood and gore was making him ill. By way of distracting himself from the carnage as much as anything, he went to the workstation. However, when he activated it, he only got a line of text on the screen in Ferengi saying that all files had been erased. "Okay, that's not good."

"What's not good?"

"Her computer's been wiped."

"Let me see that." Altoss came over to the desk, and Sonek rose and gave her the seat.

She entered several commands and then leaned back. "The entire system was cleaned out. This is just the terminal for a massive computer network—it's probably in the basement, or maybe off-site. Either way, though, it's been completely wiped out. Sekki wasn't just killed—she was purged."

Sonek let out a curse in Old High Bajoran. Whoever hired Sekki to do what she did didn't want anyone finding out the specifics. *Did they know I was onto them? Or was this just a precaution?* He hoped for the latter, only because he couldn't bear the notion that his noticing the pattern was responsible for a woman's death. The fact that the woman in question had been responsible for several deaths herself was beside the point.

"I'm sorry, Professor," Altoss said. "I guess that brings us to a dead end?"

"Looks like. It's too bad this place is empty, it might be worth searching, seeing if anything—" He cut himself off, shaking his head. "Nah, that's ridiculous. Whoever killed her and wiped the computer isn't going to go ahead and leave useful evidence behind."

Altoss, though, looked thoughtful. "Unless there was evidence they didn't know about." She took out her tricorder. "I'm scanning under the carpet, but I'm not picking up anything but the floor."

Sonek frowned, then walked over to Sekki's body, trying and failing to ignore the nausea that was returning. "The blood's soaked through the carpet. You picking that up?"

"Huh?" Then Altoss's face brightened. "Hold on." She adjusted her tricorder. "No. I'm reading the blood *on* the carpet, but not *in* it. Which means that there's something in the carpet that's masking what's under it, making us think it's an ordinary floor." She unholstered her phaser. "Stand back, Professor."

Moving to one side of the room, Sonek watched as Altoss changed the setting on her phaser, then fired it at the far end of the carpet, right in the center. She moved the beam across the room, slicing through the rug, cutting it in half. Once the beam reached the near end of the room, she deactivated it and bent over to pull up one side of the newly bisected carpet and rolled it back toward the wall.

As she exposed the floor, Sonek saw a seam in the shape of a square.

Smiling, Altoss nodded toward the seam. "Looks like a floor safe."

"Yeah, that'd be my guess, too. I don't suppose you have any notion of how to get the thing open, do you, Ensign?"

The Efrosian's smile widened. "Give me thirty seconds."

Kneeling down at the seam, Altoss scanned it with her tricorder. Then the tricorder emitted an ear-splitting noise.

"Next time, a little warning, all right, Ensign?"

Looking sheepish, Altoss said, "Sorry—forgot about your sensitive hearing."

"It's not *that* sensitive—certainly not anymore."

A second later, the square portion of the floor lowered, then moved to the right, exposing a cubbyhole. Sonek walked over to it and peered down.

Most of the space was taken up by bricks of gold-pressed latinum, several small items that looked like flat gemstones, and a padd. Ignoring the currency, Sonek grabbed the padd and handed it to Altoss. "If we're lucky, some of the data from the computer is on there."

Altoss took the padd and touched a few controls on it. After a moment, she sighed. "Afraid not. Looks like this was Sekki's light reading. According to the file list, she's got a bunch of Klingon novels on here. *The Dream of Fire. The Vision of Judgment. The Revelation of Wisdom. Warriors of the Deep Winter. Burning Hearts of Qo'noS. The Final Reflection. Charge of the* Yan-Isleth. *The Battle of* Klach D'Kel Bracht. The entire run of novels based on *Battlecruiser Vengeance.*" Altoss frowned. "Why would anyone read novels based on a serial drama?"

Sonek found his hands curling into fists. This was getting frustrating.

Suddenly, Altoss's copper face brightened. "Hang on." She ran her tricorder over the padd a few times, then entered some commands, before shaking her head. "Damn. I was hoping that there might be some hidden files on here, but no such luck."

Refusing to be defeated by this, Sonek got back down on his knees and dug around the cubbyhole, but all he found was currency. Out of curiosity, he pulled out the flat gems. Once he took them out into the light of the master bedroom, he saw that they were of various colors, but all the same size, and all only a couple of millimeters thick. They also had etchings on both sides.

"What's that?" Altoss asked.

"Looks like a type of coin," he said.

"Useless, then. A Ferengi's bound to have coins."

But Sonek was staring at the etchings. On one side were six circles, arranged in a hexagonal chain. On the other was the same phrase in several different languages, all of which he recognized:

TYPHON PACT

None of the languages surprised him. Except one.

Oh. Oh, of course.

"Dax to Altoss."

Unable to help himself, Sonek started laughing. "Now *that's* timing."

Tapping her combadge, Altoss said, "Altoss here, Captain."

"We arrived about a parsec outside the system a few minutes ago, and Lieutenant Trabka tells me you're on Thalezra. What's your status?"

"I'm afraid the Ferengi woman has been killed, and her computer records were wiped out. We found her floor safe intact, but there was nothing useful in it."

"Not quite," Sonek said.

"What's that, Sonek?"

"Captain, I think I've finally figured out what this is all about. We need to get back to Earth *right now.*"

Partial transcript of 22 February 2381 edition of *Illuminating the City of Light*, Federation News Service

VELISA: Good evening. This is *Illuminating the City of Light*, I'm your host, Velisa. It's been over a week since the Borg threat was apparently eliminated for good, and the quadrant is attempting to recover from the devastation wreaked upon it in the months leading up to the Borg's invasion. Over the past few days, we've discussed the ecological, physical, and personal consequences, and tonight we move on to the political. With us to discuss this are: Federation Secretary of Defense Raisa Shostakova; the Palais reporter for the *Times*, Edmund Atkinson; a retired Starfleet admiral and current consultant for the T'Shiro Cultural Exchange, T'Lara of Vulcan; and the chief of staff for the Jaresh-Inyo administration, Emra Sil. Welcome. My first question is regarding the Romulans—or rather, the Romulan Star Empire and the Imperial Romulan State.

SHOSTAKOVA: There is no "question." Both nations are recognized by the Federation, and we are on good terms with both.

VELISA: Yes, but I suppose the question would be, how long will that last?

ATKINSON: Until such a time as the Star Empire has rebuilt itself. After that, it's anybody's guess. They have a history of contentiousness, and none of their alliances have ever lasted long.

SIL: Once the Star Empire's back on its feet, there will be war—I suppose you could call it a civil war except, as Ms. Shostakova pointed out, they're separate governments now. But I have no doubt that Praetor Tal'Aura's first priority will absolutely be to reunite the Romulan people under one government.

T'LARA: That is an illogical assumption. The militaries are evenly split, but the Imperial Romulan State has the stronger economy. They can supplement their existing military forces with mercenaries and more easily construct new ships to replace those lost to the Borg. The Star Empire would be outmatched.

SIL: Maybe, but that's not going to stop them. The only way Praetor Tal'Aura is going to regain the trust of the Romulan people is if she brings them back together.

ATKINSON: You're assuming that Tal'Aura stays in power. She is, after all, the fourth person to sit in the praetor's chair since the Dominion War ended, and the instability that the Empire finds itself in is a good deal more likely to result in yet another regime change.

VELISA: Which raises the question of what the Federation will do if such a war does break out. The Star Empire is the recipient of Federation aid, but the Romulan State has proven to be a valuable ally—it was a State ship that sacrificed itself to save Ardana.

SHOSTAKOVA: Such would be by definition an internal matter. We would not interfere. We would provide medical and other such aid to either or both sides, but militarily they will be on their own.

ATKINSON: That's a bit harsh, isn't it? I can't imagine the Ardanans will be thrilled with that.

SHOSTAKOVA: While we are grateful for the sacrifice made by the *Verithrax,* there is no formal treaty between the Federation and either government. The alliance we made with the Star Empire during the Dominion War ended with that conflict's cessation.

SIL: Also, to be blunt, a conflict between the two Romulan governments is to the Federation's benefit. Right now, the Federation and the Klingon Empire are as weak as they've ever been. A united Romulan people would be disastrous.

VELISA: Moving beyond the "big three," what of the other nations on our border?

T'LARA: All the local spacefaring powers were affected by the Borg invasion to some degree or other. It is unlikely that any will move against us.

SIL: I disagree. The Tholians were snubbed by President Bacco when she was assembling the fleet for the Azure Nebula.

SHOSTAKOVA: It was hardly a "snub." The president was attempting to marshal a significant force to fight the Borg.

SIL: And that force was massacred with the greatest of ease, leaving most of the quadrant vulnerable to attack.

ATKINSON: Oh come now, Emra, you can't blame the president for that. Every time the Borg had attacked up until that point, it was only one or two cubes. No one could possibly have predicted seven *thousand* of them.

SIL: I'm not saying that she should have anticipated that, but do you really think that the Cardassians or the Talarians are *happy* at losing so many of their military assets in a single one-sided engagement? And then there are the Tholians—

SHOSTAKOVA: Who *refused* to join the fleet.

SIL: That's what you and I know happened, Raisa, but we're talking about the Tholians here. I seriously doubt that they're going to stay quiet. They've been antagonistic toward the Federation for as long as there's *been* a Federation, and this may give them just the excuse they need to take that antagonism to the next level.

T'LARA: A greater concern would be the Kinshaya.

VELISA: An interesting point, Admiral. Why them?

T'LARA: Since conquering the Kreel, the Kinshaya have become more aggressive. The destruction of their homeworld is only likely to make them more so.

ATKINSON: Yes, but they've only really attacked the Klingons, haven't they? What makes you think they'll move beyond that?

T'LARA: I do not guarantee that they will, but they are a concern.

SHOSTAKOVA: We have been keeping an eye on the Kinshaya, but as Mr. Atkinson says, they are unlikely to move beyond their current sphere of influence. As with the Romulans, that is an internal matter to the Klingon Empire.

T'LARA: The conquering of the Kreel represents the first significant change in the status quo between the Kinshaya and the Empire in two centuries.

SHOSTAKOVA: So?

T'LARA: So the model that has been used to evaluate the Kinshaya may no longer be tenable.

VELISA: What of the Gorn, the Talarians, the Ferengi, and the Cardassians?

SHOSTAKOVA: Our relationship with all four powers remains strong.

ATKINSON: As long as President Bacco is in office, I doubt anything untoward will occur with the Gorn—she's the one, after all, who signed the treaty with them during the Dominion War, and the Gorn respect her.

SIL: The Talarians were badly weakened by the Borg, and their usual response to being weak is to stay in their home systems and go quiet until they've built their strength back up.

ATKINSON: Cardassia will probably become *more* isolationist. They've been moving in that direction in any event, and losing a fleet in the Azure Nebula won't help.

T'LARA: I would not be entirely sure of that. Over the past year, T'Shiro has done more cultural exchange programs with Cardassia than with any other nation. Those requests—in both directions—have not abated in the past few weeks. While Cardassia is unlikely to become an enemy any time soon, nor an ally we can count on for military support, I do believe that the Cardassian *people* will have closer ties to the Federation as time goes on.

ATKINSON: I think you're being optimistic, given the Cardassians' history.

T'LARA: It is recent history that I speak of, Mr. Atkinson.

SHOSTAKOVA: I must disagree with you, T'Lara. After their experience with the Dominion, not to mention the assassination of Castellan Ghemor and the loss of the battle group that was sent to the Azure Nebula, it is my opinion that the Cardassian Union will become less involved in galactic affairs, not more.

SIL: Actually, I think you'll see a great deal of that. Most governments are going to be focused on their own reconstruction efforts. I suspect that inter-nation cooperation is going to be at an all-time low for many years to come.

VELISA: Interesting, Emra. Do you believe that will be true of the Federation?

SHOSTAKOVA: It will not. Forgive me for interrupting, Emra, but while you may be correct about other nations, it will *not* be true of the Federation. Our aid to the Romulan Star Empire, to Tezwa, and to Cardassia will *not* be reduced because of the current reconstruction.

ATKINSON: You'll pardon me if I'm pessimistic about that assessment, Raisa. It's easy to say now, only a week after the conflict is over, but even the Federation's resources are finite. And I think the billions of refugees from Andor, Vulcan, and elsewhere are not going to be pleased with some of those resources going to Tezwa or Romulus when they could be going to them.

VELISA: It certainly is food for thought. Moving on to other matters . . .

20

EARTH

President Nan Bacco half leaned, half sat on the edge of the front of her *salish* desk, headache one acting like a laser drill behind her right eye.

Just yesterday, the Federation Council had received its monthly report from the Department of Temporal Investigations. While time travel had been a proven scientific fact for centuries now, and temporal issues of various sorts had a tendency to crop up when least expected, it was something rarely attempted and actively discouraged. But right now, Nan Bacco was seriously considering getting on board *Paris One* and ordering it to do a slingshot maneuver around Earth's sun so she could go back in time about four years or so. Then she would find Esperanza Piñiero and convince her not to retire from Starfleet—or, failing that, at least try to get Esperanza not to go home to Cestus III. Either way, Esperanza wouldn't be able to convince then-Governor Bacco to run for Federation president in the next election, so Nan would still be governor of Cestus III and just be dealing with refugees like Gari was, and the rest of this nonsense would be Fel Pagro's problem instead of hers.

If this meeting goes the way I think it's going to, that's going to be a damned attractive option, she thought dolefully.

The intercom beeped and Sivak's deep voice sounded over its speakers. *"Madam President, the ambassador has arrived."*

Nodding, Nan moved around to the other side of the desk and sat in the chair behind it, partly in order to give herself more of an air of authority, but mainly because she was tired and cranky and just wanted to sit. "Send her in, Sivak."

Nan opened a drawer in her desk even as the south door to her office opened to reveal four members of her security detail escorting Ambassador Tezrene of the Tholian Assembly inside. The ambassador wore a glowing suit of golden silk from her homeworld, the interior of which was filled with the extremely hot, high-pressure gases she needed to survive.

Reaching into the drawer, Nan grabbed a fistful of its contents and tossed them onto the wooden surface, where they spread out with dozens of staccato clicks: the gemstone currency that Sonek Pran had found on Thalezra.

"When were you going to tell us?"

Silence met Nan's question.

The president shook her head. "I gotta give you guys credit. We had no idea you were planning anything—certainly not anything on this scale. But it all makes sense, doesn't it? Why the Breen, Tzenkethi, and Gorn were helping the Kinshaya at Krios. Why Tal'Aura cut off aid. And why DS4 saw all those ships going in and out of the Typhon Expanse. It's because you all decided to form a new government."

At last, Tezrene spoke, the vocoder attached to her shimmery suit rendering her voice as a harsh monotone. *"The formal announcement shall be made in a month's time."*

"Oh, you may want to step up that timetable just a hair, Madam Ambassador. You see, right now my chief of staff is downstairs having a chat with the Palais press liaison. Pretty much every news source in the quadrant is going to have the story inside half an hour: that the Romulan Star Empire, the Gorn, the Breen, the Tzenkethi, the Kinshaya, and yes, the Tholian Assembly have all banded together to form the Typhon Pact—complete with shiny new currency."

"Your intelligence-gathering skills are greater than expected."

Nan leaned forward. "I ask you again, Madam Ambassador: when were you going to *tell* us?"

"We are under no obligation to tell you anything. You were to be made aware when our ambassadors were recalled in four weeks."

Picking up one of the gemstones—a dark red one that reminded her of the color of human blood—Nan started fiddling with it between her fingers. "So you're declaring war on us?"

Several clicks and scratches emanated from the suit before the vocoder kicked in. *"No such declaration has been made."*

"Come off it, Ambassador, where do you think we *got* these gems? They belonged to a Ferengi named Sekki." Nan stood up, having grown tired of looking at the Tholian, and faced the view of the Paris skyline that she and

Akaar had been sharing last week, deliberately turning her back on the ambassador. The sun was setting, golden light dappling the buildings and the river. The Tour Eiffel glowed as brightly as Tezrene's suit.

Nan continued: "Sekki was doing everything she could to mess with both us and the Klingons. She sold the same disruptors to the Kinshaya that she sold to the Breen, she created the farantine that screwed with one of our dilithium mines, she got a loony on Capella to blow up a refinery in our topaline mine, and she worked a scam to sour our relationship with Zalda. What we had a hard time figuring out was who hired *her*—and then had her killed." She turned to look at Tezrene again. "We haven't traced how she was paid, but I assume it was your government."

"You can prove nothing."

"You're right, we can't. But we know what you're doing now. And it's going to stop."

"Perhaps. But the goal was achieved."

"The goal?"

"To hurt you as you hurt us when you did your deal with the Ferengi to leave us defenseless against the Borg. And as I told you then, the crimes of the Taurus Reach have not *been forgotten."*

Nan walked around her desk so she could face the ambassador. The heat from the suit brushed against her face. "I gotta give you credit for holding a grudge. So fine, you got your pound of flesh because I took your toys away when the Borg were invading and because you're still pissed about what happened in the Gariman Sector a hundred years ago. What I really want to know, Madam Ambassador, is why your people are part of this Pact. Playing well with others has never exactly been your strong suit." She had the same question for the Tzenkethi and Kinshaya ambassadors, but they weren't here right now.

"Because of you."

That brought Nan up short. "Excuse me?"

"The Typhon Pact exists because of you, President Bacco. When you gathered us here to convince us to join your fool's errand at the Azure Nebula, you said that we would be stronger if we stood together rather than apart. Our governments realized that this was true. But none of us had any desire to subsume ourselves to your Federation, or to the Klingons." Nan couldn't help but notice that a tone of disgust managed to make itself heard in the vocoder's high-pitched monotone. *"Therefore, we formed our own government."* Tezrene moved closer still to Nan, and the heat emanating from the suit started to become stifling. *"Weakened as you are, neither you nor the Klingons are the most powerful nation in this part of the galaxy anymore, President Bacco. And if that thought distresses you, then you have only yourself to blame."*

Her mouth suddenly dry, Nan swallowed and licked her lips. "You didn't answer my question, Madam Ambassador. Why did *you* join? It can't be because you were convinced by my words of wisdom, since you rejected the notion of joining the expeditionary force to Azure."

"The alternative was to be surrounded by a heavily armed hostile power. Instead, by joining the Typhon Pact, we assure that you *are the one surrounded by a heavily armed hostile power. I suggest you get used to it."*

With that, the ambassador turned around and moved toward the exit. Two of the security detail followed her, with Agents Kistler and Wexler staying behind.

As soon as the door closed, Nan turned around and let out a scream of frustration while she brushed her hand quickly across her desk, sending the rest of the Bloc's currency flying across the office.

"Ma'am?" Kistler asked, concerned.

Holding up a hand, Nan said, "It's all right. I just needed to vent for a second." She sighed. "Didn't help a goddamn bit, either." Stabbing the control for the intercom, she said, "Sivak, get Esperanza and Jorel up here. Looks like I'm gonna need to do a press conference pretty soon. Track K'mtok down, too. And then get Abrik," she added, referring to Jas Abrik, her security adviser, "Akaar, and Shostakova, as well as any members of the security council who are on-planet, and put them in the Wescott Room. We've got a *lot* to talk about."

"Yes, ma'am."

"And then fetch me a damned time machine."

"Ma'am?"

Nan let out another sigh as she fell more than sat back in her chair. "Never mind, Sivak. Just get it done."

Transcript of press conference given by President Nan Bacco, 12 May 2381

KANT JOREL, PALAIS PRESS LIAISON: Gentlebeings, President Bacco will be making a statement, and then will take a limited number of questions. I'm going to say the word "limited" again because I know that all of you have trouble understanding that word. It is very unlikely that she will take more than four. And now, I present the president of the Federation.

PRESIDENT NANIETTA BACCO: Thank you, Jorel. As most of you probably know at this point, the Romulan Star Empire, the Tzenkethi Coalition, the Breen Confederacy, the Gorn Hegemony, the Tholian Assembly, and the Holy Order of the Kinshaya have united to form the Typhon Pact. Yes, Gora?

GORA YED, *SEEKER:* So is this an alliance, or a whole new government?

BACCO: An alliance, but a stronger one than, say, that between us and the Klingons. For one thing, they have a common currency.

YED: A lot of those governments have a history of isolationism and xenophobia. It's unusual for them to cooperate.

BACCO: It's also unusual for seven thousand Borg cubes to invade the quadrant and kill billions. It's past time we started adjusting to the unusual. Edmund?

EDMUND ATKINSON, *TIMES:* Madam President, what changes to the Federation's foreign policy will result from the formation of the Pact?

BACCO: Can't really say just yet, Edmund.

ATKINSON: I'm sorry, ma'am, but can't or won't?

BACCO: Both, really. Honestly, it all depends on what their foreign policy is. And right now, it's the absolute least of our worries. We've got a Federation to rebuild. Sovan?

SOVAN, *BOLARUS AND YOU:* Rumor has it that you and Chancellor Martok have scheduled another summit meeting for two weeks from now.

BACCO: That rumor is both absolutely right and completely wrong—which makes it like most rumors, except for the ones that are just completely wrong. In any case, yes, there will be a summit, but it won't be just me and Chancellor Martok. We've invited the leaders of the Imperial Romulan State, the Ferengi Alliance, the Talarian Republic, and the Cardassian Union to join us to discuss an expansion of the Khitomer Accords to include some or all of those other governments. Empress Donatra and Grand Nagus Rom have already accepted, and we expect the others to answer pretty soon.

SOVAN: So does that mean that the answer to Edmund's question is that you're forming a pact of your own?

BACCO: See, *this* is how the completely wrong rumors get started. The Khitomer Accords call for an alliance between independent sovereign nations. At the moment, it relates to the Federation and the Klingon Empire, which remain two separate governments. That'll be true of any of the others of those powers who decide to join.

SOVAN: What happens to those who do not?

BACCO: Nothing at all. Maria?

MARIA OLIFANTE, PANGEA NEWS SERVICE: Madam President, with Zalda continuing to take on refugees, is it safe to say that they are remaining in the Federation?

BACCO: They were never leaving. And, in fact, thanks for the reminder, as I forgot to mention: the summit we've been talking about will be taking place on Zalda, which was at the suggestion of Councillor Molmaan. T'Nira?

T'NIRA OF VULCAN, FEDERATION NEWS SERVICE: Will this new arrangement require a renegotiation of trade agreements that exist between the Federation and the nations that now form the Typhon Pact?

BACCO: Quite likely, yes, although we have yet to receive any indication one way or the other. Secretary Offenhouse is preparing for that very possibility even as we speak. Keep in mind that it isn't as yet clear what the governing body of the Pact is going to be. In fact, I'm incredibly curious about it myself. One more—Kav?

KAV GLASCH VOKRAK, TELLAR NEWS SERVICE: If the Kinshaya are part of this alliance, does that mean they've declared war on the Klingon Empire, and if so, will the Federation be required by the Khitomer Accords to go to war with them as well?

BACCO: First off, the Kinshaya were acting on their own. One of the Pact's first official actions was to formally apologize to the Klingon ambassador to the Federation for the violation of their space. Beyond that—neither we nor the Klingons are in any shape to fight a war. In fact, I don't think anybody in the quadrant is.

VOKRAK: Will the Klingons accept this apology?

BACCO: You'll have to ask the Klingons.

VOKRAK: Chancellor Martok's son is reported to be among those killed in the Kinshaya's invasion—or, I suppose, the Pact's invasion. What if the Klingons decide to go to war even if they *aren't* in any shape to do so?

BACCO: That's all the time we have. Thank you.

EPILOGUE

The funeral took place at a community center in Valles Marineris on Mars. Rupi had grown up in that city, built into the walls of the deepest canyon in the solar system, and when Sonek and Rupi decided to live together, he had joined her there. The apartment had a glorious view of the canyon, but so did every other apartment in the city. It was built by a radical architect shortly after the Mars colony was established in the early twenty-second century. That architect had insisted that there was no reason to be, as she put it, "trapped by gravity." A network of moving walkways and escalators and lifts were built to allow easy transit throughout the city, which extended all around the entire canyon and also made it the largest city in the solar system.

The community center was built at the very top of the canyon, with a huge transparent aluminum window that looked over the widest part of the chasm. The sun was just starting to set, setting the red planet aglow.

Sonek had always loved that view.

He had returned to Earth on the *Aventine,* getting thoroughly chewed out by Captain Dax while en route. He also talked to Esperanza Piñiero and then to President Bacco, both before and after her meeting with Ambassador Tezrene.

The Borg invasion had changed the galaxy forever. It was only just starting to become apparent how much.

For now, though, it was Sonek's time to mourn the death of his wife. Family and friends had come from all over. Nobody from the *Sugihara* was able to come, as the ship was still stationed at Ardana, but a few former shipmates of Rupi's from other Starfleet assignments were present. Of course, all of the A.C. Walden Medicine Show was present, both those related to Sonek and Rupi and those who weren't. Tolik was there, along with the entire History Department, as well as a couple dozen or so other McKay faculty and students.

Best of all, though, was that Ayib was there.

There were enough people present that father and son didn't really have a chance to talk much beyond acknowledging each other's presence. After a while, however, Sonek found himself walking over to where Ayib was talking with Tolik.

"Excuse me, Gramps, but I need a moment with my son."

"By all means," Tolik said with a brief inclination of his head.

Sonek led Ayib to a back room near the commode where there were comparatively fewer people around. "It's good to see you, Ayib. It kind of sucks that it had to take your mother dying to get us together."

"There's a lot out there that sucks right now, Dad. The galaxy's falling apart around us."

"Yeah—and it's about to get weirder, believe me." He put a hand on his son's shoulder. "But the thing is, what I've been realizing these last few weeks is that it's an uncertain galaxy, and we need to stand by each other, regardless. And that means you're still my son, no matter how much we may not get along—and that I love you, and I'm proud of you."

Ayib hesitated. "I already knew that, Dad. Honest, I did. Look, we just don't get along—that's fine. The galaxy will keep spinning if you and I don't talk."

"Maybe it will. But the very last letter that your mother sent along to me said that she was sick and tired of playing go-between with her husband and her son. And now she can't do it anymore, so I think we owe it to her to try to actually speak to each other every once in a while. We don't need to be best friends or anything, but we *can* talk. Tell each other what we're doing, that kind of thing. That all right?"

At that, Ayib actually smiled, making Sonek realize that he hadn't seen his son smile in *years*. "That's fine, Dad."

About half an hour later, Sonek asked the room to quiet down. The room didn't really pay much attention, but then Sara said, "Everyone, *quiet!*" in a voice that she often used to project to the back rows of outdoor amphitheaters without amplification.

Silence descended upon the room after that.

"That's my little girl." Everyone laughed. "Folks, I just wanted to say one thing real quick, and then we can get back to remembering Rupi. You people are all family. Right now, there are a lot of funerals going on, and I suppose there are going to be a lot more by the time all is said and done. There's a lot of bad stuff happening out there, and it's likely to get a whole lot worse before it gets even a little bit better. But one of the ways we're going to get through it is to stick together. Something I've been saying to my students for as long as I can remember—and as long as they can remember, to be honest, though I wish they'd remember it more often—is that what makes the Federation work is cooperation. And that doesn't just mean being nice to each other when it's easy, it means coming together when it's hard. It means reaching out to each other when all we want to do is go home and curl up in a ball."

Sonek looked out at the huge crowd of people, all of whom were, in one way or another, family. His eyes fell on Ayib, who nodded in understanding, making Sonek realize that this was what he should have said to his son when they were alone—maybe what he should have said years ago.

"So thank you all for being here, and—well, to pull out twenty-five percent of my heritage, all of you, please: peace and long life."

"Hear, hear!" Sara said, and others did likewise.

And then Sonek's father, Kojo Pran, picked up his *jirvik* and started playing a Bajoran spiritual that he'd learned from his mother. The song was called *"Pagh Semtir,"* and it was often played when a family member died. It was a slow, dirge-like song, and about half of those present knew the words and sang along.

Sonek picked up his banjo about halfway through, and after his father was done, he led everyone in "Golden Vanity." Then Sara announced that this was getting too melancholy. "Mom would've wanted us to sing happy songs, dammit." And then she started strumming her guitar and playing "Angelsea." A'l'e'r'w'w'o'k then started singing *"Emrak sil var Emrak,"* which of course everybody knew, and then Sonek's father tried to sing "Banned from Argo," but was shouted down by pretty much everyone. Sara soothed her grandfather's bruised ego by singing "Sailing Down That Golden River," which was one of Kojo's favorites.

Then Sonek started playing "Crossroad Blues" on the banjo. Almost everyone present knew the significance of the song, and those who didn't had it explained to them in short order.

For the rest of the night, they played music and remembered Rupi and celebrated her life even as they mourned her death.

Rebecca Greenblatt took great pleasure in the surprised look on Torvis-Urzon's face on the viewer on her desk.

"Are you being quite serious, Rebecca?"

"Completely. The mine will be fully operational tomorrow morning. There are just some final tests, which are being run right now, and then Capella IV is a proper mining town again."

"You're a month ahead of schedule."

"No, I'm a month ahead of when all the doubters and nay-sayers and other pains in the ass said I would be done. I'm right on time for my own schedule."

"And there've been no explosions, terrorist attacks, crazy Capellans trying to sabotage you?"

Chuckling, Rebecca said, "Well, we've had our fair share of crazy Capellans, but I think they're starting to like us."

"Really?"

She thought about it a moment. "No, not really. But they are willing to put up with us a little while longer."

"That will have to do. Excellent work, Rebecca. You've exceeded my expectations."

"Since when do you have expectations?"

"I don't. So the odds were good that you were going to exceed them."

"Fine." Rebecca shook her head. "I'll contact you tomorrow when the tests are all done and we're up and running. Figure another week to train the Capellans, and then we can take the *Hecate* home."

"Excellent. I should have your next job ready to go by then. Out."

As the Grazerite's face faded from the screen, Rebecca punched the air. "Yes!"

Her assistant, Jir, came running in from his desk at the sudden exclamation. "What is it?"

"Oh, it's nothing Jir. Just in a good mood because Torvis-Urzon just told me that, when we're done here, I get to move on to my *next* job."

A smile pushing the edges of his cheek folds, Jir said, "That's great news."

"Damn right it is. Neither bizarre explosions nor ornery Capellans nor nosy Starfleet officers will keep me from doing my job, dammit."

"I thought that Starfleet officer was nice."

Reluctantly, Rebecca had to admit that Jir was right. Kedair was efficient and smart and actually got to the truth of why the refinery was sabotaged. And the way she took a *kligat* in the chest without flinching was just magnificent. But Rebecca wasn't willing to share credit just at the moment. "The point is, I did it. My first job as a supervisor—*this* is how I wanted it to go."

There was a spring in Fabian Stevens's step as he walked onto the *Musgrave* bridge behind Lieutenant Commander Bojan Hadžić, Lieutenant Commander Lolo, and Ysalda.

"Captain," Bojan said, "I am pleased to report that we were able to alter the structure of the farantine so it is now an inert substance."

Manolet Dayrit rose from the command chair. "You're sure?"

Bojan was grinning. "Positive, sir. The information from the *Aventine* was what did it."

"Well," Ysalda said, "that and thirty-five test runs on the *Erickson* before we got it to work right."

Fabian added, "But hey, thirty-sixth time's the charm, I always say."

Dayrit smirked at the engineer. "Fabian, honestly, I really do believe that you always say that. Good work, people. How do we apply this to the planet?"

Bojan stared at Fabian. Taking the cue, he said, "We need to modify a few torpedoes and detonate them at particular spots in the planet's atmosphere. About an hour later, the farantine should all be inert, and dilithium mining can recommence."

Looking down at Lolo, Dayrit asked, "And these modifications can be done?"

"Nnnnnnnno problem."

Holding out his hands, the captain said, "Well, what are you standing around here for? Get to work. I'll tell the planetary authorities that they can have their world back shortly."

"See?" Fabian whispered to Ysalda. "I told you we could work out a plan together."

"Fine," the Aquan said, "you were right and I was wrong. Don't get used to it."

"Testy, testy. Keep this up, and I won't tell you how the *da Vinci* made Troyius disappear."

Klag nearly choked on his *raktajino* when Laneth informed him that the *Sword of Kahless* was on approach to Krios.

Recovering quickly, he ran out of his office and stood at the fore of the *Gorkon*'s bridge. "Open a channel to the *Sword of Kahless,*" he told B'Olgana.

"Channel open."

"This is General Klag of the Fifth Fleet. Welcome to Krios."

The image of Krios spinning below them changed to that of the chancellor himself. *"Greetings, my friend, and well done! You have served the Empire with honor—and your chancellor as well. My son could not have asked for a finer warrior to avenge him."*

"The honor was ours, Chancellor."

"I have come to personally install the new planetary governor—Kaq, son of Jorvil—and to make sure that the refugees are settled in."

Klag grinned. "Oh, the refugees are more than settled in, Chancellor. In fact, we have learned that the guerrillas who resisted the Kinshaya ground troops the most were the refugees. Hundreds of them beamed down to the surface during the initial attack, and then they made themselves scarce and harried the Kinshaya after your son gave his life."

Martok returned the grin. *"Excellent. Already they defend their new home. They will be honored appropriately—as will you, General."*

"An estate belonging to the House of Lantach has been donated to the Empire. The members of that House who did not die in the Borg attack were killed by the Kinshaya's invasion. The House *gIntaq* has said that it may be used as the new governor's headquarters until a new satellite can be created."

Ruefully, Martok said, *"It may be some time before that happens. Right now the Empire has other priorities. Speaking of that, the intelligence you gleaned from your prisoners has borne fruit."*

Klag nodded. "So we have heard, sir—news of the Typhon Pact has already reached us."

"Indeed. The face of the galaxy has forever changed, my friend."

"Let it. We are Klingons, and we do not care what face the galaxy wears. We will be victorious, or we will die with honor."

That prompted a chuckle. *"Well said, General. You and your fleet captains meet me on the surface in one hour. We will install Governor Kaq together."*

"One hour, Chancellor. *Qapla'!*"

"Qapla', *General.*"

Torethirala zh'Vres swore by Thori, Uzaveh, and every other Andorian deity that she would kill that Ferengi.

If she ever got out of the prison, in any case.

The Ferengi woman had paid Thira good money (and bribed her people's government to drop the charges against her) to pull off a rather impressive fraud. Thira didn't much see the point of it, herself. Supposedly, it was to help drive a wedge between Zalda and the Federation, which struck Thira as a waste of a good fraud. But Sekki's recompense was quite substantial, even after what she had to spend to hire four hundred people to pose as evacuees (most of whom actually *were* evacuees in any case), and for that amount of coin, Thira would dive naked into a barrel full of *ushaan-tor*s.

But then she got caught, which was just irritating. The disguise she'd used should have been *perfect*. The drug had only been on the market for less than a year, and records, scanners, and efficiency were all in short supply following the Borg invasion. As was cash, since Borg weaponry wiped out the depository on Andor where Thira kept her savings.

The Johnson City Police—and how embarrassing was *that*, to be caught by locals, not even Federation Security or Starfleet, but a *city's* law enforcement—had finally allowed her to communicate with someone, and as soon as she could, she used the comm code that Sekki had given her.

When no one answered, she again swore to kill Sekki. If Thira gave her up, then maybe her sentence would be reduced. She had to get *something* out of this, especially since, in part because she got caught, Zalda was still in the Federation.

She tried several times, but there was no response. Then she looked at the officer who was guarding her while she was at the comm unit. "I don't understand, she should be answering. Look, she's a friend of mine, and she could be in great danger. Her name is Sekki, and she's on Thalezra."

The officer winced. "I'm sorry, ma'am, but if she's on Thalezra, there's not a helluva lot we can do. They're independent. Look, I can ask, but I don't know if the Thals will tell us anything."

Thira hadn't even expected an offer of that much,

but she leapt at it. *Maybe it's not so bad being captured by locals after all.* "Could you? I would really appreciate it."

He brought her back to her cell, and she didn't hear anything for several days. At that point, she realized that the officer was probably simply being polite.

After spending an entire night dreaming of throwing Sekki naked into a barrel full of *ushaan-tor*s, she woke to see the officer with a sad expression on his face.

"I'm sorry," he said, "but we finally got an answer from the Thals. I'm afraid that Sekki was murdered several weeks ago."

Oh, Thori, no. "Really?"

"Like I said, I'm sorry."

With that, the officer left.

And Thira realized that her only hope of any kind of leniency was gone.

Captain Ezri Dax welcomed the five new crew members who had come on board during their stopover on Earth, and then sent them off with their respective section chiefs. Ten others had already departed, all noncoms whose enlistments had ended and who hadn't re-upped. She was disappointed that she only got five people to replace them, but she wasn't really surprised. *It's gonna be that way for a while,* she thought with a sigh.

"Captain?"

Turning to face Spon, standing behind the transporter console, she said, "Yes, Chief?"

"I just thought you should know, we're planning to have a big jam session in the rec hall tonight at 2200."

Dax had noticed that the concerts had modulated into

jam sessions ever since Sonek Pran had been on board, though she'd only attended a couple. She was glad to see the tradition continuing even with the professor no longer around. "Thanks, Chief. I'll be there."

She departed the transporter room and headed to a turbolift. After a moment, one arrived, containing her first officer. "Sam," she said as she entered.

After the doors closed, Bowers said, "Ezri."

"You doing anything at 2200?"

"Honestly?" Bowers shook his head. "I was looking forward to a good long night's sleep."

"What if I gave you a better offer?"

Slowly, Bowers said, "It would depend on the offer in question."

Dax told him about the jam session, and how it got started.

"Huh."

"Is that a yes 'huh,' a no 'huh,' or an I'm-thinking-about-it 'huh'?"

"Just a 'huh.' I guess we aren't getting rid of Pran all that easily."

Smiling sweetly, Dax said, "I thought you were getting to like him?"

"Captain, he stole a runabout."

"For which he was duly yelled at, and for which he apologized, several times—and, I might add, for which the two officers who went along with it have been formally reprimanded. He also alerted the Federation to a threat we wouldn't have even known about for another month otherwise, and kept Zalda in the Federation." The doors opened to the bridge. "Plus he started jam sessions in the rec hall, and I refuse to consider that anything but good."

"I suppose," Bowers said. "Captain on the bridge!" he added as they entered.

Kedair was at tactical, and Dax didn't like the disappointed expression on her face. "Lieutenant?" she prompted.

"Captain, we've just received word from Starfleet Command. Your request to have the *Aventine* go on an exploratory mission is denied. We've been assigned to deliver medical supplies to P'Jem. They're being loaded right now."

Dax shrugged. "It didn't hurt to ask—and I got to remind the admiralty why they built this thing in the first place." She moved to the command chair, Bowers right behind her. "The universe has been around a very long time—it'll still be there when we're ready to look around some more."

"Aye, Captain," Kedair said.

As they sat in their respective chairs, Bowers leaned over to Dax. "You're really not disappointed?"

"Disappointment takes a lot of energy, Sam," Dax whispered back. "And mostly it's not worth it. I meant what I said—I've been around for three centuries, and in all that time, the universe hasn't changed that much."

"Are you kidding? The Federation didn't even exist three hundred years ago."

"Oh, the political landscape's changed, but that's minor. I'm talking about the *universe,* Sam. Sure, there've been some cosmetic changes, but to the universe? It's like someone clipping their fingernails. Pretty chaotic for the fingernail, but barely noticed by the rest of the body. This too shall pass." She peered at the forward viewscreen, now showing an image of Earth and its many artificial satellites in orbit. "And when it does, we'll get to see what's out there."

The hologram that projected over the lectern in the classroom showed a political map of this part of the galaxy as it now stood. The stars were rendered in white, with the territory claimed by the Federation in blue, that of the Klingons in red, and that of the Typhon Pact in yellow.

The yellow section was quite large. He'd shown such three-dimensional maps in the past in his classroom. With the way the Federation sprawled, more than one student had commented that the map looked like several amoebas having an orgy.

Now, though, it looked like three amoebas competing for the same space. In many ways, that was what it did represent.

Marva raised her hand, and Sonek called on her.

"Professor, isn't this Pact a threat to the Federation?"

"It can be, I suppose. Certainly, most every power that's a part of the Pact has itself a history of conflict with either the Federation or the Klingons or both of us."

"So doesn't that mean we need to stop them?"

"Stop them? What do you mean by that, Marva?"

Marva shrugged, then looked to the side of the room, as if the west wall would provide answers. "I mean just what I said, Professor. They're a threat—just like the Romulans used to be."

"Maybe. But how can we condemn what they're doing?"

"Like I said, they're a threat."

Sonek nodded. "All right, maybe they are. Would that justify taking aggressive action against them?"

Now Marva was getting uncomfortable. "Well, theoretically, I guess so. Yes. Yes, it would."

"So you're saying that what the Romulans did to try to sabotage the Coalition from happening back in the twenty-second century was justified, too?"

"What?" Marva's mouth was actually hanging open, as she tried to parse what Sonek had just said.

"Think about it. What the Breen, Gorn, Tholians, Tzenkethi, Kinshaya, and Romulans are doing now is *exactly* what Earth, Vulcan, Andor, Tellar, and Alpha Centauri did in 2161."

The Rhaandarite boy raised his hand. "What about the summit meeting that the president called?"

"Excellent point," Sonek said, pointing at the boy. "These people all getting together might actually make us strengthen our own alliances. The president's talking about us, the Klingons, the Cardassians, the Ferengi, the Imperial Romulan State, and the Talarians all getting themselves together and having closer ties—having us all cooperate more. See, this is what I've been talking about all this time. This is what makes what we've got so wonderful. After something like what happened with the Borg, it'd be real easy to devolve into stupid wars and pointless fighting. Instead, it's led to *more* cooperation, and that can only make all of us stronger."

"Or," Marva said dolefully, "it could mean a really, really big war where all these Khitomer Accord nations fight against the Typhon Pact and a lot more people die."

Sonek nodded, thinking about Rupi. "It might. But we have to hope that it doesn't. Which is the best we can do, because you know the thing about history is: we're still writing it." He glanced at the chronometer.

"Okay, that's it. Tomorrow we'll get back to the reading, all right?"

He watched the students file out, and thought about the future. Was the Typhon Pact the same as the Federation? The history of all six nations was one of aggression, and in the case of the Tholians, they joined solely to make life miserable for their enemies. That wouldn't necessarily make for a harmonious union akin to the Federation.

Then again, the Tellarites, Andorians, and Vulcans all had histories of aggression as well. . . .

I'll say one thing, he thought as he headed back to his office, *I'm looking forward to finding out. . . .*

2008

The DESTINY Trilogy
rocked the *Star Trek* universe

2009

The aftershocks ripple through

A SINGULAR DESTINY
February

TITAN: OVER A TORRENT SEA
March

VOYAGER: FULL CIRCLE
April

THE NEXT GENERATION:
LOSING THE PEACE
July

VOYAGER: UNWORTHY
October

TITAN: SYNTHESIS
November

2010

THE TYPHON PACT
will awaken

ACKNOWLEDGMENTS

First off, big big thanks to my editor Marco Palmieri, who first invited me to do this rather unusual *Star Trek* novel. Secondly, hugely massively amazing thanks to David Mack, whose *Destiny* trilogy made a big ol' mess that I got to start cleaning up; and to Christopher L. Bennett (*Titan: Over a Torrent Sea*), Kirsten Beyer (*Voyager: Full Circle* and *Voyager: Unworthy*), William Leisner (*The Next Generation: Losing the Peace*), and James Swallow (*Titan: Synthesis*), fellow scribes who are *also* cleaning up Mack's Mess over the next few months. All six of the above, as well as editor Margaret Clark, were immensely helpful in keeping everything consistent, and it's been great fun for us to start forging the future of twenty-fourth-century *Star Trek* together. Additional gratitude to GraceAnne Andreassi DeCandido for her usual excellent first read.

Also: Margaret Armen for the Aquans in TAS/"The Ambergris Element" and Ardana in TOS/"The Cloud Minders"; Hilary J. Bader for the Warrior's Anthem in the *Star Trek: Klingon* CD-ROM; the aforementioned Christopher L. Bennett for Maxia Zeta IV's dilithium mine in *TNG: The Buried Age* (and also for his kibbitzing on Maxia Zeta's planets' geology); Ilsa J. Bick for Samir al-Halak, Darya Bat-Levi, and Dr. Jo Stern in *The Lost Era: Well of Souls;* Carolyn Clowes for the Belandrid in *TOS: The Pandora Principle;* Gene L. Coon for

Cestus III and the Gorn in TOS/"Arena"; Peter David for the Kreel in *TNG: Strike Zone;* Fred Dekker for P'Jem in ENT/"The Andorian Incident"; Diane Duane for Eisn in *TOS: My Enemy, My Ally,* and Artaleirh in *TOS: The Empty Chair* (and also for some useful Romulan words); Rene Echevarria for Toreth and the Tal Shiar in TNG/"Face of the Enemy"; D.C. Fontana for Leonard James Akaar and Capella IV in TOS/"Friday's Child" and Shariel in the DVD commentary for TOS/"Amok Time"; John M. Ford for the Kinshaya in *TOS: The Final Reflection;* Alan Dean Foster for the Elisiar in the Power Records comic book/LP *The Crier in Emptiness;* Michael Jan Friedman for Braeg in *TNG: Death in Winter;* Sandy Fries for the Zaldans in TNG/"Coming of Age"; David R. George III for the Alonis in *The Lost Era: Serpents Among the Ruins;* Maurice Hurley for Ralph Offenhouse in TNG/"The Neutral Zone"; Heather Jarman for Uvazeh in *Worlds of DS9: Andor: Paradigm;* John Logan for Donatra and Tal'Aura (and the general Romulan mess) in *Star Trek Nemesis;* the aforementioned David Mack for T'Eama in *TNG: A Time to Kill,* Ambassador Derro in *TNG: A Time to Heal,* and for the *Aventine* and its crew, Agents Wexler and Kistler, and Ambassador Tezrene in *Destiny;* Michael A. Martin and Andy Mangels for the *w'lash'nogot* in *Titan: The Red King;* Joe Menosky and Naren Shankar for the Takarans in TNG/"Suspicions"; Ronald D. Moore for Jarok in TNG/"The Defector"; Terri Osborne for Lolo in *S.C.E.: Progress;* S.D. Perry and Britta Dennison for Kai Dava and his saying in *Terok Nor: Night of the Wolves;* Josepha Sherman and Susan Shwartz for the Watraii and the coronet of Karatek in the *TOS: Vulcan's Soul* trilogy; the creators of the *Star Trek Legacy* videogame for Ikalia; Dayton Ward and Kevin Dilmore for the *Musgrave* in *S.C.E.: Interphase* Book 1; and Phaedra M. Weldon for the city of Lejico and the crash of Cloud City in *COE: Signs from Heaven.*

Thanks as always to the actors who gave face and voice to some of the characters in this book: Jay Baker (Stevens), Shannon Cochran (Tal'Aura), Nicole deBoer (Dax), David Graf (Leskit), J.G. Hertzler (Martok), DeForrest Kelley (McCoy), Sterling Macer Jr. (Toq), Dina Meyer (Donatra), Obi Ndefo (Drex), Eric Pierpoint (Sanders), and Brian Thompson (Klag).

The usual thanks to the usual reference sources: *Star Trek Encyclopedia* by Mike Okuda and Denise Okuda, with Debbie Mirek; *Star Charts* by Geoffrey Mandel; and especially the Web sites Memory Alpha (www.memory-alpha.org) and Memory Beta (startrek.wikia.com).

Thanks to Arlo Guthrie, who has been a hero and an inspiration for as long as I can remember, and who also is a big *Star Trek* fan. But for the unfortunate circumstance of five people who contributed so much to *Star Trek* dying in appallingly close proximity to each other, this novel would've been dedicated to him, and the character of Sonek Pran certainly is.

Finally, thanks to them that live with me, both human and feline, for everything.

ABOUT THE AUTHOR

So who is **Keith R.A. DeCandido,** anyhow? Is he the author of fifteen previous *Star Trek* novels, most recently the *Klingon Empire* novel *A Burning House* and the *Myriad Universes* novel *A Gutted World*? Is he the editor who put together the *Star Trek* anthologies *Tales of the Dominion War* and *Tales from the Captain's Table,* not to mention the *Doctor Who: Short Trips* anthology *The Quality of Leadership*? Is he the writer of the *Star Trek: Alien Spotlight* comic book focusing on the Klingons for IDW, several *Farscape* comic-book miniseries for BOOM! Studios, and the manga series *StarCraft: Ghost Academy* from TokyoPop? Is he the scribe responsible for a bunch of novels, short stories, and comic books in various other tie-in universes, such as *World of Warcraft (Cycle of Hatred), StarCraft (Nova* and the forthcoming *Spectres), Buffy the Vampire Slayer (Blackout* and *The Deathless), Farscape (House of Cards),* Marvel Comics (*Spider-Man: Down These Mean Streets*), *Serenity* (the movie novelization), *Resident Evil* (all three movie novelizations), *Doctor Who* (*Destination Prague, Decalog 3*), and more? Is he a musician, the percussionist for the parody band the Boogie Knights? Is he a brown belt in *Kenshikai* karate? Or is he—*all those things?* To find out for sure, check out his Web site at DeCandido.net or read his bizarre ruminations at kradical.livejournal.com.